A BROVELLI BROTHERS' MYSTERY

THE CASE OF THE '66 FORD MUSTANG

TOM MESCHERY

CAMEL PRESS

KENMORE, WA

A Camel Press book published by Epicenter Press

Epicenter Press
6524 NE 181st St.
Suite 2
Kenmore, WA 98028

For more information go to:
www.Camelpress.com
www.Coffeetownpress.com
www.Epicenterpress.com

Author's website: TomMeschery.com

Design by Rudy Ramos

The Case of the '66 Ford Mustang

ISBN: 9781684922062 (trade paper)
ISBN: 9781684922079 (ebook)

LOC: 2022946253

Printed in the United States of America

To Ron & Don Dirito.
Thanks for all the fun and all the stories

Acknowledgments

As always, to my wife Melanie for her editing prowess and to Jennifer, publisher and editor, for her wise suggestions. I'd also like to thank all the mystery writers, alive or dead, I've read over the years that have inspired me to believe in the relevance of the mystery genre as a way to provide my readers with pleasure as well as insights into human nature and history.

The voice of sanity is getting hoarse.

Seamus Heaney

Vecchi peccati hanno le ombre lunghe.
Old sins have long shadows.

Italian proverb

CHAPTER 1
GRIZZLY PEAK ROAD

In the end, one needs more courage to live than to kill oneself.
Albert Camus

"Brovelli?"

"Yeah," I replied.

"Victor or Vincent? Never can get you two straight."

I recognized the voice of my friend, Detective Sergeant Jay Ness of the Oakland Police Department. "The Brovelli who took you for fifty bucks last Thursday with a pair of nines."

"Yeah, yeah, Victor. Look man,"

Jay coughed like he was trying to clear his throat. Jay can't tell our voices apart because we are twins. Vincent is my older brother by 32 minutes, and me, Victor Brovelli. We are known in the neighborhood of East 14th Street where we have our used car dealership as The Brovelli Boys, the sons of Big Sal Brovelli, an Italian-American icon, whose dealership he turned over to us when he retired.

Jay coughed again.

"I've got bad news," Jay said.

I had a bad feeling, but I made light of it. "What? You're going to stop playing poker and deprive me of my livelihood."

"Victor, this is serious. Get serious."

Serious dropped Ness' already deep voice a couple of octaves below bass, and in it I detected sadness. "Sorry, Jay," I said. "I'm listening." I knew that when Jay got serious it had to do with being a detective sergeant and his job with the homicide bureau.

"It's your brother, Mario. Look, there's no easy way to say this."

A knot called death tightened in my stomach. "Go ahead."

"He and his girlfriend were found at the lookout off Grizzly Peak road. It looks like ah. . . Christ. . . damn this is hard. It looks as if your brother shot his girlfriend then turned the gun on himself."

I was in our office standing at my desk, looking out onto our used car lot facing East 14th Street. Mid-morning sun trying to break through cloud-cover. The window was open. Traffic was heavy. An ambulance sounded, then a truck blew its air horn. In the distance, an airplane from the nearby Oakland Airport rose into the sky like some kind of prehistoric bird. Normally the sound of urban rock-and-roll comforted me. Not today. First the air was sucked out of the room, then out of my chest I collapsed into my chair. I shut my eyes - *impossible to breathe* - in that dark space between the eyelids and the universe an image of Mario and his girlfriend Grace appeared waiting on the sidewalk in front of San Francisco International Airport. They had been in Washington D.C. at one of the protest rallies representing PeaceLinks, a political organization Grace had co-founded a little over two years ago with another woman named Carol Hosty. Mario and Grace were full of stories about the protest, happy and energized by the expanding anti-Vietnam War movement and relieved to finally be home in time for Christmas. I heard myself whisper, "Jay, I don't believe it." What I really meant to say is that I don't want to believe it, that any talk of death of a loved one would always be unbearably unbelievable. Just yesterday, I'd talked to Mario on the phone, and he'd sounded perfectly fine.

"I'm really sorry, Victor," Jay said. "You or your brother need to come to the Alameda County coroner's office to officially I. D. the body. Cops in Berkeley are trying to contact the girl's family. One of the homicide detectives at the scene recognized your brother's name and knew I was a friend of yours. I figured it was better to call you guys than your father."

"You did right," I said. *Madonna*, Mom and Pop would be devastated. How could I break this to them? It was Monday, the 8th of December, 18 days before Christmas. Mondays would never be the same again, and there would be no joy this Christmas.The New Year would end the 1960s. Our office was decorated inside and out with bulbs and tinsel and wreaths. *Have a Jolly Christmas* was playing on our loudspeaker.

I lifted the Kelley Blue Book off my desk and hurled it with all my might at the small Christmas tree on top of the file cabinet next to the couch. The tree toppled to the floor, red, blue and white ornaments shattering in all directions.

I heard Jay yelling into the phone. "Come down, Victor. Hurry up," I brought the speaker back to my ear.

"The last thing you want is for your parents to hear about this over TV or radio," he said. "There was media all over the place."

Jay gave me the address on Fourth Street and Washington. I hung up and let my head fall between my legs, still gulping for air, tears blurring my vision. Mario was the third of the Brovelli siblings. Carlo was the first born followed by Costanza and four years later by Mario. It took four more years before Vincent and I arrived. I straightened up, thankful that I was the only one in the office. Vincent was on the lot talking to a middle-aged couple about a 1967 Ford Fairlane, and Theresa Bacigalupi, our new accountant and secretary, was at the bank making a deposit.

I stood up and walked to the open door. Vincent was turning on the charm. I could tell from here that the woman was letting herself be charmed. It's easy to charm when you have my twin's thick black curly hair, swarthy complexion that is a backdrop for gray blue eyes and a sturdy jaw in addition to an athletic body. Since we're identical twins, you'd think this description fits me too. It does, except that my face is marred by a half moon scar under my left eye that runs from the bridge of my nose almost to my ear like a hammock, the result of trying to steal second and getting tagged by a line drive that left me unconscious between bases and no longer handsome.

The husband did not appear to be as charmed by Vincent's looks as his wife. But any car salesman knows, it's the wife who makes the final decision.

Sensing me, Vincent turned and smiled. At that moment, my heart heavy with Mario's death, I felt a great affection for my twin. I mouthed the word, *important*. He waved me away, meaning he was close to a sale. I cut my hand across my throat a couple of times and waved over my head in the direction of the office. He cocked his head to the side, probably wondering what was so important that I'd interfere with a sale. He raised one finger into the air, signaling he'd be right there. I went inside and grabbed a phone. I'd let him sell his car. It would give me a chance to call Carlo and Costanza.

Twenty minutes later, I was off the phone, wiping tears from my face, in the grip of a tension headache. I'd made my sister and brother promise not to call our parents. Someone would have to do it in person, and Vincent and I were close by to our family home in the city of Alameda, across the Oakland estuary. Both sibs said they would be driving to Alameda as fast as traffic would allow.

I stared at the phone not believing the words I'd just spoken. What could possibly have happened to Mario from the time I picked him up at the airport to that moment on Grizzly Peak that he would commit suicide? I'd forgotten to ask Jay the details. I looked out the window at Vincent, still talking and gesturing. But I was seeing Mario.

Plenty of images of Mario came into my mind. Unlike our oldest brother, Carlo, and older sister, Connie, who paid little attention to Vincent and me when we were children, Mario became our defender and pal. I closed my eyes. There he was, Mario rough-housing with us on the carpet of the living room when we were kids; Mario reading to us his favorite King Arthur stories; Mario showing us how to throw a baseball; Mario taking us to Little League practices and driving us home, stopping for ice cream; Mario helping us with our homework; Mario consoling us when we were cut from the junior high basketball team; Mario talking to us about sex; Mario driving us to Saint Mary's College for the beginning of our freshman year; and Mario by my bedside, consoling me, after a line drive struck me just below my eye as I was stealing second, and the doctors were trying to decide if I would lose the sight in that eye.That I only wound up with an ugly scar and no loss of sight, I attributed to Mario's keeping my spirits up. You might ask where our father was while we were growing up. Pop was at work selling used cars or at the Italian American Club playing Briscola or Scopa with his buddies. Whatever Pop contributed to Vincent's and my upbringing, it had to do with cars and business. There were the occasional repeated quotes by well-known Italian historical figures or traditional Italian words of wisdom that he'd memorized and presented to us as fatherly advice, such as my twin's favorite: *Bisogna prima pensarae poi fare*, which means a closed mouth catches no flies.

• • •

"What's going on?" Vincent asked, walking into the office, trailed by his customers. He was staring at the tears. "Is that crying? What is this?"

I opened my eyes. How long had I been daydreaming. He asked me again. I told him.

"You asshole," he yelled. "You fucking asshole, why didn't you come out to the lot?"

Unlike me, Vincent hardly ever swears. "You waved me off."

"You think I give a rat's ass about the sale?"

Alarmed, the couple, who'd been waiting to enter the office, stepped backwards onto the lot

"Okay, okay, I'm sorry. Let's go. Jay says we need to go to the coroners and identify Mario."

Vincent scribbled a note for Theresa, flipped on the closed sign. We leaped the office steps and ran for my car, sprinting past the startled couple, who must have thought the Brovelli Brothers, or as we're often called in the neighborhood, the Brovelli Boys, were two crazy *paesani*

Moments later, Vincent was riding shotgun in my Mustang, and I was peeling rubber out of the lot, skidding on to East 14th, almost running a PG&E service truck into the oncoming traffic.I slammed the car into third and stepped on the gas. We entered the Nimitz Freeway on the High Street on-ramp, a car length ahead of a sixteen-wheeler, its air-horn blasting. In a matter of seconds the speedometer hit 80, and I kept my foot pressed firmly to the floor. Vincent yelled at me to slow down. Too late. We hit the Broadway off-ramp, and I damn near lost control, the Mustang skidding sideways before righting itself. We made it to Fourth Street and parked in a No Parking Zone. The red neon letters spelling City of Oakland Coroner's Bureau hung above the main entrance. The E of Coroner's was blinking, like it was winking at the terrible joke death plays on all of us. We took the stairs to the waiting room on the second floor where Jay said he'd meet us.

Jay's eternally exhausted face was molded into a frown. He placed his long arms around both of our shoulders and drew us into his huge chest.

For a moment we hugged before he whispered, "Let's go downstairs to autopsy and get this over."

"How did it happen," I asked. "How in the hell did it happen?"

"He killed himself," Jay answered. "What more do you need to know?"

"We want to know more," Vincent said, before I could.

"And about Grace," I said.

"Ah, jeez, guys," Jay groaned.

"Come on," I said. "We have a right. We have to tell Mom and Pop."

"Okay. It looks as if they were parked and sitting in the car. He shot her through the right temple. Then he put the gun to his own head."

"*Non ci credo,*" I said. Often when I'm stressed I respond by speaking in Italian. Before I could translate for Jay, Vincent did.

"I don't believe it either."

Jay looked pathetic. He shook his big head and began walking.

As we followed him down the hall to the basement stairs, I remembered Mario in the days after his return from Vietnam talking about the viciousness of the war. He'd been one of number of vets who'd tossed their Purple Hearts into the bonfire at an Anti-Vietnam War rally, an act that had opened a chasm between him and our pop. One of the first things he did as a political activist was join an organization to fight for gun control. He was for eliminating all private use of guns, even hunting rifles, which pissed off our oldest brother, Carlo, a member of NRA, as well as intensifying Pop's anger, already seething over Mario's anti-war stance. Pop was an immigrant who'd left Italy for America as a young married man with a wife and one baby, two suitcases, enough money to travel from New York to Alameda and the home of a distant cousin. Big Sal Brovelli kept an American Flag flying from the front porch of the family house. He would not forgive Mario's unpatriotic behavior. I'd always believed it made it worse that Pop was so proud of Mario for graduating from West Point and going off to Vietnam to fight the godless Communists.

Oh, Mario, cas'hai fatto? What have you done?

I could see Mario killing himself with pills or gassing himself in a closed car, even leaping from a tall building, but not shooting himself. No one who knew Mario would ever doubt his revulsion to firearms. And never, never would he shoot his girlfriend. He adored Grace. Grace had been responsible for helping our brother get over depression about losing his hand in the war. Grace was as firmly against war and any kind of violence as the Quakers. Mario and Grace were in the throes of a year-long ecstatic romance. Everything about their deaths was definitely not right.

Jay stopped us before we entered. "Guys, it's going to be ugly. Mario used a service pistol, a Colt 45, real powerful, real messy."

Vincent grabbed me by the arm. "Oh, man, I can't do this."

"Yes, we can," I said. We held on to each other like two old women going into church. Inside, I made the sign of the cross. Vincent started to make the sign also, but stopped half way through.

The walls of the autopsy room where Mario's body was rolled in on a gurney was tiled in pale green, supposedly a soothing color. It reminded me of puke, which I felt rising into my throat when the attendant drew back the sheet. The bullet had done great damage to that sweet face. Vincent staggered against me. We propped each other up.

I said, "Yes." So did Vincent, but his eyes were closed.

Not one minute longer. We were both up the stairs and out of the building, Jay on our heels yelling that we had papers to sign.

Fuck the papers. We left him standing in front of the coroner's building beneath the winking E – confirming some horrible dark joke on all who entered. We sprinted to my car. We had to get to Mom and Pop. From the Nimitz, we took the Fruitvale Bridge onto Alameda Island. We parked in front of the three-story Victorian house where all the Brovelli children had been raised. Before we got out of the car, I turned to Vincent. "There's not a chance on God's green earth Mario would shoot himself, Vincent. You know that." I placed my hand over my heart. "I promise you I'm going to prove he didn't."

"We're talking here," Vincent said. "You and me, Victor, you and me."

That's my twin. He'll always have my back.

CHAPTER 2

REST IN PEACE MORTUARY

. . . We are stewards, not owners of the life God entrusted to us. It is not ours to dispose of.
2288 of the Catechism of the Catholic Church

Vincent and I have seen a lot of sadness in our lives, but nothing I recall from those early years in Oakland come close to the sight of our father and mother sitting on their living room couch holding each other and sobbing. When I finished explaining Vincent and I stood facing our parent's grief, no words left. My heart was breaking.

In the corner of the living room stood a ten-foot-tall Christmas tree decorated as Mom always did with only white lights and tinsel. A Star of David at its tip. Draped over the mantle was a long cedar rope. Stockings hung there, one with each of the Brovelli children, and one for each of the grandchildren, all the names sewn on them. Carlo, the oldest, the only one of us born in Italy, a successful corporate attorney and devout conservative. Costanza, our sister, now thirty-years- old with children. Mario's stocking, painful to look at. Those stockings would remain up until January 6th when the *Befana*, the good witch in Italian Christmas lore, would arrive to give presents to the kids who were good, and a lump of charcoal to the kids who were bad. Vincent and I always being threatened with charcoal. *Those stockings, reminders of our childhood.* Mom decorated non-stop. Our home inside and out always looked like a Hallmark Christmas card. Next Christmas Mario's stocking would not be there. I wanted to say something to ease my parents' pain, but couldn't think of a single word that would help. My mother placed her hands on her hair. She pulled her hair and began to wail a string of "no's" that sent shivers down my spine. Vincent began crying. Pop's jaw clenched to stone.

The living room in which we sat, usually a place of good humor and joy, had transformed into a gloomy vault. At any moment I imagined black shutters snapping across the windows and the poinsettia decorating the top of Mom's baby grand piano wilting, and the drizzle outside turning into a rain storm.

The first words out of Pop's mouth were stunning.

"Mario cannot be buried on consecrated ground."

If I'd been close enough, I would have punched him.

The next words flew from Mom's mouth in Italian like knives aimed at her husband's heart.

"No, mai! Mario non avrebbe fatto tale violenza. Non a se stesso, non la donna che ama. Mai! Mai! Egli e tuo figlio, e vecchio pazzo. Hai dimenmticato?"

My Italian was good enough to pick up most of it. Mom did not believe Mario would commit such violence to himself or to the woman he loved. Then I think she called Pop an old fool. Pop hung his head, mumbling an apology. At that point, Mom threw her arms around him and began sobbing. And my Pop's stone face cracked like someone had taken a hammer to cement, and he too began to weep. *Madonna, mia.* I thought. Vincent ran from the room. I heard the front door slam. Frozen to my chair, all I could do was watch my aging parents grieve.

If I'd taken bets, I would have given odds Pop would have stopped crying first, but it was Mom. She wiped a hand across her eyes and stood up and squared her shoulders.

"We talk to Father Dunnican. It is 20th century. Church has changed. Mario will be buried a Catholic."

I'm a Catholic and a believer, albeit a sinful one and one not terribly inclined to give up sinning, which, until recently, had to do with a casual attitude towards the sins of the flesh. But I was pretty up-to-date with Catholic teachings. I thought my mom was right. There was something I'd read to do with persons who committed suicide not being in their right minds that allowed for burial in a Catholic cemetery. Pop's reaction was totally out of another century and crazy. But, crazy is what I imagined the death of one's child could do to you.

"We will weep over his coffin," my mom said.

Pop began drying his eyes with the ubiquitous checkered bandana he kept as a handkerchief in his back pocket, and looking less distressed.

I stood up and went to him. "Pop," I said. "Remember a year ago, you asked me and Vincent to help Sweets. You spoke to us about *Onore*, honor."

I was thinking about April of 1968 and the *casino*, the mess, Pop got my twin and me into over the arrest of Sweets Monroe for the murder of his girlfriend Winona Davis. I later referred to it as The Case of the '61 Chevy Impala. At one time, Sweets had saved Pop's life and business from a gang of Mexicans. How, remains a matter of speculations. From then on, Big Sal Brovelli felt honor bound to help Sweets, which meant Vincent and I were honor bound too. I watched Pop's forehead wrinkle into a frown. Finally, he nodded.

"This time it's about Mario's honor," I said. "Mario did not commit suicide. Mario couldn't. Vincent and I are going to prove he didn't. You can tell Father Dunnican that. There'll be a burial, no matter what. I promise."

"Victor is right."

The voice came from behind me. I looked up over my shoulder at Vincent. My twin is smart and tough and a wiling partner in some of my escapades. However, now that he's a father, he doesn't take the risks he used to. But I had a feeling that I was about to get myself into something that would require someone with Vincent's *coliogni* and my twin had some big ones, to be there when I got into trouble — a very real possibility.

"Our boys will uphold our honor," Mom said, standing up, looking down at Pop. I had never seen my mom look so ferocious. "This is not your darling Sweets who saved your life, this is the life and honor of Mario, our son." She turned to us. "*Onore*," She said. To me, it sounded like a command.

Vincent and I looked at each other. He shrugged.

"Onore," we said at the same time, our twin voices echoing through the still room, answering our mother. This time, she was in command, not our father.

"Bene," Mom said. "Now, when will I get my boy back from the police? You ask your friend, *Per piacere*, Vittorio."

"I will, Mom." I was not about to tell her what I knew about homicide cases and the length bodies were kept before being released to loved ones. But I would ask Jay if he could hurry up the process. Behind me I heard the front door open and voices. My brother, Carlo and his family entered. After hugs and more tears and grieving, I nodded to Vincent in the direction of the door.

We left our parents' home. I dropped Vincent at the lot to take care of business, and I drove to Grizzly Point Turnout. I think better when I drive, so I took highway 24 through the tunnel, the long way around. My 1965 red Mustang Luxury Coupe, has a fired up engine that our genius mechanic and part-time employee, Jitters, had rebuilt. I was driving and thinking of Mario. I didn't remember turning on the radio but found myself listening to Credence Clearwater Revival singing "Proud Mary." The word proud reminded me of Mario's girlfriend, Grace, proud of her Irish heritage, proud of her dedication to peace in Ireland and in the United States. "Bad Moon Rising" came on next, and I turned the radio off. *More than a moon was bad.*I started down the road that led to Saint Mary's College from which Vincent and I graduated. I got as far as Saint Mary's Road and turned around. I drove back the way I came back on to highway 24 going west and up through the Oakland hills to Grizzly Peak Road, approaching the turnout from the east. Driving usually helps me clear my mind. So far it hadn't helped.

The rain had stopped, but the sky remained gray and threatening. When I reached the turnout, there was still a two car police presence. A yellow crime scene tape blocked off the parking area. I pulled off on to the side of the road opposite the turnout and watched, expecting the cops to wave me away, but they didn't. Beyond the tape and over the tops of the cop cars I could see the Oakland Bay Bridge in the distance. This was the place Adila Agbo, the woman I love, and I visited often, especially if we had something serious to talk about.

The more I thought about it, Mario's death had to have had something to do with the Vietnam War. The war was increasingly turning to crap. Tricky Dicky had been elected to the office of the President and would be inaugurated on January 20th of the New Year. President Johnson was phasing out, calling for Peace with Honor, while still bombing the shit out of North Vietnam and Cambodia. Last May, the 101'st airborne division that Captain Mario Brovelli had served in had been part of the staggeringly tragic assault on Hamburger Hill that killed 73 American soldiers and wounded close to 400. According to Mario, it was a truly stupid assault that had no strategic value and only proved the futility of our remaining in Southeast Asia. The U.S still had over 400,000 troops in Vietnam. On October the 15th there was a massive demonstration and teach-in called *Moratorium to End the War in Vietnam* with an estimated 2 million

Americans across the United States protesting, the largest anti-war protest in the history of the country. It was followed a month later on the 15th of November by over 400 thousand anti-war marchers in Washington D.C. The first draft lottery took place on the first of December in Washington D.C. All over the globe people were protesting against the war.

I decided to visit Terrance Bowles, the Black Panther's Minister of Education with whom I had a reasonably good relationship. I'd done the Panthers two big favors in April of last year when the cops were harassing them. They'd paid me back for one. So, I was up one. The Panthers had their ears to the ground in the anti-war, liberal community. Perhaps now was the time to call in that remaning favor. I reminded myself to call Dila and tell her what happened. She'd known Mario and Grace because of their work in the protest movement.

I went back to thinking about what Mario was up to that could have placed him in danger. I recalled a suggestion I'd read in a book I bought a year ago called *How to be a Private Investigator.* It explained that as you embarked on your investigation, and you didn't have a clue how to start, a good idea would be to create a reasonable hypothesis and follow it to its conclusion. If the hypothesis was based on facts, there was a possibility it would segue to other possibilities. "What do you think, Dila?" I asked the windshield where I imagined her beautiful face was looking back at me. There was no answer, of course, because she was on the other side of the country, but I pretended I heard her say, *Go ahead, Victor. You're the man.* Being a feminist, Dila would never have said something like I was '*The* man.' But considering she was in New York City, I could put words into her mouth in keeping with the image I have of myself as the alpha male. "Okay," I said aloud. "Here's what '*The Man*' decided: Mario and Grace were murdered because they discovered something criminal to do with the Vietnam War and person or persons unknown would go to prison if it was revealed." The frigging Mai Lai massacre of the previous year came to mind. In September the army had brought murder charges against Lieutenant William Calley. It seemed to me, there was plenty of precedent for other kinds of criminal behavior. My hypothesis sounded good to this amateur Private Investigator, or as we're commonly referred to as a P.I. It left the door open to a lot of variations on the theme. I opened my glove box and took out a pen and an envelope to write on:

1) Pro war zealots murdered them because of Mario's stance against the war.
2) Our military or the CIA murdered them to prevent Mario from revealing a gruesome atrocity.
3) People profiting from the war such as heroin dealers or weapons smugglers murdered them.

It was a start, I thought. I put the pen back in the glove box and placed the envelope in my jacket pocket. "Thanks, Dila," I said aloud, "wherever you are and whatever you're doing." The whatever-you're-doing-part bothered me, maybe because she might be doing whatever with another man. *Nah, Brovelli, she's too crazy about you*. Still, it was the Age of Aquarius and according to the *Fifth Dimension* love was free as sunshine.

A knock on the window startled me. A cop was waving me to move on. I gave him a friendly nod and a Brovelli smile and started the engine. I shifted to first, released the clutch, and I pulled out onto the road, heading in the direction of East 14th and our lot. On the way, it struck me how ironic it was that this death, this murder occurred at the turn out, a place teens came to neck and lovers came to gaze at the sunsets and think of love and be loved, and. . . man-oh-man was I missing Dila. I slammed my hand on the steering wheel, down shifted into third around a corner. I took the next four blocks at a speed that could have got me killed if any car had crossed in the intersections on my way. A red light at the bottom the hill stopped me. I was gripping the steering wheel so hard my hands hurt.

CHAPTER 3
FOXHOLE BUDDIES

A thing may happen and be a total lie; another thing may not happen and be truer than the truth.
Tim O'Brien *The Things They Carried.*

It had been pissing rain for the last two days, which was fine with me. With the storm of Mario's death raging inside me, I wanted nothing to do with blue skies, sunshine, and fluffy white clouds. It was Friday noon, three days since Mario's death, three days devoted to family and grieving. Family on both sides either drove to our house or flew in. To my surprise, my mother's sister arrived minus her husband. Her husband, Gino Vitali, the owner of the largest Volkswagen Dealership in California, had not accompanied her. He was furious with our family, at Vincent and me most of all for the chaos that happened last year in which his daughter played a central role. That didn't matter to him. He was Sicilian, enough said.

When Italians grieve it's not like the somber Protestants or the whiskey soacked wakes and dancing of Catholic Irish. Italians grieving can be heard across continents. Vincent and I had left our family home, the sobbing still echoing in my head, and made it back to East 14th street. We told our accountant,Theresa to cover for us and walked next door to Flynn's. The black wreath was still hanging on the door, which had nothing to do with Mario, but with the death of one of the tavern's regulars

At the start of November, one of Body's Saturday night Irish dart team regulars, Danny Killian, had been shot in the back of the head, his body found in a vacant lot. Since most of us regulars of Body's tavern believed the Irish team were all members of the IRA, we speculated that the killer had been a supporter of the Protestant paramilitaries that Body called the UVF, Ulster Volunteer Force. Body refused to talk about it. Jay was the local investigative officer. He'd been assured by the FBI, which had taken over the investigation because Killian was a foreign national with ties to Sinn Fein that the UVF was not operating in the United States.

"Fooking FBI," had been Body's reply, "It was Vini, vidi and nothing. What the fook do the Hoover boys know about Ireland? All they care about is their war with the Black Panthers. I'll be telling you, Victor, that the FBI's puissant war with the Black Panthers is nothing compared to what's going to happen in me old country."

There'd been a wake for Danny Boy at the tavern with lots of Irish songs sung and whiskey drunk. From then on, it seemed that the Irish dart team was less exuberant and more watchful. I couldn't blame them.

The stools at the bar were filled. It was Friday. Being a Catholic, it was fish day. Flynn served a fabulous creamy Boston clam chowder on Fridays. Mondays and Wednesdays were Irish stew days. Tuesdays and Thursdays Body cooked his infamous *I-Dare-You-Chili*. Larry Hughes, the owner of the DoNut Hole next door and one-time professional football player for the Raiders, was bending over a bowl of chowder. Jitters and Swanee were shaking dice. Jitters was the owner of the Chevron gas station and garage and part-time employee of Brovelli Brother's Used Cars. His name was Calvin Stokes but was called Jitters for his nervous twitching and stuttering that he'd acquired as a prisoner of war during the Korean Conflict, imprisoned in one of those indoctrination camps. Jitters was never nervous around automobiles. You couldn't find a better mechanic in the Bay Area. Give him a car no matter in what condition it was in and he'd have it like new while you were still describing what you wanted done. He was currently working on a personal project, repairing a black Nash Ambassador 8 Special Cabriolet convertible with fire-engine red leather interior with walnut paneling. Jitter's dice partner was Jack Swan, nicknamed Swanee, for the Sewanee River in Tennessee where he was born. Like Jitters, Swanee was a Korean War vet. He owned the automobile detail shop a few blocks down the street. Swanee looked like a country hick in bib overalls over a beer belly and spoke in a slow southern drawl. His appearance disguised a sharp mind and free thinker. He was a member of the Sierra Club and a registered Democrat. He was married to a Korean woman.

Vincent and I waved our hellos and took a booth farthest from the door. Body brought my usual Anchor Steam and a Lucky Lager for Victor and placed them in front of us. He mumbled something about loss and left us alone. From the jukebox came the voice of Joe Cocker trying to get a little help from his friends. By now, all the locals had heard what happened to Mario, so the guys left us to our grief.

"The gun belonged to Mario," Vincent said. "It was in the car with Mario's fingerprints on it. What else could it be?"

I remembered the weapon. Mario had brought it back with him from Vietnam. He'd showed it to us and explained that he would have thrown the pistol away except it was a reminder to him of the kind of person the war had turned him into. I'd been impressed by the pistol because it had a pearl handle. I'd been curious about what Mario meant about the person he'd been turned into by the war. When I asked him, he said, and I remembered this clearly, "The truth often has more to do with what you don't do in life."

"Mario was always too deep for me," Vincent said. "But that was some frigging gun."

"Too much power," I said. In my short and, admittedly, exciting life as a P.I. last year, I'd learned a little about weapons from listening to my friend Detective Sergeant Jay Ness. "Mario would have known. He couldn't have killed his girlfriend knowing it would blow her brains out all over the car."

"That's disgusting."

"I'm just making the point that on every level, Mario could not have done this."

"Victor, I'm not disagreeing, but remember the evidence. Don't go flying off in all sorts of directions."

"You mean don't become a private investigator."

"You said it, not me."

"I'm on this even if you're not."

"I didn't say I wasn't, you *chiuccio.* Ever since last year you think you're such a tough guy P.I."

"Oh, yeah?"

"Yeah." He yelled back.

I was about to stand up and call him out and settle it the way male Italian twins are accustomed to. Probably all male twins. I won't speak for females. God knows, I needed a good fist fight to defuse my stress, but this would be bad, and I was already feeling bad enough. "Ah, *merda*" I said, leaning back in my seat. "I'm sorry, Vincent. I'm wigged out, man."

"I'm sorry too, Victor. Go ahead and tell me what you have in mind. Whatever it is, I'm in."

I took a long pull of my beer and explained my hypothesis and my plans to start the investigation by visiting the Black Panthers Headquarters in West Oakland. He was not excited about getting involved with the Panthers again. I reminded him that they had saved our asses and our business by warning us to close up shop the day Dr. Martin Luther King Jr has been assassinated. The following day lots of stores along our street had been torched or vandalized, but the Brovelli Brothers' Used Car lot had remained unscathed.

"Yeah, they're all really great guys," he said sarcastically.

"It's a place to start," I said.

He nodded, but warned me to be careful. I thought it would be best that he not get too involved as he had a baby and wife to think of. "If you can do most of the car business, I'll try to figure out what happened to Mario and his girlfriend. Does that sound right to you?"

"Fine with me," Vincent said. "But don't forget to keep me up to date."

I detected relief in his eyes. It is a blessing and curse that twins can read each other's minds.

"But the minute you need back up, you tell me." He reminded me of the time during our investigation of Winona's murder last year when he'd got me out of jam with a Mexican gangster. How could I forget, I could still feel the muzzle of the pistol jammed into my ear.

We laughed over that scary incident and ordered another round of beers. It was noon. Flynn's offered some of the best luncheon chow in town. According to Body, an Irish stew was not Irish unless it was thick enough that a mouse could run across it without getting wet. Such a vivid description never bothered the neighborhood food lovers. I had not eaten breakfast. I didn't remember if I'd eaten dinner the day before. We ordered chowder with our second beers. We finished our chowder without further conversation and returned to the lot. In the office, I tried calling Dila. I let the phone ring a dozen times before I hung up. She kept up with the news in the Bay Area, so I wondered if she'd heard. I doubted it. She would have called me if she had.

The meal and the beers were helping me to feel a little better. Vincent waved as I drove out of the lot onto East 14th, heading west toward the Black Panthers' headquarters.

• • •

There was a black mourning wreath attached to the door of the Black Panthers office. Above the wreath were photographs of Fred Hampton and Mark Clark, two Panthers who had been gunned down in their sleep by Chicago police. Whatever company was making black wreaths was bringing in some steady profit these days, when as the poet said, the center was not holding. I pulled open the door and got more than my usual angry stares. The few hey-Brovelli waves came from the Panther women, Dila Agbo's friends. Even their gestures seemed unenthusiastic. Chilly winds, I thought. Gray metal desks stood five across the four walls of the large central room. A hall opened up on the far end leading to offices and the back of the building. Telephones were ringing, typewriters were clattering. The walls of the office were covered with posters of revolutionaries, prominent among them, Che Guevara and Angela Davis. There was one of Tommy Smith and John Carlos on the Victory podium at the 1968 Mexico City Olympics, their heads bowed, black-gloved fists raised above their bowed as the American anthem was being played. I recalled a couple of fist fights breaking out in Flynn's over that symbolic gesture between supporters and detractors. Me, I didn't take sides. Piss off one group could cost the Brovelli boys sales. All right, so that's a little cynical, but our business continues to struggle in between months of solvency and the success our business helps Mom and Pop's retirement.

Black Panthers' Minister of Education, Terrance Bowles, turned from a conversation he was having and walked toward me, his hand outstretched. Bowles was a tall, slender middle-aged man with a neatly cut slightly graying Afro. His customary granny glasses sat on a thin nose. He looked like a college professor rather than one of the leaders of the notorious Black Panthers.

I smiled. He didn't. We shook. It had been a while. The minister was frowning. Frowning was a bad sign. An even worse sign was the presence of James-the-Behemoth, the minister's bodyguard and all-around gopher, standing by his right shoulder with murder-the-white-bread in his eyes. Unlike Minister Bowles, who was copasetic with my relationship with Dila, Mr. James-Many-Muscles, was furious about my dating a black woman, and were it not for the strict discipline enforced by Panther leaders on their cadre, he would have torn my Italian face to rags. It occurred to me that this fury had to do with James, like me, being in love with Dila. I wondered at some place down the road there might have to be a reckoning. My somewhat successful experience as a welterweight on the college boxing team probably wouldn't help me.

Bowles escorted me to his private office without Mr. Bad Ass. Once we were alone, I told him about Mario's death, which he already knew. He offered his condolences. I accepted them and pressed on. I explained my reason for coming. Would he help me find out what Mario was up to in the world of radical lefties?

"When are you ever going to stop straddling the fence, Brovelli? It's the establishment or the movement. You can't be friends with both sides."

"I'm not friends with the establishment as you call it. I'm a simple *paisano* business man. For Christ's sake, look where being a radical got my brother, murdered, his girlfriend murdered."

"Cops say it was a suicide. Your bro shot his woman."

"And that's total bullshit."

"Well, not being any great fan of our constabulary, I'll help. We still owe you a favor if I remember right." He sighed. "All this year, our offices nationwide have been under attack by the cops, sheriff's departments, the FBI. In Des Moines, Iowa, that office was firebombed and destroyed. You see what I'm saying? He closed his eyes as if trying to visualize his words. Bowles paused and sighed. His eyes still closed, he whispered, "Man, I'm still trying to get over the pigs shooting our boys in Chicago. Just plain criminal, but will the cops go to jail, hell no."

I'd read about the shooting death of Fred Hampton and Mark Clark earlier this month, and the subsequent full-scale attack on the Black Panthers in the City of Angels. A Christmas gift from the Los Angeles police department, I'd heard said by a few of the white cops who occasionally came to Flynn's for his famous Irish stew and notorious *I-Dare-You-Chili*. My friend, Jay, a detective sergeant for the Oakland Police Department, told me later that those guys were not his idea of policemen. Jay is a homicide detective with ethics, compared to some boys in blue who are only in the force because they enjoyed power. I remembered some of the biggest bullies in high school and wasn't surprised later in life that they turned out to be cops or sheriffs, and the ones who couldn't cut it found jobs as security guards. I wondered if at some point there'd be a way to weed the bullies out of the police departments. I only wish Jay had told these jerks to their faces.

Bowles opened his eyes and looked startled that I was still there. After a moment, he said, "We will do what we can, Brovelli."

"That's all I can ask, Terrance. It will square us."

"You might have lucked out. One of our brothers from San Jose has moved up to Oakland and is hanging out with us doing this and that. He might have been in Vietnam about the same time as your brother. His name is Tisdale."

"What's his first name?"

"Doesn't have one. Just Tisdale. Strange cat. Sniper in Nam. We're thinking he could be very useful considering all the crap that we've been facing these days."

From talking on the telephone with Dila, I'd heard her explain how the FBI had dedicated 1969 to be the year law enforcement was going to wipe the Black Panthers off the face of the earth. So far, it hadn't worked, but a new year and a renewed effort was on its way. J Edgar Hoover had announced that the Black Panthers were the most dangerous threat to internal security of the country.Dila had sited the December 1968 shooting of Frank "Franco" Diggs that began the carnage, followed on January 17th with the murder shooting of Alprentice "Buncy" Carter and John Huggins on the UCLA campus. Supposedly by the Maulana "Ron" Karenga group, a BPP, Black Panthers Party, rival, but according to her sources the guys who did it were paid by the FBI. My Dila can be pretty damn persuasive. I may not be a convert to the left, but I'd learned the hard way a year ago that cops could be brutal and corrupt while the so-called bad guys, the Black Panthers, in this case, could be upstanding citizens of their community. Okay, so they weren't overly fond of white people, which gigantic James was pleased to remind me by calling me white-bread every time we met, which, thank God, was not that often.

"Can you arrange for me to meet Tisdale?"

"I'll call the brother and set it up. He is really wary of white folks."

"Tell him I'm Italian."

"You got a sense of humor, Brovelli. That's what I like about you."

"I appreciate your confidence," I said.

Bowles said he'd call me soon. I left. The sky had cleared and become a black canopy embedded with pinpricks of stars. It reminded of a bouffant hairdo I'd encountered last year with little pearls stuck all over it. The pearls were attached to long needles that the wearer of said hairdo, a bar tender at a local nightclub, withdrew and damn near took out my eyes. I shook off the memory and gave the night sky a chance to remind me of something more pleasant.

I got in the Mustang and sat — thinking. For the last year and a half, Mario had been heavily involved in the PeaceLinks' anti-war activities. Mario had also become more active in a new movement to control gun sales in this country, something most people thought was tantamount to ripping up the Constitution. The PeaceLinks office was closed by now. I'd visit it tomorrow. In the meantime, I remembered that before Mario moved in with Grace, he and an army buddy named Charley Radley were sharing an apartment. Given how hard it was to find places to live near the university, Radley could still be living at the same address in Berkeley. Maybe he could tell me something about Mario's life. I dumped the Mustang into first and headed for the Nimitz Freeway. I took the University Street exit and headed for College Avenue. I found a parking space in walking distance to the three-story Victorian that had been cut up into three front and back apartments. I'd only met Radley a few times, but I knew I remembered he was tall skinny dude with sunken eyes, Mario had once described as war weary. He had been Mario's platoon sergeant until he'd suffered a nervous breakdown and been given a section 8 out of the army. Like Mario, Radley had also tossed his Purple Heart into a bonfire. Unlike Mario, Radley continued to use drugs and might have even been selling dope to maintain his habit. It was Mario's loyalty to his men that he never kicked Radley out and often paid his half of the rent. Charley Radley was a likeable enough guy, so I never asked Mario why he put up with him. Radley's name was still listed next to the doorbell. I pushed the button and was buzzed through. The apartment was on the second-floor front. The door was open and an old man was standing in it waiting for me, hands crossed over a large chest, his face creased in anger. He was the manager and who the fuck was I? I handed him one of my business cards. I've learned over the years that people may not like car salesmen, but they are never threatened by them.

"I thought you were one of the Communist crumbs who did this," he said, pointing into the apartment.

"I'm not a Communist, I'm Italian," I said. His face didn't register humor. "This is my brother Mario Brovelli and Charley Radley's apartment."

"I haven't seen your bother for a long time, and I haven't seen Radley or McGoffin for three days?"

"Who's McGoffin?" I asked.

"Just another Commie if you ask me. I guess he was bunking with

Radley. You tell your brother that his name is still on the lease, and he's liable for the damages."

"What damages?"

"You tell him I'm calling my lawyer."

"Look, I don't care about damages. Did Radley leave a forwarding address?"

"Didn't. These Communists come and go as they please."

I didn't bother to ask about why Communists. He obviously believed my bro was one too. "Well, I'd like to speak to Casey McGoffin?"

"So the hell would I," he said in such a way that made me think that he'd prefer shooting him rather than talking to him.

"Do you know when he'll be back?"

"Do you see what they've done to my apartment? Why would either of them return?"

I stepped around him into the apartment. The manager followed me. When I saw the destruction, all I could say was, "*Minchia,*" Someone had trashed the place.

"Communists," the old man said. "The cops are on their way. I called the FBI, but they didn't give me the time of day. Here I was giving them a Commie and. . . and. . ."His lips trembled and angry spit flew out in all directions. I ducked and moved beyond spittle range. "I always believed that Senator McCarthy fellow in the Fifties got it right about Commies."

In the Fifties I was too young to remember who he was talking about or what exactly this McCarthy character had been right about. All of the rooms had been seriously trashed: upholstery, cushions slashed, mattresses cut open, dresser drawers broken, television shattered, refrigerator door open and gooey stuff spread across the floor. Somebody was looking for something important, I thought, then thought, Duh, Brovelli. Whoever created this this mess, sure as hell was looking for something important. Following the advice of the P.I. instruction manual I'd purchased during last year's investigation, I started searching for mail or an address book, any kind of writing that might provide me with names, addresses, phone numbers. The manager followed me through the rooms, muttering about Commies, pinkos, and reds and what the hell was I looking for anyway and taking Mario's name in vain. I let him rant. I found nothing except lots of anti-Vietnam War posters and literature.

I stepped into the bathroom, certain I was not going to find mail or an address book there, but my P.I. manual stated that you get a lot of personal information out of a medicine cabinet, like if the resident had hemorrhoids, or if he or she took medication for some illness. What good that would do me, I couldn't imagine. Before I got to the medicine cabinet, I saw the blood on the floor next to a totally-wrecked commode. The trail of blood lead to the shower curtain enclosing the bathtub. I flashed on Hitchcock's *Psycho*. Nothing good could be behind it. I didn't want to know, but felt I had to. I pulled the curtain back. No insane killer with a knife, no Radley or McGoffin either, only a dirty tub and my imagination. I did an about face, almost knocking over the old man who was looking over my shoulder. I took another look at the chaos and decided in was best not to be here when the cops arrived.

I bolted for the door and down the stairs and into my Mustang just as I heard sirens in the distance. I was six blocks away before I was out of second gear. I crossed from Oakland into Alameda by way of the Park Street Bridge. I got into my apartment building on Broadway Ave. At one time it used to be a fancy hotel. The sun was setting. I was ready to hit the sack.

Or so I thought.

I was unable to sleep. I got up and began pacing and wound up standing at the living room window staring out at the billboard across the alley that featured a giant Marilyn Monroe look-alike advertising Budweiser beer. She was lit up by an overhead lamp that made her eyes sparkle. "Marilyn," I spoke aloud, "my brother and his girlfriend murdered, a few days later Mario's apartment is searched, like into little pieces. Tell me they're not related."

Why do the two have to be related? You're basing your thinking on the perhaps erroneous belief that your brother did not shoot his girlfriend and then commit suicide.

Marilyn was not actually talking to me. This conversation was a one man play in which the actor does both voices. Let me assure you that I am not a *pazzo furioso*, which means a raving lunatic in Italian. My imagination has something to do with me being a Catholic. Catholics believe in the Holy Trinity and the Transubstantiation, which makes them vulnerable to all sorts of other mysteries. In my case, miracles, ghostly apparitions, and billboard Marilyn look-a-like's. Last year Winona's ghost followed me around reminding me I was too slow solving her murder, tapping her Mickey Mouse watch as if to say, *Get a move on Victor.* On one of our trips to Italy to visit relatives in Naples, my great aunt, Maddelena, a woman I remember now as being bent like an olive tree, had read my tea leaves and pronounced, *Multi fantasmi.* I hoped that was a onetime visitation, and I'd not encounter Mario's or Grace's ghosts.

"You're just a dead film queen, Marilyn, what do you know?" I said. I dropped the blinds and went to the couch. Besides being Grace's friend from Ireland, who was this guy Casey McGoffin? I'd have to find out. I also needed to find Charley Radley. I had no idea where to start. I was exhausted. I turned on the TV as a way to distract myself from thinking about Mario. I missed half an hour of *High Chaparral.* My other choices were stupid, especially the insipid *Brady Bunch.*I went to the kitchen, grabbed a bottle of Anchor Steam out of the fridge and sat at the kitchen table. On the table was a shopping bag containing the Christmas present I'd recently bought for Victor and Gloria's baby. I took it out of the bag to examine it. I was proud of my gift, **Sports Car for Dolls**. The picture on the box showed a cool green miniature all-steel sports car with red leather interior. Sitting behind the wheel was a nine-inch Barbie, dressed in traveling clothes. The doll came with three changes of clothes. Vincent's daughter Christina was only a year-and-a-half-old, too young for the toy the saleswoman had explained. But I informed her that her daddy and her uncle Victor were in the car business, and it was never too early, *thank you very much,* to start them along the clear path to a career in sales. Thinking of my niece, a chubby raven-haired beauty, put me in a better mood. I downed the beer and grabbed another. I returned to the living room. I put on the Beatles' *Abbey Road* on my record player, went to the couch and stretched out. I was asleep before *Here Comes the Sun* ended.

CHAPTER 4
THE FUCKING PLOT THICKENS

The Game is Afoot

Arthur Conan Doyle – *Adventure off Ashby Grange*

The sun was shining when I opened my eyes. There was a hammering in my head that couldn't have been the result of the two measly beers I'd drunk last night. It took me a moment to realize it was coming from my front door. I rolled off the couch and stumbled to the direction of the noise. Someone was yelling.

"Open the damn door, you stupid dago."

Ah, the dulcet voice of Jay Ness of the Oakland Police Department's homicide division. I let him in, and he stormed past me into the living room.

I followed him, wondering what was up with my favorite cop. I found out right away as Jay turned to face me.

"Victor, goddamn it to hell, are you going to start playing fucking Phillip Marlowe again? Are you? I got to know because if you are, I'm going to have to write you a ticket for being the biggest fool in the Bay Area."

"I still don't know what you're talking about. What have I done?"

"I'll tell you what. You put yourself on a list of suspects in the disappearance of two men, Charley Radley and another man named Casey McGoffin, and don't tell me you don't know who I'm talking about because you were in in their apartment yesterday evening. You were described by the manager."

Disappearance and not murder? Why else would Jay, who was a homicide detective, be called in for a petty destruction of property or burglary?

"Jay, you're right. I was there. I explained about Radley, Mario's roommate and McGoffin, a recent arrival who was sharing the apartment with Radley. "Place was a hell of a mess. Whoever did it was looking real hard for something."

"You noticed, did you?"

"I can do without the sarcasm."

"By leaving the way you did, Victor, it makes you a suspect. The manager's description of you was not very good, but I knew right away."

"No body, no suspect," I said. "And speaking of bodies, you're a homicide detective. Why were you called in if there was no body?

"Damn it, Victor, stop sounding like some dime-store dick. I can't go through another year of you screwing around with my investigations."

"Your investigation?"

"Yeah, and I don't want you meddling."

The truth was I had only meddled once in last year's murder of Winona Davis, a onetime temp secretary for the Brovelli Brothers' Used Cars.

I placed my hand on Jay's shoulder, which seemed to calm him down. "First of all, if you recall, it was I, Victor Brovelli, son of Big Sal Brovelli, and twin to Vincent Brovelli, who, not only solved last year's murders, but also uncovered the drug connection for which you got a commendation. So who better to screw with *your* investigation? You want a cup of coffee?"

He sighed. "Yeah, hell. Why not. Sure."

"I'll plug in Mr. Coffee. Won't take a minute. I just woke up. As you can see."

"You could use a shower," he said.

Had I actually gone to sleep in my blazer with my shoes on? I took the blazer off and put it aside to take to the cleaners. "I'll be right back, and you can tell me everything." I headed to my bedroom. I took a quick shower and changed into sweats and slippers and returned. Jay was sitting on the couch, his head back, snoring. I felt bad for him. The police in Oakland as well as in all the major cities around the country, were on high alert. It was as if the country was on its way to a mental breakdown: The Moratorium and Mobilization Peace March on Washington, over 250,000 people protesting the Vietnam War, driving VP Spiro Agnew out of his mind; Charley Mansion crazies; the Chicago Seven trial, dragging on; Black Militants taking over a building at Cornell University; Police everywhere cracking down on student protests. Not to mention, Director of the FBI Hoover's bugaboos, the Black Panthers scaring the piss out of the general public. Not that there wasn't violence happening in other countries, but as Jay told me one night over too many beers, it looked like America was the commode for all the world's crap. I did not have the same negative feelings about the protest generation, not since I met Dila who was responsible for turning me left of my previous middle-of-the-road political position. I had let Jay's comment slide. I knew that in this over-heated political climate my friend was over-worked and stressed and that his sleep had been cut in half by an impossible schedule. My overweight, balding, poker-playing buddy was one of the good cops who believed in justice not simply the rule of law.

Mr. Coffee sounded the alarm. I came back from the kitchen, shook Jay awake, and stuck a mug of coffee, with cream the way he liked it in front of his nose. He took it in his hands like it was the Holy Communion chalice. He sipped and sighed.

"So," I said, "What's going on?"

"At this point, this is a simple case of malicious destruction of property."

"So why were the homicide cops called it?" I asked.

Jay shrugged and took another sip of his coffee and sighed.

"Mario and Grace are shot," I said. "His roommate and some other guy, a friend of Grace's, do a disappearing act. The apartment is completely totaled. You don't think it's coincidental? It's pretty damn suspicious to me."

Jay said. "Please, Victor, don't go speculating. Remember, Mario wasn't shot, he shot himself."

I was surprised by Jay's tone, so certain. "You wouldn't have come here, Jay, all pissed and dramatic, if you didn't think there was a connection between Mario and Grace's death and these guys disappearing."

"Yeah, you're right, the ransacked apartment is not our bailiwick. Look, if you'd only back off for a while. Let me and my boys sort through it all before you go sticking your dago nose into where it doesn't belong, I would greatly appreciate it."

Dago nose. I'd remember that for a later payback.

"Honestly, Victor, my plate is so full, stuff is sliding off onto the floor. If I have to worry about you. . . I don't want to worry about you."

"Gee, Jay. I didn't know you cared." I could do sarcasm too. I blew him a kiss, which got me a middle finger response. He was looking at me with those sad, gloomy eyes, and I was wondering that there was something else going on he wasn't telling me. Something was rotten in the state of Oakland or Berkeley or in whatever direction I was smelling.

"Jay, you're holding out on me. You're not telling me something."

"Jesus H. Christ, Brovelli. Who the hell is the detective sergeant in the Oakland Police Department, you or me? I'm the one who should be saying that to you. You're the God damn amateur."

"Right. Fine. You're alpha dog. But you're still not telling me everything."

Jay put down his cup on the coffee table and stood up.

"I'll tell you this much, and that's it. Immigration is interested in McGoffin, and Radley has a history of selling drugs. Now, it's fair warning, Brovelli. Keep out of this."

He stomped down the hall and was gone, slamming the door hard behind him. I was about to yell something nasty after him, but the phone rang. It was Terrance Bowles.

"I've set up a meeting with Tisdale. He likes Chinese food. Be at the Golden Dragon at 12:30 sharp and bring your checkbook because he'll be ordering lunch. He eats like a horse. And, remember, don't piss him off. He really doesn't like Caucasians. He's doing me a favor."

"Not another James," I said.

"Tisdale makes James sound ecumenical," he said and hung up.

"Thanks," I said into the silence at the other end of the line. *Ecumenical? James??*

My coffee was cold. I went into the kitchen, poured a hot cup and went to the bedroom to dress for work.

Saturday was barbeque day at Brovelli Brother's Used Cars. We served chicken and Italian sausages, free to all respectable customers and freeloaders in the neighborhood. I'd come up with this idea as a way of attracting customers after Pop had turned the dealership over to Vincent and me. Sometimes it worked, sometimes it didn't, but it has become a tradition. We provide water. BYOB if anyone wanted something else to drink.

For work, my closet contains four blue blazers, the same number of powder blue dress shirts with button-down colors and four gray slacks. I have an assortment of college blue and red ties with different designs. Today I wore the Blue Blazer with the nautical buttons. I was out the door by seven-thirty. I stopped at Ole's Waffle House on Park Street for breakfast, my usual three eggs sunnyside up on top of one of the largest and fluffiest waffles made in the Bay Area served to me by Mame, a tall bosomy red headed waitress, who'd worked at Ole's for as long as I could remember. Mame was named by her mother after the character in the movie *Aunty Mame.* I figured her to be somewhere in her fifties. With her youthful face, she could have easily been in her thirties.

It was eight-thirty when I arrived at the lot. The chain across the driveway was still up signaling I was the first to arrive. I unlocked the chain and dragged it aside. I parked behind our office. I unlocked the door and turned on all the interior lights. I sat at my desk and looked at the couch sitting against the wall across from me. Above it hung a map of the city of Naples where my parents were born and raised before immigrating to the United States. I enjoyed looking at the photograph. It reminded me of my heritage. Vincent told me that was stupid when I mentioned it, which, of course, turned into a wrestling match, two grown-ups replaying the whole twin-thing. We couldn't avoid it, so deeply is twinness imbedded in us, in all twins, I suspected.

The sound of an automobile engine turned my head to the window. Theresa, our accountant's totally groovy pale yellow 1967 MGB Roadster convertible was rolling in. The car was such a beauty that we'd talked her into parking it on the lot and not behind the office because it would attract customers. Theresa had agreed with a little pride-of-ownership smile. We placed a pending sale sign on the windshield, in the event someone wanted to buy it. It was sort of like a friend of mine who'd bought a failing tavern in San Francisco. He cleaned it up and renamed it Bird Cage. It did not take off the way he'd expected. Then, he got the bright idea to hire a couple of really fine chicks to come sit at the bar for a couple of hours each evening, free drinks included. After a while, the word got out that there were gorgeous dollies at his place. Soon, the bar was full of guys and where there were guys, the gals followed. The joint is thriving. So far, Brovelli Brother's Used Cars has not experienced the same growth but, as Sweets Monroe often remarks, *hope springs external.*

I watched Theresa maneuver her car into the center slot reserved for her and get out. Our cousin on my pop's side, was classic Italian with long lustrous black hair, black eyes and long black eyelashes. Her eyebrows were a little bit too thick and almost touching, which was her only negative feature as far as I could tell. Her full body would have been a Renaissance painter's ideal. Sort of a Sophia Loren-type body. If she wasn't my first cousin, I would have been putting the moves on her, *that is, before I met Dila.* Theresa entered the office, said *ciao*, went to her desk and immediately started typing. I did say Theresa was hard working, didn't I? Well, if I didn't, Theresa Bacigalupe made workaholics appear downright lazy. Vincent and I had no complaints. She'd reorganized and streamlined the files and accounting procedures that our previous accountant, Sylvia, had screwed up badly. But we had to make a few rules regarding her obsession with cleanliness and tidiness. For example: Placing our feet on our desks was okay. If I missed shooting a crumpled invoice into my wastebasket, she didn't have to leap out of her seat and pick it up. She didn't have to hang up our coats if we left them draped on the back of our chairs. In return, I agreed to put the toilet seat down, and Vincent agreed not to stick used gum under the lip of his desk. And we both agreed that after we washed and polished our cars, we would clean up behind the office and not in our bathroom, which now was decorated with photographic landscapes of her parents' native *Provencia di Napoli* and smelled like a florist shop. She approved of the large photograph of the neighborhood of Vamero in Naples, the city where my Pop grew up. Her grandparents still lived in that exact same neighborhood.

Not long after Theresa drove in, Vincent showed up.

"Good morning, Terry," he said as he walked into the office. She did not respond. Vincent winked at me. "Good morning, Theresa," he said. This time, Theresa looked up, smiled and said, "Buon giorno, Vincent." We'd tried shortening her name to Terry, but repeatedly gotten the silent stink-eye. Nobody gives stink eyes better than young Italian women, which is preliminary step before the evil eye. And whine? Have you ever heard Italian women talk, always as if they are in great need of something being denied them?

At nine o'clock, Vincent and I began setting up the barbeque. He brought out the coals, water cooler and ice. I hooked up our Saint Mary's red and blue banners to the outside of the building. When the barbeque was ready, we'd hoist it to the level of the office roof so the little triangles would signal to the neighborhood, it was chow time. While we worked, neither of us said much, Mario's death weighing on our minds. I plugged in the sound system. Vincent and I had agreed earlier that in honor of Mario, we'd play a Woodstock Medley. We settled on a couple of Santana, Joe Cocker, and Melanie hits. I went to the office and arranged the LPs in order. I added another of Mario's favorites, Janis Joplin's "Maybe." I was reminded of Dila telling me about Harlem Cultural Festival that became to be known as Black Woodstock. We'd already been dating by then. She'd flown back to New York with two of her cousins and came back raving about Aretha Franklin singing with Mavis Staples, Dr. Martin Luther King

Jr.'s favorite hymn, "Precious Lord, Take My Hand." I'd known who Aretha Franklin was. Thinking of Dila made me wish she was here with me.

Back outside, I asked Vincent if, after we set up the barbeques and got things going if I could take of around noon to work on Mario's case, which is the way I was referring to it in my mind. He told me to go for it. I had a feeling that after talking to Tisdale, I'd have a better idea of what Mario had gone through in Vietnam, and that, hopefully, would give me some direction. Why I felt that way, I wasn't sure, but I've often been rewarded by following my instincts. Or as Dila put it one time, by following my female intuition. *Ah, Dila, how you have enriched my life.*

Vincent was the chef today. I worked in the office. I spent the morning doing some cold calls with no success. Most people don't like sales pitches over the phone. But occasionally you wind up with a buyer. A salesman at an auto show told me making cold calls was like waiting for the bus to stop and asking every good-looking woman that gets off if she would like to sleep with you. After getting your face slapped hundreds of times, there'll be one who'll say yes. *Sorry, Dila, I'm trying not to be such a chauvinist, but it's tough with you all the way across the country.*

Vincent called for the meat. I went to the back-room fridge and hauled out the marinated chicken and hotlinks and took them outside. Almost immediately the aroma of barbeque sauce rose into the air. Across the street Nick Parsegian, the owner of Discount Furniture waved to me and patted his stomach. Parsegian was not one of my favorite people, a little too slick for my taste. A little too aggressive pushing sales. He was about my height with black graying hair that he slicked back with pomade. A tiny mustache decorated his upper lip over a tiny mouth, and no chin.

Joplin ended "Maybe," and Sly and the Country Stone began singing about *Taking you higher*. The cars needed a little cleaning, so I grabbed a polish rag. Two separate couples wandered onto the lot under the pretense of examining the cars, but eyeing the barbeque grills. As ordained by the Gods of Automobiles, the men asked to look under the hoods, the women wanted to see the interiors. I couldn't speak for the women, but I knew that the guys with their heads under the hoods probably couldn't tell a carburetor from a generator. When some jerk starts trying to play Mr. Mechanic with me, I love to pop the hood of one of Jitters's souped-up babies and see how much he really knows about engines. I throw a few small details about the timing or the compression. Pretty soon, the guy figures I'm toying with him and gets really embarrassed or angry. It's not a good sales technique, but fuck know-it-alls.Right now on the lot I have a cherry midnight-blue and white Impala two-door with an engine Jitters rebuilt that can go from zero to 60 in 6 seconds.My twin says he gets a hard on just thinking about it. I'm a little skeptical, since the record was set in 1968 by a Dodge Charger that crossed the line in 4.8 seconds. Even if Jitters is pushing the truth a little, that baby is on the market for big bucks. Even if it doesn't sell, car-guys stop by just to take a look at the engine. The Impala is like a shill at a blackjack table.

Theresa stepped out of the office and tapped her wristwatch. Vincent put five fingers into the air. I released the string holding our college red and blue pennants. On Vincent's signal, I raised them. Parsegian was already halfway across the street, dodging cars and trucks. Why he chose to jaywalk across one of the busiest streets on Oakland remains a mystery. We'd asked him a number of times, and he'd shrugged, like he didn't know himself. Parsegian was known in the neighborhood as being cheap. He'd never passes up a free mean. I'd heard it rumored that he had hidden wealth sort of like Scrooge in the Dickens' story. Santana's guitar's riffs sounded out over the speakers. Next door, Flynn's afternoon customers began drifting over. I grabbed a drumstick, and asked Vincent if I could go. I'd explained to Vincent earlier what I was up to. Vincent nodded as if to say better you than me. I headed behind the office for Mario's Mustang, licking barbeque off my fingers so I wouldn't soil my sports coat.

• • •

I parked in front of the Golden Dragon next to a fire-engine red Harley Davidson. Out of the midday sunlight and into the restaurant required some visual adjustment. I spotted the only Black man in the place sitting in the booth nearest the door and facing in my direction. I approached him. In front of him was a pot of tea, a bowl of soup, a side order of eggrolls and bowls of fried rice, sweet and sour pork and orange beef. A man with an appetite, I thought, but not a big man as Minister Bowles had led me to believe. Tisdale didn't have to stand up for me to know he was a shrimp. The slender fingers holding chopsticks looked like they belonged on a keyboard, not holding an army sniper rifle. His features were more Arabic than African. His dreads hung out beneath a knitted red, black and yellow Rastafarian cap. He didn't look dangerous until I slid into the booth and looked in his eyes — needle points of darkness. He did not greet me. I stuck out my hand, but he didn't respond. I shouldn't have been surprised.

I said, "I'm Victor Brovelli."

"I'm Tisdale. This is a favor I'm doing for Brother Bowles. Let's get it over with, then you can pay for my food and get your white ass outa my face."

White-ass did not sit well with my Italian personality-disorder. All right, if that's how he wanted to play it. "Any time your black-ass wants to test my white-ass," I said. "Right now, right here, or outside." I thumbed over my shoulder in the direction of the door, hoping he wouldn't pull a gun out with those slender fingers and shoot me. I watched his eyes squint. Like a fucking rattlesnake, I thought. Then, his eyes widened and a slight smile creased his lips.

"Sheeet," he said, a classic straight-razor appearing open in his hand as if by magic. "You'd be dead so fast you wouldn't feel a thing. I'll let the challenge slide, *Mister* Bro-velli, 'cause your brother was the only stand-up commanding officer in Nam I ever had." The razor disappeared as magically as it appeared. "So, what do you want from me?"

My anger turned instantly to relief, then curiosity. This was better than I expected. Tisdale not only had been in Vietnam at the time Mario was there, he knew my brother personally. He probably knew Charley Radley. Were things falling into place? I explained my hypothesis to him.

"All sorts of terrible shit happened in Nam," Tisdale said." Pausing, he closed his eyes, then closed them tighter, as if he was seeing the shit happening. "Fifty, hundred years from now, there'll be shit that's still secret." He kept his eyes closed. I waited.

"Heroin," he said.

"What about it?"

His eyes opened. "CIA mostly started bringing it over. But all kinds of officers and enlisted men got in on the action. When I was in transit on leave, I hung out at Ton Son Nhut Air Base. I saw a corpsman cutting into corpses and pulling out the intestines, then filling them up with bags of pure smack. Don't ask me how I saw it. Made me puke."

"Jesus, Mary, and Joseph, you gotta be kidding."

"Still doing the shit, as far as I know. One white guy tried to get me into it. I figured he needed a black to lay the blame on if he got caught. He was a mean cocksucker. I had no problem promising to keep my mouth shut."

"Did my brother know?"

"Captain may have. Rumors all over the place. Sheeet, everybody knew it. Probably that Texas asshole in the White House knew it. Could be using a little smack himself."

The idea of President Johnson using heroin must have seemed funny to him because he began laughing. It sounded sort of like coughing. I thought of a hyena. "Okay, drugs. How about weapons?"

"Probably best to look for that sheeet in San Diego where the big container ships from Nam come in. Around here, you'd be wasting yo time."

"I crossed weapons of the list in my mind. "Anything else?"

Tisdale nodded. "Vietnamese bitches want to get stateside. There were guys in Saigon put together a way to smuggle them in. Real young bitches too. Turn 'em into ho's."

"You mean in America, right now?"

"Why you all so fucking surprised. It's war, man. For some guys, war means money. Don't nobody think it's all about fucking stopping Com-U-nists, sheeet, waving the God damn flag around only means they scored big bread."

I had listened to Mario when he criticized the war, so I wasn't completely surprised, but heroin inside bodies, and young Vietnamese girls smuggled into America and turned into whores, *Madonna.* This sure as hell could be a motive to murder someone, say, if he was going to expose the drug dealers or the pimps.

I told him what Mario had said about how the war had changed him for the worse.

Tisdale shook his head. "Brovelli, not one soldier, officer or grunt, I knew came back himself. All got motha-fucking changed."

"What about atrocities?" I asked. "Like Mai Lai. Maybe Mario witnessed something like that and it affected his mind."

"Sure. Plenty atrocities to go around. Mai Lai? Sheeet, more Mai Lai's than anybody wants to know about. And the motha-fucking war ain't over yet. Not a day go by without some grunt raping some gook chick or shooting somebody for nothing but being a gook. The whole stinking place was one huge Mai Lai. I kid you not. If your brother wanted to put his life at risk, any soldier, for that matter, all he gots to do is write down a little of what he saw over there and wait for some government spook to snuff his ass."

"I have to start somewhere," I said.

"Somebody's word aint' good enough. Got to be in writing and witnesses. And I'm telling you now, if you start poking your nose into the heroin business, you better look out for the CIA fuckers. They be all over yo ass."

I was about to ask him another question, when Tisdale threw the chopsticks on the table, like he was disgusted with Vietnam and me and my questions that probably for bringing back all sorts of awful memories.

"I'd look into the ho's first. That's the story not many people know about. Best I can do for you. It's up to you to do the snooping, that's what y'all is ain't you ya, a snoop-dog."

He started laugh-coughing again, and I almost said something until I remembered how fast the straight-razor had appeared.

"I'll tell Brother Bowles we met, and you almost kicked my ass." Tisdale stood up and edged out of the booth, still laughing. Leaving his food and the check.

He was actually even shorter and skinnier than I first thought. How he got into the army was an interesting question, but I wasn't prepared to ask. He strode out of the restaurant. Diminutive, yes, but I felt I got off lucky he didn't take me up on my challenge.

I heard a motorcycle roar and tires burn rubber.

I failed to ask Tisdale if he wanted to buy a car, so I could write his thirty-dollar meal off as a business expense.

As I walked out of the restaurant, I realized what it was about Tisdale's eyes. The whites of his eyes were too white, and the irises so black that the stark contrast made his eyes look like bullseyes. As I walked to my Mustang, I was certain that I'd been talking to a killer. I got in my car and turned on the engine. The fucking plot thickens, I thought. Then I thought, who the fuck was I kidding. How in the world was I going to delve into the morass of that kind of criminal activity? If I was out of my league last year playing detective, I was surely out of the universe this time. I pulled away from the curb and joined the traffic. I turned on the radio.

Raindrops were falling on the singer's head. Yeah, I thought, raining on my head too.

CHAPTER 5
DELVING

One must seek the truth within – not without.
Hercule Poirot

After due consideration, I'd decided to take Tisdale's suggestion and start with the whores. The only person I knew who might have information about Vietnamese prostitutes would be my friend Detective Sargent Jay Ness. After this morning I figured it would be best to surprise him. From Chinatown, it wasn't far to the Oakland police station where Jay had his office. The desk sergeant told me he was out taking a late lunch. "He'll be at. . ."

"Brovelli Brother's Used Cars still consuming more than his fair share of our barbeque," I said, finishing his sentence.

"So you're Brovelli? Ya know, Ness was considering shooting you this morning."

"We're like brothers," I said.

"Remind your brother that he's supposed to bring me some links."

I assured him I would. Before I left, I asked him when Mario's body would be released. He made a call and told me that my parents could go to the coroner any time, just to bring identification. My mother had been on the phone with Father Dunnican working out a date for a funeral mass and burial. Whatever church said about suicide and Christian burial would not intimidate my mom. I doubted the good priest would have the courage to argue with her.When I left the police station, my watch said it was after three. The feeding frenzy at the lot would be over. Knowing Jay, he might be hanging around trying to talk to Theresa.

As I suspected, Jay was standing off to the side, talking to Theresa while she was cleaning up. Hitting on her might be a more accurate description of what my cop friend was doing. It reminded me that Jay had tried, with little luck, to date our previous accountant, Cousin Sylvia. When I first met Jay at one of Body's poker games and we became friends, somebody told me that Jay was the ugliest guy he'd ever known who could somehow get gorgeous women to marry him. He's about my height, a little under six feet. If it wasn't for his pot belly, you'd mistake Jay for a weight lifter. He has a bulbous Jimmy Durante nose and baggy eyes that make him always look sad. He's been married and divorced three times and is on the lookout for a fourth. The Brovelli family are traditional Catholic Italians down to our toenails. The institution of marriage is sacred. We'd never had a divorce in our family. It's why I've remained hesitant to get hitched, although I've been giving it a lot of thought since Adila Agbo and I started dating. In the face of marriage, I'm a coward, so it's probably a good thing that Dila enrolled at NYU to do her master's degree in theater arts and left me to pine over her. Which reminded me that Dila would be home for Christmas. Which reminded me that my telephone calls had still not reached her. We had not spoken on the phone now going on three weeks, and I was getting annoyed.

As I approached Jay, he made a face, like bug off. I smiled broadly.

"I do not like that phony smile, Victor. Whatever it is you want, I want nothing to do with it. Theresa and I were having a conversation, and you're butting in. So scram."

"Scram, who says scram these days?" I said. "Only Archie and Veronica say scram in comic books." I gave Theresa a nod in the direction of the office, and she mouthed *"mili grazi"* and hurried away. When it comes to women, Jay is not the coolest guy on the planet, which raises the question how did he wind up with three beautiful wives. A year ago, he'd competed with Sunny Badger, the chief honcho of the Satans, our local motorcycle gang for Sylvia's, affection. Badger and Sylvia were a significant part of last year's debacle that has often been the subject of some of my worst nightmares.

"I saw what you did," Jay said. "You can be that much of an asshole."

"What do you know about Vietnamese prostitutes?" I asked, hoping my sudden question would catch him off guard. A long silence followed.

"Well?" I said.

"This can't possibly have anything to do with Mario. Goddamn it, Victor, all the forensic evidence is in, and there's no question your brother shot his girl, then shot himself. End of story. Done deal. We've closed our files on it. I stamped the damn file myself, C.L.O.S.E.D."

"All right, I know you can spell. Now answer the question. I just spoke to a Vietnam vet who said bad guys are smuggling Vietnamese women into the states and turning them into whores." I watched my friend rub his temple.

"You are about to give me a monster migraine, Victor. Somebody's been feeding you a huge load of crap. Rumors, that's all. We ran them down. Coordinated with military police. Couldn't find a thing."

"Well, it sounded real the way this guy explained it to me."

"And who is this authority?"

"A Black Panther. I'm not going to give you his name. Mario was his commanding officer in Vietnam."

"Geez Louise, Victor. What kind of proof did he give you? The way your mind is operating, he could have told you J Edgar Hoover killed your brother and you'd believe it."

"Well, maybe the asshole did," I said.

"Awh, man," Jay moaned. "I gotta tell ya, Victor, you're letting your grief screw up your thinking. Trust me, there is no Vietnamese prostitute ring. And, one other thing, you better stay clear of the Black Panthers. They are becoming increasingly violent."

Something I knew from playing poker with Jay on Thursday nights at Flynn's was that he was not a good liar, so as much as I didn't like it, it sounded to me like he was telling the truth about the whores, or at least the truth as he knew it. If Jay wasn't lying, then Tisdale had been. But why would he screw with me and risk the displeasure of Terrance Bowles? The Panthers' Minister of Education, with his spectacles and tiny mustache and gray hair, looked like a college professor and spoke the Kings' English, but the rank-and-file Panthers knew not to displease him. The rumor was that two white rednecks had attacked him, and Terrance had killed them with his bare hands. I couldn't imagine it, but there was a kind of something wild in the little eyes behind the specs.There was not much chance Tisdale would talk to me again, and I'd used up my credit with Bowles. I felt as if I'd come to an intersection and had been stopped by a red light. When it turned green, which way would I go? I could drive straight ahead in the direction Tisdale had pointed me, or turn toward bodies filled with heroin, or in the direction of weapons smuggling. Or, maybe, the imaginary red light was telling me to stop for good. I needed to think. I reminded Jay he needed to bring his desk sergeant links and headed for Flynn's to have a cold brew and decide which road I would take. *Always the one less traveled*, I heard Mario telling me once, giving me advice about how to live a good life. He'd just graduated from West Point and looked super sharp and believable in his brand-new Second Lieutenants uniform, ready to go to Vietnam and win the war single handed. If that had been his road less traveled, it sure had been a dead end for him. Stopping for good was an option Robert Frost had not contemplated. I gave it a minute of consideration then decided neither would Victor Brovelli.

All the barstools were empty. The only people in the tavern were in the back playing pool. Most of Flynn's Saturday afternoon crowd was gone by now. The Saturday night crowd would not arrive until later. They were serious pool and dart players that included Body's Irish buddies, who sat around, drank and talked Irish politics and rebellion. As Brody was want to say recently about Northern Ireland, "Boys, the shiest is about to hit the fooking fan," On those Saturday nights, one took his life in his hands walking into Flynn's wearing orange. That had happened once when one *ritardato* wearing an orange sweatshirt with University of Syracuse printed on it walked in. The moron managed to escape with a few bruises, but the sweatshirt didn't.

I looked through the shadows, hoping that Flynn was next door, but no such luck. He hailed me from the end of the bar.

"Victor, me lad, before I pour you a cold one, answer me this question. What do you call an Italian hooker?" It never failed, as long as I'd been coming to Flynn's I had to suffer one of Body's stupid Italian jokes.

Body and his mother had emigrated to the U.S. from Ireland when he was a teenager. Twenty years later, he retained a thick brogue. Freckled face, carrot toped and big bellied, he looked every bit the part of the prototypical Hibernian tavern owner, either that or an overgrown elf.

"I haven't the slightest idea, but I know you're dying to tell me."

"A pastatute."

"Not one of your best, Body," I said.

But it wasn't keeping Body from laughing. For as long as I'd been coming into Flynn's I'd had to suffer his stupid Italian jokes. Most of the time I didn't mind. I had a store of politically incorrect Irish jokes in my portfolio as comebacks if I was in the mood to go mano-a-mano. Today I was in no mood. I grabbed my frosty mug of Anchor Steam that he proffered and took a stool nearest the door. I sipped and thought, and thought. I came up with no ideas for my effort, but unlike our taciturn Pop, Mario was always talking and joking. For the two of us, he was our principal source of wisdom. We saw less of him after he went to West Point. After graduating, he disappeared into the jungles of Vietnam and came home, minus a hand, a moody, unhappy and unrecognizable Mario. Until he met Grace and joined the PeaceLinks.

"Victor, Victor, you okay?"

I raised my head and looked up at Body Flynn's worried face. I rubbed my forehead where it had been resting on the bar-top. I felt tears in my eyes and quickly brushed them away with the back of my hand.

"It's tooof. Me older brother died same as me da in a shooting. He was a cop like me da. Wouldn't leave his job to come with me and me ma to the States. Me ma and me were already in the States. We got a telephone call from a cousin. I was sixteen."

Body was trying to be empathetic, but it wasn't helping.

Your beer is a wee stale," he said, pouring a new mug and placing it in front of me. I looked around and saw that while I'd been thinking, the bar had filled up, guys back from the barbeque, ready for an afternoon of pool or darts until the wives called for them to get their sorry asses home. I nodded at Larry Hughes the owner of the Donut Hole, and Flynn's token black customer. Larry had played a couple of years with the Raiders before his knees gave out. From the other end of the bar, Swanee, our detail man, waved a thumbs-up. The denizens of Flynn's were good guys. Figuring I needed space since Mario's death, they kept me out of the barroom banter.

When Body turned on the television to sports news, and somebody stuck a dime in the jukebox to "Ma Cherie Amour," I headed to the john, took a leak and departed, Stevie Wonder's falsetto trailing me out the door. I sat in my car staring through my windshield. I wanted to drive somewhere, anywhere — *off a fucking cliff*. I could feel myself growing more angry. I knew Vincent was not as convinced as I was that Mario and Grace had been murdered. I couldn't blame him. There wasn't a shred of evidence that suggested it was anything other than what Jay said it was.

From where I sat, I could see Vincent wiping down cars. The barbeque was put away. The blue and red college Go Gaels flags were down and stored. East 14th was rumbling with traffic going both ways to Oakland's city center and south toward Hayward and other small communities that would eventually give way to the city limits of San Jose. I was a city guy. I loved the sounds of motor and horn and siren. The occasional whiff of exhaust didn't bother me. The hardy street trees or city parks gave me hope, growing despite the intrusion of cement. I found the sparse lawns in front of sparse house in the neighborhood comforting for their modesty. I loved sitting on park benches, watching guys stripped to the waist playing basketball on asphalt courts, the occasional dandelion out of the surface cracks. I didn't need to buy a cabin in the mountains or on a beach like my older brother Carlo did, suffering hours of bumper-to-bumper traffic on the highways. Getaways, they called them. In this respect, Vincent was willing to join the traffic herd. He has been saving for a Lake Tahoe cabin. I give him a pass because he's a family man and likes to ski. Twins, especially identical ones, are often misunderstood. There are many clichés associated with us, but people do not pay attention to the nuanced differences. I was asked once in what way were Vincent and I different. I explained it this way: Consider comparing us to classy cars — that is to say we're not just ordinary vehicles.I'd be a Porsche, and he'd be a Rolls Royce; it's a matter of style. I'm for the back roads; he sticks to the highways.However, neither of us lets up on the throttle once we feel we've got the right of way.

I remained behind the wheel, staring out the window. I tried letting my mind wander. Give your mind a rest, I told myself. It didn't work. Eventually, it wandered back to Mario. If Jay was right, and there was no such thing as a prostitute ring, I could try to investigate the other two possibilities. But Tisdale had not been encouraging about atrocities. And as he said, atrocities were part of the scene, so many that no one was paying much attention anymore. "Gotta think, gotta think," I said to the rosary hanging from my rearview mirror. I slammed the car into first and took off. I didn't mean to peal rubber, but I was sure the squeal of my tires would have signaled Vincent that his twin was one unhappy *paesano.*

In a double-locked garage close to my apartment that I rent, I store my 1965 silver gray Porsche 365 Cabriolet hardtop coupe. I take it out on drives when I'm exceptionally happy and want to celebrate or when I'm particularly frustrated and need to think. Being car men, both my twin and I think best behind the wheel. His personality enjoys long, uncluttered highways where he can test the high end of the speedometer. I prefer driving going through the gears on roads resembling snakes. My favorite stretch is

Highway One along the Pacific Coast from San Francisco to Santa Cruz. I've driven that stretch so often I could do it in my sleep, although sleep is not advisable given that driving south the road drops off on the right straight into the ocean. After the wounds I'd suffered at the hands of some very bad dudes last year while solving the murder of Sweets ex-girlfriend healed, the first thing I did was take Dila on that drive to Santa Cruz. It was a celebration drive of our new romance. She loved those curves as much as I did. I let her drive. She was a natural. I could see her face now, glowing with pleasure, those green eyes, one a slightly different color from the other, her afro like a halo, her breathing coming fast with excitement.

I sat in front of the garage questioning whether I should open it up, pull off the tarp and head west. I finally decided against it. The sun was already going down and there would be week-end traffic. Time to head home, I thought. I'd call Dila and hope by some miracle she'd be in.

My apartment building was once a fancy hotel in the days when Alameda was an island resort for wealthy San Franciscans. You entered the front door of my apartment into an old-fashioned lobby with real oak floors, worn Persian rugs and lots of plants. There are lobby entrances to the Four Season's Florist and a piano bar called The Fireside where Deidre Delmar, an oldish bleached blonde, entertains weekends singing the Broadway tunes, her voice gravelly from non-stop Phillip Morris cigarettes. I don't hate any music, but Broadway tunes are not one of my favorites.

The door to my apartment was unlocked and opened a crack. I placed my hand on the doorknob, frightened for no reason I could think of, except. . . Except what? *Mario's murderer was in there. He was on to me, the only person between him and the perfect crime.* For a moment, I considered turning around and fleeing. For only a moment before I recognized I was thinking like a chump. *Victor, you're maybe going a little bit nuts.* If there was somebody inside, it sure as hell was not a murderer. Slowly I pushed the door open and stepped in. Keeping close to the wall, I moved slowly and quietly until I could peek into the living room. *Ma fanculo,* I thought. Sound asleep on the couch was Sweets Monroe, his skinny body surrounded by candy wrappers.

CHAPTER 6
DELVING WITH SWEETS

The fault of the burglar are the qualities of the financier.
George Bernard Shaw

With Sweets Monroe, there's a fine line between hating him and loving him. Vincent and I had been tiptoeing that line for at least six years since we took over the business from our pop. Sweets is not always as sweet as his name. The man who claims to be a direct descendant of the pirate, Jean Lafitte, cheats at cards, dresses like a clown, has a hairdo like a cockatiel, sucks continuously and annoyingly on hard candy, lies, gossips, sponges off anyone and everyone, and never pays his bar tab.However, because of his Robin Hood rep, most people in the neighborhood give Sweets Monroe a pass. Returning home and finding Sweets asleep on my couch had increased in frequency lately. Seeing him on my couch usually annoyed me. Tonight, I was happy to see him.

"Wake up," I said, jiggling his shoulder. He grunted and continued sleeping. I noticed that he was making sucking noises even though there was no candy in his mouth. Trickles of saliva on either side of his chin. *Schifoso,* I mumbled. It's the Italian word for disgusting but carries a number of other connotations like putrid and revolting. I yanked the sofa cushion from beneath his head, and his cockatiel-shaped blond hair fell back. He sat up, looking dazed.

"Man, dude, that was cruel," he said, rubbing his eyes. "I was dreaming of a faaantab-u-lus lady."

"You were dreaming about hard candy," I said.

"Sweets for Sweets, *mon frere*. What's the difference? I lick my ladies all over."

"I'm not your brother, and I don't want to hear about your disgusting perversions."

"In my heart you've always been my brother," Sweets said.

"Then you'll be happy to provide me with your burglar skills."

"Can't do it, ma man. Sweets be going straight. I was hit wit a beeg revelation, like an epiphany on the freeway to Damascus. See what I'm saying? It was your bro's death. You know, like, I could die tomorrow and what would people say? Sweets Monroe, he be a good burglar? My children wouldn't want their daddy to have that kind of legacy, *non*?"

"You don't have any children." It was a statement, not a fact. Sweets' life in Louisiana prior to moving to the Bay Area, was a cipher. He could have had three families, twenty children.

"Not that I'm know of," Sweets countered.

"True, true," I said. "And I welcome the new law-abiding Sweets Monroe, after you help me break into Grace and Mario's apartment."

"Why you want to do that, *mon ami*?"

I explained that the cops still had the apartment sealed. Sweets nodded his head when I told him that Mario could not have killed Grace and himself. He'd opened a hard candy and was sucking. As I talked, he continued to nod his head, either in agreement or in rhythm to some zydeco song pulsing in his brain. When I was finished, he stood up.

"My shit is in the trunk of my car. But I'll need a place to sleep for a couple of days."

"I thought you'd moved to a new apartment," I said.

"Got in a leettle *tete-a-tete* with the manager. I barely got my sheet out of the apartment before the cops arrived. You know how I'm not the most valued member of society in the eyes of the constabulary."

"Two nights in return for helping me."

"Four."

"Three,"

"Deal. You're the man, Victor. Go get some sleep. I'll wake you when it's time to go. "

• • •

It was going on midnight when Sweets nudged me awake.

"Get some night clothes on. I'll meet you at my car."

When I got down to the street, I was wearing a black pullover, black Levis and black Boston Celtic Converse. Sweets nodded his approval of my attire. He was wearing a black spandex long sleeved T-shirt tucked into tights one size too small and what looked like black ballet slippers.A black stocking cap was pulled down concealing his hair.

"Are you kidding," I said. "Is that the latest in burglary attire?"

"Top of the line. Skinny myself through any crack." He opened the trunk of his Cadillac El Dorado and removed a black leather gym bag and placed it in the back seat. We got in.

The Caddy was a maroon convertible. It was not one of ours, so I wasn't surprised when it took Sweets a couple of minutes to turn over the engine. Up to last year, Sweets had an arrangement with our father and us that he could pick out a car of his choosing. He'd pay license and registration and not make any payments. We would let him slide for three months then repossess the car. Sweets would wait a month, then come to the lot and the process would start all over again. This strange arrangement dated back to the time Sweets saved our Pop's life. After proving that Sweets had not murdered his girlfriend, the Brovelli Boys terminated the arrangement, figuring our debt to Sweets was paid.

Sweets turned on the headlights and pulled away from the curb. It took a block of driving before smoke stopped spiraling out of the tail pipes.

"Where did you buy this broken-down pimp car?" I asked.

"From a pimp," Sweets said.

Pimps were not my favorite subject. One had tried to kill me a year ago. He was the brother of a female bartender at the Oasis, who had tried to stab me with a hair pin the length of a pool cue.

"Got a good deal," Sweets said. "Dude was heading for San Quintin and needed some boogie- outta-town cash."

"Why didn't he drive this piece of shit out of town?"

"Had a bad generator and three flat tires."

We'd made it to the entrance to the Nimitz, and Sweets almost got us killed entering the freeway ahead of a Peterbilt 18-wheeler that he didn't see in his side-view mirror. The truck's air-horn was still echoing in my head, as Sweets crossed two lanes of traffic in third gear, his arm stuck out the window, middle-finger in the air.

"*Madonna,*" I whispered.

"It's fucking midnight," Sweets said. "Where is all this traffic coming from?"

"Probably trying to make it home safely without a *pazzo* like you turning them into a driving fatality."

Over the years Sweets had heard Vincent and me speaking in Italian that he knew pazzo meant a crazy person. He reached into his pocket and withdrew a hard candy, unwrapped it with his teeth and sucked it into his mouth. It kept him quiet until we left the freeway at Ashby Ave.

"I'm only half crazy," he said as he pulled to a stop at a red light. "And the other half is brilliant."

"You got a job to do. Stay brilliant and focused,"

"You got it daddy-o."

One time, someone had called Sweets a Cat Burglar, which made Sweets angry. Waving his arms, he'd explained that a cat burglar was a weirdo who broke into people's houses while they were asleep. "Dude gets his jollies creeping around bedrooms. A real burglar, *comme moi,* makes sure no one is home before he enters, in that way he eliminates any human factor interfering with his job. A burglar like me is like a great artiste."

Such was the case tonight that no one was at home, unless the apartment was inhabited by the ghosts of Mario and Grace, the possibility of which crossed my mind. Since Mario's death, I'd been feeling these vibes, like I'd look over my shoulder expecting to see him walking behind me. Or I'd hear a noise in the kitchen. I'd go in, turn on the lights, and nothing. But the noise had been real and so had been the quickly disappearing shadow at the corner of my eye. I shuddered, remembering Winona's ghost. I wondered if there were such a spectral presence that did not haunt but comforted?

Sweets had gotten us into the service entrance. We walked up three flights of stairs. The apartment had an X of yellow tape across it. Sweets whispered for me to wait. He placed something that looked like a dentist's pick into the lock and fiddled for a few minutes. The door opened, and we crawled in under the legs of the X.

Sweets closed the door behind me. He turned on the small flashlight and moved past me into the hall. I followed him into a large living room. I watched him move from room to room closing the drapes and the blinds. When he was finished, he gave me the go-ahead to turn on my flashlight.

"What are we looking for?" Sweets asked.

"Evidence," I said.

"Not a problem. I look for sheet that has evidence printed on it."

Sweet's sarcasm did not deserve a response.

"The cops have been through the apartment, I said. "Jay told me they didn't find any personal writing, like diaries and letters. That doesn't sound right to me, so look for any kind of writing. Pretend you're Sherlock Holmes."

"He a cop?"

"A detective in a mystery novel. You do the living room, and I'll take the bedroom."

When I was in high school, I read every Sherlock Holmes mystery. In college I discovered the classics, writers like Tolstoy and Emily Bronte.It would be unusual and maybe even comical to find reading novels such as *War and Peace* and *Wuthering Heights* in the bio of a car salesman. I could only imagine what the guys at Flynn's would say if they knew, so I've kept my love of literature to myself. I store my cache of novels in my closet in the event my twin drops by unexpectedly and gives me a lot of shit. Last year when I was trying to figure out how to be a detective, I'd bought Ross MacDonald's *Harper*, to see if I could get some tips. Since then, I've been reading detective fiction writers like Ed McBain and Raymond Chandler. Recently I bought a novel by John, D. McDonald called *The Deep Blue Goodbye*. I liked his sort of detective because he wasn't a licensed private investigator. He was how I pictured myself if I got out of the car biz and started a new career as a sleuth. That the guy lived on a boat in Florida and was surrounded by chicks cemented the picture. I felt suddenly guilty that I had thought of chicks while I was yearning for Dila. Which brought forth an image of Dila, shaking her finger at me. I could hear her voice, "We are not some kind of feathered fowls, Victor Brovelli, get that through your Italian macho brain." It made me smile. The hell with Florida, just give me Dila in any state of the union.

• • •

An hour later Sweets and I stood looking at each other with only Grace's Daily Planner to show for our effort, which I'd already gone through and did not see much that could not be explained. There were increased travel to the east coast and Midwest in the last four months, but they were all about PeaceLinks, either joining other anti-Vietnam war groups on marches or meeting with like-minded peace organizations. I would look through it more carefully later.

"Did you look in the toilet tank?" I asked. "In the movies, people hide stuff in there."

"Way ahead of you ma man."

"Is it possible they had a hidden compartment in one of the desks?" There was his and hers desks next to each other in a small second bedroom they'd turned into an office.

"A good burglar knows how to look. No hidden cubbies."

"Telephone calls?"

"Couldn't find any bills."

"How about a safe?" I asked "You know, like behind a painting."

"Checked them all out. But I'll take that painting over there. I think it's real valuable."

"How would you know? You an art critic?"

"Burglars know the value of everything from silverware, to coins, to art. Your bro has a couple of bottles of vino that's goes for a C note. I could make a profit on the painting."

Odd, I thought. Everything else in the apartment looked straight out of Ikea. "I thought you said you were an artist, not a business man."

"Dude, what I relieve the rich of goes toward making me rich. I got stocks, you know."

I didn't know and *didn't believe.* "So, now you're a financier."

He walked toward the painting. "I'm betting it's post-modern sheet. Big Kahuna artist from New York does all these kind of squiggly lines. Can't remember his name."

"You can't have that painting," I said. "We got to roll."

"We need to look in the trash?" Sweet said.

"I looked in all the wastebaskets."

"I mean outside in the trash bin."

"Right," I said. "Let's go."

We found the bins in the alley behind the building. Sweets opened it. "Up to you, Victor," he said. "I'm not dumpster diving."

I looked inside. The smell wasn't perfume, but there were only a few large plastic bags. It looked like municipal garbage had made its run. I didn't see any rats or spiders. I hauled my body over the edge. I opened the first bag and struck gold: Lots of paper and envelopes with Mario and Graces names on them. The other two bags were filled with garbage.

Kneeling in the alley, Sweets and I looked through the bag, the loose papers first. They were rough drafts of proposals for organizing marches or creating links for peace, which was disappointing. In the margin of one of the proposals, Mario had scribbled: *The first thing I killed was no kind of thing at all. It was an enemy soldier. Which is a hell of a lot easier to say than the first thing I killed was a man.* Was this a quote or an original idea? Whatever it was it was shocking. I continued looking.I had hoped that the subjects might be what I was looking for: weapons smuggling from Vietnam; heroin from Thailand making its way through Vietnam and into the United States, or smuggling Vietnamese girls into the United States and turning them into prostitutes.

I was holding receipts and six months of telephone bills. I looked through them quickly. I recognized some of the telephone numbers. Most numbers I didn't. I kept the envelopes and the article proposals and threw the bag back into the bin. My detective manual said to always take a second look at possible evidence because you want to make sure you don't miss something important.

"All right," I said to Sweets. "Let's get out of here."

"Groovy," Sweets said. "You got a real comfy couch, Victor."

I'd forgotten our deal.

In my apartment, I fitted the couch with sheets, then gave Sweets a blanket and pillow. He wrapped himself in the blanket and lay down. I poured a glass of Chianti and retired to my bedroom. No more than a minute passed before I heard Sweets snoring. He'd told me once that in prison you either learned to sleep with all the lights and noise or you came out of stir an insomniac. I took off my clothes, put on my XL 49ers T-shirt that I used instead of pajamas, stuck two ear plugs in, and got into bed with the telephone records and Daily Planner. I was still on high energy alert from our unlawful entry. Sweets claimed burglary gave him a buzz. I figured my energy had more to do with fear. I started reading going through Grace's Daily Planner first, examining each entry closely. There's was nothing there that I hadn't seen before. I finished the telephone bills. Not a single telephone number that I recognized, except the ones for the PeaceLinks office and one a week ago to our office. I didn't remember getting a call from Mario. I'd have to ask Vincent and Theresa. A couple of other numbers looked familiar, but I couldn't place them. I reread the Daily Planner. Lastly, I read though the article proposals, but found nothing in them that could conceivably put Mario and Grace in danger. I was exhausted. I tuned off the lights and lay back. I could still hear Sweets snoring through the earplugs as I fell asleep.

CHAPTER 7
PEACELINKS

Chi Non Fa, Non Falla
He who makes no mistakes, makes nothing

On Sunday, the entire Brovelli family attended ten o'clock mass at Saint Joseph's. Father Dunnican only briefly mentioned Mario's death. All the adults took communion. I hadn't gone to confession, so I hung back, but finally decided, the God that endorsed smiting in the Old Testament would understand how I ached to smite the person or persons responsible for Mario and Grace's deaths. No confession or absolution would free me of the sin of revenge. I stuck out my tongue, took the wafer, crossed myself and damned if I didn't feel better, like I'd been given the green light to smite.

The Brovelli Brother's Used Cars stays open seven days a week, so after mass Vincent headed to the lot to open up. Theresa had Sundays off. I drove home.

Sweets had departed the apartment when I returned. I vacuumed the candy wrappers and folded the blanket. Then I sat in the kitchen and reviewed Grace and Mario's telephone records. I must have been tired the previous night because many of the calls I couldn't identify were placed out of state, six to New York and eight to Washington DC that I figured had to do with PeaceLinks. There was a call to my sister that I'd missed. None to Carlo, our conservative older brother who, like Pop, was not speaking to Mario. I wondered what Carlo, the asshole, was feeling right now. I wondered what the hell could Grace or Mario want to talk to Carlo and Costanza about.

The rest of the morning I made calls to Washington D.C. and New York City. All were to liberal political groups or people, except one to

Manhattan.The destination was a nightclub called *The High Life*. Three hours' time difference. The voice that answered the phone was heavily accented, but understandable and sort of dignified. I thought it sounded Asian. He was a manager. He was busy. The lunch crowd was on its way. What did I want? I told him.

He'd never heard of a Mario Brovelli, or a Grace O'Conner. The call could have been for any customer. He hung up. I said fuck you to the phone. I'd ask Jay if he could query the NYPD and find out what kind of club this was. I wasn't sure what I thought I would find out. Maybe the mystery novels I was reading were influencing my thinking. It seemed as if the nightclubs in these books all were owned by the mafia. The non-fiction mafia would certainly be as interested in acquiring drugs, prostitutes or weapons for sale as the fictional mafia.

I dialed Vincent and explained what Sweets and I had done. He told me I was a *chooch*, a dumb fuck, for getting involved with Sweets, scolding me that Sweets' middle name was trouble and hadn't I learned anything after last year? I asked him if he remembered Mario calling a few days before he was found dead. He didn't, but would ask Theresa. I asked if it was okay to stay away this afternoon. I wanted to keep working on the case. My twin said this was *not* a case, and we were *not* detectives. Normally his criticism would have led to an argument. In the world of twins, arguments often lead to fights. This was different. It was about Mario, so he told me to go for it, but stay away from Sweets. Before I hung up, he asked if there was anything he should do? I told him to sell some cars and play with his baby, and not to forget to ask Theresa about that telephone call. He reminded me of dinner tonight at Mom and Pop's.I'd be there.

I started calling the local numbers. San Francisco numbers, followed by Marin County. Mostly, these were calls to PeaceLinks members. All of them were in shock at the news, particularly Carol Hosty, PeaceLinks co-founder, her voice of grief barely audible over the phone. Neither Carol nor any of the PeaceLinks' employees or volunteers could shed any light on what could possibly have happened. Over all, the feeling I got over the phone was that they were furious with Mario. I couldn't really blame them. What did they really know about my brother?

My other calls to Mario's friends resulted in the same shocked voices. They could shed no more light on what could have happened than any of the PeaceLinks' people. Over and over again, I heard the word, *tragic, tragic*, like some kind of drumbeat pounding in my head.

I had time to spare before going to Mom and Pop's. I called Jay and found him in his office, which was pure luck these days, with cops pulling double duty as protests continued to rise. He reluctantly agreed to find out about the High Life Club. He had a connection in in one of the Manhattan precincts stations.

I tried reading John MacDonald's *A Deep Blue Goodbye*, but couldn't concentrate. I put my legs up on the couch and closed my eyes. I wondered about the painting in Mario and Grace's apartment. I knew Mario had been living on military disability compensation, not a whole lot of bucks. Mario never mentioned Grace having much money. One valuable painting and a couple of bottles of expensive wine didn't constitute anything out of the ordinary. Finally, I dozed off. I think I dreamed of Mario, but it was one of those kinds of dreams where everything is uncertain and leave you exhausted and out of sorts after you wake up. I pulled on sweats and a hoodie and took a run along the beach as far as the dog-park and back, about five miles. That renewed my energy. I showered, shaved, dressed in some casual clothes and left for the homestead.

After dinner, which was a winter vegetable stew called Ribolita, Pop went to the mantle where his three Toscano cigar boxes rested, the green for the Garibaldi, white for the Modigliani, and red for the Soldati. Side by side they formed the Italian flag. He picked out four Garibaldi, and he and his three sons sat on the porch drinking grappa and smoking. The weather was mild for late December, but that was not unusual in Alameda, an island known to have the best weather in the Bay Area, and where the soil and climate allowed for tropical plants and flowers to flourish. At one time before the bridges and tunnel connected Alameda to the mainland, people took the ferry to our island to enjoy the sunshine. Many wealthy folks built elegant homes in an area that is now called the Gold Coast.

We did not talk about Mario. When I brought up the subject, Pop shook his massive head. Our Pop was not called 'Big Sal' for nothing. Vincent talked about sales being down. People bought books during the holidays, not automobiles. Carlo announced he was going to run for state legislator. "As a Republican?" I asked. It was a question I knew the answer to. The cigar gave me a headache. I drove home and took four Aspirin and went to bed feeling depressed. The way the subject of Mario had been avoided at dinner pissed me off. It made me feel as if my brother had died years ago instead of days ago. Sometime in the a.m. I heard Sweets stumbling in. For a burglar, Sweets made a lot of noise. He was crooning his Cajun Zydeco crap. My depression returned. I felt everything I was doing was one huge mistake after another

• • •

On Monday morning, Vincent and I left the lot in the capable hands of our accountant, and Vincent drove me to the Oakland Police Department car yard, where I took possession of Mario's Mustang. Vincent and I had found this sapphire blue '66 Mustang, and after Jitters worked the engine over, gave it to Mario as a coming-home-from-Vietnam present. We were told the car was good to go. Whatever evidence the cops needed to prove Mario had murdered, then killed himself had been gathered and documented. It meant nothing to me. I had plans for Mario's car.I drove immediately to Swanee's garage. I acknowledged our detailer's condolences and told him what I wanted.

"A new exterior paint job and new interior, except for the driver's seat?" he said, his voice rising into a question.

"Yep." I opened the driver's side door and pointed to the massive blood stain on the seatback that looked more like a rusty Rorschach test. "Clean the stain, but leave the outline." Swanee cocked his head and gave me a look, like what's up with that, but I knew. It would take a psychiatrist to figure out what leaving that stain meant.

"I want the exterior to be Signal Fire Red."

"Interior?"

"Black and ivory leather." Add whatever fine touches you feel will make the car special. You got any of those steering knobs left of Carol Doda doing her thing?" I recalled that when Victor and I presented Mario with the Mustang on his return from Nam, he'd laughed at the Doda steering knob. Later, after he'd started going out with Grace, Mario had removed it.

"Ah don't have one," Swanee drawled, "but ah know where ah can get one."

"Put one on. This baby is going to be my wheels."That got me another quizzical look. I could have added, until I solve this case, then I'm going to push it off a cliff into the ocean.

"What are you going to do about your Mustang? It's cherry."

"I'll put it on the lot for sale."

"Don't do that, Victah. Ah'll buy it. You can take this detail job off the top of the asking price."

We haggled a little, then shook hands.I left him and walked the ten blocks back to our lot.

Theresa was at her desk. I asked her about Mario's telephone call. She told me he hadn't sounded worried or anxious.

"I left a note on your desk. Maybe you should read my messages occasionally."

It was an honest criticism. I went to my desk and rifled through messages and found Mario's dated Saturday 12/6 @ 2:15 *Call me as soon as you can.* That didn't sound urgent, but it did sound as if he wasn't calling only to catch up. I'd never know. It bothered me. I sat for a while fretting until I decided I was just making myself sick. I placed a few cold calls. Called a few used car wholesalers to see if they were in need of cars. There were a couple of cars on our lot that been taking up space without attracting any buyers.Vincent stayed mostly outside where he felt comfortable in the company of our totally clean pre-used automobiles, waiting for customers. Through the window I saw two men wandered in off the street to inspect our Deal of the Week, an Alaska blue and white 1960 Chrysler Imperial with only 20 thousand miles on it that stood on a platform in the center of the lot, high enough off the ground that passersby could see it from the sidewalk. The Brovelli Brother's Used Car dealership guarantees accurate mileage. A few of our less scrupulous fellow used car dealers are not above turning a speedometer back a few miles. We don't rat them out, but we'd never send them customers.

Slow day, worse afternoon. By 3:00 p.m. you'd need binoculars to find a customer. I left the lot. Vincent was happy enough to see the back of me. His twin was one gloomy *paesano.* I drove to Berkeley and the PeaceLinks' headquarters on Shattuck Avenue. I lucked out with a parking space across the street and jaywalked to the building. I recalled the huge portrait of Bobby Kennedy that had hung above the door during last years' primaries. Kennedy was going to beat Humphrey. Sirhan shot Robert Kennedy the night he won the California primaries on June 5 of last year. I'd come down to the PeaceLinks' office for a candle light service. I'd watched the weeping and listened to the tearful speeches. I remembered feeling particularly sad for Rosie Greer, an NFL football player with the Los Angeles Rams, who was Kennedy's bodyguard. Seeing a man that huge weeping shook me. Mario spoke at the vigil. Grace spoke, and so did the woman now approaching me as I walked in the door, Grace's partner, Carol Hosty. I was nervous, heading into hostile territory. No telling after the telephone vibe I'd gotten how I'd be greeted, the brother of the man who the newspapers claimed murdered their founder and fellow political activist. The answer came in the form of a slap across my face that hurt like hell.*Minchia!* I grabbed Carol's wrists before she could wallop me again. She wrestled herself out of my grasp and took another swing. I ducked and bear-hugged her. Over her shoulder, I could see the rest of the workers on their feet, staring, wide-eyed. This anger was so out of the blue, so violent, as if I was the villain.

"Jesus Christ, Carol, stop it, stop it," I yelled. "I'm as upset as you are. Settle down." She kept struggling. By now the rest of the office employees were on their feet. I swung her around until I'd locked her down from behind. Finally, her body went limp, and she began to cry. I whispered in her ear all of my sympathies, all of my disbeliefs, my ideas. I kept it up, until I heard a tiny voice.

"You can let me go now."

"Only if you don't try to punch me out."

"I won't."

Believable voice. I let her go. She turned around and took my hands in hers.

"I'm sorry, Victor. I'm so sorry. I'm simply insane. Grace and I started this organization together. It was our baby. We worked side by side for a long time, only us. We *were* PeaceLinks. Working our asses off until we turned the corner and could hire workers. How could Mario do this? How could he?"

"We're you listening to me? Mario couldn't. He didn't murder Grace."

"I heard you; I heard you, but. . ."

"No buts," I said. "Carol, you know how Mario and Grace were. Totally in love. There's something terribly wrong. Look, can I talk to you and some of the other people. I need information, anything that will help me figure out what really happened."

"What did *really* happen, Victor?"

"I don't know, except somebody killed them and made it look like a murder/suicide. Of that I'm certain."

Carol led me into her office. She was holding on to me, so the rest of the office staff could see that I was no threat; otherwise, I'm sure they might have all jumped up and beaten me to death. She sat down at her desk. I sat opposite her, and we stared at each other. Both Grace and Carol had blue eyes, but the resemblance stopped there. Grace was tall with an alabaster complexation and raven black hair worn loosely or in braids. She dressed like an earth mother. Carol was short and compact with a body that said a once-upon-a-time gymnast. A line of freckles ran across the bridge of a tiny nose. She wore her medium length blonde hair stylishly arranged and her clothing looked more American-casual. The blonde hair looked a little too blonde, so maybe she wasn't a natural blonde. Something I might have tried to find out back in my previous dating life. The sign on the office door read Carol Hosty. Sometimes when a name is strange, I do word associations. With Carol's odd last name, I think of the word hasty, which is how I remember Mario describing her, always moving rapidly like she was late for something.

"Would you like some coffee?" Carol asked, pointing to the Mr. Coffee machine on a side table. When I first met Carol, we flirted with each other. That was before I was smitten by Dila.

"I'll pass on the coffee." I said.

"What kind of information are you looking for, Victor?"

"I'm not sure. I'm pretty much in the dark. So far, my twin and I are the only ones who believe that this suicide is bogus, and Vincent is not as convinced as I am. Bottom line, I'm investigating on my own.Perhaps you could give me an idea if Mario and or Grace or both were working on political stuff that would piss people off, you know, like embarrassing the President or screwing up some big wig's cash flow. Like that."

"In November they led a PeaceLinks group to the march in Washington D.C. They linked the White House."

I must have looked puzzled.

"You didn't see it on TV? Our group and other anti-war groups formed a linkage, handcuffing ourselves to each other around the White House fence. Police wound up having to use wire- cutters to snip through the cuff chains."

"I must have missed it."

Mario, Grace and a few others were arrested. Later, they stayed on in D.C. to protest the first draft lottery. You know the rumors are that the draft is not random. They were looking into that. One of Mario's friends works for the New York Times."

"Could be something," I said, but I doubted the government would be so upset that they'd go to the trouble of such an elaborate ruse as the one that resulted in Mario and Grace's deaths."Anything else?"

"Grace was an outspoken supporter of Sein Finn. She grew up in a slum in Dublin. She was pretty radicalized at an early age. Mario probably told you her history, coming to the States in 1966. She spent some time in Boston, but by the summer she was in the Bay Area.PeaceLinks was Grace's idea. I met her at a peace rally. We hit it off, and she asked me to join her. Grace didn't have a lot of money, and we needed a great deal more to get things rolling. I had a little inheritance that I gave her. Grace and I are partners in PeaceLinks. So here we are. I mean here I am."

Carol dropped her head and began sobbing. I was not good around crying women. Men rarely cry and when they do, it sounds phony. Women, on the other hand, even the most aggressive fem-Nazis, the second they start crying, turn into Victorian ladies in novels in dire need of smelling salts and a sip of sherry. I'd voiced this opinion once to Dila, and she'd called me a tragically-flawed male. True or not, when Carol wouldn't stop crying, my flawed male nature sent me to her side of the desk with a tissue and a shoulder to lean on. Since I was standing by the side of her chair, the shoulder turned into my stomach. She stretched her arms tightly around my waist, I let her cry herself out. When she stopped bawling and started sniffling, I took her arms from around me and returned to the less intimate side of the desk.

"God, Victor, I'm such a wreak."

She was a wreak all right, but Carol also looked frightened.

"Is there something that's scaring you?" I asked.

"Scaring me? No, no. Just that life in general is so scary."

Tears started down her cheeks. "If you start crying again, I'll have to cry too. You don't want to see a grown man cry, do you?"

Carol wiped her cheeks with her hand and smiled. Looking at Carol now, it occurred to me that if Victor Brovelli of the past, before he met Dila, had been sitting in this chair, he'd have been consoling Carol with every intention of seducing her. I don't see seduction as a wrong, but rather an instinct in the nature of all healthy males, placed there by a generous male Deity. To which, Dila would have scoffed that her female Deity would have kicked my male Deity in his supernatural *caglioni*. Dila, the radical feminist, is not a woman to mess with. Suddenly, I was overcome with a deep yearning to hold Dila in my arms.

"You can stop staring, Victor," Carol said.

I shook my head. "Sorry, my mind was somewhere else. Can we get back to Grace?"

"Not much more to tell about Grace. She was a straight forward kind of gal. Took no prisoners if she thought she was right, but was always open to other ideas."

"Was Grace involved with Sinn Fein?" I asked.

Carol shook her head.

"How about the IRA?"

"Goodness, no," Carol said. "They're the military arm of Sinn Fein. Sinn Fein is a political organization. Nothing violent about them. Grace never spoke much about Irish politics. Her emphasis was on PeaceLinks right her in the United States. Besides, this isn't about Grace. She's the one who was murdered."

The last part of the sentence was said aggressively. "Okay, so how about Mario. He's been part of PeaceLinks for about two years, right?You probably got to know him pretty well. Was there anything he was doing that you were aware of that could have caused him to have enemies?" "The last five months both of them were working hard on our America Linked Together project. Traveling like crazy from one city to another. I talked to them on the telephone a lot.

When they were home, they were exhausted. Working for peace is a hard job."

"Could they have been writing articles about Vietnam?" I told her about the papers Sweets and I found.

"The subjects would certainly cause a stir," she said. "But I would have known about it if that was their intention. As a partner, I have to approve our working schedule.I do recall Mario bringing up the subject of heroin smuggling out of Vietnam, but Grace and I decided that there were enough independent news persons all over that topic. We were sticking with peace subject, not sensationalism. You know, Grace and Mario were looking for a new apartment. They could have just been throwing away old stuff."

I was disappointed. "Damn," I said. "Is there anybody else that might be able to tell me something?"

"No one comes to mind. And I can't think of anything that would precipitate such violence."

"What about that friend of hers, Casey McGoffin?"

"A friend from Dublin," she told me.

"I hate to bring it up, but could Grace have been unfaithful?"

"You mean with McGoffin?"

"Or anybody." I said.

"Grace O'Conner, no way," Carol said. "Grace was Mario's girl right down to her pink toenails.

"Yeah, I thought so too." I stood up, and Carol followed me out of the office. I'd learned nothing that set off any alarm bells. I drove back to the lot. I'd take over from Vincent the rest of the day and give him a chance to be with his family.

I closed up around seven, and stopped for a quick drink at Flynn's. Body's night manager, Stuart Tamberg, fondly known as the "vampire" for his slicked back black hair and skeletal appearance and ubiquitous black garb, was behind the bar, which meant I wouldn't have to suffer one of Body's awful Italian jokes. A couple of locals were playing liar's dice. I sat down at the opposite end from the dice game and order a glass of Anchor Steam. Three of Body's Irish buddies were in the back practicing darts. There was a big tourney coming up this Saturday night that Body had advertised as **DUBLIN VS GALLWAY: The Eastside and the Westside of the Irish Brain.** Cute, I thought.

I finished my beer and drove home, feeling frustrated and unhappy.

CHAPTER 8
THE FUNERAL

Grave psychological disturbances, anguish, and a grave fear of hardship, suffering, or torture can diminish the responsibility of the one committing suicide
Catechism of the Catholic Faith # 2282

A bizarre mix of people attended the funeral mass for Mario. Along with family and friends of family, there were a dozen or more Vietnam vets dressed in fatigues, a few without limbs, a couple in wheelchairs. There were men and women I recognized as members of Peacelinks, Carol, Grace's close friend and partner in the non-profit, Body Flynn and the crew from the tavern and a couple of guys I recognized from Mario's high school class. Jay came in uniform. I nodded at him, he nodded back. Just before the mass began, four members of the Black Panthers in full powder blue and black uniforms, led by Education Minister Terrance Bowles, marched in and stood two to each side of the entrance, as if protecting the service from some kind of attack. One of the Panthers was Tisdale. In his uniform, he looked taller. When my pop saw them, he started to rise out of his seat, but I held his arm and told him Mom would be embarrassed if there was trouble.

"Communists at my son's funeral," he whispered in disgust.

Considering that it was a question of suicide, Father Dunnican had tried to convince our parents to have a small private family mass, but Mom and Pop wouldn't hear of it. Because of the nature of the killing wound, the casket at the front of the church was closed. The traditional framed photograph of Mario in the middle of a huge wreath of white roses rested on top of the coffin. Mom had selected his West Point graduation photograph. In Italy, white roses represent lost innocence. Vases of white and yellow lilies stood in front of the coffin. Half way through the service the wailing began. I looked for its source and saw three old women dressed head to toe in black seated nearest the side aisle. They were holding rosaries and every so often would put their heads together and wail. Like the witches of Macbeth, I thought.

My sister Costanza, sitting next to me, whispered, "*Prefiche*, this is too much."

"Professional mourners, for God's sake." I whispered back," This is America, the 20th century. I can't believe Mom and Pop would do such a thing."

"Pop wouldn't. Check out Mom."

Tears were streaming down my mom's cheeks, but her head was high, and she was staring straight ahead at the priest. I imagined her scolding him: *How dare you tell me our son can't be buried in holy ground?* I remembered her speaking to Vincent and me, *Onore, onore. You boys must do this for Mario's honor.*

The *prefiche* started up again, and soon a few of the ancient Italian woman, friends of my pop's deceased grandmother began to join them. I saw Father Dunnican, looking out from under the Eucharist he was holding up, his Irish eyes wide in disbelief at the high decibel female mourning going on. He turned quickly back to the altar, probably delighted to be facing the tabernacle and not a bunch of wailing old Italian women.

A few years back, our parents took Vincent and me to Italy to visit relatives. We arrived in the city of Naples at an uncle's house in time to be part of a *messa di suffraggio*, a special mass to honor the anniversary of a loved one's death, in this case a first cousin.Talk about Prefiche. That funeral soured Vincent and me on Italian funerary traditions. As the wailing continued and the mass stretched out into the next frigging century, all I could think of was how displeased Mario would be with this ceremony. The Vietnam War had turned Mario into an Atheist. I wondered if Mario had written a living will of some kind, any kind, expressing how he wanted us to deal with his remains. I'd read a lot of soldiers before leaving for Vietnam had.

There'd been no will or similar document that Sweets and I'd been able to find when we searched Mario and Grace's apartment. I thought of a safety deposit box. I was pretty sure Mario wouldn't have had one, but I'd check. I'd check Grace too. She'd be more likely to have one, given the valuables we'd found in the apartment.

Carlo, Vincent and I plus three people from PeaceLinks, one a large Samoan woman and two big male employees carried the coffin out to the waiting hearse. Costanza had her arm around our mother as they walked, Pop next to them, shoulders straight, chin up. I wondered if he'd gotten our mother's message and what he was thinking. I had thought that some of Mario's buddies from his company would have shown up. I'd spoken to the vets that came. They were vets for peace guys and hadn't known Mario in Nam. They were part of the anti-Vietnam War movement and admired my brother's dedication to their cause. Maybe Mario had alienated his foxhole buddies by his public denunciation of the war.Lots of Vietnam vets were still gung-ho about the war and felt guys like Mario were disloyal to their country and dishonored their fallen comrades. I have to admit I had felt a little like that, until I met Dila and she began to explain a lot of the economic and political crap that was sub-text of the war. I was not yet, as our Vice President, Spiro Agnew, would say, a knee-jerk liberal, but I was leaning in that direction.

The cortege took the Park Street Bridge into Oakland and north on 580 into the hills just above the ritzy city of Piedmont to Saint Mary's Cemetery. Tombstones, crosses and statues dotted the rolling green hills. We buried Mario under a Gingko Tree, a few of its gold leaves still clinging to the branches, not far from a statue of the Virgin Mary and an incongruous palm tree. I thought it would be nice to come visit Mario next fall when all the leaves had turned golden and shimmered with every breeze. The priest said the benediction, and we all cast dirt on the coffin as it was sent down into the grave. Mom was crying. Pop was scowling throughout the brief ceremony. As the ceremony ended, my mom took my hand, and said, "Vittorio, e tratta di sangue, non di famiglia. You understand?"

I wasn't sure, but I nodded.

"I say again in English. This is about blood, not family. Family belongs to your papa, my children belong to me. Do you understand the difference?"

I found it difficult to breath, let alone speak, so I nodded again.

"Bene, bene." she said. "For Mario, you work hard." She let go of my hand and went to join our pop.

As we were leaving the cemetery, I noticed a man standing at a distance beside a statue of an angel, smoking a cigarette and staring at us. From this distance, all I could tell was that he was tall and skinny. He began walking our way, stopped by a headstone and waited. I could see him a little bit better. If it wasn't Radley, he was a good imitation.

The crowd around the grave broke up. Most of us would be heading to the family home for the funeral meal my mom had waiting for family and friends. There would be tons of food, wine, and hopefully the *prefiche* had worn themselves out. I couldn't take any more grief.

I joined Vincent, his wife, Gloria and my aunt at the limousine. The man at the tombstone started toward us, signaling me to join him. I could see him more clearly, and it was Charley Radley. He had one of those faces people describe as a hatchet. When I met him, his hair had been long and he'd been wearing a ratty army jacket over baggy pants. Now he had a buzz cut and was wearing leathers and motorcycle boots. I leaned into the limousine and told my twin I'd see them back at the house. The cortege took off and I walked toward Radley.

We shook hands.

"It's fucked up about. Mario and Grace," he said. "I mean who could have seen something like this coming?

"I can't and I don't believe it," I said.

"I don't either. It doesn't make any sense."

"You got any ideas?" I asked.

He pitched me a non sequitur, "I'm leaving town, tomorrow. Big biker rodeo in San Diego. Me and my good friend Mr. Harley and I will be boogying down the coast."

He hesitated and looked dismal, like maybe he was going to start crying. "Mario was a good CO, and he treated me like a human being stateside. He could have kicked me out of his apartment lots of times, but didn't."

"Was it you or McGoffin that tore up Mario's apartment?"

"McGoffin. Dude came home one afternoon and went crazy. I got the fuck out of there. I knew the fucker was nuts," Radley said. "Didn't like him. Couldn't put a finger on exactly why."

"How old was he? And could you describe him?"

"I'd guess mid-forties. Average height. Black hair, real blue eyes. Kind of Hollywood handsome like, you know, ladies' man like. Big damn hands, I remember thinking he could palm a basketball."

"Anything else?"

"Yeah, you know being in the army and all, you get a feel for military. I'd bet this guy at one time was a military something."

"What about ideas? Anything that you know Mario was into that would be trouble for him."

"Just same-o-same-o. Vietnam, Nixon, the atrocities he saw, we all saw. Bothered the hell out of him. Yeah, come to think of it, Mario was stressing over something. Never asked. That was just before he met Grace. He calmed down a lot after he met Grace and joined PeaceLinks. Grace had him involved in all the peace stuff. The captain was the happiest I'd ever seen him.

"Where are you living now? I asked.

"I got a tent, a sleeping bag, and my trusty Colt Commander. Any creeps mess with me, well, hell, Mr. Colt will just put bullet in their asses."

I went through my list of possible problem areas that Mario might have gotten himself into. I mentioned weapons smuggling, drugs and Vietnamese women.

"Couldn't be difficult to do," Radley said. "Can't tell you how, but there are plenty of weapons for sale. I got into the country with my M1 carbine and an Aussie rifle, the L1A1 self-loader. Plenty of heroin smuggling going on. Could be Viet women, yeah, could be."

"If Mario knew about smuggling and was trying to stop it, would that have presented a danger to him?"

"Suppose so. Big business. Get in the way of the cash flow could cost you. People were smuggling everything, sheeet, scrap metal, parrots."

"Parrots?"

"Yeah, man. Exotic birds was big business."

Besides PeaceLinks, I knew Mario had become involved in promoting sane guns laws. Radley interrupted my thoughts.

"It would be more like Mario to worry about the Vietnamese women being brought into the United States for prostitution."

"I was told that was just rumor."

"Hell no. Young girls too. It would be just like Mario to try to expose these pimps. I heard there was a ring run by retired military police. They were really bad-asses in Nam."

This fit Tisdale's speculation, and conflicted with Jay's view that it was only rumors. "Okay, how do I run down someone I can talk to about this?" Radley frowned. A minute or so passed until he spoke.

"I have a couple of bikers I can talk to. Vietnam vets. You got a card. I'll call you before I leave."

I took a business card out of my wallet and handed it to him. He was about to leave, but stopped.

"Look, Mario was my friend, so I'll take a risk. There's talk on the street about something big going down. I'll ask around and get back to you. After that I'm in the wind. Bad moon's rising."

"I'd appreciate it," I said.

"You take care of yourself, Victor. Mario loved you and your twin. Talked about you two in Nam and back here in the states all the time. He said you guys were the craziest fuckers on the planet."

Radley chuckled, gave me a half-hearted salute, turned and walked away.

So, Jay was wrong about Vietnamese women. I stayed in place for a while thinking before turning toward the cemetery gate. I'd have a good walk before I got to a place where I could call for a cab. I was not looking forward to going to my parent's. I would have rather taken my Porsche and hit the road like Radley on his Harley in the wind. Lot's more thinking to do.

CHAPTER 9
DILA

"Amare none solo guardarsi l'un l'attro, ma guardare in sieme nella stessa direzione."

"Love is not just looking at each other, but looking together in the same direction."

Antoine de Saint-Exupery

The phone was ringing as I entered my apartment. I thought it might be Radley and hustled to answer it. To my utter amazement and delight, the voice on the other end of the line was Dila Agbo. I almost knocked over the telephone stand.

"Is this my Italian lover?" she said.

I was suddenly dizzy. I took a breath before I answered. "Italian, lover and the man who's been trying to reach you for a week?"

"Baby, I was in Boston. I thought I told you. We were performing in the high schools as part of the university's Actors Guild Arts in the Schools Program."

I do not exaggerate when I say that Dila Agbo's voice is beyond sexy. When she says 'baby' I want to cuddle. She's an actress and a playwright, a revolutionary political activist and the most beautiful creature on the planet. Her face was the first thing I saw after being knocked unconscious by a rogue cop in front of the Black Panthers' office on a day in April 1968. I was laying on a couch coming to, looking up at an angel, her skin the color of caramel, her afro like an ebony halo. But it was her eyes that drew me in. They were two shades of green, one slightly darker than the other. Her left eye had a speck of amber in the iris.

"I'm flying out tomorrow morning from La Guardia. Can you pick me up at the airport? I'll be on United out of Denver, flight 761, arriving. . ." She paused. . . "Arriving at 4:20 p.m."

It was clear to me that Dila didn't know what had happened to Mario and Grace. I had to tell her. I wished it could be in person. "Dila, I'm excited to see you, but you're coming in to some real tragedy." This time I paused. . . I heard Dila take a deep breath.

"What happened Brovelli?"

"It's Mario and Grace. They were found parked at Grizzly Peak turnout. The cops say Mario shot her then shot himself. . ." I waited to hear her reaction. None, just heavy breathing. Then yelling. "That's total bullshit, Victor, total bullshit."

I wished she was next to me so I could hug her. "That's exactly the way I feel."

"So, what are we going to do about it?"

A scene from last year came into my mind, Dila staggering down the street pretending to be a distraught drunken wife yelling across the street at me, acting the part of the aggrieved wife and I her unfaithful husband. At the time, I was being led down the opposite side of the street by two killers and a vicious murderer holding a concealed gun pointing at my back. She was making a hell of a racket and stopping traffic. The distraction had saved my life. Dila was fearless.

"We'll talk about it when you get here tomorrow. We'll put our heads together. We're a good team."

"Like a girl Friday," she said.

"And I'm Detective Saturday. I can't wait to see you."

For the first year of our relationship, we'd kept our dating a secret. Only my twin and Mario and his girlfriend Grace knew. Dila never told her parents or friends she was dating a white man. To be honest with ourselves, I suppose we'd have to admit we were both a little bit frightened, but by the summer of 1969, like the cowardly lion in Dorothy in *The Wizard of Oz*, we'd been gifted with courage. We went places where we would be seen. I told my parents; she told hers. If they were not thrilled, we were. Let me repeat, I couldn't wait to see her. I went to sleep that night dreaming of Dila.

• • •

At 4: 50 in the afternoon on the following day that I had marked on my calendar as Wednesday the 17th of December 1969 as a special day to be remembered, my wait was over. I was in the San Francisco International Airport and Dila was in my arms. We didn't give a shit who saw us kissing. It took us a while to unclench. By then, the passengers disembarking had moved on down the hall. We followed, holding hands to baggage claim. We hardly spoke until we were in my car and the Mustang was heading north on 101.

"Do you have to get right home?" I asked.

"I told my parents my flight didn't arrive until after midnight. Baggage claim and you driving me home, all takes time, so we've got hours."

"Where do you want to spend those hours? Are you hungry?"

"For you baby, so we better get moving to your apartment."

From the time I first felt truly sexual, as a late teen, I suppose, I believed the distribution of my desire over a broad canopy of females made the best sense. Unlike my twin and older sibs, I was not eager to marry and produce bambini. When it was time, sure. Maybe after I turned forty. Find a good Italian girl, preferably in her twenties and settle down. Three, four kids, who can say. Victor Brovelli was not monogamous, but I did take my romances seriously and was always faithful for the duration. Since Dila, I was no longer sure how I felt.

At the moment I was anxious to put the pedal to the metal and get to my apartment as fast as possible, and hope to hell Sweets Monroe, descendant of Jean Lafitte, was not sitting on the couch sucking of candy.

• • •

Like my living room window, my bedroom window looks out over an alley, across from which is the Budweiser Beer Marilyn Monroe-look-a-like-billboard. I pulled the blinds closed. Our sex put us to sleep. I woke up first. The bedside clock read 9:16 p.m. Dila had thrown off her covers and was naked, exposing the scarifications just above her pubis. Her father, a conservative business man but a fanatic Pan-African, had been responsible for the procedure that was done by a family doctor in accordance with the tradition of the Betamaribe people of Benin, the country from which his family originated.Specific scaring indicated tribal affiliation. But it was also performed to provide their ancestors' protection and insure good health. Usually, the scarring was done at a very young age. In Dila's case, she'd been thirteen. Last year when we first made love, the scarification shocked me. I told her that her father was cruel.Her response was pure Dila. I remembered her telling me she'd been as passionate about her African culture as her daddy. She'd explained the scarification proved she was ready for child bearing. The scarification was in the form of tiny, raised lines not much thicker than thread that looked to me when seen all together like a bird with its wings spread. At the time, she'd admitted that scarification was losing its appeal among young Africans, and was hardly ever practiced by African American. She'd told me she believed the scars stood for all things female and was proud of them.

I traced my finger over the tiny, raised flesh, following the pattern. Dila woke up and propped herself up on her pillow. She reached over to the side table and tuned on the radio to KPAT-FM. A saxophone and a bass were playing a jazz number. A year ago, when we woke up, Dila had lit a cigarette and blown perfect smoke rings toward the ceiling.

"I love you Brovelli," she said.

"When you call me Brovelli, I don't know if you mean me or my twin."

"That's so silly. Who else would be in bed with me but you? I like the sound of Brovelli. Victor sounds too much like Victory, which sort of implies, you know, your male dominance."

"So, call me Vittorio."

"I'll think about it, *Brovelli.*"

"If you want a cigarette, you left a pack of Marlborough's in the lamp stand drawer the last time."

"I gave up smoking a couple of months ago. Bad for my vocal cords."

As if the radio station was listening to our conversation, the sax ended, and a woman began singing "Smoke Gets In Your Eyes."

The world is a magical place, I thought.

"Sarah Vaughn," Dila sighed. "You're not seeing ghosts this time, are you?"

"Not so far, but there are shadows out of the corner of my eyes. I'm expecting Mario or Grace or both of them at any time now."

"I've got to be getting home soon," Dila said. "Let's take a shower together and get something to eat. We can talk at the restaurant. Is Ole's open late? I feel like a breakfast."

Ole's hours are 6 a.m. to midnight. To accommodate truckers, they never stop serving breakfast.Unless I'm late for work, I'm a regular at Ole's for breakfast. My usual morning waitress was a buxom redhead whose name was Mame for Aunty Mame, her mother's favorite movie character.

This night-time waitress should have been called Lame, her lips stress-tight, looking at us as we walked in as if she was constipated. Maybe it was because we were a biracial couple. Dila had grown accustomed to stupid people and ignored them mostly unless they said something at which point we'd *Rochambeau* to see who got in their faces. Dila and I found a booth in the back for privacy. Ms. sad-sack brought us water then stood there waiting with her pencil and pad. I ordered my usual, one fluffy waffle topped with three eggs sunny-side up. Dila ordered the same and added link sausages and English muffin on the side. At 5'10" Dila was almost as tall as me with an athletic body and ate like an athlete. Even for her, this was a big breakfast. She saw my expression and said, "What, I'm starving."

I told Dila everything I'd been doing since Jay had called me to tell me about Mario and Grace.

"Who do you believe? she asked.

"Jay swears there's no truth to the prostitute idea. But Tisdale says it's not rumors. So does Mario's ex roommate Radley who has street creds. Tisdale is closer to the streets, him being a Black Panther. He'd have access to inside criminal activities." The minute I said it, I could see Dila's eyes widen and the little amber fleck in her left eye light up.

"Why you say that, Brovelli? You think the Panthers are criminals?"

"Sorry, sorry. No, I don't think they're criminals. But Minister Bowles himself told me that Tisdale had a lot of connections in the underworld, and he insinuated the Panthers had admitted him because of his skill as an army sniper in Vietnam. And other things, I added. I was talking fast.

"Apology accepted, Victor. If you'll get up and see why our breakfast is taking so long."

I was half way out of my seat when I saw Ms. Dismal on her way holding a tray.

As usual Ole's breakfasts were amazing, and we ate without speaking. Every once in a while, between forkfuls, I watched Dila. Despite missing her dreadfully while she was away, I felt lucky, knowing she loved me and that I loved her back. Wherever our relationship took us, we had decided we'd turn ourselves over to the fates. We had worked through all the crap that came with being a biracial couple in a country that only two years before had finally struck down all the states' miscegenation laws. The Supreme Court ruling had been unanimous. I wouldn't have known that until Dila told me the first time and only time we discussed marriage. The subject is now mutually tabled until after she gets her Masters in Fine Arts next year.

Unbeknownst to her parents, who were wealthy and educated African Americans, Dila had worked as a volunteer for the Black Panthers since she was in high school and after graduating had remained with them for two years as a paid employee, also without her parents knowing. Not into violence, they'd have had a cow was how she'd put it.By the time I met her, Dila had become an important part of the Panthers' public relations program run by Minister Terrance Bowles that included free breakfasts for children, dinners for senior citizens, after school babysitting, sickle cell testing centers, medical and ambulance services and legal clinics. And her particular favorite a West Oakland cultural center for kids to learn to play musical instruments, paint, sculpt and write poems and stories. I wasn't naïve. I knew that the Panthers could and would turn violent, and that there were some factions whose behavior was criminal. I kept this to myself. Dila was ferocious in her defense of the Panthers' CORE stance which was open carry arms citizens' patrols that became known in the neighborhoods as "cop-watching." Dila believed absolutely that the Panthers had every right to arm themselves and defend themselves in the face of a concerted effort by law enforcement to destroy them. The first day I'd met her, she'd driven me back to our used car lot. There had been a loaded 30 caliber M1carbine in the passenger seat, a weapon she'd explained she had a license for, and she'd become expert at on a rifle range.I never questioned her veracity. Dila's work for the Black Panthers did not interfere with her playing in the Oakland Youth Symphony Orchestra, acting in little theater groups all over the Bay Area, and mentoring at a music camp in Michigan for two weeks during the summer. She didn't find her different lives incongruous the way I did before I got to know her up close and personal.

"What are you staring at Victor?"

"Was I? I was thinking about the time we met."

"You were coming to after that cop hit you. You called me a dark angel. You could have said black. More accurate, don't you think?"

"Dark sounds sort of villainous."

"Perhaps I am," she said and gave me a villainous look.

I said, "So, you think the prostitute possibility makes the most sense."

"I do. I didn't know Grace that well, but I know she volunteered in a center for abused women, which also took in prostitutes wanting to get out of the trade. I know that because the center hired a couple of Panthers brothers as guards. Pimps and abusive husbands didn't want to fuck with guys like James."

I double downed on that statement. James was born with angry genes and the body of a hippopotamus - both body and anger often directed at me, given that he had a crush of Dila and didn't like whites.

"You know James is really sweet, down deep."

"That's got to be really deep," I said, "like to the center of the earth."

"No, I'm not lying. He's got lot of love in him."

"Not for me, he doesn't," I said.

"Well, I didn't say he loved Eye-talians."

We eyed each other, then burst out laughing. Dila's laugh was chines in the wind.

"Oh, I sure do love you," Dila said.

I reached across the table and took her hand. "Okay, it's the hookers."

"I'll have a talk with this Tisdale dude. See if I can get some details. We have to have a better starting point."

I paid our dour waitress, leaving her a big tip, just to prove we weren't the prejudiced types.

On the way to Dila's house, she asked me if I'd talked to Renee lately. Renee was Renee Sorenson, my girlfriend before I met Dila. She was a music major in her senior year of Mills College. She was a honey blonde and looked a little like Ingrid Bergman. Renee possessed a curious fetish. Danger turned her on. When we dated, I had been glad to feed her fetish with some of the weird and dangerous encounters the Brovelli Boys had experienced selling car and especially repossessing them that often led to some harrowing incidences. You would not think of the used car business as being particularly dangerous, but let me tell you. Vincent and I had many scrapes with irate customers and just plain nut-jobs that wandered Oakland's East 14th Street. Renee's and my relationship ended when she found out I was dating Dila. Dila discovered that Renee was her friend from the Travis City Michigan Music Festival where they both mentored in the summer. "My only white female friend," Dila had told me. Dila also told me, "It's either her or me, Victor."

The choice was an easy one.

"Renee left for Europe, I think."

"Oh, yeah," Dila said. "I remember something about that. "How's Vincent? How are your folks holding up?"

Vincent was in no better shape that I was over Mario's death. My folks were barely making it. I didn't want to get into a lot of details of my mother's and father's grieving. I asked after her parents. Her mother was always polite, but distant with me. Imperious might have been a good way to describe her.I thought her father was a little looney tunes with all his Back- to-Africa stuff.We continued doing our catching-up-talk, recalling our mutual touchstones.

"How's your business?" Dila asked. "Last time you called, Vincent was getting nervous."

"Better than in November, but we're still behind for this time of year. Vincent caught a guy trying to hotwire one of our cars."

"Don't expect me to get all girly like Renee, Victor."

I explained to Dila that the night bartender at Flynn's, Stuart Tamberg, affectionately called The Vampire for his bony features, pale complexion, combed back black hair and his insomnia. Stuart lived in a small apartment above the tavern that looked out over our lot. Looking out his apartment window after he'd closed the tavern, he had spotted the car thief and called Vincent.

"So, what happened?"

"The guy pulled a knife."

"God, what did Vincent do?"

"What Vincent always does, bluff. He took off his leather bomber's jacket and waved it at the crud and started yelling, *hey toro*, like he was a bullfighter. Vincent told him that he had one chance to kill him, so he better do it right. After that he was going to stuff that knife up his ass. All the while he's waving his jacket like a bull fighter's red cape and stomping his feet and cursing in Italian. I think it was the Italian that finally scared the thief because the piece of *merda* took off running."

"That was certainly brave," Dila said.

"It doesn't end there. Vincent took after the guy. Vincent ran track in high school. He was about to catch him."

"And?"

"The *stronzo* threw the knife over his shoulder and kept running. Vincent stopped picked up knife and walked back to the lot."

"I don't get it," Dila said.

"I didn't either. I asked Vincent. He said he'd always wanted a Bowie knife."

"Jesus, Brovelli."

The conclusion of the story, which in my former life would had Renee Sorenson pawing me, found Dila and me parked in front of her house, both of us laughing like we'd just heard a really funny joke.

"You think I should come in?"

"Better not. You'd spoil my father's dinner."

We kissed. I told her I had to work tomorrow, but would call her."

I drove off, happy not to have spoiled her father's dinner.

CHAPTER 10
DELVING WITH DILA

Anche il sole passa supra il fanga, e non s'imbratta.
The sun passes over filth, and is not defiled.
Italian proverb

I was up at the crack, dressed in sweats and a hoodie and out the door for a run along the beach. I was not a daily runner like Vincent, but tried to get three runs a week. I didn't designate specific days of the week, just when I felt like I needed the exercise. The beach in Alameda is part of the bay that looks west to San Francisco's skyline and north to Treasure Island. Weather in the East Bay is normally better than in San Francisco. Today was overcast, but I would put odds on the sun breaking through by noon. I ran to the end of the beach and back, about three miles each way, working up a good sweat. Back home, I showered, and dressed for work. I stopped at Ole's and bought a large coffee to go, forgoing my usual breakfast. I was first on our lot. I unlocked the chain that crossed the driveway, drove in and parked in my spot in the back of our office. Because of Theresa's obsession with cleanliness, the office was spotless. Usually this made me feel like knocking some papers off the desk or spilling coffee on her spotless floor. But this morning I was in a good mood. Dila was back. I brought out the special sales signs and took them out to the lot, placing them on the windshields of the cars we wanted to sell fast. We were over-stocked. We needed to sell a dozen cars before the New Year in order to claim this had been a good sales year. Part of our profit goes to Mom and Pop's retirement, so Vincent and I are left to divide three fourths of the net profits. Despite the insanity of 1968, last year had turned out to be profitable. This year sales had been ho-hum. The profits would not be anything to get excited over. I started rearranging cars. Our theory was never to have cars in the same place more than two days in a row. It was Pop's idea and we kept doing it out of habit. I thought it did make the lot look a little different and maybe more interesting. My twin felt it was a waste of time. As I moved cars from one place to another, I thought of Dila. She'd still be asleep in her own familiar bed. I imagined her asleep in my bed. I imagined her asleep in my bed for life, as my wife with bambini rushing into the bedroom, yelling mommy, daddy. *Non fare l'idiota*. It wasn't entirely idiotic to imagine Dila as my wife. One of these days, it might actually happen. My thoughts were interrupted by a horn blowing. I looked up and saw Mario's Mustang driving on to the lot, Swanee behind the wheel. I went to great him. We shook hands.

"She's a beauty. All done to your specs."

I walked around Mario's Mustang, now mine, admiring the paint job. The interior was exactly how I wanted it. The driver's seat had a thin, but visible line conforming to what had been a massive blood stain. It looked a little like the outline of an island. Maybe Ireland. That would be fitting. A Carol Doda steering knob was affixed to the wheel. It made me smile. Swanee deducted the cost of his work from the price of my trusty Mustang and wrote me a check. I signed over the pink slip of my Mustang to him, feeling a little guilty to give up the car I'd driven for so long. I'd drive Mario's Mustang until I solved his murder. After that, maybe I'd sell it, or push it off a cliff into the Pacific Ocean. I drove my new Mustang to the back of the office and parked it. Every day I drove it to work, it would be a reminder of Mario. Insane? Maybe, but that's the way I was thinking.

The morning passed without word from Dila. Vincent sold a 1975 Ford Fairlane. Two customers who spent a lot of time looking left promising to come back. We knew they wouldn't. Theresa complained of a splitting headache and took the rest of the day off. I took my lunch break and headed to Flynn's. It was Thursday, Body's I Dare-You-Chili Day.

I sat down at the bar. A couple of guys from Sears were bending over their bowls, sweat on their foreheads. Body came over, and I ordered.

"You'll regret it," one of the Sears guys said." "But you'll love it to," the other guy said. Body turned and headed for the kitchen, stopping halfway there he turned back to me. I expected one of his stupid Italian jokes.

"Victor, what kind of socks do you use to plant cayenne peppers?"

Relieved he wasn't going to badmouth my heritage, which would require a comeback, something I was not feeling up to, I shook my head.

"A garden hose," he said.

The Sears guys let out fake *guffaws.*

Body was not himself. He never passed up the opportunity to give me the needle. Plus, the joke was stupid. I probably should have asked him what was going on with him, but didn't, perfectly happy to eat quietly by myself. I finished my meal and returned to the lot. I could have used the garden hose.

It was closing time before I heard from Dila. She told me to pick her up at her home tomorrow morning at 9 a.m.

• • •

We'd just driven through the toll booth onto the Bay Bridge. "Tell me where we're going," I said.

"San Francisco," Dila said. "To the Tenderloin to see a ho. To be precise, an ex-sex worker, now an iconic madam of the finest repute."

"And how do you know said madam?"

"Tisdale told me."

I was surprised. I didn't figure Tisdale was eager to help me anymore than he had. I was not going to ask Dila how this came about, but she told me.

"I talked to Terrance yesterday, and he had a chat with Tisdale. The brother was being uncooperative, according to Terrance, but when we met face to face, I was able to convince him that you were a righteous Eye-talian."

"And how were you able to do that?"

"Well, I started out telling him that part of yo family comes from the south of Italy, and it's well known that southern Eye-talians are really descendants of North Africans, and all you gots to do is look at how dark they are. . . see what I'm saying." She did a little face and reached over from the passenger side and touched my cheek.

Dila had reverted to her street talk, at which she was adept. Terrance Bowles and other African-Americans I'd met, like Dila, were also able to switch back and forth between the language of the ghetto and grammatically correct English. It was a survival technique from Jim Crow days in the South. Dila had explained that a black person would be considered uppity if he or she sounded educated in front of whites. "Blacks are natural actors," she'd said.

I had tried this Southern Italians-are-not-really-Caucasians on Dila when we first met, and I was trying to convince her to date me. So I knew she was putting me on. "I mean really, how did you get him to cooperate? I think he respected Mario, but I know he doesn't like me."

"Not exactly true," Dila said. "He just can't be in close contact with a white man for very long. That's what he told me. Vietnam was enough for him, listening to crackers talking like black men weren't real people, but damn sure needing then to cover their backs if the Cong attacked. Buddy-buddy one minute then back to being racists. That's how he explained it to me. Tisdale told me he actually gets a rash if he is in the same room with a white person for very long. He told me to apologize to you for rushing out of the restaurant the way he did."

I shook my head. Last year when I first ventured out of my racial comfort zone, I had no idea the extent to which white people had embittered blacks. When it began to dawn on me, I remembered talking to Mario about it. He'd mentioned that this was the way his girlfriend Grace had explained many Catholic Irish living in the North felt about the Protestant British. I hadn't mentioned it at the time, but I remembered thinking probably the way the Protestant Irish living in the State of Ireland felt living among the Catholic majority. But this was the first I'd heard that close contacts with whites caused black people to break out like we were poison ivy.

"Do you think this happens to other Blacks?" I asked.

"You know I couldn't say. My father often came home from big business meetings with whites and took a long shower. Probably still does. And Terrance always wears gloves if he has to meet with your race."

There were times when Dila talked about race when her voice took on a hard edge. I'd learned to ignore it. Being black and a woman, she was last in the pecking order. If sometimes her bitterness showed, she had earned it. I thought back to the first time I met Terrance Bowles in April of 1968. He had arrived with a couple of scary looking-bodyguards looking to buy a van. Yeah, he *had* been wearing black leather gloves and did not take them off shaking hands. Shortly after our mutual encounter with Oakland's Police Department's Station Defense Team, Bowles stopped wearing gloves around me, which at the time didn't register with me as anything special.

We drove through the Yerba Bueno Island tunnel and came out into the glistening white San Francisco skyline, Coit Tower atop Telegraph Hill in the distance. I had grown up in Oakland with the feeling that San Franciscans thought of east bayers as distant and disreputable cousins, to be tolerated but not taken seriously.

"So, Tisdale will help us, that's good," I said.

"I didn't say he'd be hands on. He gave me the name of the woman we're going to see."

Dila told me to take the 9th Street exit off the bridge. We were soon driving north on Polk Street. She pointed to Turk Street and said to turn right. Two blocks down, she told me to stop and look for parking.

"There on the corner is the *Blackhawk* where Billie Holiday sang her last west coast club date. Ah, man, Thelonious Monk too," she said dreamily.

I'd heard of Holiday, but no idea who Monk was. I didn't respond because it seemed Dila was talking to herself.

We took the 9th Street exit and crossed Van Ness Avenue. Many of the buildings were decorated for the Holidays. It was Friday the 19th, only six days to Christmas. Impossible to think of Christmas since Mario's death. Vincent and I were going to eliminate the Christmas music we played over a speaker at our lot, but Theresa had convinced us not to.

"You have an address for Clarita's?" I asked.

"It's supposed to be a few buildings down. No address, look for a door with parrots on it," she said.

I spotted it right away on the other side of the street. The door was black and parrots were bright green and red. From where we were standing, the birds looked like they were hovering in the air. We jay-walked. Close up, the parrots were carved in relief and were looking down on a washed-out painting of the Golden Gate Bridge. There were intricate oriental designs carved around its perimeter of the door. The building was an old five story tenement next to a row of similarly neglected tenements.

Dila pressed the doorbell, and we heard chimes coming from the inside. We waited. Finally the door opened to reveal a tiny slip of an Asian girl wearing a black dress with white apron, with a little white bow in her hair. Dila told her who we were, and that we had an appointment. The girl looked at a clipboard she was holding that I could see held a list of names. She nodded and ushered us in, pointing to a door to our right. She left and we entered. The room was dark. Dila found the light switch. What we saw was straight out of 19th century early California. All the furniture was antiques. A room-size oriental rug covered the floor. On the wall to our left hung a California Bear Flag. The wall to my right was covered with photographs in gilded frames of beautiful women dressed in long skirts and feathery hats. Some were in sepia. One in particular stood out, a blonde with luscious lips and a sneaky smile. The windows at the rear of the room were covered with heavy green velvet drapes. Next to the windows was a fireplace with an ornately-carved mantle. In front of it stood a desk that looked as if it was made from mahogany or rosewood or some other exotic wood. On the mantle was a framed sign that read:

IF EVERY MAN WAS AS TRUE TO HIS COUNTRY AS HE IS TO HIS WIFE – GOD HELP THE USA.

I looked over at Dila. She smiled.

"Check out the embroidery. This is really detailed sewing, and it looks very old."

"It is."

The voice came from behind us. We turned to see a tall silver haired woman. She was dressed in something floor length with ruffles that looked like it would have been a costume for a western movie. She was heavily made up. Her eyes were turquoise and peered piercingly through a jewel framed spectacles perched on her nose. She could have been any age from 60 to 80. It took a little concentration not to laugh. Dila stepped forward and extended her hand.

"I'm Adila Agbo and he is Victor Brovelli. Tisdale called you to say we were coming."

"My name is Clarita Wall, but you can call me Tess.

I looked at Dila. She shrugged.

"That dear boy did indeed inform me,"

I was wondering why Tess? Clarita or Tess or whomever continued.

"Dear Tisdale asked me politely if I could help you. Being polite is the key, don't you think?"

She didn't wait for an answer. "The subject he said was delicate. Please sit. We have time. Tea will be here shortly."

"We don't want to take too much of your morning," I said.

"Things don't start much until the late hours in our line of work," Clarita said.

We already knew what her business was, so we remained silent. A few minutes went by, and the little girl-maid entered pushing a cart on which was a tea set, cutlery, embroidered cloth napkins and a basket filled with an assortment of pastries. The maid served the tea and backed out of the room as if Clarita was some kind of royal presence.

"My pastry chef is the best in California," Clarita said. "He was recommended highly. I was happy to pay for his train ticket from Boston to San Francisco. We had a little establishment on the Barbary Coast then, before we moved here. Chef Wendell made the finest cakes and pastries." She looked hungrily at the remaining pastries in the basket.

I was getting a creepy feeling about Clarita aka Tess. Clarita passed the basket of sweets around. Dila and I took one. Clarita placed two on her plate, then picked out another and began munching and licking her lips. I bumped Dila's knee and made eyeballs in the direction of the door. She shook her head.

"You were looking at my photographs," Clarita said.

"We were," Dila said. "The women are very lovely."

"They are mostly of my namesake, my great grandmother Tessie Wall, the best damn madam in the history of California. *Munch, munch, sip.* "We're sitting in her residence, 211 O'Farrell Street. It has passed down through our family. Tessie was a remarkable woman. Did you know she drank the famous boxer John L Sullivan under the table? Poor man couldn't box for weeks. Some believed that had more to do with my dear grand relative's sexual prowess."

Clarita giggled. It sounded ridiculously girlish.

"During the earthquake of 1906, she turned her house of Eros into a hospital. Let me tell you we saved many lives. Our girls became nurses. We were dubbed the dark angels of mercy by the newspapers. I was never so tired in my life."

I sent another eyeball message to Dila in the direction of the door, this one I hoped expressed my growing anxiety. Somebody was crazy in this room and it wasn't us.

Clarita began munching on her second pastry, small droplets of jam matching her fire engine red lipstick slipped on to her chin. She touched her lips delicately with her napkin, her pinky finger in the air. Her glasses was hanging from a gold chain around her neck.

She swallowed and began. "Tisdale told me you were interested in the rumor going around that Vietnamese girls are being smuggled into California to be used for prostitution purposes. I looked into it for you."

Clarita sat back in her chair and took another bite of her pastry. Silence followed. There was a vacancy in Clarita's eyes, like she'd forgotten what came next.

Dila finally asked, "And what did you discover?"

"It may be true."

"But?" I said.

"If it is, it is not happening to any great degree in Northern California. Maybe in the City of Angels. There seem to be a few new girls working the Tenderloin, and they *are* Vietnamese. I had my maid who is Vietnamese investigate. According to her, the girls are not organized in any way. They have pimps, but they've been here for a while. We know them, silly little men with razor blades and little penises. The girls are too young for me to hire. I want only beautiful, mature females to whom I can provide mentorship. Any new worker for Tess Wall has to go through six weeks of pleasure training. At my expense of course. My services are for males and occasional females of a discerning nature."

"You sound very sure," I said.

"The Tenderloin is bordered by Geary Street to the north, Market Street to the south, Mason Street and Van Ness Avenue to the east and west. This is my kingdom. Nothing happens within these boundaries that I'm not aware of.My subjects keep me well informed."

Madonna, I thought. This was like listening to the Madam Mad Hatter. I was grateful when Dila stood up.

"We thank you very much, Clarita. We don't want to intrude further. We'll see ourselves out."

"You are a beautiful young woman, my dear. Dear sweet Tisdale says you are a student. If you ever wish summer employment, you'd be welcome in the house of Tessie Wall. The pay is excellent. You'd need to take my class, of course."

Dila smiled broadly. "I doubt I'll take you up on your offer, but you never know. Thank you for your time."

We left just as Clarita picked up her third pastry and brought it to her voluptuous lips.

The door closed behind us, and we were facing Clarita's maid. She handed Dila a piece of paper and walked quickly away.

We were outside before looking at the note. It read: *Quai cinq, ce soir a deux heure de matin*. Dila translated: Pier five tonight at two a.m.

CHAPTER 11
THE PLAN

Il diavolo insegna a fare pentola, man non il coperchio
The devil teaches you how to make a pot, but not its cover
Italian proverb

"We don't know exactly what she wants us to do," I said.

"Yes, we do," Dila said. "She's telling us to be at pier five at two a.m."

We were driving up the Embarcadero to have lunch at Scoma's at Pier 47 on Fisherman's Wharf, owned by friends of Pop, Enrico Scoma and his brother whose name I'd forgotten. Italians of my pop's generation all seemed to know one another. Vincent and I had eaten at Scoma's forever.They made the best spaghetti con mare in the Bay Area, rivaling our mother's according to Pop, which he would never say in front of her, in fear of losing his life. We had driven by Pier 5. There was no ship docked there. Workers were hauling boxes out of the nearby warehouse and stacking them inside a tractor-trailer. The truck driver, who was standing around smoking, would take it from there. It was called division of labor.

I turned into the alley leading to the restaurant, gave the keys to the valet and entered. It was a little past noon and the place was full. We had no reservations. I mentioned the name of Big Sal Brovelli, and we were soon seated at a table with a window view of fishing boats and seagulls perched on the pier railing. We both ordered their house white wine. I suggested the spaghetti con mare. Dila shook her head, she'd take clam chowder and crab cakes. The waiter brought baguettes and olive oil and took our order.

Dila asked, "Do you think I should tell Tisdale about this?"

"If this is what we think, smuggling in Vietnamese women, the cops should know, we need Jay," I said.

I knew Dila regarded establishment law enforcement with the same skepticism as most African-Americans, but I still believed that there were more good cops than bad, and our system of enforcing law and order was not corrupt. I told Dila, and she rolled her eyes.

"Victor, you have to see more than the Caucasian perspective."

I didn't want to get in a discussion, let alone an argument. The sun was out, the wine was perfect and there were now five seagulls sitting on the railing watching us through the window.

"Jay is essential to my plan," I said.

"Which is?"

I explained that Jay and whatever cops he could convince to join him would be waiting at Pier 10, out of sight of Pier 5 where there was a telephone booth. There was a telephone booth across the street from Pier 5.

Dila looked skeptical.

"Look, we'll be able to tell if a crime is being committed or not. We'll have night vision binoculars. So, we move in and make a citizens' arrest. But just before we move in, we call Jay, and they'll swoop in, take over and make the arrests official.If no crime is being committed, we don't place the call to them. We all go home. It will work. I'll get Vincent to join us."

"You think he would? You know, late at night and with a family?"

"Vincent is just as concerned as I am about Mario. I know my twin; he'll come."

Dila still looked skeptical. "I'll trust your intuition that it should work, but if these are criminals, it will be dangerous. Criminals have weapons."

"It's all about timing. We go in hollering, "Citizens' arrest. Police on their way! Like that. And they'll hear the sirens. . ."

Dila interrupted, "And the bad guys start shooting at you."

"Could be. but I'm betting the second they hear the sirens they're outta there. We'll save the girls and maybe catch ourselves a guy who can lead us to the top dogs."

Dila took a sip of wine and broke off a section of bread. "So?" she said before dipping it into the olive oil. "I'm still confused how you intend to make a connection between illegal smuggling of women and your brother, Mario."

I was not at all sure myself. I said, "The short answer is I don't know. The long answer is once we know this is not a rumor, but fact, we can go with the assumption that Mario discovered it and was about to expose them."

"Them?"

"The smugglers, pimps, you know." I heard myself sounding lame. "When Sweets and I searched their apartment we found a number of copies of proposals for articles on drugs, weapons being smuggled into the country and Vietnamese girls being brought to the U.S. for prostitution purposes. Granted these were just proposals, but it's a kind of evidence. I *am* Detective Saturday, right?"

"Girl Friday is listening. Go ahead, Victor."

"I'll talk to Jay. I'll tell him what we know and the time, but not the place, except that it is in San Francisco somewhere along the embarcadero."

I was about to continue when the waiter brought our meals. The aroma of the seafood and the tomato sauce reminded me how hungry I was. I gave up nibbling on the bread and began eating. Dila followed my lead. She leaned into her food like a sprinter at the starting line. I didn't recall Dila having this big an appetite. The Big Apple must have changed her attitude toward food, which was as far as I remembered about weight watching.

"They can position their wheels at Pier 10," I repeated. "Jay can stay by the phone. We'll get the number."

"The few times I met Jay, I didn't get the feeling he had a lot of power," Dila said. "Does he have friends in the San Francisco Police Department? He has no jurisdiction outside of Alameda County."

"You'd be surprised. Jay is pretty laid back, but he's well liked. He's also on the board of the California Police Officers Union. He passed the California bar examination, but decided he didn't like being a lawyer and applied to the Police Academy. He's a bit older than he looks."

"He looks plenty old to me," Dila said.

"It's just that he's out of shape."

"Alright," Dila said. "When we get back to Oakland, you go talk to Jay. We need to know right away. If he rejects your idea, I'm going recruit Tisdale. If we have to do a citizens' arrest, that fool can put a scare into people."

I knew what Dila meant, recalling how fast Tisdale's knife appeared when we met at the Golden Dragon. We finished our lunch. Our waiter brought the check. Across the top was written *Compliments of the House. Best to Big Sal, Joe.* We left a big tip.

• • •

I tracked Jay down at Flynn's. It was Friday, clam chowder. Body got clams fresh in the morning. His soup was buttery smooth and unlike a lot of clam chowders, more clams than potatoes. Jay was having a late lunch. I sat down on the empty stool next to him. His mouth was full, so he nodded. I was about to say hello when Body's voice stopped me. I knew what was coming and braced myself. I was in no mood for Body's stupid Italian jokes.

"Victor, me boyo, it's Christmas time, so would you describe for me, if you please, an Italian Nativity scene?"

"I'm waiting breathlessly for the punch line, you Irish *Chooch*."

"It has Jesus, Mary. . ."

Body paused, looked up and down the bar, smirking, then finished.

". . . and three wise guys."

"I'm holding my side laughing," I said. Body burst out laughing. So did the rest of the guys sitting at the bar, including Jay. "Don't encourage him, Jay," I said.

"You have to admit that was a good one,' Jay said.

"Yeah, yeah. Look, Jay, can we get a booth? I need to talk to you about something."

"Ah geez, Victor. I don't like what's coming. I was having a nice peaceful lunch."

"This is important. If I'm right, it could make you a lieutenant."

"It could also get me to lose my badge and my pension."

"The risk will be small, the reward great. I promise. You want me to swear on my children, I will."

"You don't have any fucking children, you asshole."

"I'll swear on Vincent's baby, how's that."

Jay sighed the sigh of the grievously afflicted, picked up his bowl and glass and stood up. We moved into the booth across from us.

"We don't want anyone at the bar to hear us, Jay, so let's keep our voices down."

"I'm not saying anything. You do the talking. No promises, you understand."

"Absolutely," I said and placed my hand over my heart. I collected my thoughts, then began. I explained my plan and asked. "What do you say?" Jay began to slide out of the booth. I grabbed his sleeve.

"Jay, our source is solid." *Okay, I was stretching the truth some.*

"Vietnamese girls being brought into our country. Mario must have found out about it. They made it look like a murder suicide."

"Who is the they?" Jay asked "And who is your source?"

"Rogue military," I lied, but the lie seemed plausible. "I can't tell you my source, but she's Vietnamese."

"This is the most harebrained scheme I've ever heard of. You want a bunch of off-duty police officers to wait at a telephone booth until you call us to arrest human traffickers. You understand in the real world, these kinds of villains carry firearms, don't you? I have no jurisdiction in San Francisco, and even if I knew some guys that might take a risk, they sure as hell wouldn't be based on rumors and a Vietnamese source you won't reveal. Couldn't that simply mean she wants to meet you there? Have you thought of that? Besides, this is Bureau of Immigration territory. You need to talk to the Feds. Way above my pay scale."

"Jay," I pleaded. He shook his head.

"I'm going up to the bar and finish my chowder. No can do, Victor. I want to keep my pension."

I could read Jay. He was not going to change his mind. "You'd make lieutenant,' I said as I headed for the door."

"You're losing it Victor," Jay yelled after me. "You might want to see a shrink."

I thought of the word, shrink, as I walked up the driveway to our office. Was I losing it?

Theresa handed me my telephone messages as I entered the office. I had ten calls. At my desk I sifted through them. All business related except for the last one from Dila, at the bottom of which Theresa had written: *Il tuo fidanzata. At her office. Call back. Good news.*

"She's not my fiancé," I said.

"Whatever," Theresa said.

I picked up the phone. "Give me a minute, will you," I said to Theresa. She stood up and left the office with a big smile on her face, like *I know what you love birds are going to talk about.*

The only office I could think of was the Black Panthers' Office where Dila had been employed and still volunteered when she was home from New York. I dialed. A voice I recognized as James the Behemoth answered. Trying to disguise my voice, I asked to speak to Ms. Adila Agbo. I said please.

"I know that's you, white bread," James growled. I imagined a bear standing on its hind legs, baring his teeth.

"I said please." The phone went dead. "*Cretino*," I mumbled. I dialed again. This time Dila picked up.

"Victor, James hung up the phone and looked like he was ready to go to war, so I figured it was you who called.'

"Yeah, he's a cretin."

"Let's hope you never call him that to his face."

"He won't know what it means."

"You ever heard of tone. He'll know. You stay clear of James."

"Not a problem. You called me. What's up?"

"Did you talk to Jay?"

"Yeah, he is not going to do it. He says he needs way more evidence than what we have to risk his pension."

"Not to worry. I've convinced three of the Panthers to join us."

"Are you sure that's a good idea. The Panthers are lighting rods right now. If something goes wrong, we'd probably run, but they might do something crazy like start shooting people."

"It's Tisdale and two of his buddies from Nam, Big Eddie and Little Edie. Both of them had serious girlfriends in Saigon. They tried to bring their girls home with them, but were blocked by all sorts of bureaucracy, that was really racist. White soldiers were given preference. They said they'd like to help if this is really about bringing Vietnamese girls in illegally. They promised they'd only bring handguns."

"Great. My mind is totally at ease."

"Do you want to get to the bottom of this or not, Victor. I'm Girl Friday doing my job. You get Vincent to join us."

"Alright. You're right. Where shall we meet? We'll take two cars. Tisdale knows how to get to Pier 5. They'll meet us there at one o'clock. Being an hour early should be enough in case Clorita's maid got the time wrong."

We hung up and I went out to the lot to find Vincent. Theresa stubbed out her cigarette and went back to the office. She had been standing close to the open window, and I wondered if she'd been listening. Vincent was talking to a customer. The passenger door to the 1962 black and white Ford Sunliner convertible was open. A woman was behind the steering wheel, looking up at Vincent. I could not see her expression, but I could guess. My twin sold a lot of cars just on his looks alone. I pretended to look busy. It didn't take long before Vincent escorted the couple past me into the office, giving me a wink. I figured fifteen minutes or so, and he'd hand the couple over to Theresa to complete the paperwork.

When I entered the office, Theresa was explaining details of the contract. They were putting down a sizable down payment, which our bank would appreciate. I heard Theresa say eleven-point five percent, which was probably the interest the couple would be paying per month. The phone rang, and Vincent picked it up and said, hello. After that whoever was on the line didn't allow Vincent to speak. I heard him mumble an occasional uh, huh. He kept turning to look at me unhappily. When he got off the phone, he pointed to the door. I followed him out and to the back of the office where he turned around and faced me. It was the face of anger.

"What in the frigging heck are you thinking, Vittorio?"

When Vincent is mad at me, he always calls me by my Italian name, and frigging is as close to swearing as my twin gets. I knew what he was talking about, but I asked anyway. "What do you mean?"

"You know darn well. That was Jay on the phone, and he thinks you've gone nuts. You can't possibly think of doing what you're planning to do tonight."

"It will be two in the morning," I said.

Vincent turned away from me. When he turned back, he wasn't mad anymore, but he looked worried.

"Jay thinks you're letting your grief for Mario screw up your judgement. According to him, you're looking for anything that will fit what you believe happened to Mario and Grace. Victor, that's like trying to fit a puzzle piece into the wrong puzzle. These illegal prostitutes, if there even are any, what do they have to do with our brother? No don't answer. I'll answer for you. *Non una cosa*, not one thing, you *babbo*."

I didn't like being called a dummy. My normal twin-reaction would have been to escalate the friction with a comeback, after which Vincent would have to respond until we came to blows. Fighting for twins is like a release value to a steam engine. Once over, all the tension is gone. But today I couldn't argue with Vincent. I knew I was acting irrationally, but what else could I do. Reason was on the side of the police report, but there was no way on God's green earth I would ever believe it.This is what a mountain climber must feel like reaching above him for a finger hold you know is there but not finding one.

"You said you'd have my back, remember?"

"Vittorio, Vittorio, listen to yourself. You have no idea what you're dealing with. Besides Dila, who else have you got going with you, not frigging Sweets I hope."

"Not a chance," I said. "Dila has rounded up a few Black Panthers."

"*Madonna*," Vincent moaned. "What is it with you and the Black Panthers? I understand that Dila used to work for them, and that she's some kind of liberal, but Victor, the Black Panthers are high on the FBI's list of priorities to send to prison, all of them. Do you want to join them?"

My inner messenger was warning me this conversation was taking us to the edge of a fraternal cliff. My relationship with Dila and quasi friendship with Panthers' Minister of Education, Terrance Bowles had already created distance between me and my twin. I was hearing, *Don't push it*. I took a step toward Vincent and placed my hands on his shoulder. "*Bene*, good, don't worry. I'll figure it out. Better anyway, now that you're a father to stay out of the trouble. I'm sure we'll be fine tonight."

The buyers stepped out of the office with Theresa trailing them. She hailed Vincent. I watched him take the temporary registration from her and lead the couple to their new automobile. He was chatting and smiling. "*Cosi, cosi*" I said to myself, *it is what it is*, and went behind the office and got in my Mustang. Vincent was shaking hands as I drove out of the lot. He saw me go and waved. I waved back.

CHAPTER 12
PIER FIVE

Don't trouble trouble until it troubles you.
Vietnamese proverb

Pier 5 sits just a few blocks up from the Ferry Building. When my father felt like eating at Scoma's, on Fisherman's wharf, our family traveled by ferry from Oakland to the Ferry Building, and on the way our father would lecture us about the building. Before the bridges were built in the 1930's, the ferries were the only way travelers and commuters could reach San Francisco unless they were coming up from the peninsula. The design of the clock tower was based on that of the iconic tower of the Seville Cathedral in the city of Seville in southern Spain. There was something about the arches of the building, but I couldn't remember. There was also a story about ghosts that roamed the building at night that I was pretty sure our pop invented to scare us.

We found parking across the street from Pier 5 where we'd parked before next to a telephone booth. We arrived before Tisdale with an hour to spare. The fog had rolled in. Low hanging wisps of it floated across our windshield like the ghosts of my father's stories.

To us East Bay guys, San Francisco was always home to the arrogant privileged. We believed San Franciscans thought they were better than us. We were the working-class side of the bay. I'd mentioned this to Dila, and she'd asked me if I'd ever been to Hunters' Point. I hadn't. She informed me that it was a neighborhood in the southern part of San Francisco that was made up of predominately African-Americans who settled there during the Second World War to work in the shipyards. Talk about your working class, she'd said.

Some time went by and a set of headlights shone through our back window. I opened my door and looked behind us. It was a dark 1969 New

Yorker 4 door sedan. Tisdale stepped out of the driver's side. The passenger door opened, and Sweet Monroe's blond cockatiel hairdo emerged.

Che cazzo, I thought. "Sweets, what the fuck are you doing here?" I said.

"Heard through the grapevine you needed help, dude. Tisdale said the more the merrier."

"Tisdale?" I said.

"Brothers at the office swore this blond-haired brother is righteous," Tisdale said. "He says he owes you a favor."

"He owes me his life."

"Don't go all drama queen on me, Victor," Sweets said.

The back doors opened and two men appeared, one very large and wide and the other short and skinny. Both were wearing black suits, black dress shirts and red bow ties – Big and Little Eddies, I presumed. Dila joined us on the sidewalk.

"We're a little conspicuous standing out here," I said. "We can all fit in your New Yorker, and we'll talk." It was a tight fit. "Here's what's up," I started. "The note given to us by Clarita's maid implied that something was going to happen at pier 5, just across the way at 2 a.m.Since we were asking Clarita about Vietnamese girls being brought into the United Stated to make whores of them, we can assume that's what's going down. Make sense?"

"Dila already explained," Tisdale said.

Dila spoke up. "Victor and I figured they have to move these women from the ship — it's got to be a boat of some kind — to some kind of vehicle. Our guess is a bus. But it doesn't matter. Whatever vehicle they bring in we'll block the exit with our cars."

"Not with my brand-new wheels," Tisdale said.

"Not mine with my Mustang either," I said.

Dila said, "That's why Victor and I convoyed here earlier and dropped off one of his beaters from the lot."

"Over there," I said, pointing to the opposite side of the telephone booth at the '59 Buick Le Sabre Estate Wagon. "It was headed for a wholesaler as a tax write off."

"Didn't think things through my man," said Little Eddie.

His voice was almost a bass. Did that mean Big Eddie was a tenor?

"That junker ain't gonna be any good 'gainst a bus or 'gainst any vee-hik-les smugglers bound to use. They'll just plow through you. Leave your ass spinning in the middle of the 'barcadero."

"And if they gots weapons like them Uzi and shit, they blow your junker up before plowing through you," Big Eddie said. Sure enough, a tenor. I almost laughed.

"Didn't you tell me you've got cops stashed somewhere?" Tisdale said. "Quick call from the phone booth over there and get their asses down here. We just the holding action."

Tisdale looked at me. I closed my eyes.

"There ain't no fuzz? Is that it?"

"My friend Jay said he wouldn't do it. I figured we could handle a citizens' arrest."

"He meant to tell you," Dila said.

As a good Catholic boy, I was raised believing in miracles. As an adult I became skeptical, but a knock on the car window made me a believer again. When I rolled down the glass and saw my twin smiling at me, and behind him the sour face of Detective Sergeant Jay Ness. Vincent was carrying the baseball bat he keeps next to his desk in the office just in case.

"Got your back, Victor." my twin said.

"God help me, if this doesn't work," Jay said. "I've stashed three of my fellow officers of the law where you told me next to the telephone booth at Pier 10. Introduce me to your fellow criminals, Victor, so I know who we're partnering with."

"Say what?" Big Eddie said.

I made the introductions.

"I'm going to say this once. If you're carrying, leave your firearms in the car. Better yet go across the street and dump them in the bay. The only shooters on our side are going to be police officers. Does everybody understand? And what the fuck is Sweets doing here?"

"I'm the brains behind this operation," Sweets said.

"You got to be kidding," Jay said. "Okay, okay. I'll walk up to Pier 10. One telephone call, and we'll be here lickity-split. We'll wait until three. If no call by that time, we're gone. Got it, Victor?"

"Thanks, Jay. I really appreciate it. You are a good friend."

"I may be a friend without a pension, so you'll have to give me a job selling cars."

To say I was relieved Jay and his crew were here, was an understatement. I was equally relieved that my twin had not forgotten the support at all cost twins make at birth and arrived with his trusty baseball bat. The bat had saved his butt and mine plenty of times. I remembered the first time. It was just after we'd taken over the business from our pop. I had gone home early and our secretary and accountant Sylvia was vising her family in San Diego. Vincent was minding the lot alone. The way he described it to me the next day, a scary hood with a scar on his cheek, and a do-rag covering his head walked into the office and pulled a switch-blade on him. "I wants all you money and the key to that blue caddy," he'd said. He was a big guy with bad teeth. I was scared." Victor is no coward, so when he told me the guy scared him, I was sure he was not overstating things. What happened next, according to my twin, accounts for my twin's long relationship with his baseball bat. Aluminum softball bat to be more accurate. Because Vincent was gone to play for his softball team after leaving work. His baseball bat was leaning by his desk next to the window. I have always loved this story and remember the details clearly as Vincent described them to me the next morning:

> *There I was, Vittorio, looking a long switchblade, my life being threatened. I still don't know what motivated me, but I grabbed the baseball bat and got into a batters' stance. "Okay, bring it on," I said. "You want me to send that melon head of yours over the centerfield wall, you just bring it on! Victor, I swear the guy looked over his shoulder like there might have been a centerfield fence and that's when I threw the baseball bat and hit him right on his melon head. The guy dropped his blade and fell to his knees. I came around my desk, picked up the bat and tee'd off on his back. When he hit the floor, I hit his legs with the bat a couple of times. Probably broke them I was so mad."*

This happened around the time I was starting a relationship with Renee Sorenson, a senior music student at Mills College who for some reason was turned on by stories of a violent nature. When I told her of Vincent's encounter with a switchblade, I received a seriously intense sexual reward. Perhaps this accounts for my remembering what happened so clearly. From that day on that exact aluminum softball bat has remained leaning in the corner by the window next to Vincent's desk.

•••

When Vincent got back, we continued our conversation about blocking the driveway with my beater.

Vincent said, "What beater?"

He said, "It's out of your share of the profits, Victor."

I was fine with that. We got back on subject.

I said, "What if we put two cars there. Would that work?"

"Maybe should be a truck." Little Eddie said.

"A truck? I can do that." I got out of the car and leaned into the window. "I'll be right back."

"Where are you going, Victor," Dila asked.

I put my finger to my lips and walked up the street. Ten minutes later I was back sitting behind the wheel of an old school bus re-painted the colors of a rainbow, its window covered by chintz curtains and outfitted in the interior to hold beds and furniture. It smelled of pot. I parked it behind Tisdale's Buick.

I slid into the front seat next to Dila.

"Victor," was all she said.

"I hotwired it. Vincent and I repo cars all the time. We're experts. Right Vincent?'

"You do realize you can go to jail for stealing a school bus," Vincent said.

Sweats said, "And they call me a crook."

"It no longer has anything to do with education except to educate its drop-in clients in the proper way of smoking weed." I said. "You should see the plants in there."

Big Eddie, Little Eddie and Tisdale were smiling. "My main man," Tisdale crooned.

I felt flattered.

• • •

Fifteen or so minutes went by, then a bus drove up the Embarcadero and turned into Pier 5, turned off its lights, but left its engine running. I raised my night vision binoculars. Two people got out of the bus and walked to the edge of the pier.

"This is it," I said. "Say a little prayer."

We waited, then we waited some more. A half an hour passed. I looked at my watch. It was two thirty-five. Jay said they'd wait until three.

Another ten minutes went by. I was getting nervous. Dila was holding my hand tightly.

"Boat coming," Tisdale announced. He was looking through a Star Light night vision scope, he'd brought back with him from Vietnam. "Pulling in. Couple of Asian men on board tying the boat off. Looks like more people coming from the cabin onto the deck. Can't tell whether they're men or women. All dressed the same. Got hats on. Gangplank down. They're starting to go ashore."

"Time to move, Victor," Dila said.

"Vincent, Call Jay," I said and slipped out of the car. I ran to the bus. The engine had stalled out. I turned the ignition, praying it wasn't out of gas. Nothing. *Ma fanfulo.* Another turn of the key, it coughed and sputtered and died. "Come on, come on, you piece of crap," I yelled, "Start!" I turned the key and it began weakly, then gained strength. I slammed the gear into low and pulled away from the curb. I made a wide U-turn across the Embarcadero and pulled across the entrance and killed the engine. I jumped out. Dila, Tisdale, Sweets, Big and Little Eddie and Vincent, holding his trusty baseball bat, were running across the embarcadero to join me,

Suddenly there was a loud voice. "What are you doing, young man? Stop in the name of the Lord!"

I was facing a large man with long white hair, wearing a black suit. Instead of a tie around his neck was a priest's white collar."Aw, merda," I said.

CHAPTER 13
Christmas

Gli uomini saggi imparano dagli errori degli altri, gli sciocchi dai loro stessi

Wise men learn from other's mistakes, fools from their own.
Italian proverb

Our family's Christmas had been a somber event with the black wreath hanging on the front door and the curtains in the house drawn. Instead of the Christmas lights being cheerful, as they normally would have been, I imagined them glowing ominously out of the darkness of the tree, ready to burst into flames. Then Christmas was over and the next day my mother stripped the tree of ornaments and strings of lights, placed them in a box and gave them to the Saint Vincent de Paul Thrift Store.Pop took the tree out to the curb. The rest of the day the pair cleaned until there was not a speck of Christmas left to remind them of this year's painful holiday. I had started to help, but my mom waved me away, it was their house, their job. I argued to no avail. As I was leaving, my mom grabbed my sleeve. "Mario needs your help," she said. Mario was beyond help, but I knew what she meant. Vincent and I had made a promise. We would not fail her.

As for Victor Brovelli, for the last week, along the length of East 14th Street and especially in Flynn's Tavern, my fiasco at Pier 5 was being referred to as Victor's Fuck-Up. The boys at the bar at Flynn's would look at me as I walked in and burst out laughing. Vincent was given a pass, but I was taking a ton of heat.

Yes, there had been illegal immigrants alright, but not young girls headed for prostitution. What we discovered that night behind the looming largeness of the white collared minister were the fatigued and frightened members of the ECVN, the Evangelical Church of Vietnam North – families. According to Pastor Reverend Cyril Harding of the Glide Memorial United Methodist Church, the North Vietnamese Communist government was steadily increasing its intimidation of protestant sects and particularly targeted the ECVN to the point that many of the members had been arrested and placed in reeducation camps. Appeals to the U.S. government to help had been ignored, thus this had been the first effort to rescue some of the most persecuted members of the church. The Vietnamese families were being herded quickly on to the bus, Reverend Harding whispering kindness into their ears, giving candy to the children. By then, I had removed the hippie school bus from the driveway. Tisdale, Big Eddie and Little Eddie had disappeared. Vincent, Sweets and Dila helped me to carry the immigrants' meager baggage off the boat for which Reverend Harding had blessed us.

•••

When I drove on to the lot, I was already there. I'd pulled the grills out from the back of the office and set them up, filled with coals, ready to go. Vincent gave me a less than genuine smile. A little later, Theresa arrived. She gave me the silent treatment and went into the office. Soon, I heard the noise of the vacuum cleaner that drove Vincent out of the office. We began cleaning dirty windshields and polishing hood ornaments, avoiding each other as much as possible, Pier 5 was still vivid in his memory: Mine too.

Dila and Sergeant Jay Ness were the only people not giving me a hard time. Grateful that he and his pals had not been called in and feeling a little sorry for my pitiful ass, Jay had made an extra effort to run down all the information available about weapons from Vietnam being smuggled into the country. Yes, he explained, it was happening, but the center of the investigative concern was in Southern California, particularly at the docks in San Diego. The military police and federal investigative agencies were all over it. He'd also found out about heroin smuggling. There was a guy on the East Coast named Larry Lucas who was the big drug honcho and well known to the FBI. In order to bring the heroin in, he had a crew of army personnel on his payroll who employed soldiers rotating home to bring the heroin in. Nothing about finding drugs in the bodies of dead soldiers. Total bull-crap, Jay had said. There was no indication that heroin smuggling was taking place in Northern California. Finally, as much as my gut told me not to, I had to admit to myself that I had allowed my grief over Mario's death to keep me from believing the forensic evidence, which concluded that Mario and Grace's death was the result of a murder/suicide.

Dila continued to support my failed Pier 5 plan. She insisted that I'd done what I needed to do for my own peace of mind. She had quoted a West African proverb, "Rain does not fall on one roof alone." I pretended to be cheered up. But I was feeling as if my roof was being struck by a rainstorm.

In five days the decade of the sixties would be over. The seventies would be without Mario. On top of everything else. I was missing Dila. Before Christmas, she'd explained that the 26th was the start of Kwanzaa, the African American year-end holiday festival. The word Kwanzaa was borrowed from the Swahili phrase: *Matunda ya Kwanzaa*, meaning First Fruit Festival. Dila explained Swahili to me as the lingua franca of most of the countries of East Africa. The holiday celebration would last seven days. Her parents, like many people of African-American descent, took Kwanzaa very seriously. Lots of her family were flying in. Her mother expected her to help decorate the house and help cook. Since I didn't have a clue, she'd filled me in on some of the main principals of the festival. Each day was represented by a theme. The first day, which was yesterday, was called *Umoja* — Unity and the second day, Kujichagulia — self-determination. I'd forgotten the rest. Along the way, there'd be gift giving and discussions about the day's themes. On December 31st, family and friends would come together for the traditional closing feast at her home. Kwansaa officially ended on the first day of the New Year. It sounded a lot like thanksgiving, I'd told her. To which she replied only when it came to lots of food. Kwansaa, according to Dila, was all about learning and being aware of one's heritage. I told her I understood. She'd told me I didn't, not in a mean way, but sort of sorrowfully. The thought occurred to me that a lot of African-Americans, like Dila, might very well feel sorry for whites for their inability to get beyond race as a way of judging humans. I didn't feel I deserved to fall into that category of white people. But maybe I wasn't trying hard enough, or paying stricter attention. Most of the Sixties, I had devoted to being a car salesman, then part owner of a used car business. I had been like a horse with blinders on running my race straight down the success track. The American way, right? When it came to racial and gender issues and all the changes going on around me, I couldn't see the horses on either side of me gaining on me until they had passed me. I needed to do some serious catching up with the times. If I mentioned this to Vincent or the guys at the tavern, they'd look at me funny, or come up with a joke or insult.

"We don't have enough sausages."

I was startled out of my thoughts by Vincent yelling at me from the grill. "Hey, Victor, we don't have near enough sausages." I'd been so deeply into my own thoughts, I hadn't noticed he'd stopped cleaning cars.

"Why don't you drive over and get some of Pop's," he said. "He's got plenty. Invite them to come over. It will cheer them up." Vincent sounded normal for once. The last place I wanted to go was to our family home, the black death-in-the-family wreath still hanging on the front door, all its shades still down. I was carrying around enough of my own grief, why would I want to add Mom and Pop's, like another layer on top of my own? But I was trying to lighten things up between me and my twin, so I said I'd do it.

I drove to our family home in Alameda and parked in the driveway. Mr. and Mrs. Luchese, Pop and Mom's neighbors for as long as I could remember, were doing something to an empty flower bed. They waved me over, but I kept walking around to the house and up the steps to the backdoor. Pop was sitting in the living room in their easy chair reading the Wall Street Journal. Mom was in the kitchen. I could smell tomato sauce. Mario's ghost was standing in the corner next to the fireplace. He was holding a family photograph taken at Carlo's wedding, the only one our pop allowed of Mario in the house since the day Mario had thrown his Purple Cross in a bonfire at an anti-Vietnam Protest.

"About time you showed up," I said. He stared at me and tapped his forehead. What the hell did he mean by that?

My mom looked up. "Victor, how nice. What did you say, dear? I missed it."

"Nothing. Vincent sent me to pick up some sausages. Would you have a few extra, Pop?"

"You know where they are, Vittorio. Got more than we'll ever eat. Help yourself."

Normally, I'd have stayed to chat, but these were not chatting times. I could see the hurt of my parents' faces. I excused myself to get back to work. On the drive back to the lot, the container of sausages sat on the back seat. Mario's ghost was riding shotgun.

CHAPTER 14
KWANSAAA

The tortoise is friends with the snail; those with shells keep their shells close together
Benin proverb (West Africa)

Since I met Adila Agbo in April of 1968, my relationship with her had been a constant learning experience and sensitivity training. I would never be able to explain this to Vincent or to my father and other older siblings, Costanza and Carlo. My mother might understand, but maybe not. By now, all my family and friends knew I was dating Dila. I was not sure if they realized how much more this was than dating. The first and only time my parents met Dila was when I brought her to our family Fourth of July backyard picnic last summer. The Fourth was always a big deal for our pop, Big Sal Brovelli, Italian immigrant and fervent American patriot.Tables were set up on the lawn. Pop barbequed burgers and dogs on the barbeque pit he'd built himself. American flags hung from all the trees along with red, white, and blue balloons.There were a lot of Italian immigrants like my pop living in Alameda, and their backyards would look just as patriotic as ours on the Fourth of July. Dila and I had strolled in acting casual, hoping not to attract a lot of attention, but one look at Dila and the buzz started. It only lasted until I made the introduction. Everybody was polite to Dila, except one of my grandmother's ancient friends who kept asking Dila if she was related to Marian Anderson, the famous African-American opera singer. If it had only been once, it wouldn't have been a big deal, but the old biddy trailed after Dila, asking the same question only phrasing it differently. Afterwards, Dila said she wasn't offended. Perhaps a little annoyed. She would have preferred if the old gal had thought she was related to contemporary black divas like Leontyne Price or Jessye Norman. I had said, *right*, as if I knew who these women were.

Not long after that Fourth of July celebration at our house, I brought Dila to Flynn's for lunch to meet my friends. I had set it up ahead of time with Larry Hughes, the owner of the DoNut Hole next door, who was black, that he'd be there on the day I brought Dila. I didn't want anyone to slip up and use the N word. If Hugh's huge body that had once played tackle for the Raiders was in the tavern, the guys would be extra careful. All had gone well. Dila endeared herself to Body by saying she supported the unification of Ireland. She had beaten all comers in darts and won a couple of rounds of beers for the house playing liar's dice with Jitters, which endeared her to the house. Before we left, the guys proclaimed her one of the guys, something she'd told them every woman wanted to be. It seemed to me Dila somehow managed not to be threatening, even though I was sure her appearance was: tall, stern, beautiful, eyes two shades of green, full lips, her afro a reminder of Angela Davis, not a soothing image for whites. Yet, there she'd been calling a bunch of white guys by their first names and giving them hugs. Jitters stammered his delight. Swanee told her to bring her car in and he'd detail it for free. Larry Hughes had been enchanted and called her sister. As I left, he'd given me a broad smile and a wink. Of course I never mentioned that Dila had worked for the Black Panthers and carried a 30 caliber M1 carbine in the back seat of her car.

To say Dila possessed a complicated personality would be an understatement. There was Dila, the actress and aspiring playwright. And Dila who mentored teenage musicians of all races in a summer music camp in Michigan with her friend, a white woman I used to date. I knew how fiercely Dila believed in the cause of African-Americans. I had never spoken of Dila working part time for the Black Panthers to anyone. She had never told her parents. I knew if push came to shove, she'd probably use the carbine she carried in her car. I tried not to think at whom she'd be shooting.

All this was by way of saying when tested by my family and friends, Adila Agbo had acted with charm and grace and with not the slightest hint of racism. The least I could do was perform up to her standards when meeting her extremely large extended family, which was where I was heading at noon on December 31st the last day of the year, 1969 for the traditional Kwanzaa feast called Karamu at Dila's home. I had left our lot with Vincent's blessing. He'd handle the rest of our annual *Last Day of the Year 40% Off Sale*. For the last four days, I'd been working up my courage. I was more than a little nervous. Scared shitless was more accurate. What was it that Ernest Hemingway called bravery? Grace under pressure?

There would be no normal Victor Brovelli New Year's Eve parties this year. Dila was required to be at home. Without Dila, I'd decided to eschew the night life. This was completely new to me. Any other New Year's Eve of my adult life, I would have been thinking of what I would wear to whatever numbers of parties I was invited to, and considering which women might be there that would succumb to my amorous moves. That was B.D. *Before Dila*. By New Year's Eve 1968, I was already dating Dila. She and I didn't celebrate that New Years together. I was still not convinced about monogamy. At the party at Body's home, I had pretended to enjoy myself, but left early *senza una donna*, without female company. This New Years Eve I was a committed one-woman-man. It was a concept that my twin and all of my male friends from college and Flynn's found impossible to believe and, as Body Flynn remarked, was depressing: *Boyo, you raised the bar of male virility. When will we ever enjoy such erotic tales again?*

The freeway was crowded. Twice I had to brake suddenly to avoid an accident. I was nervous. That was an understatement. My stomach was turning over and a few times I almost pulled the Mustang to the side of the freeway to be sick. I told myself that there was no reason for my anxiety. Dila wouldn't have invited me if she hadn't cleared it with her mother and father first. Had I cleared it with my parents in July for our family's Fourth celebration? I didn't recall, which probably meant I didn't. Was this going to be pay-back time? I put the unkind thought out of my head. Under my sport coat, I was wearing a white dashiki, a collarless embroidered African shirt that Dila had given me, over black woolen slacks. As I drove, I repeated what Dila taught me I should say to her parents when I entered the house. Kwanzaa Yenu Iwe na heri! Happy Kwanzaa. I was reasonably certain I'd forget parts of it and sound like a complete idiot. On the passenger seat was a bottle of Bertolli Classico Chianti that had won a lot of prizes this year. I had first thought to bring a bottle of Pappy Van Winkle Bourbon, but Brovelli Brother's Used Cars had not had a fruitful financial year and Pappy at five hundred bucks or so a bottle, was a tad too expensive for my pocketbook. We had a bottle that our pop had given us when we took over the business five years ago that we were told to use to toast financially successful years. The bottle stood on the top of the filing cabinet behind Theresa's desk only half empty, which was proof that my twin and I needed to work harder.

I left the freeway at Ashby Ave and drove east.

Ten minutes later, I was standing in front of the Agbo residence, a stately three-story Victorian, staring at the door bell as if uncertain of its function. "*Fottuto codardo!*" I said. I could have said it in English, but *the word coward* has more cowardice in it than English does. I said it again. "*Fattuto codardo!*"

"Was that an Italian expletive?"

I looked around trying to find the source of Dila's voice and saw a speaker above the doorbell. The door opened. Dila was looking at me, tapping her foot and pointing to her watch.

"You're almost late, Victor. I was worried you'd back out."

"We Italians are not cowards," I said.

"Come on in. We're just about to sit down for dinner."

I felt guilty. Had I procrastinated so long leaving home that I missed the pre-dinner festivities. What a *babbo* I was.

Woven straw mats with red, green and black diamond shaped designs with elephants in their centers hung on the walls on either side of the entry way. Standing on a side table on the wall to my right was a large wooden candle holder, Dila told me was called a Kinara. There were seven candles representing the seven Kwanzaa themes. One black candle in the center, red and green candles on either side. The rug on the floor was not African I was pretty sure. Persian, maybe and it looked old and expensive. It reminded me that Dila's father was a hugely successful business man. I couldn't remember if Dila ever told me what exactly he was successful at. I did remember that she told me he personally funded a trip that a group of prominent African-Americans took to visit some of the countries of West Africa where most American slaves had originated.

Dila took my bottle of chianti and placed on the table with other gifts around the Kinara. I trailed her into the dining room, feeling self-conscious.

"Everybody, this if Victor Brovelli," She announced. "He's my very good friend."

Father and mother turned in my direction as did everybody else in the room except for one old white-haired man seated at the head of the table which I assumed was reserved for Dila's father. The ancient fellow's eyes were closed, but he wasn't sleeping because his lips were moving. Praying, I wondered.

Hoping I wouldn't fuck it up, I said, "Kwanzaa Iwe na heri!"

Dila clapped and everybody in the room joined in except Dila's mother and father. Two older women, Dila introduced as her aunts Louise and Carol from Los Angeles shook my hand, their grips like stevedores, hell they were big enough. A tall distinguished gentleman with a neat mustache and a neatly trimmed goatee clapped me on the back. He was wearing dark glasses and dressed in a cobalt blue pin-striped suit over a white dress shirt with a fleur de lis tie and a matching handkerchief neatly visible above the jacket pocket. I figured he was an independent thinker as everyone else was wearing some kind of African clothing.

"You're a brave man, to enter the residence of our tribal chieftain."

I assumed he was talking about Kahil Agbo, Dila's father.

I'm Dila's favorite uncle. I'm married to this marvelously endowed lady." He placed his arm around Aunt Louise. She smiled broadly at him and said, "Oh you!"

"Uncle Daren played basketball for USC and went on to play for the Lakers," Dila said.

"Had a cup of coffee with the Lakers. Never quite made the team, but I had a great time."

"You must have played center, Mr. Agbo," I said.

"Agbo is not my name, son. My brother changed our family name to an African sur name when he elected himself our tribal chief. I'm a Williams, and so was our father."

By his tone, I could tell the name change did not sit well with Uncle Darin.

"You just like to pick on your little brother, Uncle Darin," Dila said, giving him a little push in the chest.

"You're right girl. I respect how committed your dad is, but you got to admit he goes overboard some times." He gave her a knowing look, and I figured he knew about the scarification.

He turned to me. "College center. In the pros, six-eight was too short. Anyway, I couldn't jump, which sort of screws up the myth that all black guys can leap over tall buildings and you poor white boys are left without any hops, which is also bullpucky. What sport do you play, Victor?"

Before I could answer, our conversation was interrupted by Dila's mother and father. If Kahil Agbo was tribal king, Mrs. Charlene Agbo was the queen, and she looked every bit like royalty to me, the way she was walking, sort of floating and holding her head high as if she were wearing a crown. Both of them shook my hand unenthusiastically, welcomed me into their home and wished me a Happy Kwanzaa, in English, after which Dila's mom hurried people to their seats. I sat to the right of Dila and to the left of a small man wearing an ankle length dashiki. He introduced himself as Reverend Morning. I almost said, *good afternoon,* but felt the humor might go amiss.

I noticed there was no wine on the table, the absence of which at an Italian dinner would have been considered scandalous. I asked Dila. She said some of their guests were Muslims. She added that much of the population of the countries in northern portion of West Africa were Muslim.

The toast came first, offered by the ancient wrinkled man sitting at the head of the table. Her grandfather, Dila whispered. "Whenever Kwanzaa is celebrated at our house, he sits at the head of the table. I think it sort of irritates my father." Grandfather Williams spoke so softly I could barely hear him. What I heard had something to do with the first fruits of their lives were their children. I patted Dila on her knee. Following the toast, Dila's father rose to speak.

"I would like to introduce a dear cousin from the country of Benin from where our family's ancestors originated. Rabbi Mousa Kouakou flew here to be part of our humble festival. Mousa, would you stand and provide us with a few words?"

A tall, almost skeletal man wearing a kepi pinned to his hair, rose from the table. Coming in so late, I had not been introduced to all the people in attendance, so I was seeing him for the first time. I was startled by how much darker his skin color was than all of the rest of the people at the dining room table. Must be from the Sicilian part of Benin, I thought, and almost broke out laughing, which earned me a poke in the ribs from Dila.

Rabbi Kouakou spoke with an accent that sounded French to me. "Our tribal ancestry has its roots in the country of Benin. We are all to one degree or descended from the Betatmaribe Tribe. I have lived the last decade in Abidjan, the capital of the Ivory Coast where there are two Jewish synagogues. I am here not only to join you, my American family at this joyous feast, but to be part of a forum at Stanford University on the importance of Jews standing in solidarity with African-Americans in these racially troubled times. Our previous commitment to each other's faiths and cultures is being brought into question. Not only Jews in the United States and in Israel are supporting your cause, but the Jews of Africa as well. There are more of us than you think. By our mutual suffering we have grown the hard shells of self-protection. It is imperative we support each other. You may not be aware of how many of the Jewish faith exist on the continent of Africa and how that came to be. Let us begin in Ethiopia. . ."

Ten minutes later I could tell all the people were getting restless as the good rabbi continued to provide what felt like the entire encyclopedic history of African Jewry. Gratefully, Dila's father brought the history lesson to a close with a curt, thank you dear cousin.

What followed was Dila's father speaking passionately about the goodness of the First Fruit Celebration that brought all African-Americans of all the tribes of Africa sold into slavery together as one spiritual tribe. He spoke eloquently in a deep and distinctive voice. I could imagine him commanding respect in a corporate board room. I couldn't help comparing him to my pop and his earthy pronunciation of Italian proverbs. Educated to the fifth grade, Big Sal Brovelli voice was not meant for corporate boardrooms. The thought occurred to me that the white powers that be in government and business would find Mr. Agbo, a university educated and millionaire black man more threatening than the Black Panthers. I would have to run this idea by Dila.

At the conclusion of her father's speech, Dila's aunts brought in tureens of soup, their contribution to the feast. I was told it was peanut soup, popular all-over West Africa. There were already covered dishes that when uncovered revealed mounds of a white dough. Fou, fou, Dila called it. She scooped some onto a small plate and handed it to me, then served herself.

"This is pili pili sauce for the fou, but go easy on the sauce. It's grown-up hot. It makes Mexican chili look adolescent.

I sneered. "Not a problem," I said and covered the gooey looking white stuff with a healthy spoon full. Dila smiled condescendingly.

I took a bite. It had the consistency of mud. The second the sauce hit my tongue, I knew I was in trouble.

"Drink some soup," Dila said. "It will help."

Nothing helped. I reached for the glass of water in front of me. I closed my eyes to keep them from watering. When I opened them, the room had gone quiet and the dinner guests were staring at me.

"Hot,' I said and coughed.

Everybody broke out laughing except the King and Queen. I smiled weakly.

"Not a problem," Dila said, imitating my voice.

Soup finished, bowls cleared away, the two aunts, who I decided were the King and Queen's indentured servants, brought in the main course of Jerk chicken in honor of one of the guests who lived in Jamaica. The rest of the meal was strictly African: Dohomey fish stew; yams; Jollof rice; Acaraje - balls of deep-fried black-eyed peas - and cuts of roasted goat. Dila quipped she'd test me on the names. I said, "Ha, ha." Conversation flowed with intermittent sighs of contentment. Dila leaned toward me and whispered when was I planning to announce that southern Italians were really Africans. I whispered back that I was planning to wait to tell our kids. I got a kick under the table.

It didn't take me long to realize that this dinner in a different setting and with different decorations and customs could have taken place anywhere in the world. Family and friends joined together to enjoy life, a time to keep the world beyond the dining room with all of its troubles at bay.

Desert was sweet fritters called Yovo Doko. The aunts served coffee and tea.

•••

I left Dila with her parents and family and drove home believing that the King and Queen were not impressed with me. Dila had not disagreed, but assured me that the rest of her family approved. Perhaps not Reverend Morning, who when I mentioned I knew Reverend Cyril Harding of the Glide Memorial Methodist Church, had frowned and told me that he hoped I wasn't that kind of radical. The way he put it: *Out of the Christian loop.*

I arrived at the turn off to Alameda and home, but changed my mind and drove in the direction of East 14th Street and Flynn's tavern. It would be too early for the usual New Year's Eve festivities to begin in earnest. After Dila's parents and a dry Kwanzaa meal, I needed a drink badly.

Green and white balloons covered the ceilings. Happy New Years signs were strung across the back bar mirror. It was early, but it should have been more crowded than this. On New Year's Eve I would have expected to find Body dressed up in his finest tuxedo, standing behind the bar with a pointy cap atop his red hair. Instead, Stuart, the night bartender, served me my usual Anchor Steam. I spotted Body in the back of the tavern in his bartender's apron just as he started up the stairs to his office. I asked Stuart.

"Big IRA powwow," He replied.

It was no secret that some of the Irishmen who formed the *Erin Go Braugh Dart Team* were raising money to send back to Ireland to support Sinn Fein, the Irish political party dedicated to uniting all of Ireland, but the rumor was that they were really IRA, which was the military wing of the party. Body had introduced me to two, both Irish Nationals. One of the guys with a gray pony tail was named Seamus Hallinan. His face looked like it had gone through too many boxing matches. He'd remained in my memory because he told us he was related to Vincent Hallinan, a San Francisco attorney famous for defending Harry Bridges, the head of the ILWU, the International Longshore and Warehouse Union. This little piece of history I attributed to Pop. I was a snot-nosed kid sitting around our dining room table listening to Pop rail against Hallinan, who he believed was a low-down Communist. Pop had no tolerance for fascists or communists. The other Irish guy was as short as Hallinan was tall and looked sort of like a red headed mouse. His name was Brendan Riorden. The dart team wore green and gold T shirts with a logo of an angel totting a harp on her back.

I finished my beer and asked for another. The second was almost done, when Body appeared followed by five men. I recognized Hallinan and Riorden. Body patted me on the back as he walked past me and out of the tavern, holding the door open for the other men.

"Must have been a serious meeting," I said to Stuart. "He never passes up the opportunity to entertain me with one of his stupid Italian jokes."

"He turned over the whole night's party to me," Stuart said. "He told me he had other plans."

"Doesn't sound like our party-hardy Body," I said.

I drained the last of my beer and said good night. Midnight and the fireworks were too long to wait. Before getting in the car, I checked to see if Mario's ghost had decided to drive home with me. He hadn't. This night called for a quiet New Year's Eve alone. A Victor Brovelli epiphany? Maybe.

CHAPTER 15
FANTASMI

New Years Day morphed to Jan 2, 1970

The more enlightened our houses are, the more their walls ooze ghosts.
Italo Calvino

To make up for not spending New Year's Eve with me, Dila devoted the morning and afternoon of 1970 to making me happy. This entailed driving to Carmel in my Porsche Cabriolet for a day at the beach and a lovely lunch up the coast at Nicks in Pacifica before she had to return home to her responsibilities being the daughter of the King and Queen of Agbo.

This mornings' newspaper dated Friday, January 2nd announced California had become the first state out of 50 in the United States to permit "no-fault divorce." I put the paper down and dressed for work. I thought of the engagement ring that was sitting in a strong box along with my important documents on the top shelf in my coat closet. The ring was a round, one carat diamond, very good cut set in a white gold band. Depending on my resolve or my indecision, it moved from that box and into my pocket and back into the strong box on a regular basis. Because Dila didn't know about the ring, I didn't feel guilty being so indecisive.

I drove onto to our lot at 9 a.m. I parked and came around to the front where Vincent and Theresa were standing holding mugs of coffee. I wouldn't have been surprised if Vincent had greeted me saying, Victor, you look like you've seen a ghost. Mario's ghost had vanished after its first manifestation. It had not appeared again until this morning when it decided to make up for its absence by driving to work with me. It had chosen to remain seated in my parked Mustang, or should I say Mario's and my Mustang. I wondered if it recognized the outline of the blood stain on the drivers' seat. Would it cause it to relive that terrible moment on Grizzly Peak turnout? From last years' experience with the ghost of Winona Davis haunting me, I knew better than to strike up a conversation with the Spector. The message or messages it intended to impart to me would be conveyed by pantomime. In Winona's case last year, her ghost kept taping her Mickey Mouse watch signaling her frustration with my slow detection skills. Mario's ghost sat in the passenger seat and looked straight ahead. Every once in a while, he'd tap his forehead a couple of times with his index finger. And I remembered. It was something Mario had done when Vincent and I were kids and done something foolish or were stumped for an answer to some question. The gesture was Mario's way of telling us to figure it out on our own, to use our heads.

I have never shared my relationship to ghosts with my twin. In college, I'd foolishly remarked that I liked the ghost in *Hamlet*, and Vincent had spread it around the dorm that I was I was going to change my major to literature, a surefire way to have all my drinking buddies calling me a weirdo. On another occasion, Vincent had called my interest in literature a danger to the ethos of good business men. The only person I told about last years' ghost was Dila, who'd told me ghosts or visions of the departed were very much a part of West African culture. She explained that among observers of natural religions, after death an individual lived in a spirit world, receiving a new body identical to the earthly one but with the capacity to move about as an ancestor. It didn't exactly have much to do with my ghosts, but at least she didn't consider me a danger to the ethos of good car salesmen.

There are six common words in Italian for ghost: *il fantasma*, *io spettro*; *io spiito*; *la ombra*; *le anima*; and *la apparizone*. I remember all of them from childhood listening to our pop frighten us with ghost stories while our mom wagged her finger at him for being too graphic. Later in our bunk beds, Vincent would lean over from the top bunk and call me a scaredy-cat. The more frightened I was, the more I fought him to take it back. Once in our sibling fury, we broke our bunk bed. I couldn't recall whose body, mine or Vincent's, had done the damage. Bruised and bloody, we took our pop's thrashing with gritted teeth and childish manliness, while Pop smiled at our misery. "*The ghosts made-a you do eet, eh?*" he'd said, "*Non sono io che ti sculaccio ma i fantasmi.*" We knew that he was telling us a ghost was making him spank us. Big Sal Brovelli had a sense of humor.

I said my helloes to Vincent and Theresa and I went into the office for coffee. I returned and joined them. The balloons and New Year's 40% Sale signs were up, the balloons flapping in the breeze. A sunny day, but chilly. By noon, I'd bet the weather would turn overcast. Theresa was talking about one of the cars we had on our sales list, a 1965 white and black Cadillac Calais coupe. When we hired Theresa, I was not sure how bright she was. It didn't take me long to figure it out that our cousin knew the value of automobiles without knowing a single thing about what makes them run. She would walk around a car inspecting the exterior, then open the doors and give the interior a close once-over. She would write down what we could sell the car for in a little black notebook she kept in her purse. Nine out of ten times, she'd be within a hundred dollars of the selling price. It was uncanny and a bit unnerving.

"The Cady is clean, Vincent," Theresa said. "Not a scratch. Paint job like new. All those neat luxury appointments like the built-in vanity mirror and folding center arm rest. I got in and sank into the cushioned seats. I could have fallen asleep, it was so comfy. It's only four years old. At three grand, you're giving it away. We can do better."

"I agree," I said.

"You just got here," Vincent said. "You can't agree yet."

"Five minutes is all I need to disagree with you," I said.

"Up yours," Vincent said. "I bought the car for two thousand from one of Body's Irish pals who needed the cash. A thousand-dollar profit right now would help kick off our 1970 sales year."

It was nice to be on speaking and argumentative terms with my twin again.

"I trust Theresa's instincts here, Vincent. Her track record is close to 90% accurate. Hell, the original MSRP was close to five thousand if I remember right. You know how people try to bargain down sales cars. We'll wind up selling it for twenty-five hundred and regret it the next day."

Twins possess a much greater stubborn streak than normal siblings. We argued back and forth, until Vincent finally relented. The Cady was dropped from the 40% off sale. I was suddenly feeling like life was normal. I put ghosts out of mind.

There was a big *WELCOME 1970* poster above our office door.The antennas of all the vehicles that faced East 14th Street were festooned with ribbons. Reduced Price tags were on the windshields of our selected cars. The speakers were blaring AULD LANG SYNE.

The aroma wafting from the DoNut Hole reminded me I hadn't had breakfast. I volunteered to go for donuts. When I arrived, there was already a line out the door. Larry Hughes' donuts were famous in the East Bay. Larry claimed his grandfather, a pastry chef at a New Orleans restaurant, had personally given the recipe. A friend had pointed out to Larry that his grandpa died before he was born. His reply had been, you got to believe in ghosts. After I heard this story, I confided in Larry that I also believed in ghosts, to which he'd said that most people did, but they were afraid to admit it. I had hoped to avoid thinking about ghost, but here I was waiting my turn in line and thinking about Larry's ghostly grandfather, which reminded me of the appearance of Mario's ghost. Get a grip, Victor, I said to myself. Just as I said that, the ghost of Grace O'Conner stepped out of the DoNut Hole door holding a box of donuts in her spectral hands. "*Maddona,*" I said aloud enough to startle the man in front of me who turned and said, "Say what?" I shook my head. As the ghost passed me, I reached out and touched her shoulder. She looked at me.When I touched a real shoulder, I knew I'd made a mistake. The woman had Grace's jet-black hair, but no other feature and was about twenty years too old.

"Do we know each other?" She asked.

"Sorry, I mistook you for a ghost."

She smiled as if I'd made perfect sense. She had a nice smile.

Maybe Larry Hughes was right about people believing in ghosts.

On the way back to the lot, a car pulled up in front of Flynn's and two of Body's Irish friends got out and walked into the tavern. It was far too early for anyone to be there, so it surprised me that the door was open. One of them was the guy with a ponytail named Hallinan, the other man I didn't recognize.What the hell, I'd drop in and say hello. When I tried the door, it was locked. I recalled Stuart behind the bar saying, *Big IRA powwow.*

I returned to the lot and placed the box of donuts on Theresa's desk. There were already two people on the lot checking out our stock of cars. Sales being what they were, donuts would have to wait. So would the ghosts and the IRA.

CHAPTER 16
BIG NATE'S

Even as the archer loves the arrow that flies, so too he loves the bow that remains constant in his hands."
African proverb

Dila called at three p.m. and asked if I'd drive with her to drop off Rabbi Kouakou at the San Francisco Airport to catch his flight to France and on to the Ivory Coast. Vincent told me he'd close up and to take off as long as I promised I wasn't going to go play detective. He said he'd kick my butt if I broke my promise. I told him the only thing I was going to detect was Dila. He laughed and said in that case, okay. It occurred to me that Vincent didn't take my relationship with Dila seriously. Perhaps he thought I would get over her and look in the correct racial direction for a more permanent relationship, such as a good Italian girl, like his wife, Gloria.If he knew about the ring, would he be surprised, I wondered. I considered going to the closet and getting the engagement ring. Maybe tonight at dinner I would ask Dila. I decided against it. I needed a little more time.

Traffic would be tough to the SFO airport as it was closing in on rush hour. We'd take the Nimitz freeway south and take the Dumbarton Bridge to the airport, drop the old codger off then drive up to San Francisco for dinner. I was looking forward to a night out with Dila. For the first few months of dating, we had both felt more comfortable meeting for food or movies or concerts in San Francisco rather than on our side of the bay where it was probable that we'd be recognized. It wasn't that we were afraid — well maybe a little — but we were still in that feeling-each-other-out stage of our relationship. Would we, or wouldn't we? Was this real or were we simply being curious, stuff like that. San Francisco held many great memories. The concerts: *Big Brother and the Holding Company* at the Carousel Ballroom; *Airplane* at the Fillmore. In March of '69, we saw Janis Joplin at the Winterland, and a week later Bo Diddly at the same venue. We had dressed in our finest and eaten at the Top of the Mark and dressed down for Italian home cooking in the North Beach at a little restaurant on Broadway called the 101 Club where food was served family style and the owner sang famous Italian arias as you ate.

Would he be surprised, I thought. I considered going to the closet and getting the engagement ring, but decided I needed a little more time.

I arrived in front of Dila's home. She was helping Rabbi Kouakou down the porch steps. His luggage was already on the sidewalk. I placed the three bags in the trunk of the Mustang. Dila climbed in the back, and the rabbi sat in the front.On the drive we talked about the Kwanzaa feast. I went on a little too long about how tasty the food was, to which Dila had quoted from Hamlet, "Me thinks he doth protests too much." Rabbi Kouakou talked about how America had changed since he'd last been here ten years ago. He made an attempt to steer the conversation to African Jewry, but Dila navigated him away from the subject that had almost put the Kwanzaa guests into a coma. We crossed the Dumbarton Bridge and drove north on 101, a short distance to the airport. The sun was setting by the time we pulled in at the Air France terminal. For the last half hour, the African Rabbi's eyes had been closed, but his upper body was rocking back and forth. Some form of Jewish praying, I figured. I looked through my rear-view mirror at Dila. She gave a shrug.

I nudged the Rabbi Kouakou. His eyes opened. Before I could open the door to get out, he spoke.

"You children should keep in mind an old African proverb, *A fish and a bird may fall in love, but the two cannot build a home together.*"

From the backseat came Dila's voice, "And you should know, Rabbi Kouakou, another African proverb, 'Love like rain does not chose the grass on which it falls.'"

Dila would not get out of the car to wish the Rabbi bon voyage. I could tell by the stony look on her face, she was pissed. I shook his hand. He followed the porter hauling his luggage inside the terminal.

Dila was sitting in the passenger seat when I got in behind the wheel.

"Old racist," Dila grumbled.

I pulled away from the curb and made our way around the airport to the exit leading to San Francisco. Dila suggested dinner at Big Nate's, a soul food restaurant in the Fillmore District, owned by Nate "The Great" Thurmond of the NBA's San Francisco Warriors. I agreed. We drove for a while in silence. I was a little nervous about *Big Nate's*, considering, it was a soul food restaurant in the predominately Afro-American neighborhood.I reached over and touched Dila on the knee.

"You know we're going to draw a little attention in Big Nates."

"Victor Brovelli, I sometimes worry about you," she said. "Don't forget who started our romance. We're too far into it to be worried about every little closed-minded person who looks at us sideways. Life is all about *The Do.* Remember? We're either doing our love or we're not doing. And if I feel like giving you a barbeque kiss in front of the entire restaurant of black folks that's exactly what I'll do."

You can't argue with someone who loves as fiercely as Dila.

"I can't wait for the kiss," I said. But I knew that sounded weeny.

Our first kiss happened spontaneously in April of 1968 in a small park in West Oakland not far from the Black Panthers' Oakland office. The only witnesses were two children playing in the sandbox, their grandmother siting on a nearby bench, and a teenage boy playing basketball who'd stopped to frown at us. The grandmother had called us foolish, but she said it with a smile on her wrinkled black face. The two kids, a boy and a girl, were making fakey kisses and acting silly. Since then, there have been many kisses. We had gone into our romance with open eyes, expecting we'd have to deal with racism. Both our attitudes were fuck 'em. I did not like to think that suddenly I was feeling the pressure. I felt ashamed of myself.

"Don't feel bad, Victor," Dila said, as if she had read my thoughts. "I'd probably say the same thing if you were taking me to dinner to some place where I knew there'd be no black people.""

"I feel shitty," I said.

"Just remember you're a southern Italian. You could be descended from Africans."

This made me laugh. I had made up that story about southern Italians originating on the African continent for Dila long ago, trying to convince her to date me when she'd already told me she didn't date white men.

"You know, don't you," Dila said, "that when the Italians were immigrating to the United States the white protestant racists that ran things claimed that Italians *were* Africans."

"You're making that up to make me feel better," I said.

Dila laughed one of her water-fountain laughs that sounds to me like the start of a melody. "You concentrate on the road, Victor, and I'll tell you what I learned from an attorney in New York who specializes in immigration law."

She paused. I moved into the slow lane so I could listen better without cars running up my bumper.

"During the great Italian immigration in the 1890's, the press, but also by word of mouth, circulated that "Mediterranean" types were inherently inferior to northern Europeans. Catholic Churches were burned. The immigration office was accused of allowing in a new population of Negroids that were black-eyed, swarthy, and wicked. They were talking about Italians, Victor. Black-eyed, swarthy, and wicked, can you believe that shit?"

I shook my head. My parents arrived during a much smaller wave of immigrants from Europe following the Second World War. I wondered if my pop and mom knew this history.

"In 1891 in New Orleans," Dila continued, "the chief of police was shot. Italians in the city were accused of the crime and a bunch were arrested. They were acquitted, but before they could be released a mob of white citizens stormed the jail, hauled the Italians out and lynched them."

"*Maddona*," I said. "Why ae you telling me this?

"There's real lynching, Victor, then there's lynching of the mind. We're not going to get lynched like hung from a lamppost for falling in love, but we're going to suffer a lot of mind-lynching. So, we got to man up."

"And woman up," I added.

Dila sent me her laughter. It was a light and bubbly and guiltless gift.

By this time, we were dropping down off the freeway into the city. Street lights and lights from the windows of the buildings greeted us. Night time San Francisco was postcard pretty. I took the Van Ness Avenue exit and drove to Geary Boulevard and turned left. Fillmore Street was another few blocks west.

Ty Manning, our center for Saint Mary's College when Vincent and I were students worshiped Nate Thurmond. Ty had been what I'd call a campus friend, which meant we'd pal around on campus but not off it. Ty was black. He was 6'10" and a talented player. He had not been drafted by an NBA team, which didn't seem to bother him too much. He applied to law school and the last I heard of him, he had passed the bar and moved to Washington D.C. He would have loved to be with us sitting in Big Nate's Barbeque eating ribs, coleslaw and collard greens.

We had walked in *Big Nate's* holding hands, figuring to get any looks or commentary out of the way from the start, but we encountered nothing but smiles and what-can-we-serve-you politeness. When Dila told the waitress, "Double of everything," the waitress and the other customers who heard her laughed. I laughed with them, and felt a kind of comradery of skepticism.

"Sister," the waitress said, "You mighty tall and looks in good shape but do you and you friend think you be handling that much food?"

Dila said, "Bring it on, sister."

Victor Brovelli, the only white man in the restaurant, shrugged and smiled.

There was some jazz saxophone background-eating-music, Dila said sounded like John Coltrane. I'd heard of him. The ribs were falling off the bone, the slaw was sweet with apples and a hint of vinegar. The collard greens, usually not one of my favorites, were not so bad with lots of butter but might have profited by some marinara sauce. That was me, Dila was eating her greens with Tabasco sauce and a sprinkle of apple cider vinegar. If I were digging in, Dila was digging to China.I guessed that the waitress had presented my girl with a challenge.

I can't lie. I enjoy barbeque and slaw, but I am pathetically addicted to Italian cuisine. Pasta is my soul food. I was already finished eating, watching Dila chowing down and thinking wouldn't a soul food restaurant be a perfect setting for a white man to propose to a black woman? I was imaging matrimony when the door opened and two white couples entered. The waitress called them by their first names. They hailed a few of the customers. All four were wearing Warriors' caps. They were obviously regulars. Suddenly I didn't feel so unique.

Dila looked at the white couple, then looked at me, with a knowing smile. She possessed an uncanny ability to read my mind.

"Don't say a word," I said.

"Victor, you are so obvious," she said.

We left the restaurant. Dila's appetite had been bigger than her stomach, so we were carrying ribs and slaw in takeout cartons. For tomorrow's breakfast, Dila said. The collard greens were not sitting well on my stomach. At home I'd drink a glass of chianti to smooth things out. Dila suggested that we check into the Mark Hopkins Hotel and spend the night. My stomach felt instantly better. The engagement ring remained safely in my apartment.

CHAPTER 17
HERE WE GO AGAIN

Va te nun sidisfetu e como nun s'arissi fattu.
An unfulfilled vow is as if it had not been made.
Italian proverb

I got Dila home in the morning in time for her to change and drive herself to the Black Panthers' office. It was Saturday, but she had promised to edit an article Minster of Education Terrance Bowles was writing for *The Nation*. At Brovelli Brother's Used Cars, it would be Barbeque Saturday. I intentionally didn't shower. I wanted the scent of my beloved to stay with me for the rest of the day. I dressed in my salesman's attire: light blue button-down dress shirt, blue blazer over gray slacks. Loafers. The tie was red and blue stripped. My twin would be similarly dressed except for a different tie. This is not planned. Twins just show up wearing the same clothing. I have known twins who'll go to extremes *not* to look alike, which seems weird to me. I remember the Baldwin twins. One shaved his head, and the other wore his in Rasta dreads. Vincent and I let the spirit of 'twinness' dictate our appearance.

Dila and I had agreed to meet after I closed down the lot for the night. She told me she'd drive over, and we could go from there. With last night meal still with me, I was thinking of something light for dinner at my apartment. A salad. There was also minestrone my mother had given me the day before. Nobody makes minestrone like my mom. Ever since Mario's death, Pop reported our mom spent most of her time in the kitchen cooking. She'd made enough food to feed the neighborhood. I was not bad preparing antipasti and salads. And I was an expert at opening a bottle of wine.

Theresa and Vincent had arrived at the lot before me. They were already setting up the two grills. I parked and joined them. I'd suggest to Vincent if he wanted to take off after the barbeque, I'd handle the rest of the day. I had left it to Vincent to take care of our business while I went sleuthing. I owed him some time off and I needed to get back to work. There was plenty to do. I went to the office and sat down at my desk. I began with my phone calls from yesterday. There were a couple from possible customers. Sweets had left a message that he was in need of a place to crash for a couple of nights. This was becoming a habit. I phoned to set him straight. The phone was disconnected. I heard Pop's voice, *Sweets he a good boy een ees cuore.* Sweet's heart was more like heartburn. I got to the end of the phone call slips and saw where the last two were stuck together. I pulled on them gently, and they came apart sticky and smelling of candy. *Fucking Sweets.* What was he doing in the office? I'd have to talk to Theresa. After last year's screw-up, we'd eighty-sixed Sweets from our lot. The telephone slip hidden from me was an old call. I stared at it. It was from Mario, three days before he and Grace were found shot to death. It read: *Victor, Important. Call me.* I leaned back in my chair. For a year after Mario returned from Vietnam, he was a brother incommunicado. After he met Grace and joined PeaceLinks, he rejoined the world of the living. Even so, he wasn't Mr. Social. He might have called me at home, but I couldn't remember him ever calling me at work. What could have been important? I would never know. The slip of paper lay on my desk like a single puzzle piece with no other pieces to fit around it. I folded it and stuck it in my pocket. I'd worry about it later.

For an hour I checked our inventory with the prices in my *Kelley Bluebook.* It was always a good idea to see how our pricing compared to the standards. Vincent stuck his head in the door to tell me that customers were on the lot.

Fifteen minutes later there were no customers on the lot. And no sales. Vincent and I looked at each other and shrugged. There is a truism in selling cars. If you allow a customer to leave, he or she will never return.

"We had two fish on the line, and we didn't haul them in," Vincent said.

"You let yours off the hook before I did."

I was waiting for Vincent's comeback line when I saw a police cruiser pull into the driveway. Jay was behind the wheel. The door opened and my overweight friend squeezed out. I tend to exaggerate some about Jay's weight. His middle is soft, but the rest of him is rock hard. He raised his hand and helloed us, while keeping his eyes on Theresa standing at the door. She turned and walked into the office. Jay had been married three times. Single at the moment, he was always looking for his next bride. *A glutton for punishment or a romantic fool.*

"So what brings you here on a Saturday morning of a new year?" I asked.

He pointed to the sign. "Got a couple of guys down at the station looking for cars. I'll tell them you'll give them a good deal."

"You come here this early to talk to us about giving deals," I said. I didn't mean to sound curt, but I had a funny feeling.

"Nah, I've just been to the beach in Alameda up at the north end. There's a half-naked body there. Looks like the tide brought it in. A lot of his fingers have been cut off. Burns all over the poor guy's body. No I.D."

"What makes you think he has something to do with Mario?" I asked.

"I said there was no I.D. but he still had his trousers on. We found your business card in his back pocket."

Charley Radley, I thought. I couldn't very well lie. "Yeah, it must be Charley Radley, Mario's former roommate. He was going to get back to me with some information. I gave him my card."

"Well, some crazy tortured Mr. Radley. What kind of information was he trying to find out for you?"

Jay was looking at me accusingly. I knew what he was thinking, that I was still investigating Mario's death. I wasn't, but I guess in a way I was. I hadn't counted on Radley finding anything for me, but he was probably still a druggie and streetwise. He might have found out something. Whoever tortured him must have thought he had.

Vincent was shaking his head, "You promised, Victor, no more Mario and Grace detective stuff. Haven't we had enough gosh darned bad news to last us for a while?"

Sometimes my twin sounded like Gomer Pyle on the *Andy Griffith Show*. On the other hand, he'd swear like a trooper in Italian. *Go figure?*I couldn't argue with Vincent, but I knew that whatever plans I had of dropping my investigation into Mario and Grace's deaths, was no longer an option.

I looked at Vincent. He looked at me. He sighed and said, "Ah man, here we go again."

"So, you're not going to tell me what Radley was doing?" Jay asked.

The first thing I told Jay was the truth that I'd just talked to Radley at

Mario's burial, and he'd come by to offer condolences. The next thing I told him was a lie.

"He was looking into the illegal sales of exotic birds," I said. "I thought Mario might have been trying to expose these bad guys."

"I know that is one big goddamn whopper of a lie, I've heard in all my time on the force. Who're you trying to snow, Victor?I'm not going to ask you again and have to listen to more lies. We couldn't find any relatives for Radley, so I'll need you to come down to the morgue and make an official I.D. Get in the car. I'll drive you back.

On the way to the morgue, while Jay was giving me the silent treatment, I thought of the last words Radley had said to me at the cemetery. *Bad moon rising.*

• • •

By the time Jay dropped me back from identifying Charley Radley's dead body, the **Brovelli's Barbeque Saturday** sign was in place. Theresa had strung our college red and blue Galloping Gael's pennants above the office door to signal Barbeque had begun. The aroma of grilled chicken and sausages was in the air. The crowd from Flynn's arrived first. Across East 14th Street, Nick Parsegian stood on the sidewalk waiting for a break in traffic so he could jaywalk and join the hungry mob. Jitters arrived from his gas station. Larry Hughes appeared. For such a large man, he managed to appear out of nowhere. Swanee showed up with his entire crew. There'd be a Closed Gone Fishing sign on the door of his office. How many years now had we shared this Oakland neighborhood with these people and come to know them as friends? Since Vincent and I had been in high school our pop had the two of us on the lot doing odd jobs. Flynn's tavern was called The Embers back then under a different ownership. It had been a piano bar no one frequented. Swanee and Jitters had just started their businesses about the same time pop started his. Parsigian's Furniture Outlet, the name recently changed from Discount Furniture, came on the scene the year we took over from Pop. Body bought The Embers and made it a tavern that year too and renamed it after himself. The Oasis strip club was a late arrival. The Mexican gang, The Amigos, were also a recent arrival that had come with the slow changes in population from middle class whites to people of color. The Satan's clubhouse was a fixture, the rumble of their motorcycles reminding us that our neighborhood of small businesses was not always peaceful or safe.

Barbeque Saturday ended around two in the afternoon when all the chicken and sausages were gone.

Jay had warned me not to make more of Radley's murder than the facts warranted. The subtext of the warning was don't interfere. The sub-sub text was keep the fuck away from my investigation, you've caused enough trouble already. Was there room in our friendship for a sub, sub, sub text? Jay was wrong. The only trouble I'd caused was to myself. I vowed that would not happen again. This time, I'd find out what really happened to Mario and Grace. In order to do so, I'd have to break my promise to Vincent.

CHAPTER 18
BACK ON THE CASE

In all emotional conflicts, the thing you find the most difficult to do, it is the thing you should do.
John D MacDonald Meyer's Law

Our mom had refused to go to mass on Sunday. Other than the time she was in the hospital giving birth to Vincent and me, this was a first. When Pop asked her for a reason, she refused to answer. He said he wouldn't go without her, so according to our sister, Costanza, who'd driven down from her home in Sonoma to be with them, Pop sat in his easy chair in the living room reading Friday's Wall Street Journal while mom worked in the kitchen preparing her tenth batch of marinara sauce, which would find its place along with the others in the freezer. Costanza had driven by the lot to complain that our mom's behavior was worrisome.

I told her that we should not be overly concerned because only 3 weeks had passed since Mario's death. I did not tell Costanza or Vincent that I was not on very good terms with the Almighty myself and had, like mom, skipped mass and arrived at work far earlier than we normally did on Sundays.

When Pop ran the business, he opened at 11 a.m. on Sundays, two hours later than his normal working day to allow time for him and mom to attend mass at Saint Joseph's before work. When we took over, Vincent and I changed the Sunday opening to 10 a.m. Go-getters-pop said of us proudly. Not exactly. Mostly, it was Vincent, who is more ambitious than I am and less interested in the Catholic religion than I am. He volunteered to open on Sundays to capture the elusive 10 to 11 a.m. car buyer and allow me to enjoy mass. I admit to enjoying the ritual, even though I'm skeptical of many of the church's tenets. I enjoyed the choir most of all. Saint Joe's has a fabulous group of singers. I also like hearing the Latin, and am dead-set against the idea that's being floated around to switch to English. I think the mystery would be lost, and for me the Catholic religion is all about the mysterious. I've always felt at peace in the church.

But I had skipped the mystery on Sunday and walked a few blocks west to Park Street and Ole's, found a booth in the back and ordered my usual breakfast from Mame, who I'd decided never took a day off. While I ate, I reviewed some of the more important aspects of private investigation by reading a manual on the subject that I'd purchased a year ago when I was investigating the murder of Winona Davis. Now that I had recommitted to solving Mario and Grace's deaths, I felt a review of the basics of private investigating would be helpful.

I began with the introduction that I remembered reading and enjoying. It reminded me that private investigation had been around a long time. The first P. I. agency was started by Eugene-Francois Vidoq. The guy had been a convicted criminal who turned straight and started helping the French police capture bad guys. Since he had been one himself, he purported to be an expert. That was in 1811. In 1860. in the U.S. Allan Pinkerton founded Pinkerton National Detective Agency. The guy had become famous for claiming he'd foiled a plot to assassinate President Abraham Lincoln. Lincoln hired his agency to be his bodyguard during the Civil War. For a long time after that, the Pinkerton Agency was the only one of its kind, and was involved in a great number of investigations. Mostly it seemed to be on the side of large corporations and wealthy individuals. A Pinkerton agent infiltrated the Molly McGuire's, a secret society of Irish-Americans supporting Pennsylvania coal miners' struggle for better working conditions against their corporate owners. The information the spy was able to discover led to the arrest of the members of the Molly Maguire's and the eradication of the upstart labor unions. Dashiell Hammett, the author of *The Thin Man*, a mystery novel that I'd recently read, worked as a Pinkerton agent, and was part of a group of agents responsible for breaking minors' strikes in Montana in the early 20th century.I didn't remember reading about this last year, but then I'd skimmed the intro to get to the detecting stuff I was looking for. I'd watched the movie *The Thin Man* on late night television. It starred William Powell and Myrna Loy, one of our pop's favorite actresses. The story was set in San Francisco. Powell played the detective, Nick Charles, and Myrna Loy played his young and adventuress wife, Nora. I'd explained to Dila that instead of being my Girl Friday, she was welcome to be my Nora. It had been my first half-hearted attempt to ask Dila to marry me. I had been relieved when Dila ignored my subtle proposal. Half-hearted is no way to propose. She liked the idea of being a Girl Friday because if you paid attention to her version of the original tale by Daniel Defoe, Friday was an intelligent, sexy dark skinned native woman that helped Robinson Caruso, a sorry-ass marooned white guy from Italy with a pot belly and thinning hair. She'd pronounced the name like the opera singer. I corrected her that Friday was a male, to which she replied that she wished to write from a feminist perspective. Sometimes Dila's thinking makes me laugh. I dog-eared the page about the Molly McGuires to show Body the next time I was in the tavern. He read a lot of Irish history, but maybe not about the Irish in America.

By the time I'd finished my breakfast and dawdled over a third cup of coffee, I felt I'd had reacquainted myself with investigative procedure. "Ready to go," I said to myself. Mame, who'd just placed my bill on the table asked me if I was asking her to go on a date. Before I could answer, she gave me a big wink, picked up the check and my ten spot and left.

My hour spent at Ole's had been the highlight of Sunday, the fourth day of a new year that was starting out between a new dead body and possible marriage proposals to be pretty tense.

• • •

On Monday morning instead of going to Ole's I made my own breakfast, a bowl of hot Quaker Oats with honey, washed down with two cups of coffee. As I ate, I scanned the pages of the Oakland Tribune. One article was about the Israeli capturing 21 hostages in Lebanon. The next article had to do with the numbers of dead from an avalanche in Nepal. More violence on the next page, a deadly shooting at a gas station. How do you read about violence in the abstract when inexplicable personal violence has taken a terrible toll on you and your family? I learned in college that the Greeks had an idea that great tragedy on the stage helped to lessen the woes of the audience. *Total bullshit*. I came to an article that read: "Noah's Ark Sought on Turkey Peak." Oh, yeah, who cares? I didn't know why I was bothering reading. I scanned the sports pages and put the paper down. I decided against a third cup of coffee. I telephoned Dila. I asked her to meet me later, but she declined, saying editing Minister Bowles essay would take much of her day. There was no doubt that FBI pressure was building for the Panthers. She wanted to do her part. There were times recently that I'd forget that Dila remained a committed believer in the good community services provided by the Black Panthers. She suggested dinner. We agreed on Ettore's, a restaurant we frequented often. It had been the first restaurant we'd eaten in together. Their calamari was out of sight.

I put on my blue blazer and left. There's an elevator in our apartment building, but I always take the stairs, both going up and down. It's a physical fitness thing. Outside, it was chilly and the sidewalk was damp from a late-night rain. There was a weak January sun just surfacing over the tops of the Victorian homes that face Broadway Ave. Some have been turned into duplexes, much to the distress of my mother who sits on the City of Alameda's Strategic Housing Committee. I opened the door of Mario's Mustang and checked to see if the ghost of the previous owner was in the passenger seat or in the back. No ghostly Mario. Before I got in, I traced my finger over the blood outline on the back of the drivers' side seat. *A reminder of the task ahead or some foolish symbolism I'd created to satisfy something inside me I couldn't name.* I was about to get in when I heard a woman crying. I looked around to see where the weeping was coming from. There was no one on the street on either side that I could see. *Minchia*, the weeping was coming from inside the Mustang. I slammed the door and stood staring at the car. A couple of automobiles sped by me. One blew his horn, and I jumped closer to the car in order to avoid getting hit. I finally recovered enough to look through the window. It was Grace's ghost. She was wringing her hands in her lap, rocking back and forth. I had only heard such weeping once before in my life at the scene of a major accident on the freeway where I had stopped to help. A woman was on her knees, holding a little girl in her arms, holding the girl's head, policemen trying to pry her loose of the girl and failing. I occurred to me that every time Grace's ghost appeared to me, she was crying. Whenever Mario's ghost appeared, he was tapping his forehead. I knew what he meant, but what was Grace's specter trying to make me understand? Perhaps nothing. Perhaps just plain grief. Grief for Mario or was it a greater grief of some kind? I knew so little about Graces' life.

Her weeping finally stopped, but it took me a few minutes to gather my courage to get in the car. "Grace," I said, "You have plenty of reasons for crying. I promise I'm trying my best to find out what happened." I didn't expect an answer. I turned on the ignition and the Mustang woke up. I looked in the rearview mirror, Grace's ghost was gone.

I took the Fruitvale Bridge across the estuary to Oakland and pulled into the lot by 8 a.m.I parked the Mustang in the back and headed to the office. I heard Theresa inside vacuuming. Vincent was wiping rain spots off our cars. I grabbed a towel and pitched in, but with little enthusiasm. Grace's weeping was on my mind. Traffic on East 14th was already full throttle. Across the street, Nick Parsegian was opening Furniture Outlet. Since Omar Sharifi, his partner, had died of a heart attack a year ago, Parsigian seemed an unhappy man. The only joy in his life besides selling a full bedroom set of furniture was his daughter, Meriam. The rumor going around our business district was that she was no longer a joy since graduating from high school, but a pain in her father's butt.

As I wiped windshields, my thoughts returned to Sunday morning at Ole's and the idea of mystery. I was fine with leaving the Catholic Church a mystery, but not the violent death of Mario and Grace. That was a mystery I intended to solve.Yes, I was back calling it what I first believed it to be — a murder. Charley Radley's torture and drowning death made my mind up for me. If you counted the execution murder of Body's Sinn Fein pal, there were way too many unexplained homicides in one small neighborhood of East Oakland. When I had pointed this out to Jay, he shrugged and said, "Maybe."

"No fucking maybes," I'd said. "Certainty."

He'd just shrugged again, which annoyed me. Didn't they train them at the police academy to be wary of coincidence? Maybe Jay had been on the job too long and was getting rusty.

I was roused out of my thoughts by Vincent calling to me that there were customers on the lot. He took the couple, I took the singleton male.

Normally Mondays are slow, but things were looking good after I sold a '57 Ford Fairlane that I'd taken in on an Olds Super 88 convertible in November of last year. The buyer, a middle-aged man told me he worked as a shoe salesman at Sears. He had bad credit so the bank would not accept the contract. The Brovelli Brothers' Dealership would have to carry the note ourselves for 26 %, interest, high but not exorbitant since we were the ones taking the risk. A guy defaults on a loan, there is not much you can do about it except reposes the car. Usually it's in pretty bad shape, dirty on the outside and nasty on the inside. You can count on dents and scratches. We might sell the car again, but our best solution would be to discount it to a wholesaler. They don't give a crap what they put on their lots.Considering the interest the shoe salesman would be paying monthly, there was a decent profit in the sale as long as the guy kept up his payments.

I crossed my fingers and turned the paperwork over to Theresa. She'd finish up. Then it was my turn to present the keys to the proud new owner of a Brovelli Brothers' immaculate pre-used automobile. I escorted him to his vehicle and waved him on his way. I watched him turn onto East 14th Street and nearly lose a bumper to a Langendorf bread truck. The expletive I uttered was in Italian, a language I find that has more force when it comes to expletives.

By noon, not another customer had come our way. Theresa and Vincent took their lunches first. They said there was a special at *The Grotto* at Jack London Square. They asked if I wanted them to pick something up for me. I told them when they got back, I'd eat at Flynn's. After they drove off, I looked at the open door to the office. If I went in, I'd have to do paperwork or make cold calls, so I stayed on the lot with the cars. For me, being around automobiles is comforting. It's maybe the way some people feel about nature. I'll take a Bugatti type 101 coupe over a giant Sequoia any day.

A few vague ideas were forming in my mind. Body might be able to help me make sense of them.

When Vincent and Theresa got back a little after one, I headed to Flynn's. Monday was Irish stew day. As I pushed open the door. All the booths were filled and most of the stools at the bar.There was an open stool next to Larry Hughes. Let me rephrase that. There was half an empty stool next to Larry's enormous buttocks. I perched. Larry grunted a hello with his mouth full and scootched over enough so I could get comfortable. I raised my hand to get Body's attention, steeling myself for one of the Irishman's stupid Italian jokes. He nodded, disappeared in the back and came out with a bowl of stew and a frosty mug of Anchor Steam, placing them in front of me and walking away.

"What's eating him?" I asked.

"What do you mean? Hughes asked.

"No stupid Italian joke."

"Does seem strange," Hughes said.

He stuck a huge spoonful of stew in his mouth and chewed. I took a taste of my stew and washed it down with beer.

Hughes said. "Stuart came by for donuts. He told me Body is real upset about his fellow Irishman getting himself killed. He doesn't think the cops are trying very hard to figure out who shot. . . you know. . .I can't remember the dude's name."

"Neither can I, but I don't come down here on Saturday nights much when the Irish were playing darts and talking Irish politics."

I called Body's name. He looked at me and signaled if I wanted another beer. I waved him over.

"If you're not going to harass my ass with your stupid Italian jokes, I could use a little information."

"Ah, so it's an Italian joke me boy-o is missing? I got one right here on the tip of me tongue."

I groaned.

"How do you know you're an Italian?"

I waited.

"When you're 5'4", can bench press 325, shave twice a day, but you still cry when your mother yells at you."

"Not bad," I said, thinking there was some truth about Italian men and their devotion and fear of their mothers. Not my sweet and gentle mom, of course.

"Thought you'd appreciate it. So, what kind of information can a poor tavern owner provide you?"

I turned to Hughes. "Larry, what you hear here, stays here. If Vincent gets even a sniff that I'm back to being a detective, he'll brain me with his baseball bat."

Hughes raised his hand and swore silence. As long as he kept shoveling stew into his large mouth, there'd be no problem with silence.

"What was the name of your Irish pal who was shot to death?" I asked. "I forgot."

"Danny Killian. What's your interest?"

"There's been another killing, a one-time roommate of Mario's. A Vietnam vet by the name of Charley Radley."

Body picked up my bowl of stew and mug of beer and beckoned me to follow him down to the other end of the bar that a group of salesmen from Sears had just vacated. As they walked by, I recognized the shoe salesman I'd just sold a car to. I grabbed my spoon and napkin, excused myself to Hughes and followed Body.

"I hadn't heard about this killing." Body said as I sat down. "A man came in three days ago who called himself Charley. He wanted to know if a guy by the name of Casey McGoffin frequented my establishment. I said he didn't. This Charley guy said he was asking at all the Irish pubs in the area. It was important, he'd said, and would I give him a ring if the fellow dropped in. He wrote his name and phone. Just his first name. Like what did he expect? That I asked all the men who come in here for a beer what their fooking names are?

"Do you still have that number?" I asked.

"I do, but first you need to tell me what's going on in that wee dago mind of yours."

"I was going to let things go, Body. Mario, Grace, the whole *fottoto casino, the whole fucking mess I got myself into*. Everybody was giving me the needle. I felt foolish. Even when I knew I shouldn't stop investigating, I did. I acted against my better instincts. When the cops found Radley, his fingers were cut off. Somebody was torturing him to get him to talk. That's when I said to myself, Victor get back to detecting."

"So, what's this all about?" Body asked.

"I don't know. But whatever it is, it has got to do with McGoffin. And McGoffin had to do with Mario and Grace. And McGoffin is an Irish national recently arrived in the states. And if I'm right, your Irish friend that was murdered was an Irish national, not an Irish American, am I right?"

"Right you are, boy-o. Danny Killian, me cousin on me mother's side, arrived six months ago."

"All the bodies are connected somehow. I've lost a bunch of days and who knows how many clues I could have discovered by now that I missed."

"How can I help, Victor?"

"I need to talk to your Irish pals. And I need to know what's been eating you lately. Stuart told me you've been staying late in your office. Except for Saturdays, you've never done a night shift that I remember. He said you slept overnight on your office couch."

"It's Ireland,' Body said.

He was going to continue, but just then the door opened and a group of PG&E repair crew entered and filled the bar stools around us.

Body touched his finger to his lips. "Come back at six when Stuart starts his shift. We'll go to me office, and I'll tell you what's going on in me unhappy country."

CHAPTER 19
IRELAND

26 + 6 = 1 (Refers to how 26 provinces of Ireland plus 6 in the North, would equal one unified Ireland.)

Back in our office, I called Dila and asked her if a late dinner, at 9:00 p.m. would be okay with her. Yes, she said. It would give her more time to finish editing, since she'd lost an hour when the cops stopped by unannounced, the last part said with dripping sarcasm.

"I swear, Victor, they had no warrant and when we asked for one, they just laughed."

The officers sounded like the so-called Special Defense Team that had harassed the Black Panthers last year. These days, the Los Angeles police were calling such units SWAT teams. The Acronym stood for *Special Weapons and Tactics*. I knew that in early December the LA SWAT team had shot it out with the Black Panthers while serving a warrant for illegal weapons at the LA BPP's headquarters. There was no longer a similar rapid response team in Oakland. It had been disbanded after Minister of Education for the Black Panthers, Terrance Bowles, furnished photographs to the press of some of the rogue cops inciting a riot at the Little Bobby Hutton candlelight vigil. I was the one who'd taken the photographs and given them to Dila, who in turn gave them to Bowles. The unit deserved to be disbanded. A lot of the Bay Area's finest agreed. Jay had told me at the time not to condemn the entire barrel because of those rotten apples.

"Sounds like Oakland PD has got itself a SWAT team," I said.

"I put away my carbine," Dila said. "But I'm bringing it with me to work tomorrow."

"Don't do that. Please." In my mind I envisioned Dila in the middle of a shootout, rising up above an overturned desk firing her carbine — bullets flying everywhere. "Don't do it Dila."

Just because I'm a woman, is that it, Victor? All black women these days know how to protect themselves."

"All Black Panther women, you mean," I said.

"I guess, but some of our white and brown sisters *knows* how to handle firearms."

I ignored Dila's grammar, having experienced before the unusual verbal transformation that Dila went through whenever she spent time working at the Black Panther's office. It didn't take long before she'd dropped formal English and began speaking Ebonics. I thought it had something to do with Dila being an actress, internalizing her role. Something about all the world's a stage. Dila said goodbye, made a kissing sound and hung up. For a while I stared at the phone, remembering the time Dila and I discussed racial identity. She'd shifted into Ebonics and said to me, "*Yo, Victor, remembah, am proud ta as Afracha blood ahn mah veahns.*" It had taken me a moment to translate. She was proud to have African blood in her veins. I sometimes questioned which role in life Dila was playing. Was she acting the part of an upwardly mobile woman, while her real self was a Black Panther chick? It was moments like these over almost two years of our relationship that I wondered if I would ever learn the truth, or if I even really wanted to.

I joined Vincent on the lot. He was looking to the west where a cargo jet was landing at Alameda Naval Air Station and another one was taking off.

"What's up?" I said.

He didn't turn around. "Gloria is all excited about an afternoon show called *All My Children*. It's a stupid soap opera, and I'm watching planes carrying troops and equipment to Vietnam."

"Maybe she's making a point," I said.

"Lot of people dying over there, Victor,"

"Lot of people dying over here too," I said.

• • •

Body's office was a lot fancier than I expected. The desk he was sitting behind looked mahogany and antique. The room size rug was definitely something from the Middle East. Parsejian would know. The wall behind him was covered by a huge tricolor green, white, and orange Irish Republic flag. There were photographs of Ireland covering one wall some in black and white, some in color and on the opposite wall hung two landscapes, one of a lake and the other of an ocean coast with canoe like boats resting on the beach. Both looked like they'd been painted at sunset.

"Me brother painted those," Body said.

"Damn good."

"Too bad the Jaffa bastards killed him."

I didn't have time for a translation. "I thought you told me your brother was in the police and died in a shootout during a bank robbery."

"True, he was in the Garda. It was the fooking Provos committing the robbery."

"What city are the photographs of?"

"Derry."

"Why Derry? I thought you lived in Dublin."

"Well, now. I might have got my geography mixed up. Dublin is a little more upscale, if you know what I mean."

I shook my head. I could feel myself growing angry.

"I suppose it's the truth you be wanting?"

"That would be nice. We've only known each other for . . . "

"Since I bought the place," Body said, "That would be six years."

"Six years of putting up with your stupid Italian jokes."

"I've got a good one handy, boy-o, if you've a mind to listen."

"I'll pass. You said something about the truth."

"It's like this. When I came to the United States, me ma says let's not say we're from the North. She'd grown up in Dublin, and we'd lived there when I was a wee babe, before me da got a job policing in Derry. Right now, Derry is as at the heart of the conflict. Some are calling it The Troubles again after the first uprising against the Brits in the old days fighting for independence. The violence is growing. Give a year or two and all hell will break out. The Brits would like Americans to believe that since the Republic of Ireland was established there's been peace in Northern Ireland, but that's a bunch of shiest. The Catholics in the North have been taking shiest from the Protestant Loyalists forever. Anyway, I went along with me ma and said we were from Dublin. But I grew up in Derry and all my mates are still living there, except for my cousin who's now dead. Me mates Seamus and Brendan are from Derry, but I didna know them then. They've been after me for a good year to help them raise money for the cause."

"Who?"

"You remember, the dart team guys, Seamus Hallinan and Brendan Riorden. I introduced you."

"Right. So, what cause are you talking about," I asked, as if I couldn't guess.

"Well, not Sinn Fein. They're just a bunch of chin-wagging politicians."

"So, you're telling me that you are IRA? Is that it? Hell, Body, you could have told that to me at the bar with all the seats taken, no one would have been surprised.All of us figured you were involved in Irish stuff. So why are we up in your office being secretive?"

"It's what me cousin told me. He was a sort of a big shot in the Derry IRA. He was sent over here to make contact with all the fundraising groups to warn them that the UVF or UDF have an assassin in the United States whose job is to disrupt the fund raising."

"UVF UDF sounds like something electrical. What do they stand for?"

"Ulster Volunteer Force and Ulster Defense Association. They're bad-ass paramilitary organizations. UDF probably the worst. Up to recently they've only operated in Ireland, but there have been a couple of incidents in Boston and a couple of other cities on the East Coast that have their grubby paws all over them. In Boston, one of the best fundraisers, Billy Malone, was found shot to death. Turns out the killing was done exactly the way it happened to Killian. You may not believe this, and I sure as hell didn't at first. . . "

Body stopped talking and rubbed his un-razored jaw. I waited.

"Look, this may sound impossible to you," Body said. "But Mario's girlfriend, Grace. . . "

"What about Grace?" I asked, feeling queasy in my stomach.

"Grace may have been all peace and love about the Vietnam War, but she supports Sinn Fein when it comes to Northern Ireland. Me cousin only met her the one time. He was guessing she was IRA. He was going to broach the subject the next time he saw her, but, well, Grizzly Peak happened.

"Not IRA," I said. "It's not possible. She was the founder of PeaceLinks."

"Me cousin doesn't lie. Killian told me just before someone put a bullet in his pate. Whoever this assassin is, he's no longer on the East Coast."

"So, are you all in danger? Was Grace in danger?"

"Looks that way. Grace, rest her soul, doesn't have to worry anymore."

Was it possible I wondered that Grace could have been a member of the Sinn Fein? That was not unreasonable. But could she be IRA, a group committed to violence to unite the North to the rest of Ireland? *Not a chance.Grace, the earth-mother, in her long tie-dye skirts and sandals, her long black hair kept in place by a headband of peace symbols. Grace who'd brought peace back into Mario's life. Grace the idealist who never stopped marching to end the war.*

"So, you see why me lads and I are a wee bit spooked these days. Kind of looking over our shoulders, so to speak, see if some Ian Paisley-loving hit man is catching up with us. We're just a bunch of fundraisers. I know the fellows in the tavern think we're IRA, but we're not."

"Who's Ian Paisley?" I asked. I realized that I knew absolutely *merda* about Ireland.

"He's a Protestant minister nutjob who leads the Ulster Loyalists in the North. Defended all the *orangie* bombings. Some fooking man of God he is. So, you know now why we needed to meet in my office rather than at the bar. This is between you and me, boy-o."

"Do you have any other shocking news to tell me?"

Brody shook his head.

"You want a wee dram, before you go, Victor," he said, pointing to a bottle of Irish whisky on his desk.

"Nah, better not. I'm going out to dinner. Thanks Body."

"Ach, with your Dila. She's a pisser."

"She is that," I said as I left.

The fresh air cleared my head as I walked back to the lot. I wondered what I'd thanked him for. I was definitely not thanking him for the information about Grace, as incredible as it sounded to me. I knew I would have to find out if it was true, and if so, what it meant about their deaths.

CHAPTER 20
ETTORE'S

Niente di importante puo essere deciso a stomaco vuoto
Nothing important can be decided on an empty stomach
Big Sal Brovelli

Dila and I began as we always did when we ate at Ettores with Calamari Bruchetta, with tomatoes and goat cheese, and grilled the way our father, Big Sal Brovelli, claimed was the only way to eat squid. For entrées, Dila chose lasagna and I had my favorite linguini con vongole, the clams the size of silver dollars. For wine we usually go with Chianti, but tonight the owner had persuaded us to try a Charles Krug, Sauvignon Blanc. He'd assured us that very soon the wines from our Sonoma and Napa Valleys would be as good if not better than French wines. While we munched on our appetizer, I explained to Dila what Body told me about Grace. Dila didn't seem to be surprised.

"The Panthers always did their due diligence before trusting white organizations that claimed were sympathetic to us. We vetted the PeaceLinks and its leadership. I've read the report recently helping Minister Bowles. There was not much in the way of background on Grace. She'd only been in the country since 1966. She was born in the city of Gallway, which is on the west side of Ireland. She went to a nun's boarding school for girls before moving to Dublin where her history ended, until she shows up in the United States. That's all about her that the Panthers could find. No birth certificate, just a school record. Once she arrived in the United States, she became dedicated to ending the war in Vietnam. She was also a practicing Catholic who never missed religious services. I don't know if that's significant."

"We call them masses," I said.

"Yeah, those," Dila said. "And as far as Minister Bowles could ascertain, Grace was a pretty die-hard Irish Nationalist. I'd have to assume that was true while she was in her home country. There wasn't any information about why she immigrated. Maybe Mario told you."

"You know, I never asked. I guess I didn't see any reason to know. Mario and Grace were totally in love and good for each other, why would I be curious about her past?"

"Most Irish in America are supporters of the Republic of Ireland and want to see the country united. Sinn Fein would have financial difficulties if it wasn't for the money raised in America."

"And, according to Body," I said, "the IRA would have less weapons to fight the British if they didn't have the money from Americans to buy them."

We stopped talking as the waiter took our plates and the empty Calamari dish. I poured more wine. It was really terrific. I was not a connoisseur of wines, but I could taste the difference between ordinary wine and the good stuff. I'd have to tell Vincent, who took his wines more seriously than I did.

"You trying to get a po black gal drunk so you can take advantage of her, *mastah*?"

"I'll accept that you're black. Dila, my angel, but poor you're not and as far as being your master, it's clear to me who's been in charge from the start, and it's never been Victor Brovelli." Dila laughed her fountain tinkling laugh. *Music to my ears.*

We clinked glasses. "To us," we said.

"What's our next move, Girl Friday?" I asked.

"Minister Bowle's article is taking longer than I thought, so I can't help a lot. It's long and important and has to be right. You need to explain to me what you think the connections could be. Body didn't say for sure that Grace was Sinn Fein. Now if you can prove she was IRA, I can see how the anomaly would make you suspicious. But, here's the thing, Victor, suspicious of what?"

"I see what you mean. And that's the question I first asked myself. But the more I thought of it, the more I got that unexplainable and annoying car noise in my head. Remember my telling you last year when we were trying to solve Winona's murder, there was a point when something I couldn't name began to irritate me. Clickty clack in my brain and an irritation in my stomach. I couldn't shake the feeling."

"I *do* remember. I have a rattle in my car right now that my father's mechanic can't figure out where it's located. I'm getting so frustrated, I'm about ready to sell the piece of junk."

A car salesman doesn't pass up an opportunity like this. Her '64 Ford Galaxy was definitely sounding a little iffy. "Why not use it as a trade-in on another car. We'll make you a good deal on a sweet silver 1960 Mercedes 190 SL."

"Maybe when I get back in the spring," Dila said. "I don't think I can take the irritation all summer. Don't try to sell me tonight, okay. Let's stay on subject."

"And the subject is? I'm not making the connection, or understanding how Grace's Irish back ground has anything to do with how she died."

"Well, there you go, darling."

"Go where?"

"You need to do more research on Grace," Dila said. "I'm not sure how you do that. You wouldn't happen to have any Italian relatives that live in Ireland?"

I was sure Dila asked the question as a joke, but I thought it was worth asking Pop. Mom had relatives living in Norway. Pop's army of cousins lived spread out all over, from Germany to Staten Island, New York, where they pronounced Calamari, Galamah. *Weird.*

The waiter approached with our entrees, which ended our conversation.

After a couple of minutes of eating, Dila put down her fork, took a sip of her wine and said. "It seems to me Body and his pals are your best source of information. You might want to talk to someone in the Irish Consulate in San Francisco."

"Good idea," I said. I still wasn't sure how Ireland fit, but Dila's instincts were sharp. I took a sip of wine and continued eating. The background music was an Italian melody I recognized from one of Pop's favorite albums. Lots of accordions and violins. The subject of the tune might have been Sorrento.

"What would the Irish Consulate be able to tell me?" I asked

"They might be able to give you some facts about place and date of entry." Dila said. "Like what kind of visa she had, student or work. From which city her travel originated. Did she fly into New York City or D.C.? You need to get as many facts as you can first. You don't use guesses, only hard facts. Then you brain storm. Here' something I do when I'm stuck on an essay. You write down all the facts you have on Grace, not just the ones the consulate gives you but from all your sources on index cards and spread them out on a table. Then you separate the ones that fit together from the others. But don't discard the facts that don't fit. It's possible some of them may fit into the pattern later. That's what you're looking for — a pattern."

I had used one of Dila's brain-storming strategies last year. "I'll try it." I said.

We had finished our entrees.

"What shall we have for dessert?" she asked.

We ordered flan to share and coffee. We ate our desert slowly and savored our coffee.

The waiter brought our check. Dila insisted on paying her share. A year and half into our relationship, and I still was not used to being told she didn't need to have a man open doors for her, or pull out chairs for her at a table. And she had her own money and would pay her fair share. Recently there'd been a feminist protest in Berkeley in which women tossed all manner of female items: bras, corsets, false eyelashes, makeup, into a Freedom Trashcan. Similar feminist protests were going on all over the county. Miss America contests were taking a huge hit from feminists. I had been noticing an increase in women-put-down jokes from some of the guys at Flynn's. "At least they don't tell queer jokes," Stuart Tamberg had quipped.

We were the last customers to leave.

I said, "Your place or mine?"

"You know that's a stupid question, Victor."

"You mean your father would object to my sleeping over?"

"He'd chop you into little pieces with his sword."

"Your father owns a sword?"

"It's a Betamaribe tribal ceremonial sword. It's totally mean-looking."

"Guess it's my place then," I said, thinking maybe I should find a telephone booth and call ahead to see if Sweets hadn't broken into my apartment, which he did whenever he needed a place to crash. If that damn Sweets was there, I'd chop him into little pieces with my butcher knife. It would be a ceremony I'd enjoy.

Even though we were close to the university, we had the sidewalk mostly to ourselves. It was a clear night in the East Bay. You could actually see a few stars. But to the west from San Francisco, a fog horn was warning ships approaching the Golden Gate Bridge. When we got in my Mustang, I leaned over and kissed Dila.

"Start the engine," she said. "You're wasting time."

CHAPTER 21
LIES AND UNTRUTHS

A lie is the best kind of a clue."
from *How to be a Private Investigator* by Oscar Medford

This morning I woke up remembering that something Body had told me last night didn't fit the facts. By the time I drove into the lot in the morning, I was anxious to talk to my favorite Irish tavern owner, but he didn't open until 10 a.m. I parked the Mustang in the back of our office and told Mario's ghost to enjoy a siesta or whatever ghosts do when they're not haunting you. I left him with a word that it would be helpful if he'd talk to me. I paused for an answer but didn't get one. I turned the corner to the office. To my left was my twin standing in front of a car that looked somewhat familiar. I called his name as I walked toward him. He didn't respond. I wondered what he was concentrating on so intently. As I got closer, I knew. There are times in a car salesman's life when no matter what's going on around you, tragedy or joy - an eight on the Richter Scale earthquake or Michael Anthony knocking on your door to tell you you're a millionaire — when nothing else matters except for a brother pointing to a 1937 Ford Deluxe Station Wagon, a classic Woodie, and saying, "It's ours." It was so beautiful I felt myself holding my breath. The body was dusty blue with horizontal wooden door panels of golden pine. The white walls were spotless. I stepped past Vincent and opened the front door. All rich chocolate colored leather interior — absolutely immaculate. All it needed was a surfboard strapped to its top.

"The engine is blown," Vincent said. "But Jitters say he knows where he can find a replacement. I dipped into our rainy-day-money. I didn't think you'd mind."

"Mind? Are you shitting me?" I grabbed Vincent by the shoulders and planted a big kiss on both cheeks. "How? When?"

"Jitters, who else? He called me yesterday. He didn't have the do-re-me because he's putting all his bread into the cabriolet."

"When it's running, what do you think we can sell it for?"

"Let's not sell it, Victor. Let's put it on a platform where passersby can see it. I'm betting it will bring in customers, just wanting to take a closer look."

At first, I thought I should ask Vincent how much of our rainy-day fund, he'd used, but I didn't. My twin was right, this Woodie would have every car junkie in the Bay Area burning rubber to get to our lot. It would become part of our dealership, like our Saturday barbeque lunches. I'd talk to Theresa and see if she could find a newspaper guy who'd be interested in this car as a story. There weren't a lot of '37 Ford Woodies this clean around.

I clapped Vincent on the shoulder. "When you're right, bro, you're right. Congratulations." I gave him another hug. "We'll build a higher platform," I said.

"The tow truck dropped it off here instead of at Jitters," Vincent said. "Jitters will come get it with his own truck. In the meantime, feast your eyes."

I did, until Theresa yelled from the office that the Morris Bank and Trust was on the line. Vincent wheeled around and sprinted, beating me to the door. As beautiful as the Woodie was, for the Brovelli Boys, Morris Bank required our full attention. Most used car dealers had favorite banks. Another way to put it was that most bankers that loaned to car dealers had their favorite dealerships. Champ Simpson at Morris Bank loved us. And, as the as Smokey Robinson song goes, we seconded our devotion. How do I know about Smoky? Well, I do date a woman who knows everything there is to know about MoTown.

I listened to Vincent speak into the phone. Mostly he was nodding his head and agreeing. After he cradled the phone, I asked him what that call was about.

"Champ is coming by at noon to check our stock."

From time to time, banks come to inspect cars we bought through their line of credit to see if they were still unsold. If one of their cars was sold, we were obliged to pay back the loan on the day of sale before we could take our profit. Champ, or if it was another banker, and Vincent or me would inspect each of the cars the bank technically owned and check vin numbers just to be sure cars and their vin numbers matched.These periodical checks by the banks were done because some dealers, finding themselves in cash flow problems would not report the sale of their bank owned automobiles promptly, holding on to the money as long as possible. Pop had never done this, nor had we.

"How many cars do we still have on the lot that belong to Champ?" I asked.

"Eight. No problem. They're good cars. Champ knows we'll sell them. I could have sold one yesterday, but there wasn't enough profit in it for us."

•••

Four hours later, Champ departed, satisfied all the vin numbers checked out, and I was sitting at the bar at Flynn's, having had to suffer one more in a long line of bad Italian jokes. This one required me to answer the question of why Italy was shaped like a boot. I didn't know and didn't care. At least Body was acting more like Body and less like a man being hunted by killers. It was Chili on Tuesday. After telling me the answer to the joke that you couldn't fit all that crap into a tennis shoe, Body had placed a bowl of his notorious I-Dare-You chili in front of me along with my usual frosty mug of Anchor Steam. By the time I finished my lunch and my tongue stopped burning, the bar had cleared out enough that I could ask Body the question that had been bugging me. Abbot and Costello, two local Yellow Cab drivers that never missed Body's tavern lunches, were sitting to my right. Nobody knew or cared what their real names were. That they answered to the famous comedians' names meant they must not have cared either.

I definitely needed their big ears gone before I talked to Body.

I took my time eating. Larry Hughes, who'd been sitting at the end of the bar stood up, wiped his brow with a handkerchief and left, followed by Swanee and couple of salesmen from Sears whose names I always forgot. Abbott and Costello, seated to my right, were eating and sweating. Abbot turned to me. "You know, Victor, Body claims the reason his chili is so hot he mixes a chili from some freaking Asian country called a Bhut chili in with his Mexican chilies."

I'd heard this before. Body had spent some time traveling all over the world when he was, as he'd said, a lad.

"Yeah, "Costello said. "Tastes so good, how come it hurts? If I eat one more bite, I'll burn to death." Costello rose from his seat. Fat Abbot did the same.

A couple of stragglers finishing their meals, but mostly playing liars dice, remained at the end of the bar. I waved to Body.

"Ah, me boy-o, tell me. . ."

I held up my hand, "Stop, you've already tortured me. You only get one shot at me a day."

"It's too bad, Victor. I remembered a good one."

"Save it for tomorrow," I said. "I want to ask you about Grace."

"I told you everything me lads found out."

"Yeah, but you said they had Grace growing up in Derry, Northern Ireland. But she told Mario she'd been raised in Dublin. Last night Dila and I had dinner, and she told me that the Black Panthers researched the PeaceLinks."

Body frowned.

"They do that for any group that supports them. Being cautious, I guess. Anyway, that research included Grace and Carol as founders of the group. Their research had Grace O'Conner born in Galway and going to a nun's school there until she left for Dublin to find work. But there was no record for her in Dublin. A big blank until Grace shows up in the U.S."

"Look, Victor, I told you all I can about me lads. They're Sinn Fein, raising money for the cause. They don't need any publicity. I guarantee you they're pros. They don't make mistakes."

"If that's the case, Grace lied to Mario. And, somehow, she managed to fool the Black Panthers with some phony records."

"Looks that way, Victor. I can tell you, given both Hallinan and Riorden call Derry home, they were a bit surprised about Derry. I thought I told you they never got a chance to talk to her.Who knows, they might have had mutual friends."

"You did tell me," I said. "Could you ask them about Galloway and nuns' schools?"

"Be happy too. They'll be interested."

The dice-throwers called for another round of beers, and Body left me. I heard the phone behind the bar ring. Body lifted the receiver. He listened, hung up and went to the kitchen. He came out minutes later holding a paper bag in his hand. He placed it in front of me.

"Got a call from Vincent. He wants chilli. It's double-bagged but it's plenty hot."

"Why would Grace lie?" I asked.

"Do you know what her passport says?" Body asked.

"There was no passport found in their apartment. I'm going to the Irish consulate tomorrow to see if they have any records. It's just too strange. And it must mean something. My P.I. manual states that a lie is the best kind of a clue."

"That's the kind of reading that's going to piss off your brother something fierce, Victor. If he finds out you're back to being a P.I. he'll be after you with that shillelagh of his."

"It's a Wilson baseball bat," I said. "And don't you say a word."

"Me lips are sealed, boy-o. And by the way, don't count on the Irish consulate giving personal information to you. You'll be lucky if they don't give your Italian ass a big boot out the door."

I told Body to screw himself and left with Vincent's chili.

• • •

An hour later I was in San Francisco standing in front of a desk in the Irish Consulate looking down at a red-haired maiden asking me what she could help me with.

As it turned out, absolutely nothing. But I didn't get a boot in my fanny.

CHAPTER 22
THE IMPORTANCE OF BURGLARY

I may be a burglar, but I'm an honest one, more or less.
J.R.R. Tolkien

Sweets Monroe claims the Brovelli's are the only family he ever had. What he really means is our pop, Big Sal Brovelli, is the only family he had. Count the rest of us out. It was this poor-abandoned-boy-sob-story that kept our pop believing that one day Sweets would rise up like the Phoenix out of his desultory life, cut his hair, give up womanizing and burglary, become a business man, pay his taxes, and join the Lions Club. I could have told Pop, *fat chance*, the principal reason being Sweet loved being a burglar. He thought of it as a performing art. Imagine, he said to me once, the aesthetic required moving soundlessly through a window. I was pretty sure he meant skill, but didn't correct him. It's always impressive when a guy who never finished high school uses a word like aesthetic. There was no doubt Sweets Monroe was as skilled at burglary as Nureyev was at ballet. He stole from the rich and gave to poor women with kids. No doubt he left enough for himself, which seemed fair to me.

Sweets was laying on my couch, having entered my apartment while I slept and made himself comfortable. After my initial annoyance that tempted me to pour water on him, I shook him awake. I could see he was wearing his full-body black tights, the black head covering rested on his chest. His blond cockatiel hair was at a slant that reminded me of a row of wilted flowers. One eye opened.

"Daddy-o," he muttered.

"If I was your daddy, I'd shoot myself."

"Hey, man, I was exhausted. Big house in Saint Francis Woods. Been checking it out for a while. Found a lot of nice treasures."

"Don't tell me, you and your apartment manager had a falling out."

"No, nothing like that, but my conscience was bothering me."

"Make sense, Sweets. I don't like to guess."

"Well, it's like this, that house was full of goodies. . . ah, man, I got some jewelry that's worth at least ten grand, and an antique silver flat wear set, easily three big ones. I was in heaven. All the stuff almost too much for old Sweets to carry. I was feeling bitchin until. . ."

Sweets closed his one open eye.

"Go on," I said. I had a bad feeling.

"Mon frere, you understand, you, that I don't discriminate between the rich, like I don't play favorites."

I nodded.

"As I was getting ready to leave, I spotted an old Bible. I'm no expert, but I knew that was deep into antique land, real leather cover, gold filigree lettering."

"So what's the story you can't seem to spit out." My bad feeling felt worse.

"I drove home. I was sorting through my acquisitions. I opened the bible and there was an inscription inside in a language you're familiar with."

Italian + Saint Francis Woods, = ? I did the math. "*Minchea,* don't tell me, Sweets. You didn't?"

"Like I said, Victor, it wasn't planned. I had no idea Carlo lived in Saint Francis Woods."

My eldest brother, Carlo, was a highly-paid corporate attorney. Six months ago, he'd bought a mansion in the Swanky rich neighborhood of Saint Francis Woods in the part of west San Francisco called the Sunset. I could have bought four decent cars for what the housewarming party cost. Carlo was still not talking to me because I had brought Dila with me. She hated Carlo's politics, but she'd agreed to go. "Cause a little commotion," she'd said with a wicked smile. She didn't, thank God, except with one of Carlo's partners who she called a greedy misogynist.

"You see, Victor, I had to bring your brother's things to you so you can get them back to him, discreet like, you dig?"

"I'm going to dig your fucking grave, Sweets, that's what I'm going to do. You dig?"

"Don't be like that man, we're like brothers. Maybe not Carlo, he's kind of a dick, but you and Vincent. And don't forget, Mario loved me."

"Don't start with Mario."

"You mind if I have one of those beers in your fridge?"

I couldn't help myself. I started to laugh. If nothing else, Sweets Monroe had some big *coglioni*. I went to the kitchen and came back with a bottle of Anchor Steam. "Here, you *retardate*." He opened the bottle with his teeth.

I'd been thinking of something since yesterday. "Sweets, I'll get this back to Carlo and make you a hero in his eyes, but you owe me one."

"How you going to do that, *mon frere?*"

"For Christ's sake, stop calling me your brother."

"Okay, okay."

"I'm going to tell Carlo you were scouting the neighborhood and saw a burglar enter his home. You waited until the dude came out and stole all his stuff back from him."

"Sort of lame. He'll never believe it."

"Maybe not, but he'll have his stuff back. And no one to blame since you didn't know the creep. And what does it matter, he hates you anyway. You have nowhere to go in his eyes but up. Where did you put the stuff?"

"In your front closet. It's all there."

"Okay, I'll get these back to the dick."

We both laughed.

"So, my man, I'm guessing you need my fine burglary skills."

Most of the time I could convince Sweets to help me break into places I needed, but this was going to be a hard sell. "Yeah, you're going to help me break into the Irish consulate."

"You mean a government building?"

"Not our government."

"Yeah, but no matter. That's a federal offense. I don't want anything to do wit J fuckin Hoover."

"What you're really telling me it's too difficult for you."

"Did I say that? Not so. *Moi,* I could break into the White House — if I wanted to."

"It's not like an office building," I said. "The Irish have their consulate in a mansion in the Pacific Heights district in San Francisco. It's a neighborhood you're familiar with. I know for a fact you've broken into a number of those mansions."

"I'll pass, Victor. Right now, according to everything I've read, things in Ireland are getting really hairy. They're bound to have some serious security."

"A consulate is not like an embassy, you *chooch*. It's mostly approving passports and public relations. The offices are on the first floor, and the living quarters are on the second."

"Well that does it, people asleep while we're at work. That would be beneath me. I'm not a cat burglar."

"Okay, I tell Carlo you broke into his house, and he presses charges."

"Ah, man," Sweets groaned.

• • •

I spent the rest of the morning working. Dila and I drove to Jack London Square for lunch. Afterwards, I told Vincent to take the afternoon off. Gladly, he'd said. He could get in a round of golf before going home. If Vincent is not talking cars, he's thinking of how he can improve his golf game. Vincent's hero a local, named Bobby Lunn, who'd been playing some real great golf on the PGA tour. When I asked him Lunn and not Palmer or Nicklaus, he'd told me those fellows set the bar to high. He could imagine himself playing like Lunn. I enjoyed playing golf, but enjoyed boxing and rugby better.

After Vincent took off, Theresa kept eyeing me, until I finally let her go early. I closed up the lot at seven and drove home. An hour later I was in bed with the curtains drawn and asleep. I wanted to be alert for our breaking and entering.

CHAPTER 23
THE TROUBLE WITH THE TROUBLES

The only way to escape from a problem is to solve it.
Brendan Behan

I'd had five hours of sleep untroubled by ghosts and woke up at one a.m. rested. In less than an hour, later Sweets and were parking in the Pacific Height neighborhood.As Sweets modestly put it, this burglary was going to be a piece of cake. He claimed that the people who lived in the exclusive neighborhood called the Pacific Heights in which the consulate was located were so arrogant that they often failed to activate their alarm systems. His claim proved true. At two in the morning, we climbed in a ground floor window facing a secluded backyard. The egress required only some caution. It was the interior that became problematic, the problem being a gentleman in his bathrobe asleep on the couch in his office. Mr. Consul General, I'd presumed. To which Sweets' whispered response had been *mathefuckah.* True enough, an expletive I repeated in Italian. Sweets, however, had not allowed the gentleman to interfere with our goal.

• • •

The following morning, I was first in the office, having barely slept. Our breaking and entering had provided no evidence to clear up my concerns about Grace. I was rolling my pen through my fingers, thinking about what kind of fallout there'd be once the break-in was reported. What the media reported would not likely reveal the true story. There was no way I could ask Detective Jay Ness to find out, and did I really want to know anyway. We had tied the consul general securely to his couch with his mouth duct-taped. Sweets easily picked the file cabinets' locks. I'd found a copy of Grace's passport and visa attached to a bunch of information about PeaceLinks.

The Passport stated Graces' Birth place as Dublin, which didn't surprise me. The only thing that was a surprise was her age. Her passport said she was 38 years old. Her PeaceLinks bio stated she was 30 years of age, which is what age Mario thought she was. I could write that off as female vanity, or I could add it to my growing misgivings about Graces' identity. I had found no information on Seamus Hallinan and Brendan Riorden, Body's *lads* on the Erin Go Braugh Dart Team, which I found suspicious. Were they in the country illegally? I felt that the break-in effort had resulted in little progress, except for Sweets saying he never wanted to see me again after having put his life in danger of being investigated by J, fucking Hoover. I had told him that meant I wouldn't wake up mornings and find him sleeping on my couch. To which he'd answered, our Pop's couch was better. This he'd said to me at four in the a.m., laying on my couch, a pillow beneath his head and one of my blankets tucked around him.

I was wondering what I'd really ever believed I would find in the Irish Consulate, when I was jostled out of my reverie by Theresa at the door greeting me with a cheery *Ciao, Vittorio, come stai?* She didn't wait for me to tell her how I was — worried and tired — but went straight to the storage room and returned with the vacuum cleaner. I stood up, gave her a thumbs-up, gathered the 20% off signs from my desk, and fled the office. Vincent was just driving in. I waited for him to park.

"You look like shit, "Vincent said. "You and Dila better stop acting like little bunnies into the wee hours. It's not like you just met, you know."

Maybe my twin was trying to be funny, but it didn't sound that way. Twins often pick fights with their other halves for no reason other than some code in their genes requires an occasional sibling confrontation. The intensity of ours had diminished as we grew older, but I remained ready, willing and still able. Today I was too tired. I left him staring at me and went off to place the sales signs on the cars we most wanted to sell today.

The rest of the day passed routinely. One sale, a 1957 Chevy Bel Air convertible to a retired Master Sergeant, who'd told us he was planning to drive cross-country, and always wanted to do the drive in a convertible. We took his DeSoto sedan in trade. He wrote us a check for the balance. A cash deal always makes the Brovelli Boys happy.

At noon, I pushed open the door to Flynn's.

I didn't need to adjust to the change of light as I walked in to know the voice and its intention, something that had become a ritual.

"Victor, me Boy-o, tell me why do Italian men wear mustaches?

"I haven't a clue, you Irish prick."

"So they can look like their mothers."

The men seated at the bar erupted in laughter. I sat down on the corner stool next to Swanee. Still laughing, Body placed a bowl of creamy Boston clam chowder with a package of oyster crackers in front of me along with a mug of Anchor Steam. Swanee was digging in next to me. It looked like he'd dumped all the entire bottle of Tabasco in the soup. He looked up, staring and said. "Needs a little spice."Swanee claimed Korean cooking was hotter than Mexican or Indian. He admitted that Body's chili might compete. He had brought some of his wife's pork cutlets to one of our Saturday barbeques as a gesture of neighborly solidarity and to prove a point. The chops were drenched in a red sauce that Vincent gave me the opportunity to taste first, seeing that I was one minute older than him.One bite and my tongue wanted me to shoot itself. Later, Swanee had admitted that in Korea, *Donkatsu* sauce was called *Donkatsu of Death*. After I finished the chowder, I asked Body if he had a minute to talk. "Private," I said.

Tamberg, the night manager, often referred to as the Vampire because of his gothic looks and his nocturnal habits, was having his breakfast at the other end of the bar. Body spoke to him, then pointed to the last booth in the back where a couple of guys were just leaving. I joined him.

Before I could say anything, Body began.

"I know this has to do with Grace and me lads, and I'll say this from the start, don't get them involved."

"But they involved themselves, telling you that Grace was born in Derry. What did they expect, that I wouldn't be interested that she'd lied to Mario? Come on, Body, I only need a little of their time. I promise you I don't give a damn if they're really IRA. And don't bother telling me they're not. I know they're in this country illegally."

I didn't really know this, only that there were no records of them entering the country on file at the consulate. "Don't ask me how I know, I just do. I need as much background on Grace as I can put together. All of a sudden Grace O'Conner is a cipher. O'Conner might not even be her name. I also need to find out what they think of Charley Radley's murder. You guys can't possibly believe his torture and murder is not connected to the torture murder of your cousin Danny Killian. Who, by the way, was also in the United States Illegally. If I remember correctly, the three of them all showed up pretty much at the same time six months ago, right?"

"Victor, I wasn't about to bring up Hallinan and Riorden's names up to the coppers. As for Danny, I asked Jay what the Oakland police had found out. Nothing. We looked into the connections between Radley and Danny ourselves as well.What do you think we're fooking stupid?"

"Jay and his fellow fuzz aren't always right, you know. Talk about being stupid."

"Now don't go insulting me. Meself and the lads felt Radley got on the wrong side of his motorcycle buddies. The Satans are into a lot of shiest. If Radley presented a danger to their various enterprises, well, hell, they wouldn't waste any time putting him down. Look, we couldn't figure out what the torture was about, except that usually means whoever tortured him wanted to find out something Radley knew. you don't have to read cop thriller novels to figure stoof like that out. You've had some run-in with those Satans fookers last year, so you got to remember how they are."

At the cemetery, I was sure Radley hadn't mentioned that there would be members of The Satans riding with him to the motorcycle rally down south.

"Okay, you've got a point." I said. "Your lads might not be connected, but what if they are?"

"Tell me if I'm wrong, Victor, but didn't you tell me that Radley was going to look into something about weapons being smuggled in from Vietnam?"

"That's right. But isn't the IRA interested in weapons."

"Weapons have nothing to do with me lads, Victor. I keep telling you they are Sinn Fein, but your ears are too small. For the last time, boy-o, Sinn Fein is a political party, not military. Granted, the money they raise goes to a lot of things, weapons included. I've never once heard my lads talking about weapons."

"And I'm telling you it doesn't matter to me what they are and what they're about. This is about finding out what happened to Mario and Grace. Mario was a great guy, Body. You know that. I remember one afternoon you and Mario at one of our Saturday barbeques yakking it up, like you were life-time buddies."

"He was a very smart man. Mario was, that's a fact. Ah, shiest," Body said, sighing and rubbing his forehead, "I'll have the lads in my office tonight at 10 P.M. They'll answer your questions. But this will be it. Agreed?"

"Agreed. Thanks Body."

Body slipped out of the booth and returned to the bar. I got up and left the tavern. On my way back to the office, it occurred to me that Body might be more in command of "The lads" than I had previously thought. He didn't say he'd *ask* Riorden and Hallinan if they'd meet with me, he said they would be there, like he'd order them. More and more this investigation was beginning to have something to do with the Troubles in Ireland. I began composing the questions I'd ask Body's *Lads*. I'd only get one shot at them. I'd have to do a lot of thinking between now and 10 p.m.

By the time seven o'clock rolled around, and we closed the lot, I had the questions I wanted to ask Hallinan and Riorden in mind and a plan of action that would begin with my conversation tonight. If I wasn't satisfied with the answers I received, I needed Sweets help again. For the first time in my life, I hoped Sweets had not left my apartment.

CHAPTER 24
THE LADS

Niente di violente e permanente
Nothing that is violent is permanent.
Italian proverb

Dila and I had just finished a pizza at Angelo's on Shattuck Avenue, and we'd order a couple of cannoli for dessert. The waiter brought coffee. While we waited for the cannoli I explained about Body and tonight's visit with his two Irish friends, and what I was hoping to learn about Grace. I thought Dila would be upset that it was looking as if Grace O'Conner might be a card-carrying member of the Irish Republican Army. Not at all. She didn't even seem phased that Grace had lied to Mario.

"The Black Panthers support all revolutionary movements in the world." Dila said, "If it's true Grace is IRA, she had every right to remain below the radar. The BPP library has current information on all the active liberation fronts. What I've read about Ireland these days, their revolution is sharing the same time line as ours. Sinn Fein, the political party, needed to be goosed, just like our beloved NAACP. God bless them, they just keep talking and marching and getting beat up, and hoping the white government will deliver on some of their promises. True here and true over there."

"Violence never works," I said.

"Victor, sometimes violence is the only option that's left."

Once again, the image of Dila with her carbine came to mind. It scared the hell out of me.I changed the subject.

"What do you think of my plan?"

"Hard to say. You're counting on Sweets."

"The way I figure, tonight, Body will counsel his lads to tell me just enough to satisfy me, but not everything. I want to know everything. I believe they know way more about Grace than she grew up in Derry.

"And you don't think Body and his pals will be straight with you?"

"I don't. That's why when our meeting ends, Sweets will follow them home. I couldn't very well ask them exactly where they lived, could I? Once I know where they live, Sweets and I can break in and search their place for more information. I'm betting I can find more out."

"Sweets looks like a cockatiel. He'll be too easy to spot. Let me follow them. If they see a woman in a car behind them, they won't think anything of it. Remember, I'm your girl Friday."

Dila made sense, but then there could be some danger.

She continued to argue that she'd be far less conspicuous than Sweets.

"If these guys are pros, they'll spot Sweets behind the wheel. Didn't you tell me they came to a few Barbeque Saturdays? Sweets is always there. Right? They'll remember him, trust me."

The waiter arrived with our cannoli. I didn't want to blow tonight's opportunity, and I felt that time was not on my side. My detective manual stressed that the further time separated you from the crime, the harder it would be to solve it.

"Okay," I said. "But you have to promise me to be careful."

Dila looked up, a splotch of chocolate on her lip. I reached over and wiped it off with my napkin.

"Don't worry, Victor. Even if they see me, they won't think a black woman is following them. Men don't pay much attention to women unless they're trying to hit on them.See what I'm saying."

I thought that was unfair, but didn't want to get into a conversation about gender. "Got it," I said. "The meeting is at ten, so you should be parked a way down the street, but close enough to see people walking out."

"How will I know who they are?"

"Two possibilities. If, for some reason, after the meeting they walk out with me, then you'll know, and if they stay in the tavern, which is more likely, I'll be out first and wait with you to point them out."

"Do you know for sure they're not going to take public transportation?"

"Not likely. Body got a loaner from us for Hallinan, a Ford Galaxy. I had Jitters tune it."

"We're set then," Dila said. "Aren't you going to eat your cannoli?"

"I'll split it," I said

• • •

At ten o'clock on the dot I entered Flynn's. Tamberg was behind the bar. He pointed to the back stairs. I knocked on Body's office door and walked in. Body and his two lads, Hallinan and Riorden were throwing darts at a target on the wall to the left of Body's desk.

"Practicing," I said.

"Boy-o, it's the English we'll be playing Saturday night. The Duck and the Fox Club or the Hen and the Skunk or some British shiest like that."

"This is America, don't forget, no wars on neutral soil."

"We'll be fighting with these," Hallinan said, lifting up his dart and throwing it into the bullseye."

"Impressive," I said.

Body said, "Let's have a wee dram and get this talking over with."

He opened the door to the closet and pulled out a portable bar, with a sink. A small refrigerator fit beneath the bar. Body placed one ice cube in four glasses and poured three fingers of Irish whiskey in each. He passed them to us. "*Slainte,*" he said.

Hallinan and Riorden responded with *Slainte agatsa*, which I knew meant to your health in Gaelic. The three drained their glasses. I'm a wine and beer man. I prefer my heat-on developing over time, not all in one rush, which is what happens to me if I drink the hard stuff.

Body looked at me sorrowfully. "Boy-o, you'd be a sad Irishman paying such disrespect to whiskey."

"Perfectly happy being a good vino-drinking Italian and beer-drinking American," I said.

"Let's not let it go to waste," Riorden said, reaching for my glass that I'd placed on Body's desk.

"Go for it," I said.

Body said, "Lads, you may be wondering why I called this meeting."

His lads laughed.

"I've told you what's gone on, my friend Victor and his family have suffered a great loss. As Irish, we know what a loss of a family member can feel like. So, if we can help Victor, let's try to the best of our ability."

I had not heard such a canned speech since college when my twin ran for student Body president. Probably the reason he lost. I could have embarrassed Body with some evil remark about lack of orginality, but decided to let this performance play itself out.

"Right you are Body," Riorden said. "How can we be of service?"

Who the hell wrote this script, I wondered.

Body nodded. "Victor believes that Grace O'Conner's past has something to do with their suicide as well as the deaths of me cousin Danny and the other guy, Radley, I was telling you about. Is that about it, Victor?"

It was my turn to nod. "How about bringing me up to date on what's happening in Ireland," I said. "And what you guys are really doing here. I know you're not Sinn Fein."

Hallinan stood up from the couch. He held his empty glass out to Body. "A wee dram more to whet my tonsils, Body, if you please."

Body poured, Hallinan drank, then began talking.

"First of all, you're wrong. We *are* Sinn Fein," he said, pointing his empty glass at Riorden. "But we may not be for very long. As of December, over half of the official IRA has split away and formed the Provisional IRA. The Officials that are left are mostly Marxist-Leninists. The Provos have got the popular sympathy in the North. We Catholics are fed up with the shiest the Protestants have been feeding us. There's already fighting. I can't speak for Riordan, here, but I'll be thinking hard about joining them. Meanwhile we still work for Sinn Fein, raising money for the cause."

"And doing a fine job of it," Body said.

And lying, I thought. "All right, so you're Sinn Fein, whatever. What I'm interested in is how you came to research Grace O'Conner. Okay, she's Irish, but were you suspicious of something?"

Brendan Riorden spoke up, "She came with your brother to a dart contest in San Francisco. She was cheering for our opponents that night, the Dubliners from The Shamrock Tavern. We talked some. I couldn't be sure, but she didn't talk like a Dubliner, kind of posh, they are, nothing of the Gaelic in it."

"Ach, you're being a snob," Body said. "There's good Gaelic spoken in Tallaht and Clondalkin."

Hallinan interrupted. "You may not know this, Victor, but there's a unique local dialect for each of the 32 counties in Ireland and that includes the North. The North is pretty easy to pick up. Brenden and I were both born in Derry, but moved away when we were children, but folks still can tell our roots are in Northern Ireland."

"It wasn't just that," Riordan said. "There was something about her. Lots of mother earth hippie malarkey, but I could tell she was no peacenik, too intense, her eyes were."

"So, the way Grace spoke alerted you. But you got a feeling and that made you research her?" I turned to Hallinan. "Aside from the way she spoke, did you also have the same impression that she was not genuine?"

"Riorden pointed some things out. Yeah, it did strike me that there was something not quite right with Ms. PeaceLinks. Not phony-like. Doing what we do, you get a feeling and learn to trust them. She was real, but real about what?"

"How about you Body?" I asked.

"I've not been to Ireland since I was a boy."

"That's not an answer."

"Best I can do, Boy-o."

"Let's move on," I said. "You two guys did what first?"

Hallinan said, "You got to understand, Danny Killian had already been murdered. We were on edge and on the lookout for anything that seemed out of place. I called Sinn Fein in Dublin. They have good records. There was a group photograph at the dart contest with her in it. We wired it to our lads in Ireland. No O'Conner came close to the description I gave of a Grace O'Conner ever being enrolled in Sinn Fein.She's such a stunner, they wouldn't have been mistaken. They did find some general information like a driving permit, employment records and such."

"So, she lived in Dublin."

"Yeah, not for long," Hallinan said.

"What about Gallway?" I asked.

"What about Galway?" Hallinan replied.

I explained about the Black Panthers vetting Grace and what they'd uncovered.

"We would have been told you if they'd found she'd been from Galway," Hallinan said. "Since Killian was murdered our office has put all of us on alert. The word is out that UVF is prowling."

"Like the mad dogs they are," Riorden added.

"Or the UDF, damn their souls," Hallinan said.

"Body told me that you guys discovered Grace O'Conner was born and grew up in Derry."

Both of Riorden and Hallinan looked at Body. "Our esteemed Mr. Flynn told you wrong. "O'Conner is a common name. All we had was a snapshot of her. I wired it to our lads in Derry. A couple of them thought they recognized her, but they were pretty sure her name wasn't O'Conner. But to be honest, we have no real proof."

"Tell them about McGoffin," Body said.

"Aye, this is from our Dublin lads. She had written the name of a cousin by the name of McGoffin on an employment form as next of kin. Bit odd, that since it's a mostly Scot Ulster surname. I'd be asking myself why she'd have a protestant cousin?"

"We checked out the McGoffins from Derry," Riorden said. "There were some pretty hard-ass UVF guys by that name. That's not to say there aren't any Catholics named McGoffin."

I closed my eyes. This information supported my suspicions. I opened my eyes; The Lads were staring at me. "How about the IRA? Did you find out if she was one?"

"We know for certain she's not Sinn Fein. No woman by any other name matched her photograph."

"Okay," I said, "Let's assume Grace O'Conner is IRA."

"Can't do that," Hallinan said. "We checked with contacts in the IRA. No one that fits Grace's description is enrolled."

"I thought you said you were Sinn Fein." I said.

"We have contacts. We're all fighting the same bloody Englishmen."

"Okay," I said."Let's assume that she's part of this new group you say is called the Provisional IRA. What would she be doing in the United States that would have to do with The Troubles?"

"Boy-o, that's not the problem that I see. Grace and Carol run the PeaceLinks legitimate like." Body said. "It's the McGoffin thing that worries us the most."

I saw Hallinan frown at Riorden and Riorden shrug back. What was the meaning of that interchange?

"Are we through here, Victor?" Body asked.

I felt there had to be more. "How about some guesses first," I said.

Riorden said, "If McGoffin is UVF, then my guess he's the one who murdered Killian."

"I second that," Hallinan said. "Too coincidental. He shows up, Killian get assassinated."

"Are you saying that Grace and McGoffin. . . I stopped talking. The thought that Grace might be related to a murderer seemed too odd.

Body said, "Nah, Victor, not saying anything like that at all. Like I said, there are lots of Catholic McGoffins, aye lads?"

"Aye," they both said in unison.

I had a lot to think about and didn't have any more questions for them. I thanked Body and his lads and left.

Outside, there were wisps of fog, unusual for the dryer climes of the East Boy, I walked quickly down the street where my Girl Friday was waiting for me, seated behind the wheel of her Toyota.

CHAPTER 25

ANOTHER BURGALRY, BUT WHO'S COUNTING

La note e per amore e furto.
Night is for love and burglary.
Sicilian proverb.

Another successful Brovelli Brothers' barbeque was just ending. The 5th Dimensions were telling us it was the Age of Aquarius, only the sun was not shining. Earlier, Vincent sold a 1962 two- door Cady El Dorado hardtop for a little over five grand, 50% down. The rest of the day, he was walking around with a big silly grin on his face. He was ear to ear smiling after he sold a forest green Pontiac GTO Coupe. I sold a 1963 Chevy Impala 2 door hardtop with a pink and white exterior to Verna Bacigaloupi, Theresa's cousin, the owner of Pinky's Hair Salon in Hayward, the next town south of us. She said she was going to have the interior completely reupholstered in pink. I recommended Swanee.

I was happy for the profit we'd made because I had paid Sweets to figure out the best way for us to break into the *Lads'* apartment. Sweets insisted the fee he was charging was for consulting, and I could write it off on my taxes. Last night, Dila had followed Hallinan and Riorden to a five-story apartment building overlooking Lake Merrit. The Lads lived on the third floor. We planned to break in tonight because Saturday night at Flynn's was dart competition and our targets would be hard at it trying to beat the Brit dart team, and afterwards, drinking beer and singing sentimental Irish songs into the wee hours. It was a semi-finals contest that was scheduled to begin at 8 p.m. They wouldn't be home until 2 a.m. at the earliest. I felt confident Sweets could get us in and out with plenty of time to spare. My only concern was that I'd allowed Dila to talk me into letting her join us. Her argument had been that a woman was better able to spot details. "Do men see dirt?" she'd asked. I told her I considered that a trick question. Surprisingly Sweets hadn't objected. He claimed the best burglar he'd known was Tootsie Boucher from Baton Rouge from whom he'd learned a lot about burglary and making love. My imagination was never creative enough to visualize any woman going to bed with Sweets. But I grant there is no explaining women's choices. A recent *Readers Digest* poll of a cross section of American women had revealed that Henry Kissinger was high on their list of sexy males. When I'd told Dila this, she'd responded with *you're talking about white women. No black women would stoop so low.*

Dila called from the Black Panthers' headquarters to ask me if I could give her a ride. Her car refused to start, and the verdict was something wrong with her carburetor. I asked Vincent if I could take the rest of the day off. He was in a good mood and told me to have fun. Traffic on the Nimitz was already heavy by 3 p.m. Before my exit there was a slowdown that turned into standstill. My radio was on and raindrops were falling on BJ Daniel's head. In the distance I could see airplanes landing and taking off from Alameda Naval Air Station. The Vietnam War was raging.

I arrived at the panthers' office late. Dila and I had been a couple now for over a year and the Panthers were used to seeing me. Some of them had started calling me "token." I was always slightly nervous walking into their office.I stepped through the door.

"Hey Dila," someone hollered, "Token is here."

If this had been Flynn's tavern, I would have had a comeback, but I must admit I was still not exactly comfortable among the Black Panthers, particularly James the giant, who had been hostile to me from the beginning. I stood there grinning, hands in my pockets, trying to look cool. The office walls were covered with posters of Malcolm X, Elijah Muhammed, Eldridge Cleaver, and a huge photograph of Muhammed Ali. In 1967 surround by a bunch of elite black athletes like NBA's Bill Russell and the NFL's legend Jim Brown. Ali had refused to be inducted into the military for which he was convicted of draft evasion and sentenced to three years in prison and banned from boxing for three years. The poster read: *I Ain't Got No Quarrel With No Vietcong.*

Dila entered from the back room accompanied by Minister of Education Terrance Bowles. He reached out his long arm at the end of which were long slender fingers that looked like they belonged on a concert pianist. But I'd seen the minister ball those fingers into a fist on a number of different occasions, a few that had included the police.

"You're just the man I need to see," Bowles said, as we shook hands. "We're starting a free medical clinic and ambulance service. We need two vans, one that we can retrofit into an ambulance and the other with three rows of seats.

I told him The Brovelli Boys had the van with the seating arrangement, but would have to find one he could strip into an ambulance, although I didn't believe it would be too hard. I told him I'd call him. We shook hands on the deal. I visualized Vincent adding up the profits. The Panthers were not cheap and never bothered to negotiate. The profit would be sizeable. Dila took my arm and we walked out of the office. I was closing the door when I saw James from the back, his huge arms crossed over his enormous chest, glaring at me.

Once we were seated in my car, Dila leaned over and kissed me.

"Where's your car?" I asked.

"We got it towed to a garage down the street."

"I'll get Jitters to come get it. He's the best."

"No, don't go to the trouble," she said. "They already called to say it was the carburetor and they'd put a new one in by Monday. We support our neighborhood businesses. We're going to have a long night. Why don't we get something to eat then go to your place for a nap."

I could have skipped the food and gone straight for the nap, but I waited patiently. Dila's definition of a nap was worth the wait.

• • •

A few minutes after midnight, Dila and I were dressed head to foot in black as per Sweet's instructions. I'd had chosen an older model dark blue Olds four door sedan off our lot to use tonight instead of driving my Mustang, which would be more easily recognized if something went wrong. We drove to Sweets' apartment. He was waiting for us at in alley next to his building carrying a backpack. With his face half hidden and his cockatiel hairdo covered by his all-elastic black spiderman outfit, Sweets looked surprising athletic. He got in the backseat and I pulled away from the curb. I drove to the Lake Merritt district where the Lads' apartment was located. I parked a block away. Sweet brought a small canvas bag out of his backpack and began placing things it if. I recognized a set of lock picks and a can of spray paint in the event there was a security camera in the apartment lobby.

"What is that?" Dila asked.

"A bump-picking set," he answered. "Best tool for getting in apartment front doors. You insert one of these leetle ends into the lock, and bump, Voila, you're in."

"Like bang?" Dila said.

"*Oui*, I use my knee. The key creates the action, the bump knocks the pins into place. I say, 'Sesame, *ouvre-toi*,' Open Sesame, and that's it."

"Shouldn't we be going?" I asked.

Sweets took the canvas bag and stepped out the car. Dila and I followed. We walked quickly to the front door where Sweets did his bump thing and the three of us moved into the lobby and to the stairs. On the third floor, Sweet approached the Lads' door, then waved us back. He bent to examine the lock. He took an envelope and a pair of tweezers out of the bag. Using the tweezers, he picked something out of the door jam. He lifted the tweezer so we could see.

"A hair stuck in the jam," he said. "If someone was to break in, the hair would drop. They'd know they'd been creeped. These guys are pros. He placed the barely visible hair into the envelope.

"When we leave, I'll put it back. Can't fool a Cajun, *non, non, non*." He looked back at us and smiled. He turned his attention back to the lock. It took no more than thirty seconds and we were inside the apartment staring down a dimly lit hall. We were each carrying small flashlights. The hall opened into a large living room. To the right was the dining room and the kitchen, to the left another hall that had to lead to the bedrooms and bathroom. Sweets made sure the Venetian blinds were closed tightly.

"Bedrooms first," I whispered.

Sweets said, "I don't know exactly what you're looking for but I'll poke around in the bathroom for anything that looks like it don't belong."

What we found was one very large bedroom with two queen size beds and a cot. The other bedroom was smaller, but there were four cots there instead of beds. All the cots had blankets and were neatly made, blankets stretched tightly.

"It looks as if there were a bunch of people sleeping here not two," Dila said.

I nodded. "Let's search the rooms together. *A quattr'occhi* as my pop likes to say. Four eyes are better than two."

Fifteen minutes later, Sweets joined us.

"Nothing in the bathroom. Not even a condom. Are these guys monks, or what?'

"Or what," I said. "You see those cots. That one over there? It's made tight like it's done in the military. I know because that's how Mario made his bed after he came home from West Point. Top blanket so tight, a coin will bounce on it."

"You *did* tell me they were IRA," Dila said.

"They swore they weren't," I said.

"Have you found anything that you're looking for?" Sweets asked. He was looking at his watch.

"Don't worry," I said. It's not even one "o'clock."

"Look at this," Dila called from where she was kneeling beside an open bottom dresser drawer. I joined her.

"Newspaper clippings," she said, handing me a folder. They were all from 1966 about the petrol bombing in April of that year of a Catholic primary School. Four little girls and two little boys had been burned to death. The Ulster Volunteer Force, more commonly referred to by their initials, UVF, had been blamed for the bombing. According to one of the articles, the bombing was committed to protest the Catholic-Protestant Reconciliation Meeting called by Prime Minister of Northern Ireland, Terrance O'Neil. There were editorials deploring the violence. The UVF denied they were responsible. They blamed a splinter group calling themselves the UDF, the Ulster Defense Force.

Dila handed me another folder. In it were more newspaper articles. These were from 1965. The first one was about a bombing of the Crow's Nest, a pub frequented by Protestants. The owner, Sean Trimble, and a husband and wife, Mr. and Mrs. MacDowell, were killed. Dila handed me another folder dated 1968. The RUC, the Royal Ulster Constabulary had attempted to disperse a Catholic civil rights' march. Riots had broken out. There were many injuries and some deaths. An editorial claimed this would be remembered as the start of the modern-day Troubles. I'd heard Body talk about the Troubles of the early 20th century when the Irish fought the British for independence.

Sweets looked over my shoulder

"Looks like you got something," he said.

"I think so," I said. Dila was handing me another folder. "We don't have time to read all these. I need to read them carefully."

I tapped Dial on the shoulder, "How many more folders are there?"

"Just two more," She handed them up to me. One was dated 1969. The label read PEACELINKS.

Sweets said, "I got me a camera."

I pivoted. "You have a what?"

"A camera, bro. All burglars carry cameras."

I didn't ask him why. "Get it," I said.

I was tempted to sit down and read, but time was not on our side. We couldn't count on the Lads staying in the tavern for last call. Sweets returned the camera, one of the smallest cameras I'd ever seen. Dila spread the articles out on the bed, and Sweets began taking pictures.

We had one folder to go when Sweets stopped and placed his finger to his lips. "I heard a car. I think it stopped in front."

Dila rushed to the window. She peeked behind the drapes. "It's them," she said.

"*Minchia,*" I said.

Sweets said, "Put the folders back. Follow me."

Dila and I followed Sweets to the living room window. He slid it open and climbed out onto a balcony. He leaned in and smiled.

"Fire escape. All these old buildings had to have one." We followed him out on to the balcony.

Back in the car, I asked Sweets to give me the negatives. He said he knew a guy who could develop them fast.

"How fast?" I asked.

"I'll wake the dude up," he said.

I was anxious to read the articles. I had a feeling the answer to Mario and Graces death were somewhere in those folders.

CHAPTER 26
THE RING

Vivi con passione, Ridi di cuore, Ama profoundamente.
Live with passion, Laugh out loud, Love deeply.
Italian proverb

Rather than have me drop her off at her house, Dila spent the night with me. We were both exhausted, but managed a little gentle love-making. There are times when I looked back on our year together, it seemed to me most of our love making was gentle. But maybe gentle was not the right word. Careful came to mind. That's not to say there wasn't passion, but it was tempered by both of us paying attention to each other's needs. I'd never experienced this kind of sex before. Being an Italian male, I was raised to believe women sat in the passenger seat, and men did the driving. I could not make sense of this change in seating arrangements, unless it had something to do with our being an inter-racial couple, that our success or failure as lovers somehow would make a difference. When I'd expressed this idea to Dila, she'd replied, "Yes, a difference, but let's not go too deeply into figuring it out. Let's ride the air currents." And I'd said. "Right, I'll take my hands off the wheel and let the car drive itself." I was not being funny, but I remember Dila laughing, and saying that she had a drivers' license.

We were both awake by seven in the morning. The church bells at Saint Joseph's were ringing, which was a reminder that my family was still in mourning for Mario.

The Italian custom calls for parents of dead children to spend six months in mourning with the heavy mourning period lasting 30 days from the time of death, which had been over a day ago. However, I would have bet my mom and pop would still be wearing black. I was feeling that maybe I should go to mass.I asked Dila if she wanted to go to mass with me. We were sitting on the couch in our bathrobes drinking coffee.

"Good Baptists don't go to Catholic masses."

"What about our children?" I asked. Dila looked startled.

"What children? Who said anything about children?"

"Hey, I was just speculating. I meant when we have children, what religion will we raise them in?"

"Who said anything about marriage?"

"Oh," I said, which was all that came to mind.

"Are you asking me to marry you?"

"Wait here," I said. I stood up and walked to my bedroom closet. I opened my safe and withdrew the engagement ring. "*Abbiamo fatto trenta, facciamo anche trentuno*," I whispered. which is sort of like saying in for a penny, in for a pound. I gathered my thoughts, took a deep breath, and walked into the living room. I stood in front of Dila, then knelt. I opened the box holding the ring and held it out. "I love you Dila. Will you marry me."

"Aw, *Minchia*," Dila wailed.

I began to laugh. "Did you just swear in Italian?" I was still holding the open box.

Dila burst out laughing, then she started crying.

"What?" I said. "This is supposed to be the happiest day in a woman's life."

"Victor Brovelli," she said, hiccupping and wiping her eyes. "I thought we weren't going to, *hiccup*, talk marriage until I was finished grad school."

"I changed our minds."

"You changed mine too?"

"As an Italian's wife, you'll have to get used to things like that," I said, smiling. Dila began crying again.

"I'm kidding, I'm kidding," I said. "Come on, Dila, it's not a hard question. We've been together for over a year. The racial crap is behind us. We know we can deal with it."

"Why now, Victor, why now? Why not three months from now, a year from now?"

"I don't understand the question," I said.

"The now is important — *hiccup*. This very minute is important. I need to — *hiccup* — know what motivated you to ask me today? Why today?"

I stood up and sat down beside her. The open ring box was still in my hand. I placed it in her lap.

"There is no why, Dila, all there is, is. I loved you the first time I saw you bending over me with a damp cloth in the Black Panther's office. I called you my angel. You're still my angel. I'll let Vincent buy me out of the business. I'll go back with you to New York. I'll find a job selling cars. But I can sell anything. First, I need to sell you on marrying me, *capisci?*

"I understand," Dila said.

DIla had stopped crying, but she wasn't smiling. "Okay, Adila Agbo, what's wrong? What's worrying you?"

"There's nothing wrong with our being married. It's just. . . "

I saw Dila's gaze shift over my shoulder to the window, as if beyond the window was the answer to my question if only I bothered to turn around and look.

"Did I ever tell you about my interview to get into Columbia?"

"You meant NYU?"

"No, NYU was my second interview, Columbia was my first."

"So? What does this have to do with our marriage?"

"Maybe nothing, maybe everything. See, the professor interviewing me was this white male, probably in his mid-fifties. He asked me point blank, like he had no idea about how much I wanted to write and direct plays, why a woman was applying for admittance to their MFA program? And when I began to explain about my love of the art, he interrupted me."

Dila paused. She took a deep breath and continued.

"If you can believe it, what he meant was why was I bothering when I would be married and having children. When I'd told him I didn't understand, and believe me Victor, at the time I really *was* confused, the misogynist ass clarified. I still remember exactly what he said. Dila's voice dropped an octave: *Women never finish these advanced degrees, my dear, because they get married and start families.* "I wanted to go across the desk and grab him by his throat."

Dila's eyes were now tearless and blazing angry. She'd once explained to me the kind of self-defense training all members of the BPP went through. That interviewer was lucky Dila had controlled herself. I was about to ask her again what this had to do with our marriage, when the light bulb went on. "Ah crap, Dila, our marriage won't change anything for you. I promise. We'll be careful. No kids until you're ready." I was speaking Italian family planning heresy. But I didn't care. Let Vincent and Carol be the baby makers.

We stared at each other. I smiled, then Dila smiled.

"I'll hold you to the promise," she said.

"Just hold me," I said.

"Not a problem," she said, and wrapped her arms around me.

"I may not make you a good wife," She whispered, "but I'll make you a great Girl Friday. I will always have your back."

As if I had any doubts.

I was awakened during the night with the realization that Dila had not really said yes.

CHAPTER 27
MYSTERIES & CONUNDRUMS

Vidi ch'un s'afaccia quarcchi fungia
Keep watch for the appearing mushroom (Beware the unseen obstacle)
Sicilian proverb

I dropped Dila off at her home in time for her to attend church with her parents, and in time for me to be late for work. Vincent met me with a sour look. Theresa had Sundays off. Pop's theory about selling cars on Sundays was that people felt good after going to church and what better way to keep those good spirits alive than to go car shopping. We'd sold enough cars on Sunday to allow for the possibility that Pop was right. We grew up with Pop's theories and endless Italian proverbs.

I was sitting in the office running my pencils through my fingers, thinking. I should have been thinking about being married to Dila, but my mind was back at my apartment where Sweets had telephoned to tell me that he'd left the contents of the negatives he'd had his friend develop on the living room coffee table. I knew better than to ask how he got into my apartment. The more I probed into this *casino,* I had no doubt the more dangerous this mess would become. There were already three murders. One of Pop's proverbs came to mind: *La migliore armature e tonersi fuori portata.* The best armor is to keep out of range. Good advice, but I knew I wouldn't follow it.

By eleven and no cars sold, Vincent asked me if he could take the rest of the day off. One of Vincent's golf buddies had called with a noon T time. After Golf, Vincent's wife had arranged a Super Bowl IV party. As Vincent headed to the door, I said, "Don't think too long before you putt." When it comes to golf, Vincent is very suggestable. He gave me the good old Italian flip me off sign, his fingers brushing against his chin. I smiled and gave him the good old American middle finger. I watched him drive off the lot — a happy man. I play golf, but don't understand why the majority of men, like my twin, pay such homage to a day at the links.But that's just cynical me. Get out in the fresh air, chase a little golf ball around. *What the hey*. It felt good doing something for Vincent. Lately, I hadn't been pulling my weight at work, and he hadn't complained. I decided I wasn't being entirely altruistic. By staying at work until closing time, I was putting off reading the articles Sweets had left for me that were increasingly looming darkly in my imagination. At the moment, my annoying unexplainable-car-noise which served as my male instinct or as Dila had once told me substituted for female intuition, was rattling like crazy.

The day dragged. No customers. Normally, I would have been able to take a lunch break at Flynn's but on Sundays there would only be chips and peanuts. I called The Golden Dragon for chow mein and potstickers. I called Dila. Her mother answered and told me Dila had taken the bus to do some work at PeaceLinks. It was a fiction Dila had maintained over the years rather than confess she worked for the Black Panthers, which would have frightened her parents. Dila's parents were committed to their African heritage, her father most of all, proud of his tribal roots in the country of Benin, but the Agbos were also wealthy, conservative and opposed to violence. I called the Panthers' office. Dila told me she'd promised her parents to have Sunday dinner with them and would take the bus home. Before hanging up, I said, "I'll love you to the 'Twelfth of Never.' She laughed and hummed a few bars of "My Guy," by Mary Wells.

I stared at the phone and wondered if getting married turned two normally sane people a little loopy.

To keep busy while I waited for my food, I went out on the lot and picked out the three-seater van I would sell to The Black Panthers. I knew where there was a Pepperidge Farm bread delivery truck I could pick up cheap and let Jitter do his magic on the engine. There would be enough profit in the van that we could sell the truck cheap. The Black Panthers thought well of us, but the way the county was going, who could tell. Best to stay on the good side of all the sides. Dila would tell me I was being a political weeny, but I was not about to put our business in jeopardy. Pop and Mom's retirement came out of our profits. *La famiglia e tutto*. Family is everything. Since Dila and I were going to be married, she'd come to realize we Italians were right to put family above politics or anything else.

My Chinese arrived. I paid and gave the driver a buck above the normal tip. I took a bottle of Anchor Steam out of our refrigerator. I finished my meal and cleaned up. At three I watched the Kansas City Chiefs upset the Minnesota Vikings 23 to 7. There would be a lot of Monday morning quarterbacks in Flynn's tomorrow analyzing the game to death. Pop's Sunday theory had not worked today. Not even any lookers. I turned off the office lights and locked up. I drove out and parked at the curb. I secured the chain across the driveway entrance. I encountered a fender bender at the drawbridge to Alameda, and had to drive to the next entrance to the island to get to my apartment. I was torn between curiosity and anxiety over reading the contents of the folders.

The folders containing the negative copies were stacked on the living room coffee table along with a bunch of hard candy wrappers, evidence that Sweets had stayed a while, probably reading the articles. I went to the kitchen made coffee and returned. I was met by Grace's ghost sitting on the couch her hands in her lap, looking dolefully up at me. Those startling blue eyes, so common to the Irish called Black Irish, were filled with tears. Always, their messages were the same, Grace's sorrow, Mario pointing to his forehead. I understood Mario's message. I didn't understand what Grace's ghost was trying to tell me.

"What? What?" I said to my ghostly presence. "I'm doing the best I can. I'm not a real detective you know." Last year's ghost never spoke, so I didn't expect this years to either. The tears spilled from Grace's eyes and ran down her cheeks. "Go ahead and cry," I said. I don't know what to tell you." I lifted the first folder of the stack. It was labeled Grace O'Conner. I waved it in the direction of Grace's ghost. "Whatever secrets you've been hiding, I'm about to find out. So you might as well confess." I took a sip of coffee. When I looked up, Grace's ghost had disappeared. "I didn't think so," I said. I opened the folder.

I scanned the article about the bombing of the Crow's Nest. In the margin, I wrote: *McGoffin and Grace???? Pub owner, Trimble and Grace??? What do they have to do with each other????* The next article was a brief history of the growing problems between Catholics and Protestants, leading up to 1969, when all hell broke loose in Northern Ireland. By then Grace O'Conner was already in the United States and established as a peace advocate.

The next article went into great detail about loyalist killings that began as early as 1966. According to the writer, the public was misinformed that there had been a climate of relative calm and even hope of peace before the violence of 1969. As proof, there were a couple of paragraphs about the Hotel Malvern Public House shooting and the death of Peter Ward. I wrote: *Peter Ward and Grace????* The next article was about the April 1966 petrol-bombing of the Catholic primary school. Why was this lengthier article here along with the newspaper clippings? How was Grace connected to this event? I speculated. If Grace had been from Derry instead of Dublin, could she be related to any of the victims of that fire? If that were the case, it would certainly be a motive for her to join the IRA. But then the Lads had found no evidence that Grace had ever been a member of the IRA.

I went on to the next article in the folder. It was about a man called Gusty Spence, the leader of the first UVF the Ulster Volunteer Force. There was a photograph of him in a dark turtle neck shirt and leather jacket. His eyes were covered by sunglasses. From the photograph he was young, 30 years old, the date written at the bottom of the photo, and handsome in a kind of bad boy Marlon Brando sort of way. At the time of the formation of the UVF, he'd stated: *From this day, we declare war against the Irish Republican Army and its splinter groups. Known IRA men will be executed mercilessly and without hesitation.* I read on. His education ended when he was fourteen. By then he was a member of The Church Street Lads, a Church of Ireland group and the Junior Orange Order. I assumed these were groups that supported the Protestant cause. Spence joined the British Army in 1957 as a member of the Royal Ulster Rifles. I kept reading, although I was not sure why. The guy was a fanatic Ulster loyalist. What could possibly be the connection between him and Grace? I wrote: *Gusty Spence and Grace, adding multiple ????*

The next item in the folder was a photocopy of a birth certificate for Fiona Devlin, born 1933. Who the fuck was Fiona Devlin? Was this Grace's real name? But the dates didn't seem to make sense. On Grace's passport, it had listed her age at 40. If Grace was Fiona, her age at the time the passport was issued, 1967, would be 34. *Minchia!* What the fuck. So far Grace was from three cities: Galway, Dublin and Derry and was three different ages. She was IRA and she wasn't IRA. Was Grace really a peacenik or was she a *fugazi*, a fake.

The sun was going down. I turned on the reading lamp and kept reading. Grace's ghost reappeared and huddled at the other end of the couch with her hands clasped tightly in her lap, her eyes downcast. *Ghost tears.*

"I'm so sorry," I whispered. It didn't stop her crying.

I kept reading. There were three handwritten pages about the Magdalen Laundries. I'd never heard of them. How were they connected to Grace? The pages informed me that the Magdalen Laundries were industrial schools for young women who'd become pregnant. These unfortunate women were sent to these schools to have their babies and learn to be laundresses. When they were first created, they were called Schools for Penitent Females. In the margin of the page, someone had written the word, CRUEL in capital letters. Talking about the nuns? Probably. I went to a Catholic elementary school and could vouch for some pretty mean sisters. My third-grade teacher, Sister Mary Josephus, for example, who brandished the sharpest ruler in the universe that always managed to find my knuckles or those of my twin. As I continued reading, I expected to find something about Grace. Why else would Hallinan and Riorden have included the Magdalen Laundries in their research? The reason for it remained a mystery. I placed the three pages back in their folder and opened the next one.

If the contents of the previous folder confused me, the next one confused me more. I was looking at a map with three locations on the California coast circled, starting in the north with the harbor at Fort Bragg followed by Monterey Bay Harbor, and further south, the harbor in Saint Louis Obispo. For each of the harbors there was a name of a company that offered deep sea sports fishing: The Sea Turtle in Fort Bragg; Harpoon Annie's in Monterey; and in Saint Louis Obispo, Wooster and Sons. At the bottom of the page there was telephone number followed by the name: Big Daddy. I looked at the phone on the coffee table. I could dial, but what did Big Daddy signify? If I were in an espionage movie, I thought, this would be a code. Or it could mean to ask to speak to Big Daddy. Big Daddy fucking Warbucks or Big Daddy in *Cat on the Hot Tin Roof*? It had to be ten years or so since the movie came out. I remembered watching it in college when I took a seminar on American playwrights that cost me a lot of shit from my twin and our business major buddies who were ceaselessly on my case ever since I foolishly admitted I enjoyed the Great Literature course that was a four-year requirement for graduation. I remembered falling in love with Elizabeth Taylor. But Burl Ives as Big Daddy had always remained front and center in my memory. I decided Big Daddy had to be a person. As soon as I called and someone answered I'd say Big Daddy, then see what happened. I dialed. The phone rang four times before I heard a voice.

"Yeah,"

"Big Daddy."

"Be right back,' the voice said.

There was something about the voice.

"Midnight tomorrow," the voice said. "Harpoon Annie's. Don't be late."

The voice hung up. I'd heard that voice before, but I couldn't put a name to it. *More mystery.* I wished there was a way to trace the number. If I knew where it came from, it would help. What would be the best way to find that out? Being a cop, Jay could do it easily. But would he do it? I doubted it. He'd guess right away this was about Mario. The last time I talked to Jay about Mario, he threatened me that he'd arrest me if I fucked with his investigation. By the set of his jaw, I knew he wasn't kidding. Still, I pondered a little. What if? What if I could get Theresa to promise to go on a date with Jay? He was crazy about her. That would do it, but would Theresa agree? She'd have a heart attack if I proposed such a thing to her. What if? I looked at Graces' ghost.

"What if I offered her a raise?" I asked the spirit. "What if I said, I'd fire her?" The ghostly presence, no longer weeping, continued her silent vigil.

"Ma che fai," I said, "What are you doing, Brovelli, talking to the departed?"

I had to find out the location of the telephone number somehow. I turned my attention back to the folders. The last folder was about PeaceLinks. Newspaper articles and detailed research. Some of the research had to do with the initial investment to get the organization up and operating. An early bank statement revealed a checking balance of $58.000. That was enough to buy a decent three-bedroom home and have ten grand left over. The account was in Grace O'Conner's name. *Another frigging mystery.*

Another mystery was the schedule of protest events Grace and Mario had been a part of in 1969. They had traveled to more cities on the East Coast than I had originally thought, Boston, Philadelphia, and Baltimore. These were photocopies of the PeaceLinks typewritten schedule. It included days of arrival, hotels, times of events, departure dates. There were handwritten references to restaurants and taverns. Next to them in parenthesis were days of the week and specific times of the day. There were lots of details about city tourist sites and shopping centers and little drawings of streets and cross-streets. Why such scrutiny? I was sure this was not Mario's handwriting, which had a backward slant. Next to the maps was a handwritten comment, *What the fook?* Which, considering the spelling, could only have been written by either Hallinan or Riorden, mystified as I was by such details.

I started at the beginning with the first folder and reread everything. Hallinan and Riorden definitely thought something was hincky about Grace. There were multiple references to people they spoke to in various cities in Ireland, first names only and no telephone numbers.

It looked as if Bodys' *Lads* had queried just about every splinter group of Irish Nationalists in the Republic and in Northern Ireland and had found no one who remembered a Grace O'Conner. Some thought they recognized the face in the photograph, but couldn't give her a name. I started to question if Grace was Irish or some other nationality pretending to be Irish.

There had been one night when Dila entertained me by acting out scenes from various plays. For French plays she spoke in a French accent; for a Spanish play, her accent was pure Castilian Spanish. She even made me believe she was from Italy when she acted the role of a flirtatious woman in an Italian melodrama. A good actress could fool you. But could Grace have fooled Hallinan and Riorden who swore Grace's accent was from Derry? I leaned back on the couch. Much to my relief, Grace's ghost had disappeared, gone to weep elsewhere.

What to do next? I decided I would have to go to Harpoon Annie's in Monterey. I had no idea what I would discover there, but I felt it would be something important.

CHAPTER 28
THE FBI

Anyone who isn't confused, really doesn't understand the situation.
Edward R. Murrow

Dila and I were still in our bathrobes. I was drinking coffee and listening to Dila confirm her airline reservation for midnight on Saturday the 17th for New York City and already feeling lonely. Dila hung up and sighed. I hoped that the sigh was meant she too would be lonely. *Shared loneliness, right?* Dila left me and went to the bedroom. I heard the shower. She returned later dressed in her customary African garb that she wore whenever she worked in the BPP office. Dila dressed as an African Princess made me wonder how she could have managed over the years to keep her working for the Black Panthers a secret from her parents who were certainly no fools. Had they never telephoned the PeaceLinks office to speak to their daughter? It was a thought that had occurred to me often, but never broached with Dila. Now that Dila was in graduate school in New York City, the ruse was no longer needed. Even so, the minute Dila returned to the Bay Area, back she went to the Panthers to work for Minister Bowles. Bowles was around the same age as her father, but on occasion I found myself jealous of their relationship. Those moments passed quickly as I had come to admire Minister of Education Terrance Bowles, and I loved his helper deeply. To my surprise I had discovered my love for Dila had a lot to do with my respect for her. She found no contradiction in her loyalty to the more violent doctrines of Black Panthers and the non-violent strategies of Doctor Martin Luther King Jr and teachings of all the other black empowerment movements, while being in love with a white Italian used car salesman. A complicated woman was my Dila, no doubt. But perhaps she was no more or less complicated than other black women.

I remembered Dila quoting from W.E.B DuBois once when we were in a discussion about race. It had stuck with me like a lot of what Dila told me. DuBois had been asked specifically to talk about African American womanhood. His answer was as close as I could remember that he doubted that no other race of women could have done what black women have done under these devilish circumstances. No, that was not exactly the way he'd put it. He'd been more eloquent. His quote came back to me: *I sincerely doubt if any other race of women could have brought its fineness up through so devilish a fire.*

Dila roused me from my thoughts by handing me a cup of coffee.

"Hot directly from Mister Coffee," she said.

I took the cup. She sat next to me. As we sipped, I filled my Girl Friday in about my recent discoveries. Dila agreed that we should go to Harpoon Annie's. I told her no way was she going. *Big mistake.* I should have known not to command Dila. It was like ringing a bell at a boxing match. Dill lit into me with enough rhetoric to blow away the best debate team. I was no verbal counter puncher, so I quickly threw in the towel, acknowledging it would be smart to have backup. I knew after our Pier 5 escapade my twin would not help, and Sweets was really only good for breaking into places. I was relieved when Dila promised to remain hidden far enough away while I met with whomever the unidentified voice belonged to.

"I need to be at work in an hour," I said. "What's on for you today?"

"Terrance made some revisions to my revisions," Dila said. "He's added a whole new wrinkle. The article is going to address the bogus voluntary manslaughter charges that Huey Newton was convicted of. Terrence thinks the information we'll bring to light in the article will put the pressure on for a new trial."

In July of 1968, a short time after Dila and I met, Huey Newton, one of the founders of the Black Panthers Party, had been charged with the shooting death of an Oakland police officer. The felonious assault and kidnapping charges had been dismissed. At the trial, he was convicted of voluntary manslaughter. Newton was serving his 15-year prison sentence. The consensus in our East 14th neighborhood was that Newton was guilty. Jay, who knew the dead officer from their time together in the Police Academy, was particularly in favor of Newton's conviction. But I wasn't sure my friend was right. I'd witnessed firsthand some pretty nasty tactics employed by the police department against the Black Panthers. And there was supposedly evidence that the FBI had targeted the Black Panthers and would stoop to any means to destroy them.

When law enforcement is brought up, Dila's face changes from angelic to satanic. I changed the subject. "When do you plan to tell your parents we're getting married?"

"When do you plan to tell yours?"

"I asked first."

"I'll cut cards for who goes first," Dila said.

"Not funny. I'm being serious."

"Jeez, Victor, being serious is not any fun."

I stared. She stared back. Then smiled wickedly. "I told them at Sunday dinner. My father said he was going back to chapel to talk to our minister. My mother said it was inevitable. My Aunt Louise, you remember her from Kwanzaa, said we'll have some cute children. That's when my dad got up from the table and stormed out the door."

"Stormed. Did you say stormed?"

"It wasn't a hurricane," Dila said.

That did not reassure me.

Dila stopped talking and cocked her head like she was studying me for a part in a play. "So big fellow, the ball's in your court."

I tapped my watch. "I'm late for work."

Dila laughed. "Coward," she said. "Call me later and headed to the door.

I dressed for work in my customary blue blazer, over a white shirt and gray slacks, college blue and red tie. I put the coffee cups in the sink and unplugged Mr. Coffee and left. The weather was overcast.

• • •

Nothing distracts a car guy from his troubles faster than selling three vehicles for a good profit. Vincent and I were in the office enjoying one of the best Monday sales we'd ever had, Mondays being the slowest sales day of the week. *L'unomo che fa la spesa per un'auto il lundi ha una virago come moglie.* Who shops for a car on a Monday has a virago for a wife was one of our pop's sayings. I'm sure he made that one up. I had sold a 1960 Chrysler Imperial with an Alaska-blue-and-white interior, and Vincent had sold a 1960 all-white Super 88 Olds convertible and a gunmetal gray 1955 Chevy 3100 series pickup. The buyers had made substantial down payments, which meant the bank would carry the paper, which mean an instant payday for the Brovelli Brothers. We were tempted to bring down the bottle of Pappy Van Winkle bourbon that sits on the self behind Theresa's desk to toast our special Monday. I remembered how that bottle had contributed to my solving the murder of Winona Davis last year. We decided against bringing the bottle down since the month so far was nothing to brag about.

It was going on four and I hadn't eaten. Vincent and Theresa had brought their lunches. I left them to hold down the fort and headed to Flynn's

I was already seated at the end of the bar closest to the door before Body noticed me.

"Ah, Victor, me boy-o, I've been saving this one just for you. Mind you, there were a couple of dagos in an hour ago I could have used this joke on, but they might have taken offense."

"Get it over with, then get me a beer and stew if there's any left."

"Right you are. "Why are Polish jokes so short? Answer me that."

I shrugged.

"So Italians can get it."

A few of the guys at the bar that were listening chuckled. I glared at them. I heard Body laughing all the way back to his kitchen. He returned with a bowl of Irish stew and a mug of Anchor Steam. For all his joking, Body did not look happy. I figured it had to do with his Lads. Behind me the door opened and closed. I felt a slap on my back. I turned to see Jay and two men.

"Victor, I'd like you to meet Sam Brothers and Les Corbett from the Federal Bureau of Investigation."

Just what I needed, I thought. I tried to sound polite and put out my hand that was shaken forcefully. Neither of them smiled. There were three empty stools and Jay and the FBI agents sat down. Jay introduced them to Body. Body asked them to send his regards to his old friend J Edgar. I didn't think the two agents thought Body was funny. Body mouthed the word assholes and left to get the stews and draw three Budweiser drafts.

I leaned over Jay and asked the agents if they were investigating the shooting of Body's friend and dart team member, Danny Killian.

"Yes," the guy named Corbett said.

"What happened to the other agent that was working the case?" I asked

"Williams was recalled back to D.C. We're replacing him."

"Any luck so far?" I asked.

"Not that we can talk about."

"Hush, hush," I said.

"Very," Corbett answered.

"How's the car business?" Jay asked, changing the subject.

I didn't take the hint. "I heard Killian was IRA. Is that true?"

Body came back with the stew and drafts. He frowned at me and shook his head.

Before Body could leave, agent Brothers said. "I see a couple of Sinn Fein posters, Mr. Flynn."

"You can call me Body. I told the other agent everything I know. I hope I'm not going to have to talk into a wee tape recorder again."

"We've got all we need, Mr. Flynn. It was just an observation."

"Well, now. I've been observing that not much arresting has been done for shooting me friend."

"We'll get the villain, don't you worry, Mr. Flynn," Brothers said.

My observation had been that apart from Brothers being bald and Corbett having a full head of brown hair, there was not much in the way of bodily or facial differences between the two. They could have been related. Both of them had square faces and were jut jawed. Both of them looked like they could run the marathon. While I ate, I listened to their conversation. It was mostly about the anti-war protests in the Bay Area, particularly those that were taking place outside military facilities. When their conversation stopped, I taped Jay on the shoulder.

"Any news about the Radley killing?"

"Nothing," Jay said. "A gang thing, we think. He was a motorcycle guy. Could be any of those assholes, the Satans, the Druids, who knows. Drugs maybe. He had some coke residue in one of his pockets."

"It seems unlikely that Mario would have a coke-head for a roommate," I said.

"You think your brother Mario was a stand-up guy, do you?" Agent Brothers asked.

I didn't like his tone. "You want to show me your Silver Star, asshole?" I asked.

"Whoa," Jay said. "Calm down Victor. No harm, no foul, right."

"Yeah," I said. "Lots of harm." I stood up and left the tavern. If I hadn't, I would have had to punch that guy's jut jaw. The door to Flynn's opened and

Jay was standing next to me with his arm around my shoulder. "Everybody in law enforcement is on edge, Victor. The world is confusing enough under normal circumstances. These last few years have not been normal.

"Yeah, I get it," I said, but. . ." I was about to say something snarky about the agents, when it occurred to me I need to ask Jay for a favor. "Lots of pressure," I said. "Tell them I apologize."

"Atta boy, Victor," Jay said. He slapped me on the back — again. He turned to go back into the bar, but I grabbed his sleeve.

"Jay, I need a small favor," I said.

"Shit, I knew you were being too nice. What is it?"

I pulled a scrap of paper from my pocket and gave it to him. "I need to know where this telephone call originated."

"Let me guess. This has to do with Mario, right?"

"Not exactly."

"Not good enough, Victor. I know you too well. Can't do it pal."

I played my hole card. "What if I can get you a date with Theresa?"

"Don't put me on, Victor. I don't think she likes me."

"I know for certain she doesn't dislike you. She's a big opera fan. If you take her to the opera, she may just start liking you."

"I hate opera," Jay said.

"Consider Theresa's voluptuous body," I said.

Jay smiled broadly. "I might get to like opera. You think you can talk her into it?"

"Not a problem," I said, knowing that it would be. "Now how about the telephone number?"

"You get her to agree to a date, and you'll get your address."

"Solid," I said. "Apologize to the two assholes, and I'll get back to you."

I walked back to the lot thinking of opera. My mom and pop were big opera fans as were most of their friends. Opera is in Italian blood. Not in the blood of my generation of Italians, I didn't think. Back in the office I called my mom. Keeping my voice low so Theresa couldn't hear me I asked her if she could get tickets to an opera. It didn't matter which one. She told me she could, but opera season wasn't until fall. *Oddio,* I said. "That's too bad."

"Vittorio, you never like opera, what's so important?"

"I need them as gifts for business reasons."I didn't want to lie too much. Lying to your mother is a big no-no for Italian men.

"Well then, you are in luck, *figlio mio*. There is a special performance of *Nabucco* at the San Francisco opera house this Friday and Saturday. Giorgio Tozzi will be singing. It's being sponsored by the National Italian American Society."

"Can you get me two tickets?"

"Your father and I are not ready to go out in the public, so you can have ours."

I told my mom I'd be by to pick the tickets up. I thanked her *milli grazie*, made lots of kissing sounds and hung up. On the lot. I told Vincent I'd be right back and took off running.

I caught Jay just as he was leaving Flynn's. I asked the two agents if Jay and I could have a moment alone. They wandered up the street. When they were far enough away, I told Jay about the tickets to the opera, *Nabucco*.

"You're in like Flynn," I said, forgiving myself for the stupid pun. "Theresa will be unable to turn you down. I'm going to pick up the tickets after work, and I'll drop them off at the station. You go have a chat with Theresa."

"I hate opera," he said.

"But you love Theresa. Right?"

"I *could* fake it."

"Good. Now, let me tell you a little about *Nabucco*, so you don't sound like a *ridardate*."

• • •

I was back in the office waiting for Jay's call. After I'd provided him with a quick summary of the opera, he told me he'd get back to me before the end of the day. I told him I'd soften the ground a little with Theresa, talk him up a little, what a sweet guy he was. I did more than that.

I admitted to Theresa what I'd done and offered her a bonus at the end of the month based on our net monthly profit. That we might not have one was a consideration. But if worse came to worst, I'd take money out of my own pocket. She grumbled and called me a *chooch,* but once I mentioned the *Nabucco* tickets she agreed. One date, she said, holding up her index finger, *uno, capece?* I told her I understood perfectly, and I loved her like my own sister.

At five o'clock, Jay called.

"Are you sure you're ready to find out where your caller called from?"

Jay sounded worried. "Give it to me," I said.

"If you insist, but you're not going to like it."

"Oh, for Christ's sake, Jay, stop being so fucking dramatic. Where did the call originate?"

"Just down the street from you, Victor, from The Satan's club house."

CHAPTER 29
HARPOON ANNIE'S

We have the will, we need the guns.
Anonymous, Provisional IRA

In my imagination, Harpoon Annie's was a wooden one window shack, stuck on the end of a pier. In reality, it was a sleek modern concrete building with portholes for windows that took up the entire space between two piers. Dila and I were in a parking lot across the street, crouched behind Mario's Mustang. Both of us were dressed in black burglar clothing that Sweets had provided us. I was looking through Sweet's night vision binoculars. It was 11:36 p.m.by my watch. Every once in a while, Dila would nudge me and ask if I saw anyone. I could have told her I saw Mario's ghost sitting on an oil drum near the entrance to the building next to the pier, but decided not to complicate an already tense situation. Yesterday's revelation that the *Big Daddy* telephone call had come from The Satans' Club house had added another unanswered question to my long list of unanswered questions. *Our long list, Dila had reminded me.* It still was bugging me that I couldn't match the name to the voice on the phone. The Satans had been a big part of last year's investigation into the murder of Sweets' girlfriend, Winona Davis. I would have immediately recognized the voice of their leader Sunny Badger, but he was among the not so dearly departed, and I had never heard the voice of the Satan's new honcho, Champ Kowalski, Sunny's top henchman, known more for brass knuckles than words. Since taking over The Satans, the word around East 14th Street was of increased drug deals and violence. When asked about the motorcycle gang, Jay said the police department's priorities were anti-war protests and the Black Panthers. I suddenly wished that I had explained to Jay what I was doing and convinced him to have some of his fellow officers ready if I got into trouble. Given the Pier 5 fiasco, I knew what his response would have been. I was increasingly anxious about Dila's presence. I lowered my binoculars and turned to her. Her 30 caliber M 1 carbine was cradled in her arms. She looked like a guerilla freedom fighter from some South American country. She was wearing fatigues and boots. She was fiercely beautiful.

"Maybe we shouldn't be doing this," I said.

A voice came from my left, "Whitey, you've never been more right."

It was the voice I couldn't place from the telephone, I turned. "Tisdale," I said.

"That would be me." He was pointing a handgun at us. "You drop that carbine, Sister Agbo, or I pop yo white ass bo-friend."

Dila placed the weapon on the ground.

"The minute you said Big Daddy, I recognized your voice, Brovelli. I figured there was a problem if you knew the password. So Little Eddie has been following you."

Little Eddie stepped out of the shadows. He was holding a large gun. It looked like the kind Jay used, a Colt 38 special revolver.

"Hi Little Eddie," I said and instantly felt foolish hailing him as if that gun barrel was not pointed at my chest and the look in Little Edie's eyes was not malicious, and we were all friends.

"Is this some kind of joke, Tisdale?" Dila said. "You can't be serious pointing a gun at me. You're a Black Panther. I'm going to have a word with Minister Bowles."

"I'm a Black Panther when it suits me, sister. And you sleep with a white man, so don't start with we're tribal and shit. Y'all start walking."

Tisdale pointed across the street in the direction of the pier.I reached for Dila's hand. We made it across without being shot, which was not a reason to be optimistic. Tisdale had sure fooled me. Something illegal was happening, but what was it? I figured it wouldn't cost me anything to ask except maybe my life.

"This is a pier. There are boats. By the anxious look Little Eddie's face studying the horizon, I'm betting you're smuggling something. Drugs, right? While you were talking to me at the Golden Dragon, you knew massive amounts of drugs were coming into this country from South East Asia. Right?" I paused for a reaction. When there wasn't, I continued, "And Mario and Grace must have found out about it and you killed them and made it look like a suicide."

"Fuck you Brovelli," Little Eddie said. "You have no idea what you're talking about. Mario be a good commanding officer. Why would we kill him?"

It had never occurred to me that Little Eddie had been a soldier in Vietnam. Perhaps Big Eddie had also been in Nam and all three in Mario's platoon.

"What is it, heroin, cocaine?" I asked. Dila squeezed my hand. She mouthed, "Don't push it."

We were at the front door of Harpoon Annie's. A large van turned the corner and drove slowly in our direction. The sign on the side said: *Safe Moving and Storage*. It passed us, picked up speed, and turned at the next corner.

"That be them," Little Eddie said.

The *Them* were most likely drug dealers. We were going to be witnesses to a drug deal. Then, I thought why would they need a moving van to haul drugs? Whatever was going down, Dila and I would not live through it. I had to think of something. The van appeared and drove toward us. This time slowly pulling to the curb. The curbside door opened, and I saw an Irish face I recognized - Seamus Hallinan. From the driver's side, came Brendan Riorden. *Minchia.* What in the hell was going on? With a sickening feeling, the thought came to me that every discovery I'd made so far had been intended to mislead me. Tisdale was not who he really was. Neither were the two Irishmen walking toward us. The fact that Radley was tortured before being killed was proof he must have been someone other than the simple army grunt he claimed to be. Grace was already the central mystery. What about Mario? *Oddio,* what if Mario hadn't uncovered some illegal activity, but been a part of it? I shook my head as if it would somehow help me focus. How long had Mario told me he'd been off the hard stuff? If Mario was involved, how could I have been so wrong about him? As fast as that thought came to me, it disappeared. *Mario, a criminal? Ridiculous.*

"Fooking Christ, Brovelli," Hallinan said as he saw us, "what are you doing here?"

"He called with the password," Tisdale said. "I did what I had to do, And after the shipment arrives, you know what has to happen."

"Sin Fein. Raising money, what a joke," I said. "You two are just a couple of drug dealers." Suddenly I was angry at myself for being duped, but also for placing Dila's life in jeopardy.

Riorden laughed. "What are you talking about? This is about. . ."

"Shut your hole," Hallinan said. "Look, let us take care of these two. Let's get our deal done, and we'll all be happy."

"Can't do that whitey," Tisdale said. "These two are taking a boat ride." He pointed west toward the bay where a light had appeared out of the fog bank. "Your merchandise will be here soon. I'll need to see cash."

Hallinan frowned. "I don't call you by the names I've heard your people are called," he said. "So I expect the same respect from you. I'm going to let the slur pass because this is business. But just to be sure we understand each other."

Hallinan reached inside his jacket and withdrew a handgun.

"Now we are both armed," he said. "Brendan, escort Mr. Tisdale to the van and show him what's in the suitcase. Then we'll all wait for the wee boat to arrive."

"Keep these two covered Little Eddie," Tisdale said and walked away with Riorden.

I looked at Dila and mouthed, "Any ideas."

She shrugged, then she gave me a little wink. *Oh, God, I should never have asked.*

Tisdale returned smiling. "All's good. We be rich as fucking Mid-ass," he said. "We wait."

I could now make out the shape of the boat, a fishing trawler. I guessed the large shadow standing at the bow was Big Eddie.

"Once, the boat ties up at the pier, we need to move fast," Tisdale said. "You back your van on to the sidewalk as close the pier as you can. I have a couple of guys on board who'll help you unload the crates and carry them over.

"If this isn't about drugs, Riorden, what's it about?" I asked.

"We're soldiers. You make an educated guess," Riorden said.

"Guns," I said. There was a sudden movement to my right. I turned to look and saw Dila dropping to the ground in front of Tisdale. She hugged his legs and wailed. I'd heard this plea before. A year ago. Oh, shit, I thought, it's Shakespeare time.

"Don't kills me, Tisdale," Dila moaned, "Ahm a good sister. Really I am. Kills Brovelli. I won't say nothin. I'm a Black Panther. You're my brotha, Ohhh don't kills me."

Tears were streaming from her eyes. She was gulping for air and pleading at the same time. She kept tugging on Tisdale's pants. *Madonna mia,* I knew what she was doing. A year ago, she had saved my life by acting the role of an aggrieved and drunken wife as two gangsters were about to cut me up into tiny pieces. I wanted to rush to her and stop her, but another part of me told me to let this performance go to the final curtain. Tisdale kept trying to loosen her grip. In the process, he dropped her carbine, and at that moment Dila drove her fist up between Tisdale's legs. He let out a grunt, doubled over, bent to the ground like a Muslim praying. Little Eddie was standing with his mouth open. I didn't need an invitation. I leaped at him, slamming my head into his face, his nose making a smooshing sound. Dropping his pistol, he fell backwards bringing both hands up to cover his face, blood spurting between his fingers. Dila had the carbine in her hands, and I was holding Little Eddie's big revolver. I got up off my knees. Hallinan was pointing his handgun at me, but he was smiling.

"Good performance, eh Riordon?" he said. "Young lady, you should be in the movies."

He was about to say something else, when I heard a noise like a car backfiring and Hallinan's smile disappeared in an explosion of blood and brains. His body landed prone on the sidewalk in front of me. It took me a second for the attack to register, then I yelled to Dila to take cover. Riorden was already crawling on all fours toward the oil drum on which Mario's ghost was sitting, impassively watching the action unfolding in front of him. Tisdale was limping and hopping across the street, holding his crotch when the bullet slammed him to the asphalt. Whoever the rifleman was, he was fast. Another shot hit Riorden's foot, and he flipped over but kept scrambling backwards, pumping his legs, yelling in a language I knew to be Gaelic and dragging the suitcase of money. The next shot pierced the oil drum. The next shot ricocheted off the sidewalk, and I heard Dila scream. Almost simultaneously another shot hit Riorden, and he yelled, "Ah, ya fooking Jaffa." I jumped to my feet and ran to Dila. She was holding her side. There was a lot of blood. Another bullet ricocheted off the sidewall next to me. I knew I shouldn't move her, but I had to get her to safety. I lifted her under her arms and dragged her behind a stack of crates. I tore open the side of her blouse. *Oddio*, I thought. The wound was large and full of blood that was running down her side onto the cement. I took off my jacket, folded it, and pressed it over the wound.

"Dila, keep your eyes open, listen to me. We'll stop the bleeding. You're going to be okay."I was suddenly aware of sirens sounding in the distance. "Cops," I said, my emotions soaring."We're going to get you to a hospital. Don't worry. I'm here."

"You're getting dark, Victor," Dila said.

My angel's eyes closed, and I began my first and not my last prayer to the Virgin, *Holy Mary, Mother of God. . .*

CHAPTER 30
GUILT

It senso di colpa non lascia spazio all'amore
Guilt leaves no room for love.
Italian proverb

I was sitting in the operating room waiting area of Monterrey Peninsula Community Hospital. My eyes were closed, and I was holding my head in my hands. my emotions ranging from fear for Dila's life, to anger at my own foolishness, to deep pangs of guilt, to thoughts of revenge against the unknown shooter and back to fear and guilt, the cycle repeating itself. I didn't realize I'd been crying until a nurse touched my shoulder and offered me some tissue. She told me the doctor had finished operating and would be out soon to talk to me. I had told the ambulance driver who brought Dila and Brendan Riorden to the emergency room that I was Dila's husband. Later, after the doctor had examined Dila and explained the seriousness of her wound, I called Dila's parents. I could feel the anxiety and anger in her father's voice as he told me they would be driving down immediately. His last words to me were that I'd better not be there when he arrived. Or something to that effect. Screw him, I thought. Victor Brovelli was going nowhere. Where would I go without Dila? I was suddenly aware of an old woman sitting in the corner of the waiting room. She was dressed in black, a black shawl over her head. She was very old. Her wrinkled fingers were holding a rosary, and she was saying her beads, her lips moving over the silent words. I knew her as my mother's great aunt, Maddalena, from a trip to Italy my parents gave to my twin and me for a high school graduation present. The lady in black had read my tea leaves and pronounced that I would see *molti fantansmi,* many ghosts.

"May I have your rosary," I asked. "I need to pray." The old woman held the beads out to me. As I reached for them, I heard her say, *"Il senso di colpa non lascio spazio all'amore,"* I didn't understand completely, something about guilt and love. I asked, but she'd disappeared. The rosary felt heavy. For a moment I thought I would drop it. *You can't drop a rosary. That would be a sin.* I stared at my vacant hand. Perhaps I was going crazy. I felt a tap on my shoulder and whirled around, expecting another ghost. It felt almost sane to see a real human being, the same nurse who'd spoken to me before.

"We're you speaking to me?" she asked.

Her eyes said kindness, but her frown said concern. I wanted to tell her that I was only talking to my mother's great aunt, who'd been dead for a decade. I closed my eyes and took a deep breath.

"I'm okay. Sorry, I was talking to myself. I'm worried."

"Doctor Simmons is one of our finest surgeons. Your wife will pull through. There's nothing you can do for a while. Why don't you go to the cafeteria and get something to drink or eat. Or take a walk. Get out of this waiting room for a while."

"I'll do that," I said. She smiled and left. To myself, I whispered, "Probably not."

A half hour later, when the elevator door opened and Kahil Agbo and his wife stepped out, leaving the waiting room didn't seem like such a bad idea. The second he saw me, his face turned tight with anger, the muscles of his jaw throbbing.

"You're not needed here you, you. . . "

It was as if he'd forgotten my name.

"I have every right to be here Mr. Agbo, Mrs. Agbo. Dila and I are engaged."

"You have been trouble from the first day my daughter met you. You don't think we know what happened last year when you almost got her killed, trying to save you. You think we don't know you influenced her to work for the Black Panthers. All the rubbish about PeaceLinks."

I felt dizzy. Me, influencing Dila to work for the Black Panthers? What was wrong with that picture? White basically apolitical middle-class Italian used car salesman somehow proselytizing for the most notorious Black organization in the country? Was this weirdness the result of shock? I looked at Mrs. Agbo. She was not smiling, but she raised one eyebrow. I thought it best not to respond. Better to be apologetic. It would not be hard since I was feeling intensely guilty anyway.

"I can't begin to tell you how sorry I am. I accept complete responsibility for what happened." I paused. He stared at me. I wasn't sure what else to say. I blurted out, "Mea Culpa." That got Mr. Agbo's attention.

"If that's Italian for you're a culprit, I'll second that," Mr. Agbo said. "I want you out of this waiting room. We don't want to see you. We don't want to hear in English or Italian or pig Latin. Are you some kind of Communist?"

More weirdness. This time Mrs. Agbo took her husband's arm.

"Kahil, get control of yourself. Victor is right, you know they *are* engaged." She pointed to the chairs. "We'll take a seat. Victor, you sit over on the other side, away from Kahil. We will wait for the doctor. We will pray and act like sane human beings. Adila is strong. She will survive. My baby girl will get through this. Do you understand, Kahil? Do you understand, Victor?"

We both nodded and I turned away from them. Charlene Agbo had always seemed regal and logical. For the first time I saw her fire and knew where Dila got her flames.

An hour went by. Finally, the door to the operating wing opened and a doctor came out. Mr. Agbo leaped to his feet. His wife followed. I trailed behind.

The doctor stepped past them and spoke to me. "Mr. Brovelli," he said, "Your wife came through the operation. She will recover. She'll need lots of rest."

I heard both Mr. and Mrs. Agbo say something at the same time, but it was if their voices were coming from a distant place. I could hear the doctor asking who they were. I heard myself ask, *when can I see Dila?* I could hear Mr. Agbo say, *he's not her husband.* I could hear Mrs. Agbo say, *he's her fiancé,* and feeling only slightly grateful that I was not some hobo who'd wandered in off the street. I could hear my brain telling me, *Stay calm. Dila will be okay*. That's all that mattered. I could hear the doctor explain that there would be no visitors for at least four hours. I heard the elevator doors close behind me.

•••

The next thing I knew I was standing in front of the nurses' station asking in which room would I find Brendan Riorden. I was told visitors were not allowed. "Hush-hush," the nurse said, "Police business." She placed her finger over her lips.

I gave her my Brovelli smile, full dimples. It didn't work. But I'd seen her eyes shift to her right when she said no visitors. I walked away. When she returned to her paperwork, I moved quickly down the hall in the direction her eyes had sent me. At the end of the hall, I spotted a police officer sitting in a chair outside a door. I took out my wallet and opened it. I squared my shoulders, stuck out my belly and did my best imitation of my friend Detective Sergeant Jay Ness' swagger. The officer rose as I approached. He looked younger than me and unsure of himself. I held up the open wallet and marched quickly through the door before he could say anything. Inside, I waited to see what the officer would do, counting to ten before I felt safe that my impersonation had worked. Dila was not the only person who could act. Riorden was sitting up in bed. His eyes were closed. One leg was in a cast and elevated.

"Fooking bullet broke a bone, Brovelli," he said.

"Your eyes are closed. How did you know it was me?"

He opened one eye. "I trust me instincts. Besides, doctors and nurses have a way of entering the room. And I can smell *garda*. That's coppers to you yanks."

Both of his eyes were now open. "Do you have any idea who was shooting at us?" I asked.

"Of course. There's only one possibility. A fooking UVF or UDF assassin, that's who. Probably the same one who killed Danny Boy Killian, rest his soul."

"Do you have a name for this assassin?" I asked. I had one in mind. I figured he was thinking of the same name.

"I'd put money on that roommate of your brother's, McGoffin. I think he tortured and killed Danny Boy Killian too. Newly arrived Irishmen can't hide. He was no business man.And the name, I tink we mentioned it, is more common in Northern Ireland.

How did McGoffin know what you IRA guys were upto?

"Who the hell knows. Ireland is about to go up in flames. Both sides have spies. It was no coincidence McGoffin shows up in the Bay Area, sniffing around. It's very likely he learned something from that Radley fellow. It doesn't matter anymore."

I was reminded of something I'd read out of my how to be a private investigators' handbook that there would always be lose ends that an investigator would never be about to tie together.

I changed the subject. "So, you're really IRA and you're here trying to buy guns to take back

to Ireland."

"Right you are boy-o. The shiest is about to hit the fan back home. But there's no reason to mention such speculation to the coppers, is there? You have no proof you know."

"What about the trawler with the guns in it? Didn't the cops seize it?"

"No. Must have heard the shooting and turned the boat back out to sea. Our shipment is out there somewhere."

"I know the name of one of Tisdale's guys. He was on the boat."

"Who's Tisdale?"

"That's the name of the gunrunner who was selling you weapons. He's a Vietnam vet and a member of the Black Panthers."

"I thought we were dealing with a motorcycle gang called the Satans."

"Maybe you were," I said.

I couldn't imagine why a man such as Tisdale who hated whites would have anything to do with a bunch of racists like the Satans. It had been a question on my mind ever since Harpoon Annie's when Tisdale showed up with his gun and death on his mind. Still, the phone call had been traced back to the Satans' office. There were a lot of questions that needed answering. "Did the cops get your money?" I asked.

"I hid the suitcase before the cops arrived. I don't know how long it will stay there before someone finds it. That's why I can't get arrested. I need to get our money back."

"You can't walk," I said. "Where did you hide it? I'll get it and give it to Body."

Riorden looked at me and smiled. "So kind of you, boy-o to offer, but I tink its better if the guys on the dart team help, not that I don't trust you."

I shrugged. "Your call." I said. "Tell me, is Body IRA?"

"Nah, he's part of a network of American supporters, that's all. A fine fellow, he is."

"When you were shot the second time, you yelled something, like you were calling the shooter a name. What was that?' Riorden looked puzzled, then his face brightened.

"Ach, you mean Jaffa. It's a bit of history to you, yank. Jaffa is a seedless orange."

"The color orange, I get it."

"Not exactly. In 1688 Prince William of Orange at the Wall of Derry. After the battle, the arsehole restored Protestantism to England and Ireland. I've always thought of the seedless part as having no bollocks, but that's just me crude-self talking."

In the silence that followed, Riorden's eyes closed, and I thought he might have fallen asleep.

His eyes opened and he said. "I've been tinking about the shooter."

"What about him?

"That there were probably two shooters."

"Go on," I said.

The first two shots were meant for Hallinan and me. Hallinan's head was a bullseye, but I got hit in the leg. A trained UVF or UDF assassin would never have missed me. The second time I was crawling fast, but the gunman got me leg anyway, a hard shot if they were shooting as I suspect they were from that ridge above the street.Then, there were our two gunrunners we were buying from. They were gunned down by a real marksman. But you were out in the open and the shooter missed you."

"That shot for me hit Dila," I said.

"That would be your girlfriend," Riorden said. "I saw. Is she alive?"

"Yeah, but the operation was difficult."

"Sorry to hear it. That was some fine acting she did. Had me believing she would leave you hanging."

"She's an actress," I said. Leave me, never, I thought.

"That shot meant for you that hit her must have ricocheted. You see what I mean about two shooters? One was a trained rifleman, the other not."

"I do. If McGoffin was one, any idea who the second shooter could have been?" He was about to answer when the door opened and a nurse entered.

"You need to leave, sir," she said. "The Doctor is on his way. You can come back later."

"A name." I said. Riorden shrugged.

"I'll give it some thought," I said. "Let's see if we can come up with a likely candidate."

He nodded and I left. The cop guarding the door looked like he was taking a nap. As I walked down the hall, I passed the doctor heading for Riorden's room. At the nurse's station, I waited for the elevator to take me down to the emergency and the operating room waiting area. I was about to press the button, when the elevator opened and a doctor in his white coat stepped out.

He hailed the station nurse. Rita. "Is my gunshot patient ready for me?" he asked.

I didn't need to hear another word. I turned and sprinted by him and down the hall. The officer seated by the door didn't have time to stop me. I was inside Riorden's room, staring at the dead Irishman. His throat had been cut, his chest and the blanket around him covered with blood. I pivoted into the arms of the police guard, who had followed me into the room. I brushed him aside. "He's been murdered," I yelled and ran out the door as fast as I could in the direction of the exit sign at the end of the hall. Slamming through the exit, I two-stepped down the staircase, my feet barely touching, and out into the parking lot, just as the fake doctor leaped into a dark Ford Galaxy. The driver pulled away from the curb and sped for the parking exit. I didn't get the license plate number, but I could see the driver was a woman.

When I returned to the hospital, the napping police guard placed me under arrest and cuffed me. I tried explaining, but he shook his head. I could only imagine what his commanding officer would say to him for allowing a man to be murdered while under the protection of the Monterey County Police Department. When his commanding officer finally arrived, along with a dozen or so other cops, what I heard was this: "Trooper, you're going to be pulling elementary school crossing guard duty for the rest of the year." I was hoping for the rest of his time on the force.

• • •

It took the intersession of Detective Sergeant Jay Ness of Oakland's homicide division, who had driven down to Monterey plus the statement by the officer guarding the door that in the brief time I was in the room, I couldn't have been the killer.

After arranging for their daughter to be transferred to Merritt Hospital in Oakland, Mr. and Mrs. Agbo left. Dila was taken from recovery to a private room. When I tried to visit her, I was informed that Mr. Agbo had promised to sue the hospital if I was allowed anywhere near his daughter. Jay drove me to my car parked across the street from Harpoon Annie's. On the way he tried to cheer me up. It didn't work. I felt like shit.

"I can follow you, if you'd like, "Jay said. "You look a little shaky."

"I'm fine, Jay. Go on. I'm going to take the coast highway home. Do a little thinking." I stepped out of the car.

"You sure now?"

"I'll be fine,"

Jay drove off. I got in Mario's Mustang, but didn't start the engine. A thought occurred to me. I was pretty certain I knew where Riorden had hidden the suitcase of money. For a while I stared at the front of Harpoon Annie's. The sidewalk was blocked by police barricades and yellow crime scene tape. There was a sheriff's car and what looked like plain clothes investigators. Tourists were stopped on either side of the barricades, gawking. By now, local news had probably informed the public about the gun battle that had raged there during the night. I saw Riorden's hiding place. There was no way I could get the suitcase. Maybe if I came back late tonight. I put the Mustang in gear, pulled out of the parking lot and drove away.

Both Vincent and I find driving helps us empty our minds so that we see things more clearly. My twin uses speed and the freeway to clear his mind. I prefer the roads with plenty of curves that force me to concentrate on shifting gears, establishing a rhythm and a mental escape. Thoughts come to me in bursts. I wished I was in my Porsche Cabriolet instead of Mario's Mustang. I was particularly conscious of the imprint of blood that looked like a Rorschach test against which my back rested and my mind depended. It was a reminder that I would never stop until I solved the murder of my brother Mario and his girlfriend. A psychiatrist would probably come up with a more accurate reason for me leaving the stain on the seat. Then there were my *fantasmi.* I wondered what a shrink would say about them. I looked in my rearview mirror, surprised to be driving alone and not accompanied by the ghosts of Mario or Grace.

By the time I reached Pacifica, I was exhausted. I hadn't slept, and I was hungry. I stopped at *Nicks* for crab cakes. They did not serve Anchor Steam, so I settled for a Pabst. Looking out the window at the Pacific Ocean, I was reminded that Dila and I had eaten here last summer and stayed overnight at the motel next door. We'd made love, walked on the beach, made love, eaten the largest mussels I'd ever seen, cooked in garlicy broth on a bed of linguini and served with chunks of crusty French bread. We'd finished off a bottle of Pinot Grigio from a winery in Napa. There had been people who stared at us. We smiled at them, too happy with ourselves to take offense. Thinking of Dila happy and healthy and now in the hospital, put an end to my appetite. I left the crab cakes half finished, paid for my meal. I drove back to Highway One, entered the highway and stomped on the gas.

CHAPTER 31
SOME PIECE OF WORK

Anche un pomodoro puo insegnarti qualcosa
Even a tomato can teach you something
Big Sal Brovelli

Vincent and I were standing on the lot facing each other. The morning sunshine behind Vincent darkened his face but did not obscure his dark anger.

"You *cazzo*. You lied to me. You promised after the screw-up at Pier 5, you were done with investigating."

Cazzo means all-purpose prick. It is odd that Vincent, who rarely swears in English, will curse like a trooper in Italian. But I deserved it. I *had* promised. Somewhere there is a rulebook for male twins that states they do not apologize to each other. In the event of a disagreement, the first rule calls for staring angrily, the second calls for cursing one another, the third requires pushing each other back and forth; the final rule calls for a fist fight. I was told by a wise ass one time that only Italian twins resort to fists. To which, I remember replying that wrestling was weeny. I do not believe the rulebook for female twins includes physical violence, but I might be wrong.

To tell the truth, I was a little pissed at Vincent for not driving down with Jay. Didn't he swear he'd have my back? In the hospital, I could have used some twin brother emotional support. But I couldn't really blame him. Jay had explained I was safe and no harm had come to me.

"Vincent, I know I broke my promise. I apologize." The apology so startled my twin that his eyes widened in surprise. After taking a moment to recover, he spoke.

"You feeling okay, Victor?"

"I'm okay. This has been an insane time. What happened at Harpoon Annie's is the screw-up of screw-ups. Dila is in the hospital recovering from a gunshot wound. Four people are dead, and this has turned into some kind of international criminal investigation. Jay told me to expect the FBI to bring me in for questioning. The frigging FBI, *merda!*"

"I didn't know about Dila," Vincent said. "I'm happy she's going to be okay."

I didn't tell Vincent about the suitcase of IRA money or Riorden's hiding place.

We were standing near the office door. We hadn't noticed, but the door was open, and Theresa at her desk was probably listening to everything I told Vincent. Theresa was not a gossip, but she and my mother were close. This was nothing I wanted my parents to know. I took Vincent by the arm and led him onto the lot among the cars. I stopped at this week's loss-leader, a 1955 Packard Clipper that was on display next to the platform in the middle of the lot that strategically displayed our classic Woodie, its horizontal golden pine panels inviting passersby to come take a look and be amazed. And if they noticed the loss leader, well the price was right.

Vincent asked, "So?"

"I don't know what to do." I must have sounded pretty forlorn because Vincent's face softened. How long can twins stay mad at each other? He placed his hands on my shoulders. "I'd normally tell you to drop the whole thing, but I have to admit this sounds too bizarre to be a simple Victor Brovelli kind of *casino.*It looks like we need to put our heads together. Twin brains, are better than, you know. . ."

"Half a brain," I said, completing the joke we often said to each other.

"It's too early for Flynn's," Vincent said. "You want to get some breakfast?"

"Ole's?"

"Too far away. Let's go to Lenny's. I'll take my car. I can't stand to be in Mario's Mustang with that bloody stain on the back of the seat you left. If Mom knew you did that, she'd tell you you're inviting a curse."

I was pretty sure my mother would have understood the symbolism. As much as I wanted to solve Mario's death, my mother doubled my intensity. The word *Onore*, coming from my mother's mouth had never sounded more like Honor. Last year, my father had intimidated us with his sense of honor. This year it was my mother's turn to use honor, but this time to galvanize out resolve.

"Just the outline, no blood," I said.

"You still might be cursed."

"Fine, your car then," I said. I already felt cursed. We walked to the back of the office where our cars were parked. This year Vincent was driving a bronze and cream Chrysler Town & Country with 440 ci V8 engine. A year ago after his baby girl had been born, my twin explained to me that being a family man, he needed the security of a wagon. Being a family man hadn't stopped him from taking the Chrysler on to the freeway and seeing how it felt going 100 mph — my twin, the speed junkie.

Heggenberger Road led to the Oakland Airport.I couldn't remember ever taking a flight out of Oakland Airport. Dila's flights to New York always left from San Francisco International. There was a parking space in front of Lenny's. The last time I'd eaten at Lenny's was with Sweets a year ago when he formulated a plan to save his butt from going to prison. That fiasco seemed so long ago in light of the far more complicated and dangerous one I currently found myself in.

I followed Vincent in. We took the furthest booth from the door. The same lipless and chinless waitress that had served Sweets and me last year arrived with menus with as many pages as *War and Peace*, all having to do with pancakes and waffles. She placed a menu in front of us, looked at me for a second, then said, "Aren't you a friend of Sweets Monroe?"

"Yes," I said, "how did you know?"

"I remember the first time you and that knucklehead came in. I'd just gotten the job here."

"Great memory," I said.

"He's some piece of work," she said. "You guys want coffee?"

"Coffee and cream for him, black for me" I said. I didn't need to respond to Sweets being a piece of work. I could have said he was a burglar, but she probably knew by now. It's all over the neighborhood. It drives the cops nuts because they can never catch him. The name tag on the waitress's uniform read, Tammy. We looked through the menu that featured varieties of pancakes and waffles and toppings to satisfy any carbohydrate addict. Most items would require a ten-mile run to work off some of the effects. As breakfasts go, this place didn't hold a candle to Ole's. Tammy came back with the coffee and took our order. I couldn't bring myself to order my Ole's usual, so I settled for an avocado and bacon omelet. Vincent ordered the blueberry pancake special that came with two eggs and bacon. I could have told our waitress ahead of time, over easy, burn the bacon and bring him jam instead of maple syrup. Knowing each other's tastes is part of being a twin. When we were kids and before the scar on my cheek, nobody could tell us apart. We relished confusing people, especially our teachers. Vincent had once taken an algebra test for me because I would have failed it. He deliberately missed a few to make sure the teacher did not become suspicious. A gentleman's C was fine with me.

Tammy tore off our order form. She turned to leave, but pivoted back. "Sweets comes in regular. I swear to God I never seen a guy eat and stay skinny like him."

"He's got a tapeworm," I said.

"Of the brain," she said and left us to place the order with the cook.

For a while we drank our coffee, staring over each other's shoulders. Behind Vincent on the far wall above the window was Oakland Raider banners surrounding what looked like a team photograph. The Raiders had just lost the AFL Championship on January fourth 17 to 7, which cost most of the guys at Flynn's a lot of money.

"So, you going to tell me the whole story, or are you going to keep staring off into space?"

"You were doing the staring, not me."

"Don't start it, Victor, don't start being an ass. If you want my help you need to begin where you left off, after the Pier 5 *casino* when you promised me no more being a detective, *capisci?*"

I understood. Duly chastised, I started at the beginning and after food and two more coffees ended at the hospital emergency waiting room. It was, as I'd read about some autobiographies, the unvarnished truth. But I am skeptical of such claims and wondered what else was driving my desire to find the truth behind Mario and Grace's deaths. Was it the excitement of being a detective? Last year I'd had to admit to myself as I worked on the murder of Winona Davis that investigating was more satisfying than being a car salesman. I'd even thought up a name for my efforts and had written it on the inside cover of my private investigator's manual: *The Case of the "61 Chevy Impala*. A few months into our relationship when I felt more secure about it, I had shown the title to Dila. I remember saying to her, if I ever gave up selling cars, I'd get a private investigators license. She'd *hrumphed* and patted my cheek, a little condescendingly, I thought.

"You are in a whole lot of *merda*," Vincent said.

I said, "What?"

"Are you listening?"

His words brought me back to the present. "Sorry," I said.

Vincent said, "There's a lot of stuff that doesn't make sense."

"You're telling me." I said. "It's like I feel I'm on the right track, then find out I'm off the rails."

"I don't get who these people are," Vincent said. "I thought Tisdale and his two buddies Big and Little Eddie were Black Panthers. Now you tell me they're some kind of gunrunners. Could the Panthers have gone into the weapons business? Newspapers and broadcasters are all predicting there's going to be a war between whites and Negroes."

"African-Americans, you mean."

"Whatever," Vincent said "Then the Irishmen who convinced you they were fundraising for the Sinn Fein turn out to be IRA agents here to purchase weapons. Are there no guns to buy on the East Coast? Lot closer to Ireland?"

"Not if they're guns from Vietnam?" I replied.

"Okay, so what's up with Radley?" Vincent asked. "I know he was in Mario's platoon in Vietnam and shared an apartment here. He winds up tortured and murdered. Why?"

I had no answer for Vincent except that Radley's killer was probably McGoffin. Vincent continued questioning me. For every question my twin raised, I shook my head. "What really threw me," I said. "Is that the telephone call I made about the weapons delivery was traced to the Satan's clubhouse. The Satans would never have allowed a black man to set foot within ten feet of their front door. You ever see the inside of their clubhouse, all those Nazi flags?"

"When were you ever inside?" Vincent asked.

"You've forgotten, Sweets and I. Where we stowed Winona's body."

"*Oddio*, I forgot. Vittorio, sometimes I think you have a death wish."

"I'm beginning to believe I attract dead bodies. You think I'm cursed?"

The voice came from above us. "I think you need Sweets Monroe, to help you."

I turned in my seat and looked up at Sweets.

"How long you been standing there listening, you *babbo*?" I asked.

"You know, Victor, it's not polite you calling me a dope. Especially since I can clear up one of your mysteries."

"Oh, really. Well, I guess you better sit down and tell us."

"Move over Vincent," Sweets said.

"Sit next to Victor. I have problems with your dandruff."

"Unkind, Vincent, unkind. I wash my hair every night. You going to finish that pancake, Vincent?"

"You touch that pancake and I stab you with my fork," Vincent said.

"Forget the pancake," I said. "What do you know that we should know?"

"You two geniuses can't figure out how Tisdale took your call inside the Satans' clubhouse."

"Correct," Vincent said.

"I'll need to order some food, first."

Before I could say anything, he called Tammy by name. She arrived with her pen and pad in hand, a forced smile on her lips.

"You want your usual, Sweets, darling?" she asked, accent on the *darling*.

Double on the pancakes, angel. These two fine-as-wine gentle-mens are paying."

Tammy looked at me and rolled her eyes. I nodded. Vincent shook his head.

"Put it on my bill," I said.

"Our bill, don't you mean," Vincent said, scowling at me.

"Twins share."

"Not for burglars," Vincent said.

This is called Twin Repartee. I had at least two more come-backs in store for Vincent, but I had more important stuff on my mind.

Tammy left, and I turned to Sweets, grabbing a fistful of his shirt and pulling him toward me until we were nose to nose. "The food's on me, but I'm going to be truly pissed if what you tell us is not good news."

"*Mes bons freres*, my good brothers, not to get your shorts in a tweest. The answer is really simple."

"Spit it the fuck out," I said, tightening my grip on his shirt.

"Okay, okay. Be that way. Now if you'll kindly let go of me, I'll proceed."

I released him. He sat back, wiping my fingerprints off his yellow Hawaiian shirt.

"You wrinkled the parrots, you see Victor, their leetle heads, they say you hurt dem."

"That's the ugliest shirt I've ever seen. Tell that to your parrots, now get on with it or I grab their little heads again."

"Okay, you one beeg tough guy," Sweets said. "The answer to you is simple, *non*? The Satans, those badasses, are not in town. They haven't been for the last two weeks. They're down in the Mojave Desert at a motorcycle roundup. All the bikers west of the Rockies, they be there. Their clubhouse is locked up."

Before I could respond with something sarcastic, Vincent asked, "So what does that mean?"

"Don't be a donk, Vincent," Sweets said. "It means Tisdale set it up. Picking locks, no problem, *oui?* A making a safety net. Beside the telephone call, I'll bet he left other clues pointing to the Satans. Any blowback with the deal, would be traced to the Satans, not to him."

"Or the Black Panthers," I said. Vincent frowned.

"You one smart detective, you." Sweets said.

CHAPTER 32
THE WORLD ACCORDING TO JEAN LAFITTE

The night sky always pointed me in the right direction. Still THURS JAN 15
Jean Pierre Lafitte

"You can't possibly eat all that," Vincent said.

Instead of skeptical, I thought my twin's voice sounded more like he was in awe. I had seen Sweets at his trough plenty of times before. The oink could scarf it down, to be sure. To describe Sweets as a pig at his trough is accurate only as it applies to his eating habits, considering he looks like a human cockatiel. I counted ten pancakes. That meant Sweet's "usual" was a stack of five. Atop the stack were three over-easy eggs that Sweets immediately broke so the yolks disgustingly dripped down the sides of the pancakes like a bad paint job. There were three separate plates on the side: one with three link sausages, another of bacon, while the third held two toasted English muffins. The waitress had refilled our coffee mugs and brought a mug of coffee for Sweets to which he'd added cream and five packets of sugar.

As he buttered his muffins, Sweets said, "The theory of dots was passed down to me from my momma as far back as her great *grandpere*, the corsair, Jean Lafitte. You can apply it to anything, even criminal behavior. Like you guys are trying to figure out a crime, the leetle dots can hep. You dig?"

Jean Lafitte was a pirate and smuggler who did his dirty work in the Gulf of Mexica in the first decade of 19th century. I could imagine Vincent adding and subtracting years in his head. Some version of the Lafitte story, I'd heard often enough that I could probably recite it by heart. But I'd never heard about the little dots. I also knew from experience that Sweets, braggart that he was, also possessed a keen mind, albeit convoluted, self-serving, and often mendacious. He had once told me that although he had very little formal education, he had earned a PhD in Burglary. Since he had already provided us with the solution to one of our mysteries, I wanted to see if he had solutions for the others. God knows there were enough of them. Vincent's brow was still wrinkled over the Jean Lafitte time-line.

"Corsair is just another word for pirate," I said.

Sweets ignored me. He took a huge bite of pancakes. Syrup dripped on the head of the red and green parrot on his shirt. He swallowed and continued talking.

"Great grand papa, he be knowing it was all about connecting the dots if you wanted to solve problems. Which ships were sailing with good stuff and the ones sailing with molasses and sheet like dat, you know like food, not gold doubloons. Anyway, he was problem solver. For him it was the leetle dots. There was one set of dots like measles, all random. . ."

Vincent was holding his hand over his mouth, trying not to laugh. I shrugged. He shrugged back.

". . . like measles dots weren't worth trying to figure out. Different on every body. Nothing a smart corsair could count on. The other kind of dots were up in the sky. They looked random like the measles dots, but if you look real care-ful, you could see bears and scorpions and sheet like dat."

"Would you get to the point. I'm growing old here," I said.

"I'm almost there, daddy-o, but I got to eat. These pancakes get cold quick."

"I'll buy you more," I said. "Talk!"

He stuffed his face and chewed. Vincent and I waited.

"So, you have the nighttime sky dots,' Sweets continued. "You in good shape now. You got to look real careful like and see what the dots turn into. We got those weapons dots in a pretty picture: rifles, pistols, bazookas, hand grenades, sheet like that, right?"

Madonna mia, I thought. "Okay, we got the picture. So?"

"So, Victor you got to go talk to your bud in the Black Panthers. Tisdale was a crook and probably working for himself, but there had to be a whole bunch of upfront money to cover the cost of the weapons shipment. The dudes on the procurement end don't just let a shipment of killing stuff go without getting some bread.'"

"You're saying the Black Panthers were in on this deal?" As I said it, I remembered Dila telling me how the FBI was waging a war against the

Panthers and the Panthers had no recourse but to fight back. Thinking of Dila reminded me she was in the hospital because of this weapons deal, and I could feel my heart starting to race.

"Connect the dots, Victor," Sweets said. "Look at the picture. Did the Irish guys have cash with them?"

"Yeah, a suitcase full. Full of greenbacks. I saw it when they opened it to check. Before all the shooting started."

"There you go, dude. So where did the up-front do-ray-mi come from? Panthers are the only logical answer. They the beeg dot."

"Okay, when we finish here, I'll have a talk with my guy."

"That be Minister Bowles," Sweet said. "Man's cool. He'll give you the straight scoop." Two more mouthful of pancakes found their way into Sweets' mouth along with a chunk of sausage. His cheeks filled up like one of those puffer fish. Vincent turned his head away.

I reached over and took Sweet's plate of pancakes and slide it over to Vincent's side of the table. "Don't let him have another bite," I said, "until he finishes connecting all the fucking dots." I slid the sausages, bacon and muffins over too, but not before Sweets grabbed a piece of bacon and managed to fit it into his already full mouth.

"You buy me another breakfast?" he mumbled. Be cold by the time I finish."

"I'll buy you ten breakfasts as long as you stop eating and keep talking," I said. By now, Vincent's was leaning back in the booth, his hands folded across his chest, shaking his head.

"I'm paying Vincent," I said. "Let's hear Sweets out."

"*Ma che fai,*" Vincent said.

"I'll tell you what I'm doing, bro, trying not to screw this investigation up — again"

Vincent sighed. I said, "Continue, if you please, Mister Monroe."

"So, Victor, we've connected the dots that have to do with Tisdale, and you got a picture, right? Like Orion or the Big Dipper. We're not through, there is a whole other picture to figure out. The Irish guys and who shot them is not it. That's too simple. They be IRA, the IRA are Catholics, so the shooters must be Protestants. Been fighting it out since that dude nailed a whole bunch sheet to a wall and called the Pope a mutherfucka."

"Alright," I said. "McGoffin was the shooter according to Riorden. Nothing new, Sweets."

"Yeah, McGoffin," Sweets said. "If he is an assassin, then he was sent over to America to kill Catholics."

"You mean IRA," I said.

"Catholics, Victor, Catholics. All this sheett is about religion. Don't let the politics confuse you."

"Let's move on," I said, "What's next. With the dots?"

"You got to connect the Grace dot to the McGoffin dot. You see what I'm saying? You put those two together and all the other dots fall into place like a constellation. Now you can follow it over the ocean like Jean Lafitte to your destination."

Vincent had unfolded his arms and was leaning forward listening and for the first time looking interested. Maybe he was imagining Sweets more kindly. I couldn't find any fault in Sweets' reasoning, even though in didn't seem too different from what I'd been thinking. I remembered my earlier conversations with Hallinan and Riorden in Body's office. They believed Grace was from Derry. If that was the case, McGoffin, being Grace's friend, could have been from Derry too. Derry was in Northern Ireland and the center of a lot of the struggle that was brewing between the Irish that wanted to remain politically connected to England and the Irish that wanted the North to become part of the Irish Republic.

It had already crossed my mind briefly that Grace was not for the Irish Republic as she'd claimed. But it had seemed unlikely. Now I asked, Sweets. "Are you suggesting that Grace was a protestant, a supporter of British rule. In which case, like McGoffin, she could be an Ulster Volunteer Force agent?"

Sweets smiled and nodded.

"Can we prove it?" I asked.

"After you go see Minister of Education Bowles," Sweets said. "You go to Flynn's and get that Irish prick, Body, to find out everything about McGoffin."

Vincent said. "This is making some sense. Perhaps Mario found out Grace was lying about who she was. And maybe she was not such a peace advocate at all."

"What else could she have been doing?" I asked.

"What about spying?" Vincent replied

"Can I have my pancakes back?" Sweets asked.

Vincent shoved the plates toward Sweets. The syrup had congealed around the stack.

I waved at waitress Tammy. She came to our table and I said, "Give this guy all the pancakes he wants." I took two twenties out of my wallet and put them on the table, "Until this runs out," I said. "Then he's on his own." Forty bucks would keep Sweets busy chewing for a while. I pushed Sweets out of the booth and stood up. "Let's go, Vincent, we got work to do."

Grace and McGoffin. UVF. It made sense, but I was missing a dot that would connect everything. I thought of McGoffin being driven away from the hospital. *A dot?*

CHAPTER 33
CONNECTING SWEETS' DOTS

Falsehood flies and truth comes limping after it, so that when men come to the undeceived, it is too late, the jest is over and the tale hath had its effect.
Jonathan Swift

Minister of Education, Terrance Bowles was not in. They didn't know when he'd be back. According to one of the secretaries at the Panther's office, he had received a telephone call and he and behemoth James had left in a hurry. My next stop was Flynn's.

Jay was sitting at the bar when I entered. He was talking to Body. Body's face looked grim.I knew what they were talking about. It was the reason why I was there. As the door shut behind me, Body looked up. He shook his head and walked away. Given the circumstances, I had not expected one of his stupid Irish jokes, but I didn't expect to be ignored either. I felt anger well up inside me. Did Body have the nerve to blame me for what happened to his IRA buddies? It didn't matter if he thought they were Sinn Fein or not. It was all about the violence back in the country of his birth, which reached our shores. By God, I was going to find out how much it had to do with Mario and Graces deaths. Not to mention to what extent their cause had endangered the life of my fiancé.

Without looking back, Jay patted the empty seat next to him. I sat down. Body was at the other end of the bar, ignoring me. I shouted, "If you've got a minute, I'd like an Anchor Steam, that is if you're not too busy." Jitters and a couple of other guys sitting at the bar stared at me.

Jay put his hand on my shoulder, "Cool down Victor, I just told him about Hallinan and Riorden.

After giving me the finger, Body left for the kitchen.

"If the stupid Irishman would take a second to think about it," I said, "he'd realize those guys were trouble from the beginning. All the dart playing and Irish drinking songs. Irish eyes are smiling crap. They were down in Monterey to receive a shipment of weapons to take back to Ireland and kill Protestants. Except that Protestants can be Irish too. Going to kill their own kind."

"That's what you say." Body yelled. "There is no proof they were in Monterey on the waterfront for that purpose. It's reasonable to assume it, but we don't have any tangible evidence."

That was true. Both men were dead. The moving van they arrived in was leased by a company called Free Trade International, a bogus company. "Was there anything in their van that could be evidence?" I asked Jay.

"Not a thing. Two surfboards in the back. They could have been there looking for some midnight surfing."

"Give me a break," I said. "In a moving van? What about the money?" It had slipped out and I wanted to kick myself. "There must have been money," I added to cover up my mistake.

To my relief, Jay didn't pick up on it.

"There *was* no money," he said. "Nothing that the local police could find."

I was not certain why I was keeping quiet about the cash. If it was where I thought it was, I wasn't planning keeping it, but perhaps I could use it in some way to help me solve this case. *Case. What case? I was no Private Eye. Perhaps a make-believe-one.* I put my head down on the bar. I felt Jay patting my back and heard him telling me not to get discouraged. Everything becomes clear over time. I just wasn't letting time do its job. It felt like hours but it was only minutes before the aroma of chili peppers made be raise my head, and saw Body standing behind the bar in front of me with a frosty mug of Anchor Steam in his hand. He put it down on the bar next to a bowl of his I-Dare-You Chili.

He said, "We'll talk later, you Italian prick, when I get over being mad at you,"

He walked away. I knew better than to try to call him back. I'd wait until tomorrow. After this morning's breakfast I was not hungry, but ate half the chili anyway. The beer went down cold and satisfying. Jay asked about Dila. I'd called and been told she was stable, but still in intensive care. I told him I was driving down to visit her this evening. He offered to drive down with me, but I explained I wanted to be alone so I could think. It was a partial truth. I offered to buy him another beer, but he had a meeting. There were a number of protests scheduled for the weekend. Also, FBI agents were in town and needed to be briefed.

"About the shootout in Monterey?" I asked.

"Small potatoes compared to their concern about the Black Panthers, but don't be surprised if you get a visit."

"What's up with the Panthers?" I asked.

"Lots of stuff I'm not privy to. You know how secretive the FBI can be. They are really worried about the Black Panthers' increasing membership."

I remembered Dila mentioning something about Panthers' membership recently. Had we been alone or with some of her theater friends? She didn't hang with the Panthers socially, not that she wouldn't, but she was trying to keep her work with the Black Panthers a secret from her parents. Which hadn't worked, given what Mr. Agbo had said to me at the hospital. Ironically, it might have been the other way around. They might have known it all along and kept their knowledge a secret from their daughter. It seemed to me that in 1970 the African American community was divided among a number of groups with differing ideologies: the separatists of Elijah Mohamed, the armed resisters of Malcom X and the Black Panthers, and the followers of Doctor Marin Luther King Jr, who advocated a more Gandhi type approach to political and social activism. But what did I really know? As much as I tried to understand, I always felt I wasn't getting it, not completely. It was as if being white impeded my understanding of other races.

Jay stood up, slapped me on the back and told me to keep my powder dry. I told him to not let the FBI depress him, and I'd see him around. I finished my beer, put money on the bar and left. I walked slowly to the lot and the office where I called the Black Panthers to see if Minister Bowles was back. He was and agreed to meet me at six o'clock at the Panther office.

While I had been at Flynn's, Vincent had sold a 1960 Corvette. He told me the sale had made up for the morning spent watching Sweets eat. Thank God for Vincent. If our business was counting on me to sell cars, we'd be in bankruptcy. Maybe, I thought, I should get a private investigators license and leave the lot to Vincent. If I was being honest with myself, there was a lot about being a detective that excited me.

I would leave such thinking for another time. I filled Vincent in on my confrontation with Body and my upcoming meeting with Minister

Bowles. Like Jay, he cautioned me. Vincent believed the Panthers were violent and unstable. It was the belief of the majority of white people in the area and probably the country. I didn't disagree, but my take on their violence was that they were counterpunchers. I boxed a little in college, so I knew something about the strategy: let your opponent throw the first punch or two while waiting for the right opening to retaliate. The police and the FBI were definitely throwing the first punches. If that was the case, I wondered when the Panthers would decide it was time to counter-punch. I didn't see a lot of peace moving forward into the year. It was only January, and racial tension was high.

Vincent said. "Victor, you're not going to let this go, are you?"

I shook my head. "Not anymore."

My twin left me and went out on the lot. I knew Vincent was angry with me, but I also knew he'd be with me if was being threatened. It's comforting feeling to have that kind of absolute certainty about another person, sibling, friend or lover. There were two people in the world I knew had my back, my twin Vincent and my lover, Dila. I was pretty tired. I lay on the couch below our pop's photograph of Naples. I intended to only take a little nap, but I fell sound asleep. I woke up with a blanket covering me.I'd been dreaming of ghosts. I looked at the clock, and it read 5:30.It was already dark outside. Theresa was not at her desk. Her desk was clear of all paperwork, which meant she'd gone home.The blanket was probably Theresa's doing. I stood up and went to the door. Vincent was moving cars around. The theory was that you didn't want the lot to look the same every day. He had already replaced our loss-leader with a new one, a 1962 MGA 11 coupe.

I grabbed my sport coat and the keys to the Mustang. I stepped out into the din of rush hour traffic on East 14th and the distant roar of the Nimitz freeway. Street lights were already on. I told Vincent I was late for my meeting with Bowles, and Vincent waved me on my way. Most of the freeway traffic was headed out of town. Going into downtown, traffic was moving reasonably well.

I made it to west Oakland just as the big hand on my watch hit six. The door to the Panthers' office was locked. I knocked. A couple of seconds went before the peek-hole opened and an eye looked out at me. I recognized the very ferocious eye of James the Large.

"I got an appointment with Minister Bowles," I said before he could say anything that had to do with the color of my skin. Another couple of seconds passed before the door opened. I walked in past James, giving him my best smile for which I received back his best scowl. Minister Bowles was standing at the back of the office looking at a map of Oakland. He didn't turn around, but said my name.

"Victor, the Black Panthers are planning three new clinics, here, here, and here," he said pointing to three places on the map. "The more medical needs are taken care of off the grid the less the big hospitals can gouge poor black folks. We'll be giving lectures on sickle cell anemia and venereal diseases.

I thought that was a great Idea and told him.

He turned around and faced me. "Big James and I just got back from Monterey, visiting Sister Agbo. Let's talk in my office."

I followed him. In the time I'd known Bowles, he'd never invited me into his office. It was small and windowless. His desk faced the door. Two straight back chairs were placed in front of the desk. Next to his desk was a metal filing cabinet on top of which stood a wooden African sculpture of an elongated head. It looked old. The wall to my right was taken up by one long bookcase. The opposite wall held a framed painting of an African. Next to it hung a large poster announcing the ten-year anniversary of the start of the Mau Mau Revolt 1952 – 1962. The floor was covered by a beige rug with the word UHURU woven in red into its center. The office looked spotless, as if someone had recently vacuumed and dusted. Theresa, our neat freak accountant, would have approved.

Bowles sat down behind his desk and nodded in the direction of a chair. I sat. He did not look happy. I waited for him to begin.

"You placed Sister Agbo is a tough spot, Victor."

"I couldn't have stopped her coming with me," I said. "She is very stubborn. You must know that."

"I need to know what the hell was going on down there. What was Brother Tisdale and Little Eddie doing? Why were they shot, and who shot them?"

"You have no idea why they were there?" I asked.

"Don't fuck with me, Victor. Our association with you and your automobile dealership has been mutually beneficial, but the Black Panthers are fighting a war and two of our Warriors are dead and you know the cause. I want to be informed. Our organization is at a crossroads. 1970 will mark the year we finally gain some freedom or. ..."He paused. "If we don't, the war begins."

"By war, you mean fighting with guns, right?"

"War is self-explanatory," he said.

"Tisdale was selling weapons to the IRA," I said. "The Irish are also fighting a war, you know."

"Don't be condescending, Victor."

"It's the truth," I said.

Bowles leaned forward, placed his elbows on the desk and cradled his head in his hands. His eyes narrowed.

"If you are lying, Victor, I'm going to call James in here."

I acknowledged the threat. James was the last person I wanted to see. I told him the entire sequence of events beginning with Dila, Sweets and I breaking into Hallinan and Riorden's apartment and ending with the final violence at Harpoon Anne's.

"Those were our weapons," Bowles said. "The Black Panthers paid for them. The deal was Tisdale purchased the weapons with half our money. The other half was due on delivery."

"Who has the other half?"

"Luckily we do," Bowles said. "But we would have given it to Tisdale to complete the deal when we take possession in two days."

"Your money and the Irish money. That's a lot of cash," I said. Bowles knew what I meant.

"Are you telling me that Tisdale was running a scam on us? He was a brother. This is hard for me to believe."

"Believe it," I said. I explained how Tisdale got into the Satan's office, so that if things went south for some reason the finger would point to the motorcycle gang and not him.

"Where are the weapons now?" he asked.

"On a fishing trawler somewhere with Big Eddie. That trawler is probably down to San Diego by now, maybe Mexico."

"Big Eddie was in on this too?"

He sounded like a father whose son had just disappointed him.

"If it had worked," I said, "the IRA would have your guns, and Tisdale would have had a shit load of cash. Theirs and your half. You'd never have seen him or the two Eddies again."

Bowles leaned back, mumbled something under his breath and slammed his fists on the desk that brought me out of my chair.

"Tell me who the shooter was?" he demanded.

"We think there were two shooters, members of the Ulster Volunteer Force, the UVF."

"This is not going to go down well with our brotherhood. This is messed up. No weapons and no money."

There *was* money. I felt a twinge of guilt. I thought Bowles looked frightened. It made sense. It was a good bet that Minister Bowles would be held responsible for the loss of not only the weapons and the money but also for the loss of respect. The word would get out that the Black Panthers had been ripped off. I probed.

"Did Tisdale approach you with this plan to get weapons," I asked.

"He did. He'd just returned from Vietnam. He said he had a connection to an ex-Vietnam vet who knew a guy who knew a guy. I can't remember the name, something like Reilly or Raymond."

Or Radley, I thought.

"I gave Tisdale the go-ahead. A couple of days later, he brought us a crate of brand-new M1 carbines. He said he had hand guns and grenades as well as ammunition."

"Do you remember the date Tisdale came to you with the idea. I was thinking maybe the guy who I know believed must have been Charley Radley hadn't wanted to give Tisdale the information, but had been persuaded. That meant it was Tisdale who tortured and killed Radley and not McGoffin.

"I couldn't tell you exactly, but I could check our banker."

"You work with a bank?"

"Not exactly, not what you'd call a traditional bank."

"Are you going to get into trouble over this?"

Bowles shrugged. "Can't say I'd blame the brothers for being angry with me. I trusted Tisdale. I vouched for him."

Ah, crap, I thought. I shook my head.

"What's the problem, Victor," Bowles asked.

"Nothing. I might be able to help you."

"I'm listening."

I was not sure if I was doing the right thing. I hesitated. Bowles stared at me. Finally, I told him I believed I knew how he could recoup his money and probably make a little profit, given that the Irish probably paid a lot more for the weapons than the Panthers.When I finished, Minister of Education for the Black Panthers stood up.

"We better get started driving," Bowles said. "It might be a good idea to bring James along."

"Yeah, good idea. And maybe he should be packing."

"James has a private investigator's license and can carry a pistol legally."

Oddio, I thought - James the behemoth, a fucking PI.

CHAPTER 34
JUSTICE VERSUS THE LAW

Sit magna tamen certe lenta ira deorum est
But grant the wrath of Heaven be great, 'tis slow.
Juvenal

Because of an accident, traffic going south on Nimitz was bumper to bumper. It took us nearly two hours to get to San Jose. I was okay with it because I knew we'd probably have to wait once we arrived in Monterey.

We arrived at the waterfront docks as the clock on the dash read 10:18 p.m. I turned into the parking lot across the street, parked and switched off the headlights. The waterfront sidewalk was still alive with people probably leaving the seafood restaurants and curio shops. The area around Harpoon Annie's was still barricaded and taped off. Tourists were walking around the barricades. There were too many people to allow us to retrieve the suitcase of IRA money. If it was still there, the big question. What if some bum looking for stuff had looked inside and found it. I imagined the bum handing out 100-dollar bills to his pals.

"We'll have to park and wait," I said.

"What if the suitcase is not there?" Bowles said. "We'll have wasted our time sitting around."

"I'll go over there," James said from the back seat. "I'll pretend like I tripped, knock the oil drum over. If it's there, I'll grab it and boogie,"

In the two years that I've known James, this is the longest speech I've heard him utter. "Good luck with that," I said. "Have you noticed the cop car parked down the street? If I'm not mistaken, that's a security guard in front of Harpoon Annie's."

"Damn it to hell," Bowles said. "It makes sense. Multiple homicide took place here. There are probably going to be round the clock pigs."

I ignored the pig comment. Jay had once told me that the first time he'd been called a pig, it had hurt his feelings. After that, it was just anger. I didn't blame him. Dila and I had gotten into an argument over her use of the pejorative. She'd said, she'd try not to use the term around me. She wasn't always successful.

"You got any ideas, white bread?" James asked.

"Honest to God, James, if you call me White Bread one more time, I don't care how fucking big you are, we're going to duke it out."

James started laughing as if I'd told him a terrific joke.

"I apologize for my racially insensitive brother, but the question is worth answering," Bowles said. "This is your show, Victor."

"Give me a minute. I'll come up with something. In the meantime, I'm going to drive to the back of the lot so we won't be noticed." I started the engine. I kept the lights off as I backed out and turned. There was a parking space half hidden under a row of eucalyptus trees. I backed in so we were facing the wharf. We could still see the front door of Harpoon Annie's, the pier, and the oil drum.

We sat in silence. Bowles took a pen and small notebook from the inside pocket of his jacket and began writing in it. My thoughts turned to Dila. A half an hour passed. I heard James snoring. Bowles looked up from his writing.

"James can sleep standing up."

I didn't care to talk about James. "Who was the man in the portrait in your office?" I asked.

"Dedan Kimathi. He was the leader of the Mau Mau rebellion in Kenya in 1952. Jomo Kenyatta gets a lot of the credit for liberating Kenya from British colonial rule, but without the terror that Kimathi inflicted on the colonists, Kenya would have waited a lot longer for her independence."

"I always figure you weren't into violence as much as. . . "

Bowles finished my sentence. "As my more violent brothers, you mean?'

"Yeah, I guess. You're always writing articles describing all the good stuff the Black Panthers do in the neighborhood."

"And rightly so. It's important that the word gets out we're for solving problems for our people, but make no mistake, Victor, if push comes to shove, I'll be on the front line. So will Dila. I hope you know that about her. I never hire anyone I'm not absolutely sure is willing to die for our cause."

I shook my head in disbelief. "You'd ask her to die?"

"She asked herself three years ago when she applied for the job, and answered it herself. I think you two are being very brave, and I know she loves you, but Dila's heart is with her people, first and foremost. I don't mean this to disrespect you, but if there was a choice she had to make between you and our people, you would come in second. Dila was politicized long before she met you. And just so you are aware, I know she keeps her association with us a secret from her parents. Good people but delusional with all that Back to Arica bullshit. We earned our rights to be Americans off the sweat of our backs in the cotton fields and by the scars on our backs from the masters' whips. And we're still earning it with the lynching in the South and the police brutality all over the country.

I didn't know what to say. I stared out the window, angry, but at the same time knowing he was right, that if I came between Dila and her cause, the love of my life would not choose me. It hurt too much for me to think of it and put it out of my mind.

The streetlight in front of Harpoon Annie's illuminated the door and the oil drum. If that light were out, I thought, and the security guard no longer there, even if there were a few people wandering around at the other end of the block, we could get the suitcase.

"I have a plan," I said.

"Okay," Bowles said. He turned around in his seat and slapped James' knee.

"I was awake," James said. "I heard. White toast has a plan."

"You're too clever for me, James," I said.

"Let's hear it," James said.

"We need to get the street light out. Can we do that?"

"I have something in my backpack that can get that done," James said.

"What is it?" I asked.

James reached under his jacket and withdrew a snub-nosed revolver.

"That little shooter won't work," I said.

"He pulled out the little revolver and placed it on the seat, then he reached into his pack and brought out a police issue 6 in magnum revolver and a silencer.

"This will do it," he said. He fitted silencer on to the barrel of his pistol and held it up. "I have marksman trophies in handgun competitions."

More insights into a side of James-the-Large that broke the stereotype

I had of him as only a strong-arm bodyguard with little between his ears. I didn't know if I liked being wrong about him.

"I'll need to be a little closer."

"How about where that motorboat is parked?"

"Should do it," James said.

"What do we do about the cops down the street and the security guard?" Bowles asked.

I'm betting the cops will go on a coffee break sometime after they see all the tourists are gone. They'll' be back, but we'll have a window of opportunity."

"How about the security guard?" James asked.

"That's for Minister Bowles and me to handle. We will walk out of the parking lot staggering like a couple of drunks. This is something I learned from Dila. She saved my life once by acting like a drunk woman. It's a long story. You and I, Minister Bowles, will stumble across the street to Harpoon Annie's and pretend we think it's a tavern and we need a drink. I'll take him out with a right cross. We check the oil drum, grab the suitcase. You have our back, James."

"No," Bowles said. "No need for fists. I'll put him to sleep with a quick karate chop."

"Okay by me. That would attract less attention. I haven't boxed since college. I might be a little rusty."

James said. "Check it out. I just saw the cop cars' taillights go on. They might be leaving."

"They are," I said. "They'll be back. We can't waste any time. Let's go."

"There are still people down the street," Bowles said.

"If the cops come back, we're screwed," I said. "We got to do it now."

Bowles took off his tie and jacket. I took off my jacket and messed my hair up. James stepped out of the back and took off at a trot down the side of the parking lot toward the boat, the revolver at his side. Bowles and I waited until James was in place then started walking. At the boat, I said to James, "You shoot the light out and Minister Bowles and I will begin our Shakespeare routine."

James took aim. I heard a sound like someone spitting tobacco and the street lamp shattered, glass falling in splinters to the sidewalk. The security guard ducked, then moved through the dark toward the streetlamp. Bowles and I began stumbling forward. We were in the middle of the street before the security guard noticed us staggering toward the front door of Harpoon Annie's. Bowles pretended to trip then regained his balance and began singing, "13 Barrels of Beer on the Wall." I put my arm around his shoulders and joined in. There were 17 bottles of beer on the wall by the time we were at the door, rattling the handle and calling for someone to open up because we were two thirsty gentlemen from Missouri.

The guard hurried toward us shaking his head.

"Hey fellows, this is not a tavern. You better move on down the street. There are a couple of restaurants that way that keep their bar open," he said, pointing down the wharf.

He was looking at us as if to say, not that they'll serve you in your condition.

"Are you sssshure this ish not a tavern?" I slurred, Bowles began rattling the handle again and yelling to open up. The security guard moved in to stop him.

"Hey," he said.

That was all he said. Bowle's hand flashed through the air. He caught the guard in his arms and placed him seated in front of Harpoon Annie's door.

"Let's go," he said.

I reached inside the oil drum, felt something wiggle, and almost cried out. A rat leaped out. I shuddered. I reached in again and sighed with relief. The suitcase was there where Riorden said he'd hidden it. I handed the suitcase to Bowles.

"I'll be thanking you for me money," I voice behind us said. I looked up. Bowles spun around. A man was pointing a pistol at us. It looked like the kind I saw in Second World War movies used by the Nazis.

"You must be Mr. McGoffin," I said, in a much calmer voice than I felt.

"And you're that Eye-talian younger brother of Mario Brovelli called Victor. He talked a lot about you and your twin. Very proud of you two he was."

"And you tried to kill me and almost killed my fiancé."

"In war, civilians die," he said.

Bowles held the suitcase up and cradled it against his chest. For a stupid second I thought that Bowles believed the suitcase might stop a bullet.

I said, "There's a cop car checking this area out since you shot everybody; they'll be turning the corner any minute."

"Ach, if that be the case, all the more reason you hand over that suitcase you're holding Mr. Black Panther.

"You killed two of our brothers. We'll hunt you down."

"If you want to come to Ireland, you're welcome to try, but I'll have me money."

"It's not yours," I said. "It belongs to the IRA. You're Ulster Volunteer Force."

"Fook the UVF. It's the UDF that will be using this money. He raised the weapon that I now remembered was called a luger and pressed the tip of the barrel against Bowles temple. I glanced in the direction of the parking lot to see if I could see James. Where the fuck was he?

"Now I'm going to count to three and when I reach two, I'm going to pull the trigger and you'll be missing your black head. One. . . "

"Give him the suitcase," I said to Bowles. Bowles raised an eyebrow and shook his head. I saw McGoffin's mouth form the word two but the number didn't come out. What did come out was a spurt of blood. Just as the Luger fell from his hand, it fired. I grabbed Bowles and pulled him away.McGoffin fell forward. clawing at his chest and landed on his face. Bowles's shoulder was bloody.I heard feet running. James was suddenly next to us. He kicked the pistol away from the fallen Irishman.

"You okay, boss?" He asked.

"He could have killed me," Bowles said.

James said. "He was so close to you. Had to take a chance."

I knelt beside McGoffin and turned him onto his back. He was alive, but the wound looked deadly where it had torn through flesh and bone before exiting. He would not survive. I placed my face close to his. "Did you kill my brother and Grace and make it look like a suicide?" I asked. He shook his head and tried to say something, but all he did was cough blood.

"You're dying," I said. "You might as well tell the truth."

James said, "We need to get the hell outta here, Brovelli."

I barely heard him. McGoffin's mouth opened. He closed his eyes then opened them, "Ach, you silly bugger," He groaned, "Why would I kill me own wife, the most beautiful woman in Ireland." His eyes closed again. This time they didn't open.

James had me by the arms lifting me up. "Man's dead. We got to move."

"I got to talk to him," I yelled.

"He's fucking dead. There's nothing you can say to him."

Bowles was already stumbling half way across the street, carrying the suitcase of money with his good hand. James grabbed my arm and pulled. I let him, and we ran for the parking lot. I slid behind the wheel and started the engine. As I pulled out of the parking lot onto the street, I could see the fallen body. The ghost of Mario was staring down on the dead Irishman. I stepped hard on the gas.

CHAPTER 35

WHEN IRISH EYES ARE CRYING

Dress suitably in short skirts and strong boots, have your jewels and gold wands in the bank and buy a revolver
Countess Markiewiez October 1915

It was Sunday, the 18th of January.My parents and I were in Saint Joseph's waiting for 8 a.m. mass to begin. I was guilt-ridden over involving Dila in my problems and her getting shot and almost dying. I needed to go to confession. Three confessionals were to the right of the aisle we were sitting in. All were in use. When a woman stepped out of the middle confessional, I got up and hurried inside. I didn't care if it was our parish priest, Father Dunnican, who'd recognize my voice. I needed absolution. The drive to confess is transfused into Italian Catholics through mothers' milk. I'd told this once to my twin, but Vincent had scoffed that he was as Italian as I was and never felt the need. I confessed everything to a priest whose voice was new to me. I even confessed stuff that I didn't do, like Bowles karate chopping that poor security guard who was just trying to do his job. I confessed that James was probably sorry for shooting McGoffin, but the priest didn't feel he could absolve in absentia. I walked out of the confessional not feeling much better, but did my penance anyway, six *Hail Mary's* and six *Our Fathers*. I had expected more. Once last year, a priest made me do the Stations of the Cross on my knees, which was hell to pay on my trousers.Today, I would have walked the road to Santiago di Compostlla the whole way on my knees if only God had seen to it that Dila had not been shot.

The mass began with the Penitential Rite, which is an acknowledgement that everyone is a sinner and has sinned to some degree during the week. At communion I took the wafer on my tongue. It was hard to swallow.

Afterwards, I dropped Pop off at home, and Mom and I drove to the cemetery to visit Mario's grave. My mom placed a bouquet of white roses against the tombstone. For purity, my mom said. Maybe, I thought. She held my hand as we walked out. I left her at the front door. Before she went in, she said, "Vittorio, soon you will know. You will tell me the truth." I kissed her on the cheek. I didn't have the words to say we might never know. I thought I knew enough, but there were loose ends.

By noon I was sitting in Mario's Mustang at Grizzly Peak with the motor off, looking out to the bay and the silver bridge that connected Oakland to San Francisco. Out of my side window I could see to San Francisco's Coit Tower and the tops of the Golden Gate Bridge, the tops rising out of a layer of fog. I could just make out a string of barges being pulled by a tug boat and a fishing trawler making its way toward the Oakland docks. From this distance, they looked like toys. I imagined Big Eddie in one of them, its hold filled with all sorts of military hardware.

I leaned back in the seat and closed my eyes. The results of the confessional and communion were wearing off, replaced by sadness and a growing frustration that I could have done better, or that I had missed something important. My thoughts returned to Dila.

On Saturday, Dila had been transferred from the Monterey County Hospital to Highland Hospital in Oakland. When I tried to see her, Mr. Agbo met me at the door of her room and told me she didn't want to see me, and I was no longer welcome in his home. I didn't give a crap about his home; I was only interested in the person behind the door he was standing in front of. He told me he was hiring a bodyguard. I couldn't knock my future father-in-law on his ass but I was sorely tempted. I left figuring he'd cool off. I'd give him until Monday.

I had decided to come here to the scene of Mario and Grace's deaths. I still refused to believe they were a murder/suicide, but I wasn't sure what else to call it. McGoffin naming Grace as his wife had really thrown me into a pit of self-doubt.

"All right, Victor," I said to the windshield, "what do you do now?" If I sat here long enough, perhaps the Gods of Private Investigators would shine down on me and provide me with some kind of inspiration. A half hour later I could still think of nothing. Other than the crucial question whether Mario and Grace's deaths were suicide or murder, another question that was not resolved was who Grace O'Conner really was. Was she the wife of Casey McGoffin? A wife is a definition only of a certain marital status and responsibility. At the moment of dying, people normally don't lie. But maybe McGoffin and Grace were separated. Divorces I'd heard were damn near impossible to get approved in Ireland. They still had to be friends; otherwise, she wouldn't have convinced Mario to take him in as a roommate. No divorce might mean that McGoffin still thought of Grace as his wife.

There was only one person I could think of who might know something about Grace's prior relationships, Carol, Grace's partner in PeaceLinks. Would she be willing to reveal any of Grace's personal information?My thinking was interrupted by a car pulling in and parking. It was a white AMC Rebel with a red racing stripe. I was familiar with the Rebel. It had a 390 ci V8 engine with 340 hp and was referred to as "The Machine."I expected to see the occupants get out so they could see the view better. But they didn't. A moment later, the car began to rock and roll. Ah geez, I thought. I was reminded of the days I would drive here with Renee Sorenson for the same rock and roll purpose. It seemed strange to even think about making love in a car. I would never have considered it with Dila, and she would have thought the front seat of a car lacking in imagination. I turned the ignition and put the Mustang into reverse. I took the curves down to Oakland. I had decided to talk to Carol at PeaceLinks. This being Sunday, I doubted that the office would be open, but the pursuit of peace might call for a seven-day workweek. If somebody would be in the PeaceLinks office, my guess was it would be Carol. If the office was closed, tonight might be a good time to get the best Cajun burglar in the world to work his magic. Maybe there'd be some files or other information about Grace.

I heard my twin's voice in my head a few days ago: *You're not going to let this go, are you Victor?*

I parked in front of the PeaceLink's office and got out. I could see Carol through the plate glass window standing in front of a table with files in her hands.I knocked on the window. She looked over at me. I mouthed the words; *I want to talk to you.* She waved in the direction of the door. It was open. As I entered, Carol smiled, but I didn't detect any happiness in the smile. She looked tired. There were shadows under her eyes. Her blonde hair, usually neat, looked as if she'd forgotten to comb it this morning. She was wearing sweatpants and a Stanford University hoodie. A briefcase was open, and I saw there were a number of files in it.

"You went to Stanford?" I asked.

"Status symbol. I never went to college. You graduated from Saint Mary's College, right?"

"Class of '65."

"I haven't made coffee," she said.

"We could go down the street. Coffee and a bite to eat. I'll buy. I'd like to talk to you about Grace."

Carol shook her head.

"Please," I said. "There are some important questions I need to ask you, one in particular. You're the only person I can think of who might have an answer."

"I don't really need the caffeine, and I'm not hungry, Vincent, but I'll try to answer your question if I can."

Carol might not have been hungry, but she looked like she'd lost weight and could use a meal. I remembered the first time I'd met Carol over a year ago in the Peacelinks' office. Mario had introduced me. We'd sort of flirted with each other. If I hadn't met Dila, I probably would have taken my flirting to the next level of persuasiveness.

"How about a desert?" I asked.

"No, honestly. I have a lot of work to do. I'm way behind."

I wasn't sure how to word the question. I decided on a statement that she'd have to address in some way. "I got this from an impeccable source that Grace was married when she was in Ireland." I stopped to gauge Carol's reaction. She didn't seem surprised, but maybe I was just hoping she wasn't. She didn't say anything, just looked at me sadly. "Is this true? I asked. "Please tell me the truth, Carol."

Finally, she asked, "How did you find out?"

The relief must have shown on my face because she reached toward me and took my hand. I couldn't tell her about McGoffin. "Do you know who she was married to?"

"Some guy she met when she was a teenager. He was abusive and dangerous. She had no folks, no one to help her. She ran. To Dublin, then to England, from there to America."

My instincts were telling me, *Victor, you're not getting the whole truth.* "You said Dublin. Does that mean Grace grew up somewhere else?"

"Derry, in Northern Ireland. It took a year of us being friends, you know, before Grace opened up about her life. You don't need to know any more, Victor. It's an old story for lots of women; you're young, you marry your prince charming, find out he isn't such a prince. After the first beating and the next, you either take the abuse and resign yourself to living a crap life, or you run. Things may be changing in America, but Ireland is still a pretty dreadful place for women. Grace chose to run."

"Until he found her? In America? All the way across America to here?" This was a question not a statement because it seemed strange to me that an abusive husband would travel across the ocean to find a woman who'd left him long ago. "Why now?"

Carol remained stoic. After a moment or two, she frowned. "You better tell me what you have found out, Victor," she said quietly. "Is there something I need to know?"

The scene in the parking lot of the hospital after McGoffin had cut Riorden's throat came to mind and the image of the woman driving the getaway car. *Oddio,* I thought. Then, I thought, *nah, not possible.* Then I thought, *well yeah, could be very possible.* All the while Carol was staring at me. I stared back at her, not knowing what to say. What could I say? McGoffin's dying breath?

Carol spoke first. "Are you being a lawyer, Victor? Did you already know the answers to your questions about Grace being married? Were you just fishing for confirmation?"

"Something like that," I said.

"Like what?" Carol asked.

"Like, you know," I said. Now I *was* fishing. Carol's face turned angry. She reached into the briefcase, and I watched as if in slow motion as she withdrew a snub-nosed revolver.

"You must have seen me when we were driving away from the hospital," she said, pointing the gun at me.

The revolver may have been small, but it started to grow larger the longer Carol pointed it at my chest. "No, no, Carol, I had no idea the driver was you," I said, "That's the truth, but I do know now." For Christ's Sake, Victor, I thought, that was not a very smart thing to say. If I'd expected this from Carol, it must have been concealed in my subconscious. I was staring at a gun and an angry woman, perhaps a murderer. Carol? *Minchia!*

"We better go into my office, Victor. There's more to this than you realize." She pointed the way with her revolver.

"Can you point that gun in another direction?"

"Don't give me any trouble, Victor. If you do, I'll shoot you. You know, I could have shot you in Monterey at the waterfront. I'm an excellent shot.My daddy bought me a pistol when I was 14. He put a rifle in my hands when I was 16 and taught me to shoot. I missed you on purpose."

"Well, one of those misses on purpose hit my fiancée," I said, suddenly I was the one angry. "Dila's still in the hospital recovering."

"I'm sorry that happened. I had to shoot, or be shot myself."

I had to think of about that for a moment. "*McGoffin.*"

Carol shrugged.

We entered Carol's office. I was thinking that Victor Brovelli was truly the victim of some kind of Italian curse to have two women, one last year and Carol this year, pointing a revolver at me with violence on their minds.

Carol pointed to a chair. "Sit. Place your arms behind the back of the chair.

"How about I make some coffee?" I said.

"Don't be a wise ass, Victor." she said.

Carol brought out handcuffs from a desk drawer while keeping the pistol trained on me. She cuffed my wrists. My arms stretched the way they were, my shoulders instantly began to ache. "These hurts. How about loosening the cuffs?" I asked.

"Can't do that. I've heard all the stories about you and your twin from Mario. I want you very secure. I don't want any more deaths. But I don't plan to be arrested. All I ever wanted to do was live in peace. I thought I would be able to do that until Grace found me. And where Grace went, McGoffin would not be far behind. I was a fool to believe her that she'd rid herself of him. Dumb."

"Was Grace Ulster Volunteer Force?" I asked. Rolling a suitcase out from behind her desk, Carol said, "Not UVF but Ulster Defense Force. UDF makes UVF look like peaceniks."Carol lifted her coat off a wall hook and slipped it on. She took a small mirror from her purse and began fussing with her hair. Up close I could see the roots of her hair were not blonde. I wasn't sure, but they looked reddish.

"You're not a blonde," I said. "You're Irish, aren't you? Carol Hosty is not even your name, is it?"

"Not Carol. Hosty is our family's original name a long time ago. It derived from Mac Oiste. I guess that's why I chose it. Sentimental. Didn't think it would be a problem. Probably I should have chosen a Polish name or Italian." She smiled. You don't need to know my real Irish name."

Suddenly it became clear to me what it was about Grace's Daily Planner that bothered me. Sweets' dots, I thought. I hadn't connected the trips to the East Coast and Mid-West in November and December to Body telling me about the assassinations of two Sinn Fein fund raisers. The thought so stunned me that I closed my eyes and hung my head. From the darkness behind my eyes, I heard myself say, "Grace worked for the Ulster Defense Force as an assassin. And you knew about it."

"If you'd known McGoffin," Carol said. "He recruited me in 1965 and Grace the following year. He married her a month later. Oh my, he was a handsome devil. Ireland at that time was starting to turn into a tinderbox. Grace was so beautiful, he used her like bait to attract certain people, military, political.They'd follow Grace right into McGoffin's line of fire."

"Did Mario know this?" Without answering my question, Carol continued.

"I began to have misgivings, not Grace. She was a Northern Irish Provo patriot or fanatic.

I recognized where McGoffin was headed and caught the first train out of town. I can tell you this, Victor, Grace did not object to the killings. They were British soldiers mostly IRA, Sin Fein. Grace's parents had been caught in a gun battle and shot by the IRA. Grace was committed to a Northern Ireland remaining Brit.

"Are you making excuses for Grace?" I asked.

"Not at all, Victor. You simply need to understand everything is not black and white. But Grace had a tipping point. We all do. You wouldn't have read about it over here, but there was a firebombing of a Catholic elementary school. McGoffin told her there would not be anyone inside."

"She firebombed an elementary school?"

"Little girls were burned to death. The guilt was too much for Grace. She left McGoffin and Ireland. She planned it carefully. At least that's what she told me when we met again in Boston. How she found me, I'm still not sure. I was happy to see her. We'd been really close in Ireland. One night over too many whiskeys, she confessed to the elementary school bombing. It scared the hell out of me. I told her we should head for the west coast. There were too many Irish in Boston. I was ready for a change of scenery anyway, and I thought that we could renew the relationship we had in

Ireland. Grace was a really special woman. We wound up in Oakland and started PeaceLinks."

Carol shook the gun at me like she was trying to make a point.

"But she met Mario," Carol continued. "Anyway, it probably wouldn't have worked for us."

By now my head was spinning. I felt like I was listening to something out of an espionage thriller disguised as a romance novel. "Why PeaceLinks?" I asked.

"It was Grace's idea. She felt it was a good place to hide under cover of an Anti-War Peace Organization. To tell the truth, I think Grace was also trying to do some good. You know, doing penance for past sins and all that. Do we ever really atone? That's what I thought. Not too long ago I found out differently."

"What does that mean?" I asked.

"Grace couldn't escape her past. And, perhaps, when she was forced to make a choice, she chose the past instead of the future."

"Carol," I said. "You know what happened to Mario and Grace, and how it happened, the real story. Before you kill me, I must know. I can't die without knowing."

"I'm not going to kill you, Victor. And, unlike Grace, I *am* going to escape my past."

If Carol disappeared, I had no idea how I'd ever find out. I took a gamble. "It must have been McGoffin." I paused. "And maybe you helped him." I was reaching, but I knew the instant I said it, I'd hit a nerve. I only hoped that the nerve didn't change Carol's mind and put pressure on Carol's trigger finger.

But I was surprised by her reaction.

"Oh, Victor, Victor, Mario was so in love with Grace, and maybe I was too, still in love with her. It had nothing to do with McGoffin, not really. Mario didn't die at the Grizzly Peak turnout. Grace shot him in his car in the parking lot outside this office window."

Finally, finally the truth. For a moment my fear left me, and all I felt was relief. Then the fear returned. What if Carol changed her mind and shot me. I wouldn't be able to tell my parents that Mario had not committed suicide. This was on my mind when something else occurred to me, something Carol had just said. I should have kept my mouth shut, but didn't. "You just said that Grace loved Mario. Why would she shoot him?"

"No, I said Mario loved Grace. And yes, Grace loved Mario all right — in her own way. She might have gone to jail for him, but as strange as this may sound to you, she wouldn't allow her love to interfere with her Protestant cause.

I'd heard something like this before, but I was too upset to figure out where or when. I said, "But you told me that Grace had left the cause."

"No, I said, she left McGoffin. There's a difference." Carol checked her watch. "It began in this office. It was evening. All the employees were gone. Mario had just left too, but I guess he came back for something. We didn't hear Mario return. Grace and I were arguing over McGoffin. I was furious that I had been suddenly drawn back into his political extremism. He heard all of it: her assassinations, the children at the elementary school, McGoffin. That she and McGoffin were married. He was devastated and angry. It was awful what he said, what *they* said to each other."

In a lifetime I would never forget what I was hearing. What could Mario have been thinking as he listened to the woman he loved who'd lied to him and used him. If Carol had stopped and not said another word, I would have been okay with that, but I was caught up in the fury. I wanted all awful details. And Carol, it seemed, wanted to tell me.

"Mario told Grace he was going to talk to your friend, the homicide detective, I don't know his name. Grace yelled that he couldn't do that. He stormed from the office. She followed him. I saw what happened from the window."

"And that was?" I asked.

"Mario got into his car. Grace got in the passenger seat. They continued yelling. Then she pulled a pistol and shot him."

Listening to Carol, my heart was racing, my lips dry, and I was having a hard time breathing.

Carol continued, "I ran outside. Grace was still holding the pistol. Victor, she was sobbing, but what was frightening was her gun hand was perfectly still. I had a hard time taking the pistol away from her."

"Can't be the end of the story, can it? They had to get up to Grizzly Peak somehow," I said

"It was my idea to stage a suicide. Grace and I moved Mario's body into the passenger side. I covered the blood with plastic and drove the Mustang. Grace said Mario liked to go to the parking area at Grizzly Peak when he wanted to think things out.

Like me, I thought. Perhaps I got the idea from Mario.

"Grace followed in my car. I removed the plastic, and we replaced Mario in the driver's seat. I positioned the pistol in his right hand. Right hand, right temple. End of story."

"Except you shot Grace," I said. "And made it look like murder/suicide."

"McGoffin was dead," Carol said. "That left only Grace between me and complete freedom. Now you know, but you don't have an ounce of proof, except my story. I don't want any more killing. I'm going to disappear. You're going to spend an unpleasant rest of the day and night attached to this chair. When our office employees show up for work Monday morning, you'll be found, no harm done. By then, I will be out of the country, somewhere this time, where no one will ever find me. Grace had been living a lie for a long time. . . "Carol paused as if she was thinking. Then she shook her head. "The Cause might have had Grace's soul," Carol said. "But not her heart. If this is at all important to you, Grace loved Mario. Mario loved Grace. That's all you need to know, ever, on this earth. And they died together."

I looked at Carol. Her eyes moist. "Why are you telling me this?"

Carol didn't answer me. She duct-taped my legs and arms to the chair, stuffed a hanky in my mouth and duct-taped it on.

I was thinking, what if Carol was lying? What if she'd killed them both? The events as she'd described them made sense, but I felt there was more.

Carol tested my bonds to see if I was secure.

"Victor," she said, "while you're waiting to be rescued, I'm sure you'll come to the realization that telling the police about me or pursing me will not be to the advantage of your family. They need closure, don't you think?"

With that question hanging in the air, Carol Hosty, or whoever she was, walked through the office door and locked it. I heard the front door slam. It too would be locked. I knew I'd be found so I wasn't worried. It was time to worry about how much Vincent and I would tell our parents. *Closure*. Maybe for my parents. Not for Victor Brovelli.

CHAPTER 36
PATIENCE

I beg you to have patience with everything unresolved in your heart and to try to love the questions themselves as if they were locked rooms or books written in a foreign language.
Rainer Maria Rilke

It was Barbeque Saturday at Brovelli Brothers Used Cars. I was standing in the office looking out the open window. The voices of Peter, Paul and Mary leaving on a jet plane were competing with the laughter and chatter around the grill.The aroma of barbeque chicken and Italian sausage was wafting through the air. I was waiting to relieve Vincent at the grill. The day was partly sunny. Warm for January. East 14th was filled with the cacophony of urban sounds, music to my ears.Buses rolling, cabs starting and stopping, cars honking, an Ambulance siren whooping, pulling traffic to the sidewalk. Going the opposite direction, was a member of the Satans in his black leathers, bent over the handlebars of his Harley. The gang, back from their trip south, were undoubtedly unaware that in their absence their clubhouse had once again been used to commit a crime. In the distance I could see the air cargo planes taking off and landing from the Alameda Naval Air Station. There might very well have been the angry voices of protestors outside the fences of the Navel base — the Vietnam War still raging, protest growing in numbers and intensity — but heard only in my imagination. Somebody in my real world was gunning his engine at the corner stop light.

When I was in college and trying to keep my love of literature a secret from Vincent and the rest of the business majors, I'd read Rainer Maria Rilke's *Letters to a Young Poet* and *The Duino Elegies*. Why was I remembering this now? Because, driving to work this morning, I had been thinking about what Rilke said about patience and the stuff in your life that that remained unresolved and at some point, in the future I would have do something about. Thinking of what that might entail had kept me worrying until I'd pulled into the driveway of our lot and saw life in the near future in front of me. After all the events of the last few months since the death of Mario and Grace, I remembered thinking how much I was looking forward to some degree of normalcy.

Normalcy as I viewed it form our office window was a lot filled with good looking automobiles and a Saturday filled mostly with our fellow business men and women from the neighborhood who rarely missed our weekly barbeques. You couldn't miss Swanee in a crowd with his bib overalls and red bandana. I spotted Detective Sergeant Jay Ness of the Oakland Police Department talking to Cousin Theresa. Their night at the opera had gone surprising well. It didn't seem to me that Theresa was as unhappy with Jay's overtures as she'd been before. I should have been outside trying to talk people into buying a car. Had this been any other Saturday, I would have, but I was content where I was enjoying the peace and thinking.

Three Saturdays had passed since I'd been found in the PeaceLinks office duct-taped to a chair with my hands cuffed behind me and smelling of urine. When I told the employees who discovered me on Monday morning that it had been their boss, Carol Hosty, who had done this to me, they didn't believe it, but once they saw the empty wall safe with all the cash gone, they changed their minds because Hosty and Grace were the only ones with the combination and unless Grace's ghost had made off with the cash, Hosty was the only possible culprit. They wanted to call the police. It had taken all my powers of persuasion to convince them and the other employees and volunteers who arrived that it would be best not to report this incident to the authorities. Since Hosty had left all the funds in the bank account, PeaceLinks could continue operating. They would get more donations. I promised Brovelli Brothers Used Cars would pony up. Wouldn't it be a shame, I'd argued, if all the good work they had accomplished came to a sudden and ignominious end as a result of all the terrible publicity that would have to come out about Carol Hosty and Grace. I didn't go into a lot of detail, but I was persuasive. Finally, three of the oldest serving-paid-employees agreed to take responsibility of the organization. I'd suggested a couple of scenarios that would account for

Carol Hosty's sudden disappearance. They said they could do better and thanked me for not making a big deal about my overnight travail. At which point I had bid them good luck and driven home to take a long shower and get some much-needed sleep.

The following day, I explained to Vincent that I thought it was best not to go into too much detail telling our parents what happened to Mario. All they really needed to know was that Mario had not committed suicide. And who shot him. Of course, we would have to explain that we had no proof, and they would just have to trust us. I didn't think that would be a problem. Costanza and Carlo would have to told, but Pop would swear them to silence. Vincent approved, saying it would be closure. *Closure*, I was starting to hate that word. That evening Vincent and I drove to Alameda to our family home. We sat at the kitchen table with glasses of wine. Across from us, Mario's ghost leaned back against the kitchen sink, one ankle crossed over the other. He looked pleased, or I liked to believe he was, as I told our mom and pop the truth according to Victor Brovelli.I explained that Grace was not the person Mario thought she was. In reality, Grace was a Northern Irish Protestant extremist who was using Mario and PeaceLinks as a cover while she went about her nefarious business. My mother was astonished that she had believed Grace would be a perfect wife for Mario and wondered how she could have been so wrong. Both Vincent and I said we felt the same way. Our father grumbled about Protestants. Our mom said she would visit our parish priest in the morning and let him know he needn't worry that Mario's grave was not legitimately holy. She assured us she'd not explain any more than that. The look in her eyes told me she was eager to set her local parish priest straight. I was certain that Father Dunnican would be sufficiently chastised.

As we were leaving, my mother pulled me aside out of Vincent's hearing. "Vittorio, how long have you been seeing Mario?"

I was about to act the innocent, when she placed her hand on my cheek and patted me. "*La verita, per favore.* Mario was with us listening. I saw you look over a few times to the kitchen sink. I saw him there. So handsome. He has come to me too, but mostly in my sleep. He said just now as you were leaving that he and I would talk later when I go on my walk to the beach."

"Mama," I said, "the truth is that Mario never talked to me. He just followed me and watched me. He just watched me. Not a word, not a sign of approval or disapproval. I saw Grace's ghost too. All she did was cry and wring her hands."

"*Colpevolezza,*" my mother said. "Guilty of what she did to my boy."

"I wish Mario would have spoken to me. It would have all been so much easier."

"Is it not possible that by finding out the truth and upholding the honor of your family, you made it possible for Mario to speak to his mama. It is what I think. *Ti son grato. Ti amo, Vittorio*"

• • •

Of that evening with our parents what stood out in my memory was my mom saying she was looking forward to talking with Mario – he was free from purgatory, she'd said. There would be so much to discuss. I was unsure about purgatory, but I had left the house feeling a great burden had been lifted from me. Smiling, I imagined my mother walking along the Alameda esplanade talking to Mario's ghost. Perhaps people walking past her would smile at the pretty, old woman talking to herself. Or perhaps they would worry. Perhaps word would get back to my father that his wife was getting a little senile. I was sure his pop would already have heard from his wife of these conversations and being Italian would except *fantasmi* as a normal part of life. I wondered what Mario and our mother would talk about? Secrets, no doubt, that only sons and mothers shared. Perhaps ghosts could comfort as well as haunt.

The weeks that followed that time with our parents had been difficult and frustrating. Thinking back to what Carol had told me about the Ulster Defense Force, I half expected a member of the UDF to show up, seeking revenge for McGoffin's death. But no such agent of death arrived. Both Body and I were interviewed by the FBI. It had taken up most of a day. We both felt there was no reason to tell the FBI that Grace was the assassin who'd killed Body's friend Danny Boy Killian and other East Coast IRA fund raisers. They were mostly interested in what I could tell them about the Black Panthers, and were angry when I wouldn't cooperate. In their war with the Panthers, I made it clear Victor Brovelli was a civilian noncombatant.

My frustrations as well as my concerns about the case was magnified by my worrying about Dila. I had attempted to visit her at Highland Hospital. Each time I was turned away. I made my final attempt in disguise and reached Dila's floor only to find the door to her room guarded by James, the largest Black Panther in the universe. He'd been hired by Dila's father, which I believed was the height of irony. Any idea I entertained that James was less antagonistic to me because of our shared experience at Harpoon Annie's was soon dispelled when he told me if I came close to the door, he'd break both my skinny white legs. I was at a complete loss trying to figure out Dila's silence. I had managed to get a couple of messages to her, but she did not respond. It was driving me crazy. What could the problem be? She couldn't possibly blame me for her being shot. It had been Dila herself who'd insisted on coming with me to Monterey. In my mind I could picture Dila that night holding her 30 caliber M1 carbine, looking beautiful and ferocious. Patience, I told myself. Everything would work out once she got home. But that had not happened. When Dila was released from the hospital, I went to her parents' home and was turned away once again by Behemoth James and provided with a message from her father that any further attempt by me to see his daughter, he would get a restraining order. I could not believe Dila would put up with this. My engagement ring, I hoped, was still on her finger. It was not so crazy that her father was actually keeping his daughter prisoner in her own home. I imagined he bedroom door locked. James standing in front of it, with his huge arms crossed. *Oddio*, my imagination was running away with me. Finally, I told myself this was just one more insane development in a series of insane developments.

Today's familiar barbeque scene from our office window uplifted my spirits. Parsigian's Furniture store across the street comforted me. He was having a sale. He always had a sale. Body's tavern, its sign at night flickering *Flynn's* in green lights comforted me. So did the DoNut Hole next door to Flynn's. The sweet aroma of fresh-baked dough comforted me. And further down East 14th, there was the Satan's Club House that we all would have preferred not dwell amongst us, but we would point out to visitors the way you would a bearded woman in a carnival. I could walk in the other direction and be comforted by Jitter's gasoline station and repair shop. I'd drink bad coffee while Jitters regaled me in his stuttering voice with stories of the world's fastest hotrods. I knew most of the people who worked in this area by their first names. I knew their family members and had shared in their griefs and their joys. I had worked on East 14th Street helping Pop since I was a teenager, this was my second home. I wanted Dila to live in this home with me.

As for Mario and Grace's death, I imagined myself at some point in my life, perhaps if I ever became a licensed private investigator, tracing Carol Hosty's whereabouts. For what purpose, I wasn't sure. Perhaps revenge. The Old Testament kind — a life for a life. Perhaps to bring a murderer to justice. Was justice suddenly so important to me? I recalled Carol's last words to me: *Mario loved Grace. Grace loved Mario.* Then she'd added that was all I needed to know. How could that be? How could I leave it at that, so simple, yet so complicated? I couldn't. I made a promise to myself: Carol, wherever you're hiding, *I'll find you*. Vincent and I will find you. The Brovelli Boys never break a promise.

I heard Vincent calling me. I put on my barbeque apron, ready to spell him, but he was waving his hand in the direction of the street where a Yellow Cab had pulled to the curb. Vincent was smiling. A woman was getting out. It took me a second to register who it was, then I was out the door, running to Dila.

The End

About the Author

TOM MESCHERY is an ex-NBA player for the Golden State Warriors and Seattle Sonics and retired high school and college English teacher. A graduate of the University of Iowa's Writers Workshop, he has published five collections of poetry. Meschery had been inducted in the Nevada Writers' Hall of Fame. He has also traveled extensively in West Africa coaching basketball and lecturing. *The Case of the "61 Chevy Impala* is the first of his Brovelli Brothers Mystery series. The Case of the '66 Ford Mustang is the second novel in the Brovelli Brothers' series. Tom Meschery lives in Sacramento, CA with his wife, the painter, Melanie Marchant.

Printed in the USA
CPSIA information can be obtained
at www.ICGtesting.com
LVHW032247170324
774745LV00037B/1257